And all Yancy knew was that he wanted to see her again. There was something about her, something different . . .

Dana opened her mouth as if to say something. Maybe that was his undoing, seeing her moist lips part, compliments of the full moon. Hell, he didn't know at the time what came over him, what triggered his knee-jerk response, nor did he care. His base instincts took control.

He reached for her and, with a rush of an electric current charging through him, crushed her lips against his. For a moment, she stiffened, which made him only increase the pressure. With the full force of her breasts pressed against him, there was no time for anything now except to give in to his rising tide of lust.

Their ragged breathing rivaled the sound of the rising wind . . .

"Simply captivating . . . a gripping emotional tale and a wonderful love story."
—Julie Garwood,
New York Times bestselling author
of *Castles* and *Saving Grace*, on *Sweet Justice*

"Popular romance writer Mary Lynn Baxter makes a perfect ten-point dive into women's fiction. . . . Ms. Baxter has constructed a dramatic, riveting, and emotionally complex novel that should land on the bestseller list."
—*Affaire de Coeur* on *Sweet Justice*

Also by Mary Lynn Baxter

Priceless
Sweet Justice
Hot Texas Nights

Published by
Warner Books

One

Seventeen Years Later

Mrs. Balch, the B&B innkeeper, eyed her guest, an anxious expression on her face. "Is this room okay? If it isn't—"

Dana Bivens held up her hand. "It's just what I had in mind. I'm sure I'll be as comfortable here as I would at home."

The older woman's anxious look was replaced by a smile. "Wonderful. It's our aim to please."

"Well, you've certainly done that."

The instant Dana had turned into the graveled drive, she had been enchanted. The two-story white house with its twin chimneys on each end sat on a hill surrounded by lush greenery.

Once she'd stepped out of the car, she had turned to stare at the immaculate grounds, watching as a tiny squirrel scampered about. But then her eyes had switched to a budding rose tree. She had thought nothing could be lovelier until she spotted several dogwoods nestled together, their branches heavy with a blizzard of blooms. Dana had watched for a breathtaking moment as the soft breeze turned the fragile white petals into shifting cards of light. No place could compete with Virginia in the spring.

"If you need anything, why, you just let me know."

Dana forced her attention back to the moment and smiled. "Thanks, I will."

When she was finally alone, Dana looked around her room at the Inn of Monticello and grinned like a schoolgirl, eyeing the cherrywood step stool that allowed access to the high-canopied bed. *Quaint* was the word that jumped to mind because of its Civil War flavor. Still, it was a warm room with feminine delicacy.

When she'd called to make her reservations, the innkeeper had told her that there were five rooms with private baths, each with a different amenity. Dana had chosen the lilac one that had a screened-in porch.

She'd always wanted to stay in a bed and breakfast but had never had the opportunity. Rather than choose a motel for the several weeks she would be in Charlottesville, she had opted for a more homelike and personal atmosphere.

Maybe that homing instinct, that need to have roots no matter where she was, came from never having had a real home. She thought of her rented home in Richmond and smiled, though for a second it was a pained smile. She'd hated leaving it. She had worked so hard to make it warm and comfortable, with cottage blinds that let the sunlight pour through the windows, plants all over, brightly cushioned furniture, and memorabilia that she'd collected on her journalistic ventures.

And to think—she'd have to leave that home, her friends, everything, if she moved to Washington.

Feeling her stomach suddenly turn over, Dana eased into one of the highbacked chairs. Another unsettling thought hit her with renewed force: What if this test assignment with *Issues* magazine didn't work out? Why did the stakes have to be so high?

Without wanting to, she thought of a friend who had been lured away from a secure newspaper job for a glory one with *USA Today.*

"Can you believe it, Dana?" her friend had cried when she'd been notified.

"Knock 'em dead, Susan!" Dana had responded. "Show those men that you can tackle the gritty stories just as well as they can."

Only she hadn't. Susan had slammed her head against that glass ceiling quickly, and had left the newspaper brokenhearted and down on herself.

Dana didn't want that to happen to her. It wouldn't, she vowed. She'd do what she had to do to get to the top of her profession and stay there, even if it meant returning to this area and a town she hated in order to research a story on a man who stood to be the next Nobel Prize winner.

Pushing aside that unpleasant thought, she decided to call her friend April Merriwether, whose friendship had survived all these years of separation. She couldn't wait to let April know she was back in town, nor could she wait to ask her old friend if she knew anything about Dr. Yancy Granger.

No one was home. After the beep of her friend's answering machine, she said, "Hi, guess who's back in town. I'll call later."

Dana felt restless. She wanted to go outside and enjoy the beautiful day, but she had work to do. Reaching for her folder, she sat back, curled her feet under her, and began reviewing her research notes on Yancy Granger.

She had in her possession two major articles. The one on top was from *The New England Journal of Medicine.* In a nutshell, the writer praised the forty-two-year-old Dr. Granger as a brilliant OB/GYN surgeon, currently being considered for the Nobel Prize in medicine for his work in infertility.

What she wanted was something about the man himself, about his personal life. Dirt, to be exact. *The NEJM* made it sound as though he could walk on water.

Dana knew better. No one on this earth was that perfect or lily white. She had to find his Achilles' heel. She knew he had one; Wade Langely, the senior editor of *Issues,* had all but told her so. Still, she felt a twinge of shame that she was digging for a dark side. But that was her job—to expose the bad along with the good.

It wasn't like her to second-guess herself. She'd been given this assignment because she never hesitated in her work. In fact, she considered herself a predator, always on the prowl for the perfect story. If that meant slamming in for the kill on someone or something, she would do it. In her business, those who didn't go for the jugular got their own throats cut.

Feeling her eyes begin to tire, Dana took her reading glasses out of her bag and put them on. *Time* magazine also had a story about Yancy Granger. It touched on his personal life, pointing out that he had graduated from the University of Virginia summa cum laude, then gone to Johns Hopkins for his medical degree.

Following years of research, he returned to his hometown of Charlottesville to set up practice and teach, putting that research to use. Shortly thereafter, a women's infertility clinic was built away from, but in association with, the University of Virginia teaching hospital. It was stressed that Dr. Granger divided his time between the two facilities. Now, though, it seemed his goal was to attach a hospital to the existing clinic.

The article went on to say that Yancy Granger was from old Virginia stock, but that it seemed his cometlike rise to prominence was due to his hard work and tenacity rather than to his name.

"Sure," Dana murmured, finding that hard to believe. Once an aristocrat, always an aristocrat, was the unspoken motto of Virginia high society. Certain family names never failed to open a multitude of doors that were forever closed to average people like herself. Granger was one of those names.

Before she shut the magazine, she studied the doctor's color photo. No doubt about it, he was handsome in an offbeat sort of way, with incredible blue eyes that were almost scary in their intensity. He looked like a man who not only did everything with passion but who reveled in a brash arrogance that even his picture couldn't hide. For some reason, Dana shivered.

Still, she was glad to have that mental image of him. She liked to know her subjects personally and to know what they looked like before meeting them.

"Ready or not, Dr. Yancy Granger, here I come. And your life's about to change."

First, though, she had to refamiliarize herself with her surroundings. The rest of the day was too valuable to waste.

Seventeen years. Had it been that long since she'd been here? Now that she was back, it was as though she'd never left. While some things had changed, others had not. The beauty of the town had remained intact. The size certainly had not. Its fifty-thousand-plus population made it a thriving metropolis compared to what it had been when she'd visited and worked here.

The University of Virginia was Charlottesville's claim to fame and its biggest employer. But it had other tourist draws as well: Monticello, Thomas Jefferson's home; licensed farm wineries from which Charlottesville had gained the title "Wine Capital of Virginia;" and last but not least, the lure of the Blue Ridge Mountains.

To the southwest was the tiny town of Batesville, where she'd been born and raised. She wondered if it, too, had grown. Maybe she should find out. No, she wasn't ready for that. Not yet, anyway. For now, it was enough that she was back in Charlottesville.

Ten minutes later, Dana stopped for gasoline, pulling into the first convenience store she came to. She had to wait to pay. At the time, she didn't know what made her turn toward the voices behind her.

Two men occupied one of the tables. Both were drinking coffee and both were smoking, one a cigarette, the other a cigar. She turned away and held her breath. But the clerk behind the counter was so busy chewing her gum and chatting with her present customer that Dana feared she might burst.

It was then that she heard one of the men say, "Yeah, not only does my wife think Granger can do no wrong, he apparently thinks the same about himself."

Dana's investigative antenna rose, and despite the foul odor, she released her breath and listened.

"Hell, Fred, tell her to stay away from him, then."

"I wish I could," the man responded, his tone glum, "but she's hell-bent on having another baby."

The man called Fred chuckled, then scratched his head with vigor. "Correct me if I'm wrong, but isn't that your job?"

The other man glared at him. "Don't be an ass. It's not me, it's Liz. This doctor keeps telling her to take her temperature, to do this, do that."

"Maybe you just oughta adopt."

"I don't want no other man's kid."

"So be patient, then, Ken my man. Maybe the good Dr. Granger can work a miracle after all."

Ken's glare strengthened, then he snorted. "I don't like the arrogant s.o.b. From what I hear, he's too busy trying to raise money for that hospital to do his job. Then there's rumors of his appetite for women."

Fred chuckled. "Seems to me you'd best have a chat with your wife."

"Yeah, right," Ken retorted. "Only—"

"Ma'am?"

Dana jerked her head around and stared at the clerk, whose face was pinched with impatience. No wonder, Dana thought, realizing that two other people were now waiting behind her to check out.

"Sorry," Dana muttered, offering her credit card, which seemed to add to the woman's displeasure. She slammed the card into the gizmo, all the while mumbling under her breath.

Back in her car, Dana reached for her pad and made a note of that conversation. Apparently, not everyone in this town looked on the good doctor as a deity.

Dana drove around the city, amazed at what had changed and what looked exactly as she recalled. She was sure that the dress shop her mother had loved wouldn't still be there, but she turned onto the street anyway.

The shop was not only there, it looked the same as it had all those years ago when her mother had craved new party dresses.

Dana hadn't been more than ten years old, but she remembered the place vividly, as if it had been seared into her brain. That was because it had.

Dana braked her Honda and peered up at the sign: BEAUTIFUL THINGS. And there had indeed been beautiful things, but she hadn't been allowed to have any of them. That had been made plain from the get-go.

Dana remembered her mother trying on every dress in the store while she looked on, dressed in clothes that were too small and too wrinkled to have been worn in public. Her tennis shoes had had holes in them.

"Mrs. Bivens, would you like for me to pull some things for your daughter to try on?" the sales clerk had asked one time. "We—"

"Mind your own business, lady!" Clare Bivens lashed back.

The clerk turned beet red, while Dana peered down at the floor, wishing it would open up and swallow her.

Later, in the car, her mother suddenly grabbed her by her hair and shook her. "What did you say to that woman?"

"Nothing, Mama," Dana whispered, tears pricking her eyes.

"Don't you ever embarrass me like that again. You hear?"

"Mama, you're hurting me!" Dana cried out.

Her mother yanked harder. "I'm gonna hurt you a lot worse. That's a promise."

Clare Bivens had kept that promise, too, that night . . .

Dana fought off and finally escaped the endless darkness associated with those buried memories. Yet she continued to sit there, too devastated to move. That secret place inside her where she had hidden her pain all these years had suddenly been exposed to the cruel glare of daylight.

Run! Go back to Richmond, to your old job at *Old Dominion* magazine. You don't have to stay here. You don't have to do this. Yes, she did. She had two weeks' vacation coming, and she was going to use it to full advantage.

Besides, she prided herself on being responsible, reliable,

and dependable. She had committed herself. She'd always had an obsessive need not to let anyone down, especially herself. She didn't intend to start now.

As much as she hated this town and the memories it held, she wouldn't be sorry that she'd come back.

Still, as she drove back to the inn, emotion was thick in her throat and tears flooded her eyes. But not for long, she swore. She'd unpack, shower, dress, then go out for dinner.

Tomorrow she'd start her work.

Two

Dressed in a silk button-down caftan, Vida Lou Dinwiddie made her way down the circular staircase in the Dinwiddie mansion and didn't stop until she reached her office at the rear of the house. She went immediately to her desk, where a cup of hot coffee awaited her. Folding her arms over her silicone breasts, she hugged herself. God, she loved being waited on, being pampered.

Money. There was nothing like having money. It could buy her anything, even Yancy Granger. Her eyes strayed through the open door into the parlor, where a huge portrait of Alfred Dinwiddie hung in reigning glory. She had considered having the painting of her late husband removed but decided against it.

She owed the geezer too much. She'd snagged him, a multimillionaire, the last of an old Virginia family, when he was in his seventies, with a bad heart to boot. Perhaps aided by her voracious sexual appetite, Dinwiddie had died of a heart attack within months of having changed his will, leaving his fortune to her.

Vida Lou blew the portrait a kiss, then sat down at her desk and concentrated on her to-do list. As chairwoman for the fundraising committee for the proposed women's hospital, she was planning yet another shindig to collect money for her pet project.

She smiled to herself. It wasn't the project that was her pet—it was the doctor who would run it. She didn't give a whit about the hospital except as a means to an end. That end was Yancy Granger.

She was in love with him, the result of his having spent one night in her bed. And what a night it had been. The fact that he hadn't touched her since—six months ago, now—didn't matter. Once she'd had a taste of his body, she was determined to have more. But he had other ideas.

"This was a mistake," he told her the moment he'd gotten out of bed.

Her body turned cold as she watched him reach for his jeans and scramble into them. "You can't mean that."

"The last thing I intended was to hurt you, but—"

"Then don't." Vida Lou heard the desperate note in her voice and hated herself and him.

"You know it's a mistake to mix business with pleasure."

"After last night, how can you say that?"

When he looked at her again, his eyes were dark, unreadable. "It shouldn't have happened," he insisted.

She wanted to strike him.

"Look, I'll take full responsibility for stepping over the line here. I just want us to go back to being friends."

"I'll be whatever you want me to be," she whispered, swallowing her anger and her pride. Then, holding out her hand, she added, "Just as long as you don't stop fucking me."

"I told you that's not going to happen again," he said with obvious disdain.

At first Vida Lou's fury ran strong enough to plunge one of his surgical knives into his black heart. But again she cooled her temper, realizing that there were more ways than one to get what she wanted.

And she wanted Yancy Granger, not just in her bed but as her husband. So she decided to play his little game for a while, until he returned to his senses. In the end, she wouldn't be denied. Yancy would see the light and come back to her, especially when he saw the megabucks that she intended to raise for his hospital. He'd be beholden to her then.

However, she was growing weary of his stubbornness. He refused to so much as touch her hand, for God's sake. She truly had intended to curb her sexual appetite and abide by his rules, but this silliness was getting to her. At times—now, for instance—the urge to see him alone was so powerful that she couldn't fight it. Hence the phone call she had made earlier.

With clammy hands, Vida Lou opened her desk drawer and took out a mirror; she wanted to make certain she looked her most desirable. Perfect, she thought with a smile, flipping a bleached blond curl back into place.

She had never felt or looked better.

Dr. Yancy Granger's chest tightened. Margaret Davenport was one of his newest patients; he'd been seeing her for several months. She flew in on a regular basis from her home in California, convinced that he was the answer to her prayers.

At moments like these, he hated his job.

"Well, Doctor?" she asked in her sweet-toned, hopeful voice.

He sat down behind his desk, clasped his fingers together, and said, "I'm afraid I have bad news. Your ovaries are badly damaged."

Her eyes widened as her hand flew to cover her mouth. Still, he heard her muffled cry before he spoke again. "You're going to have to have a hysterectomy. I'm sorry."

"You're sorry!" she cried. "Is that all you can say?"

"I know how hard this is for you. I also—"

She lunged to her feet. "How could this have happened? You're supposed to be the best! You're supposed to be able to perform miracles!" She began to sob.

Yancy stood, came around to stand beside her, and tried to offer words of comfort. "It's not the end of the world, Margaret. You can adopt—"

Her head came up, and her eyes struck him like chips of glass. "And you can go to hell!"

Before he could say another word, she raced out the door, slamming it behind her.

Yancy didn't know how long he stood in the middle of his office, his heart and his head pounding. When he heard the knock on the door, he walked like an old man back to his desk and sat down.

He figured it was Brodie Calhoun, the hospital's chief of staff—the last person he wanted to see.

Seconds later he heard the knock again, only louder. He knew it wasn't Calhoun. He'd have knocked once, then barreled inside.

"Come in," Yancy snapped.

A young man dressed in a sheriff's uniform walked in. "Uh . . . you Dr. Granger?"

"Who wants to know?" His tone was surly, but he didn't care. He was in a surly mood.

"I do, sir. I'm here to serve you with civil papers."

Yancy stood. "What?"

The young deputy coughed, shifted his feet, but he didn't say anything. Instead, he handed Yancy the papers. Before Yancy could respond, he turned and walked out.

Yancy mumbled a curse as he ripped open the envelope. Moments later he looked up and took a deep breath.

"I'll be a son of a bitch!"

The threatened malpractice suit had become a reality. One of his worst nightmares had come true.

Three

"Dr. Granger, I need to talk to you. In my office."

"Not now, Brodie," Yancy said, passing him in the hall of the University of Virginia Hospital. "Later."

"No, not later," Calhoun sputtered. "Now!"

Yancy stopped and faced Brodie. "What is it?"

"What in hell's going on between you and Vida Lou Dinwiddie?"

"Nothing," Yancy lied, wondering what Brodie could possibly know. "Why?"

"I just spent an unpleasant ten minutes with her on the phone. She said you won't return her calls. Is that true?"

"Yeah. So what?"

"Megabucks is so what! Who in hell do you think controls the purse strings? If you want money to buy that land for the new hospital, you'd best get off your high horse and call her back."

Yancy's eyes were hooded. "You've made your point."

"I certainly hope so." Brodie paused, then added, "Now get back to work."

Yancy stormed into his office, not bothering to sit down. Instead he went to the window, and stared outside, watching the rain lash against the pane. When had that started? He hadn't even noticed the storm.

He thought about heading home, calling it a day. But the

day wasn't over, and the notion of going to his lonely, austere condo further blackened his mood.

As much as he hated to admit it, the idea of *any* lawsuit becoming a reality unnerved him. He despised that feeling, especially since his nerves were usually like steel.

He hadn't so much as flinched when the rumor of a paternity suit involving him and one of his patients had circulated. Hell, he knew that was hogwash. He'd been right. Nothing had come of the gossip. It died a natural death. A sarcastic smile crossed Yancy's lips as he thought about that degenerate doctor, an infertility specialist, who had recently made headlines by impregnating some of his patients with his own sperm.

It was a sick world out there, all right, and while he certainly wasn't without his faults, taking advantage of his patients wasn't one of them.

The malpractice suit, however, was another matter, even if it was just as ludicrous. It stemmed from his having performed an emergency C-section on a woman who had toxemia. As a result of that condition, her baby died; hence, the woman had looked for a scapegoat. He was that scapegoat. He'd been accused of operating while intoxicated, an untruth that seemed to gain strength with each passing day.

Yancy knew what had happened. Someone had seen him drinking Perrier with a twist at a party and had assumed it was alcohol. Shortly thereafter, the emergency had occurred.

He had enemies. Lots of them. He hadn't gotten where he was in the medical profession by being a nice guy. When it came to doing what was best for his patients, he didn't give a damn whose toes he stepped on—those of other doctors, nurses, anyone who didn't do things as he thought they should be done.

That hadn't always been the case. He had entered medical school wanting to be a doctor, but the passion had been missing. Only after that life-altering incident on the rain-splattered road had he become focused and committed to his profession.

He'd been determined to be the best doctor he could be, at whatever cost.

It hadn't been easy. At times he'd wanted to throw in the towel, but he hadn't. Now, all those long nights of studying and working in hospitals until he was ready to drop had paid off.

One of his dreams was on the brink of becoming a reality—a hospital for women that specialized in gynecology and infertility. The Women's Clinic was already established; he practiced there several days a week. If the committee was successful in raising the money, the adjoining land would soon be the site of a small hospital. Both facilities would fall under the auspices of the University Hospital.

It wasn't that he didn't like operating at the big hospital. He just wanted more—an upscale facility that catered only to women's special needs. In addition, he wanted a place to continue his infertility research.

Besides, many of his patients complained about the huge University Hospital, mainly because its proximity to the campus made access difficult for them and their families.

At this point in his life and career, Yancy cared only about pleasing his patients. With that in mind, he couldn't afford the stigma of a court battle.

"Ah, to hell with it," he finally muttered.

He was just wasting energy by anticipating something that wasn't going to happen. Given time, that lawsuit would fizzle out like the others had. Besides, until the new hospital became a reality, UVA couldn't run without him, its chief gynecological surgeon. Brodie Calhoun wouldn't let anyone touch him.

He groaned suddenly, his thoughts switching to Vida Lou. *She* could touch him, all right, where it hurt the most. He scowled.

Thank God, Brodie wasn't on to his little secret. If he were, Brodie would understand his reluctance to talk to Vida Lou.

Damn! How could he have gotten into such a mess? How could he ever have slept with her in the first place? At the time, the reason had been simple: She'd caught him in a weak moment, just after he'd had a hellish day in surgery and had heard the first rumors of a possible malpractice suit against him.

Now, even he couldn't buy that excuse.

To add to his mental agony, Vida Lou was under the misconception that he'd slept with her because he wanted her in his life. That couldn't have been further from the truth. Although she was wealthy now, it was common knowledge that Vida Lou had earned the money on her back, then simply got lucky and married the poor bastard.

Her brazen, sluttish ways so repulsed him that he could barely look at her, despite the fact that she had spent thousands on various plastic surgeries to make herself sexually attractive, lifting everything in sight. She looked fifteen years younger than her true age. And with her bleached blond hair, she could almost pass for a younger Linda Evans.

While money had taken the woman out of her background, it hadn't taken the background out of the woman, but she refused to face that. She wanted to be well thought of, to have a good name in the community.

That was impossible, for everyone in Charlottesville knew about her. As one blue blood put it, "That woman's just as filthy with money as she ever was without it."

Yet, through her own tenacity, she had gotten herself appointed chairwoman of the most important civic project to hit the town. That had been a coup in itself, considering the odds against her.

Yancy had always resented being an aristocrat, for he knew how shallow the caste system was. His opinion of the upper crust was "a bunch of flakes who hung together because they all had a lot of grease." Only he didn't have the "grease." He lived off his income as a physician, even managed to save some, but was far from wealthy.

Orphaned while a freshman in college, he had found himself poor for the first time in his life. When his parents died, he had come to know the facade they had lived behind—robbing Peter to pay Paul, selling off pieces of their estate to pay the bills, leaving him with more financial obligations than assets.

He knew what it was to overcome the obstacles involved in that degree of snobbery. While he might admire Vida Lou for her gumption in bucking the same establishment, that in no way should have evolved into anything personal.

Making the project become a reality was well within her power, which was a legitimate cause for concern and the most asinine reason for sleeping with her.

As much as he hated to admit it, Vida Lou Dinwiddie and her obsession with him was a brewing shit storm that could cost him dearly.

Four

Dana hated to dine alone. She had hoped to have dinner with her old friend, but April hadn't returned her call.

Reluctantly, she had decided to try the new restaurant in town that Mrs. Balch had recommended. Since the spring air was chilly, she'd chosen a pair of silk slacks and a matching sweater. She felt she looked her best—not that it mattered, she thought with a rueful smile.

Now, sipping wine as she waited for her grilled chicken salad, she scanned her surroundings. Her eyes stopped on a table occupied by a man and a woman. At first it was the woman Dana noticed, most likely because she was so striking, with a thin, model's body, wispy bangs and close-cropped brown hair, and a sprinkle of freckles across her nose. But on closer observation, the woman looked hard and angry.

Surmising that the man with her was the source of that anger, Dana focused her attention on him. At the moment, his profile was all she could see. Yet he looked familiar—so familiar that she felt a shiver of uneasiness run through her.

She averted her gaze, her face flooded with unwanted color. She felt not only uneasy but . . . something else. Recognition? A sensory response? Of course not. Neither was possible. She shifted in her chair to get a better view of him. His features were chiseled, and his expression hinted at some damaged vulnerability that told her he'd seen hell. Still, he was good-looking in a raw, rough way.

But she was immune to his kind of potent attraction. She always had been, always would be. But dammit, there was that niggling feeling that she'd seen his face before. But where? She shifted still more. That was when his startling blue eyes met hers.

She jumped as if jolted by electricity. *Time* magazine. The man staring at her was Dr. Yancy Granger.

In the flesh.

Damn, but she was a magnificent creature—one of the loveliest he'd ever seen, and he'd seen many.

Her face was dominated by smoky gray eyes, porcelain skin over high cheekbones, and a full, sensual lower lip. Her hair was dark, almost black, glossy, shoulder length and free flowing. The facial package was strong, yet powerfully alluring. Its force was irresistible; akin to an open fire compelling him to place his hand over it.

He wished he could see the rest of her. She appeared tall and lean but well-endowed. Her red V-necked sweater called attention to the shape and swell of her generous breasts.

Suddenly he felt uncomfortable. He had a hard-on the size of a lethal weapon. Damn! It was at that moment, while he was squirming, that their eyes connected for the briefest of moments. His squirming intensified and this time, he winced as though he had just stuck his hand in that goddamn fire.

Who the hell was this woman? He knew he had to find out.

"You didn't hear a thing I said, did you?"

Yancy turned back and faced his ex-wife, who was staring at him with raw hostility. He'd done it again—waded into a pile of crap that was so deep he needed hip boots. For someone who was supposed to be an expert on the opposite sex, he'd sure made some stupid moves lately.

Would Misty be the next to exact a pound of his flesh? If

so, it would serve him right. When the hell was he going to learn that he couldn't take women at face value? They seemed to always say one thing but mean another.

Misty had called and insisted on having dinner with him. She'd sounded so innocent, so charming, that he hadn't seen any harm in it. The thought had crossed his mind that maybe they could be friends now, having been enemies for so long.

When he'd decided that their marriage was a big mistake and would never work, guilt had gnawed at him because he'd never loved her. And she'd known it. He'd been attracted to her, but love—hell, he hadn't known what the word meant, and still didn't.

But then, she hadn't loved him either; he'd found that out as soon as they had started divorce proceedings. She'd made it quite plain that she'd married him for his performance in bed and his potential to make lots of money.

Now, two years later, they rarely saw each other except at medical conferences or other chance meetings.

"Sorry," he muttered, "you're right. I didn't hear you."

Her thin lips became thinner. "You haven't changed one iota, you know."

"How's that?" Yancy asked in a bored tone, knowing what she was going to say. Damn, the one evening he didn't have to work, and he opted to spend it with his carping ex-wife.

"You're just as self-centered and arrogant as you ever were—more so, in fact."

"Dammit, Misty." His temper was on a short leash.

She smiled. "You were and still are the best in bed, you know." Her smile turned intimate. "You used to think that about me, too."

"Things have changed."

Her expression changed suddenly. "Damn you, Yancy!" she said through clenched teeth.

"Sorry, that was out of line."

"You're not sorry and you damn well know it."

"Look, Misty—"

She held up her hand. "Don't try to make me feel better. You couldn't when we were married and you can't now. Besides, now I have someone who loves me more than he loves himself."

"I'm glad," Yancy responded in the same bored tone.

"I suspect I'll marry him."

"So why this meeting? You need money for the wedding?"

Her lips curled in an unfeminine snarl, and for a moment she looked as if she might reach across the table and claw his eyes out. Lord! Yancy thought. What a fiasco.

"One of these days, Yancy, your mouth and your attitude are going to get your ass nailed. But in answer to your question, no, I don't need money. The man I'm planning to marry just happens to be filthy rich."

"Good, because I don't have any cash to spare."

"That doesn't surprise me. All yours is probably going into that almighty hospital you think you have to have. Then the great Dr. Yancy Granger will truly be immortalized."

"You don't know when to quit, do you? But then, you never did. I pity that poor bastard who's about to take you on."

"You'd best pity yourself instead."

"If you don't stop dancing around the mulberry bush and get to the point, I'm outta here."

Misty stared at him for a long moment, as if trying to decide what to say next. But when she finally spoke, her tone rang with confidence. "I've just heard the news."

"What news?"

"Don't play dumb with me."

Yancy shrugged.

"The Nobel Prize. That's the news I'm referring to."

He laughed, but without humor. "Surely you don't think I have a chance at that?"

"With your arrogance and luck, yes, I do."

"Well, put your mind at rest 'cause it ain't gonna happen."

"Suppose it does?"

Yancy shrugged again. "Then I'll be one happy sonofabitch."

"What about me?"

An eyebrow shot up. "What about you?"

"I should share the honor and the money."

Yancy was too stunned to speak. All he could do was stare at her while a smile toyed about his lips. "I gotta hand it to you, Misty, you've got balls, more than most men I know."

"Thank you."

"You're welcome."

"So, now back to the part I played in your success."

Yancy leaned forward. "What I accomplished in the field of infertility I did on my own, and you damn well know it."

"That's not true! I helped you with some key research." Her tone was as terse as her expression. "And I want what's coming to me. It's not open for debate, either."

Yancy smirked. "People in hell want ice water, too, but they don't get it."

"We'll see about that. And remember that I warned you."

"That works both ways. You helped: I'll concede that. But the original idea wasn't yours. So I'm warning you that should I win, which again is a big *if,* I don't intend to share it with you or anyone else."

Misty stood, rising to her full five-foot-ten height, then leaned over and said for his ears alone, "Don't bet on it."

Before he could offer a suitable comeback, Misty turned and strode out of the restaurant.

"Damn," Yancy muttered, lifting his glass of Perrier and taking a big gulp. It was at times like this that he wished he had a glass of Crown Royal on the rocks. But those days were over, and no matter how much he craved a drink, he couldn't, wouldn't, ever take another one.

He didn't know how long he sat there brooding about that disturbing conversation with his ex, but it didn't matter. What mattered was that he'd thought they might be friends. He cursed. The problem was that she knew too damn much about him. His mood soured even more.

Only after the waiter asked if he wanted something to drink

did he shake himself out of that sour mood. Hell, Misty was just blowing hot air. She wouldn't make good on her veiled threat, he knew. But if she tried any mud slinging, he would have no choice but to retaliate. She had her own skeletons in the closet, and he wasn't beneath exposing them if she continued on this path.

Ah, to hell with her! Whatever she might threaten, it wasn't worth worrying about. She had worked with him and contributed—he wouldn't deny that. But the ideas that had prompted his research had originated in his mind. He'd best not get too cocky, though, he reminded himself. A woman who felt cheated was liable to do anything. Vida Lou had taught him that.

Yancy's eyes strayed back to the attractive woman who still sat across the room. She looked every bit as delectable as she had earlier, only there was something else. She looked as lonely as he was upset.

He thought for a moment, then asked himself, Why not? Why should he let Misty completely ruin his evening?

Shoving back his chair, he got up and made his way to her table.

He noticed that her eyes were gray with thick lashes. Close up and personal, she was even lovelier than he'd first thought.

"I couldn't help but notice that you're alone. Would you like to join me for coffee?"

Her smile was not only stiff but cool, as though it hurt her to make the gesture. "What about your lady friend? What would she say about that?"

God, even her voice was a turn-on; it had the same husky appeal as Kathleen Turner's. He could feel himself getting hard again. "First off, she's not my lady friend," he said in a rush. "She's my ex-wife, and she won't be coming back."

Dana smiled for real this time, and he was sure that smile could warm the coldest day of any winter.

"If you say so."

"I say so."

A loaded silence followed. Finally, he said, "Well?"

"Why don't you join me, Dr. Granger?"

He was taken aback that she knew his name. "I'm afraid I don't have that same pleasure of knowing who you are."

"Dana Bivens."

He sat down but didn't extend his hand. Maybe it was because she hadn't extended hers first. Too bad; he would've liked to touch her. "How did you know who I was?"

"Easy. Everyone in town knows about the infamous Dr. Yancy Granger."

For a moment his eyes twinkled. "Uh-oh. If that's the case, then I'm in trouble."

"At least you admit it," she said, laughing.

That laugh radiated a potent seductiveness that didn't escape his senses. Who was this woman? "So do you live here, in our fair city?"

"No." She paused, toying with her lower lip. "I'm a journalist, actually."

He almost didn't hear what she said. He'd been concentrating on her sultry, dark-haired beauty. "Can I assume you're here to do an article?"

"Absolutely."

"Do you like your work, Ms. Bivens?"

"Do you like yours, Dr. Granger?"

He grinned. Sharp lady. She'd picked up on the censure in his tone.

"Mind telling—" The waiter suddenly appeared at Granger's side.

"Sorry to interrupt, Doctor." With an apologetic look, he held out a cordless phone to Yancy.

Dammit! "Granger here." He listened for a moment, his stomach tightening. "Now?" he demanded. "At the clinic?"

He listened a moment longer, then said, "All right. I'm on my way."

After he handed the phone to the hovering waiter and the man scurried off, Yancy turned back to Dana. She smiled. "You have to go."

The fact that she smiled deepened his regret. Of all times

for that particular patient to show up. But he couldn't afford not to attend to the matter—his work always took precedence over his play. He felt another stab of regret, thinking that this woman would make one helluva playmate.

"Yeah, I have to go," he said slowly. "A VIP's at my office."

She nodded, then reached for her purse. "I should be going too. Another time, perhaps?"

"When?"

Their eyes met.

She shifted her gaze, then swung it back to him. "Soon."

"Where can I call you?" Granger pressed.

"I'll call you."

Something strange yanked at his gut, then, which both excited and angered him. What was the matter with him? Hell, he couldn't afford to get involved with another woman, no matter how badly he wanted her.

"Come on," he said, almost choking on his inner rage. "I'll walk you to your car."

They strode in silence through the clear night air. Unfortunately, it wasn't the air that held his attention, but rather the subtle scent of her perfume and the way her slacks hugged her hips, causing them to sway as she walked.

She gave the word *sexuality* a new meaning, only he'd bet his ass she didn't know it.

And all he knew was that he had to see her again. There was something about her, something different. . . .

She stopped suddenly and looked up at him. Because he hadn't been paying attention, he bumped against her. For a second, he was too stunned to move, probably because he'd felt a nipple jab him in the chest. God!

He cleared his throat and was about to apologize when their eyes locked, blue on gray. This time neither broke the stare. His tongue seemed to have gone numb. All he could think about was that eraser-hard nipple and his erection, wondering if she'd felt the latter.

"Uh . . . sorry," he finally murmured, yet he still couldn't move or take his eyes off hers.

Dana opened her mouth as if to say something. Maybe that was his undoing, seeing her moist lips part, compliments of the full moon. Hell, he didn't know at the time what came over him, what triggered his knee-jerk response, nor did he care. His base instincts took control.

With a rush like an electric current charging through him, he reached for her and crushed his lips against hers. For a moment, she stiffened, which only made him increase the pressure. With the full force of her breasts pressed against him, there was no turning back from his rising tide of lust.

He heard her moan deep inside as he nudged her lips apart with his tongue. Apparently, it was that boldness that made her act. She jerked her head back and pushed him away, her eyes wide and frightened.

Their ragged breathing rivaled the sound of the rising wind.

"I don't make a habit of this," he managed to get out, more shaken than he cared to admit, even to himself. "I—" He couldn't go on. The truth was that he didn't know what the hell to say. She turned and opened her car door, but not before he saw that her hand was shaking. He placed his over hers. "When can I see you again?" His voice sounded thick and deep.

She raised her eyes to his and whispered, "I'll be in touch."

He stood there like some flat-footed idiot, knowing that he should already be at the clinic.

Yet he still didn't move until her taillights disappeared.

Five

Sweat drenched Yancy's body and clothes; even his green surgical scrubs hadn't escaped the abuse. The nurse wiped his brow above his mask. Finally yanking it off, he stared at the two resident doctors across from the patient, who returned his stare as if Yancy were the devil himself.

"Don't just stand there with your fingers up your butt," Yancy snapped. "Finish, then close her up." Without so much as a backward glance, he turned and walked quickly out of the OR.

He didn't make it far before he had to stop and lean against the wall, taking deep, gulping breaths. Sweat continued to ooze out of every pore on his big body. He wouldn't have to jog this evening, he thought inanely.

"We nearly lost her back there."

Yancy looked up at Carl Parker, the surgeon who had operated with him and who had followed him out.

"What's this 'we' bullshit? You were the primary on this one. What the hell happened, Parker? If I hadn't gotten there when I did, that woman would've bled to death."

"I—" Parker's face turned the color of his hair, burnished red.

"If this ever happens again, I'm going to report you. Do you understand that?"

"Look, Granger," Parker sputtered, "just where do you get off—"

Yancy got in his face. "I get off running the OR in this hospital, and if you or any of my staff fucks up, the board looks to me!"

"No one's perfect," Parker responded, a bitter twist to his lips. "Not even you."

"That's where you're wrong. *I am perfect.* The sooner you learn that you'd better be perfect too, the sooner we'll get along. Now get your ass back in there and check on those residents."

When the doctor didn't move, Yancy yelled, "Now!"

Parker jumped as if he'd been shot and rushed back through the swinging doors.

"Hey, Granger, Calhoun wants you in his office. Gonna get your chops busted again, huh?"

"Go to hell, Marsh!"

The heart surgeon just laughed, then he sauntered down the hall, not missing a step.

Yancy took the opposite direction, walking briskly to his office. There, he plopped down on the cot in the corner and buried his head in his hands.

He knew that he should feel remorse about the way he treated his colleagues and underlings, only he didn't. In this business, there was no room for sentiment. He was a hard taskmaster; he had to be, otherwise he couldn't have lived with himself. When dealing with human life, there was no room for error. More often than not, there wasn't room for a second chance either.

In the future, those who worked under him would thank him. Hell, he'd had a tough old bastard in med school who had stayed on his ass until he'd gotten it right. As a result, he felt confidence in his ability, which was what he wanted for his students.

Yancy loved his work. He loved making the ill well, loved seeing the tears of joy in a woman's eyes when he told her she was pregnant.

But those rewards didn't come easily. There was a price to pay. God, he knew that.

Yancy peered at his watch; he had about forty-five minutes until he had to be back in surgery. His next patient was a woman who had a tubal pregnancy. She was older and hadn't yet had a child, but she still had hopes of doing so. He hoped he could make that possible.

He gave his head a savage twist and jumped up. Neither his body nor his mind could stay still. He looked at his hands and noticed they were trembling. If only some of his cronies could see him now, especially Parker.

"Aw, fuck 'em," he muttered.

He knew what was wrong with him. Dana Bivens. He wanted to see her again. He wanted her in his bed. But there never seemed to be time for anything he wanted anymore. All he did was work and return Vida Lou's phone calls.

Damn that woman. Like Dana, she was driving him up a wall, only for different reasons. Yet he needed Vida Lou, needed her expertise, her aggressiveness, to build the hospital he so desperately wanted. Once that happened, he wouldn't ever have to see her again if he didn't want to, nor would he have to deal with incompetents like Carl Parker. At the Women's Hospital, *he* would pick the staff.

In retrospect, Yancy realized that the same thing could have happened to him. In fact, it had, which was why he tried so hard to see that no other doctor experienced that kind of hell. Perhaps he'd gone a bit overboard with his criticism of Parker. Perhaps he could've used more diplomacy.

Still, Parker's mistake could've been avoided. He had deserved to have his balls busted, and Yancy wasn't sorry he'd busted them. Yet he knew that part of his volatile reaction stemmed from inside, from his own frustrations.

Yancy's thoughts drifted back to Dana Bivens. Like a fool, he'd kissed her. Even now, he felt another rush through his body. She had tasted so good, smelled so good, and felt so good. But then, most women he chose to see fit those criteria. So how had Dana managed to do what others hadn't been able to? She had turned him inside out, made him long for things he had no business longing for.

Maybe it was the way she'd responded to him for that one split second when her lips had been as hot and pliant and greedy as his. The top of his head had nearly come off. He hadn't wanted it to stop there. He had wanted to—

Was that a knock on his door or the pounding of his pulse? Yancy stilled his thoughts and listened. The sound came again.

"It's open," he said.

His secretary peeked into the room. "Dr. Calhoun's waiting for you."

"Thanks, Abbey. Tell 'im I'm coming."

Yancy massaged the back of his neck, took a deep breath, and walked out of his office, his expression as dark as a thundercloud.

Dr. Brodie Calhoun rubbed the tiny bald spot on the top of his head, still unable to believe it was there. In fact, he'd messed with that tiny dome so much that it felt raw, but not nearly as raw as his temper.

Damn Yancy Granger. One of these days he was going to put that doctor in his place. Sure you are, Calhoun told himself with a rueful smile. He didn't intend to give up, though. Someone had to keep trying to put a stopper in Yancy's mouth. And he was that someone. If he didn't, the hospital could end up in a world of hurt.

There were times when one had to play the game. The problem with Yancy was that he refused even to be on the team. It was *his* way or the highway. If only his chief gynecologist and surgeon weren't always so angry, so driven, as though he were running away from himself.

Actually, Brodie worried about Yancy, especially in relation to the hospital board.

"If it takes licking any of those board members' asses," Yancy had said, "then you can forget it."

That was practically the first thing Yancy said when he'd

first come to the University Hospital. To date, he'd stuck with those words, much to the chagrin of the board and the staff.

But what can I do? Calhoun asked himself. The University Hospital was damn lucky to have Yancy Granger, and if that specialty hospital of his became a reality, it would bolster the economy not only of Charlottesville but the entire county.

He stared at the ceiling as if asking for divine intervention. He just wished Yancy would be like the other doctors—do his work, then go home to a wife and kids. Brodie scoffed at that picture. Even if Yancy wanted to be like other doctors, he couldn't. He was on a sphere all his own.

Brodie had tried to explain this to the hospital board, but they were having a hard time with Yancy's attitude and the controversy that surrounded him.

The hospitals grapevine seemed to work nonstop, and most of the time Yancy was the source of that gossip. It seemed that he relished stirring up trouble, as if to prove that he was the best at what he did. Brodie suspected that Yancy was determined to prove that he could make it on his intelligence and talent rather than the Granger name.

If only someone could tame just a little of the man's wildness, his arrogance, then his job as chief of staff would be so much easier. Most often it was hell, like now.

He feared that Yancy might have gone too far this time.

"If you've called me in about Parker," Yancy said, striding through the door, "you can forget it."

Brodie glared at him. "Dammit, next time knock."

"This had better be fast. I have to be in surgery in exactly—"

"For once, sit down and shut up."

Yancy looked at him for a long moment, then shrugged. "All right, but again, if this is about Parker—"

"It's not about Parker, although he just called to report the ass-chewing you gave him in front of anyone within hearing range."

"So? The sniveling bastard had it coming. That woman could've died."

"I'm glad you said that."

"What the hell does that mean?"

Brodie felt himself start to reach for his bald spot, then jerked his hand down. "Need I remind you that people have died under your knife, too?"

"All right, Brodie, get to the point."

"Wipe that smirk off your face."

A muscle twitched in Yancy's jaw. "What the hell's going on here?"

"Lawsuit. Does that jar something loose?"

Yancy didn't so much as flinch. "Yeah. So what?"

"So what? How can you sit there and act as if it's nothing? Hell, Yancy, I've always thought of you as a friend. I've even gone to bat for you against the board—numerous times. But at this moment, I'm tempted to just hand you over to them."

"Look, you gotta trust me on this. The lawsuit *is* nothing."

"The baby died, for chrissake!"

Yancy bolted out of the chair and slammed his palms on Brodie's desk. "Don't you think I know that?" His nostrils flared. "Don't you think I live with that every day? I don't need you or that sanctimonious board to judge me!"

"Well, I'm sorry, but that's life, my friend. And right now they're willing to hang your ass out to dry."

"Just tell 'em to calm down. That I'll fix it. I wasn't drunk when I did that emergency surgery. Hell, I hadn't even been drinking."

"Still, there are witnesses—"

"I don't give a rat's ass how many witnesses there are," Yancy flared. "It's just a trumped-up charge that's gotten blown way out of proportion."

"While that may be the case, we, you, and the hospital have to deal with it. It's bad publicity, but then I shouldn't have to tell you that."

"So what?"

"The board chewed on my ass for twenty minutes about you and the suit, that's what. And I want to know what you're going to do about it."

"Like I said, fix it, as in make it go away."

"Now, why doesn't that give me any comfort?" Brodie asked.

"Because you're the eternal pessimist."

Brodie snorted. "This is serious, Yancy. *I'm* serious."

"So am I—especially since I did my job to the best of my ability. No one could've saved that baby. By the time the deadbeat husband finally called 911 that night, the baby's condition had already deteriorated to critical. I'm not God."

Again Brodie snorted. "You sure about that?"

"Yeah, I'm sure," Yancy responded in a suddenly tired voice.

"Okay, so what do we do? How do we get you out of this mess?"

"Not to worry. It's being taken care of even as we speak."

Brodie felt his spirits rise, yet his tone held suspicious caution. "By whom?"

"The best lawyer my malpractice insurance can buy."

"And just who might that be?" Brodie asked, his voice still cautious.

"Old man Tremaine's son, Rooney, who practices in Richmond."

Brodie felt the blood in his veins turn to ice water. "Surely you're joking?"

"Nope."

"But that's absurd!"

"I thought it was a stroke of genius, myself."

"But that's a clear conflict of interest. What with Shelby Tremaine owning the land in question—"

"Rooney doesn't own the land. And like I said, he's the best."

Brodie's features hardened. "What if it does compromise the deal? What if old man Tremaine decides he doesn't like this messy affair you're involved in? More to the point, what if he doesn't like the fact that you're involving his son? You know how he guards that family name."

"Then I'll just have to figure out a way to make him change his mind, won't I?"

"Rooney'll never take the case."

Yancy got up, walked to the door, then turned back, smiled, and said, "Wanna bet?"

Once he was alone, Dr. Brodie Calhoun sank back in his chair, fear growing like a malignancy inside his head.

Six

Dana punched the pillow one more time. Then she flipped over and stared at the ceiling. Dr. Yancy Granger was the sole reason for her discontent and her insomnia.

Too bad he hadn't turned out to be old and ugly. If he had, she'd be safe on two fronts. She wouldn't be thinking about him on a personal level, and she could take advantage of his medical expertise.

It was ironic, she thought. Here she was in a town that claimed the best infertility specialists in the field, yet she didn't have the courage to do anything about it. If only she could muster up that courage and settle once and for all her fear that she might be infertile. Following the accident, she'd been a mess mentally and physically. She didn't know if she could get pregnant again.

Dana suddenly gave her head an abrupt shake. What on earth was she thinking? Granted, she wanted the answer to that nagging question, but *not* from Yancy Granger.

Feeling disgusted, she looked at the clock. Seven. She considered getting up and making her way downtown to the treasure she'd stumbled on among the boutiques and antique shops—a tiny restaurant that served delicious pastries and dark, strong coffee. But her body refused to move. She decided to turn over and try one more time to fall asleep. She needed all her wits about her today. She planned to get started on her job.

Dana groaned, as color flooded her face and her heart began to pound. Dammit, why did her subject have to be the charismatic Dr. Yancy Granger? She still couldn't believe she'd simply stood there and let that man kiss her.

Why hadn't she knocked the stuffing out of him and then bolted? That thought hadn't even entered her mind.

What had entered her mind was that his kiss hadn't frightened her. Instead, she'd felt intense heat and exquisite pleasure, especially when his tongue had eased into her mouth and she'd felt his erection. Even now she shuddered with emotions that memory evoked.

Granted, he was attractive. So were a lot of other men. But she'd rarely gone out with any of them, and she sure as hell hadn't let them kiss her. Rooney was the only man in years who had gotten within touching distance.

What was so different about Yancy Granger, other than his strong, aristocratic good looks? She didn't know; that was the scary part. She pictured him in her mind as he'd been in the restaurant.

When talking to his ex-wife and *not* trying to charm her, he'd been different. Gone were the easy-listening voice and the disarming smile that had thrown her heart out of rhythm. He'd looked somewhat older than his years and battered to the point of grimness.

Yet she couldn't seem to stop seeing that errant strand of hair that grazed his forehead. But it was his eyes—and what eyes they were—that had left their mark. Not only were they unique in intensity and color, they seemed to have the power to cut through all her defenses.

She would have to tread carefully around him for more reasons than one. Her reaction had been knee-jerk and out of proportion. He had already gotten under her skin. He both repulsed and fascinated her—repulsed her with his aggressive charm and fascinated her with his arrogant daring. Both were lethal.

Such behavior would not happen again. Since she'd lowered her defenses and allowed the unthinkable to happen, the playing field was no longer level. She had broken a cardinal rule: don't become personally involved in the story or with the person. Had she compromised her work before she'd even started?

She had predicted that he wouldn't be an easy subject to interview. But he would be a challenge.

Dana punched the pillow again. Harder. Stop thinking about that jerk! His potent masculinity had the power to seduce any woman, including herself. Her anger blazed.

Had she lost her mind? Yes, for a moment last night, she had. Worse, his wet, hot kiss had left an unfamiliar ache between her thighs.

She pressed her hand against her stomach, which felt queasy. She'd hoped for fireworks; that's what a good story was all about. She had been sent to dig into the heart and soul of Dr. Yancy Granger, to find out if he was truly deserving of the Nobel Prize as well as all the notoriety and homage that had been paid him.

She had always enjoyed dodging the Scud missiles that were so much a part of her business, as long as those missiles didn't involve her personally.

Not only did she have Yancy Granger to contend with, she had Rooney Tremaine as well. Rooney had met her at the airport following her return from her interview with *Issues* magazine.

He had taken her to a French restaurant for dinner. They had barely been seated when he'd looked at her with his heart in his eyes.

She had shifted her gaze because she couldn't return that look, although she wished she could. He wasn't as handsome as a lot of men she'd known, but that didn't matter. He had everything going for him. He was a gentleman and a successful attorney who owned his own firm. He also had plenty of money and the pedigree behind that money.

However, none of that mattered, either. She just didn't love him. She knew that he wished she felt more than fondness for him, yet he hadn't pushed, for which she'd been thankful. But judging from the way he had continued to stare at her, she wasn't sure how much longer she could stave off the inevitable.

She hated to hurt him. He'd been so good to her and for her. But she realized that nothing stayed the same and that once they reached a certain point in their relationship, it would change.

"I missed you, you know," he'd said into the building silence.

Still she hesitated. "And I missed you."

"But something's going on. Something's wrong. I can feel it."

He reached for her hand and she flinched.

Rooney's lips thinned. "Dammit, I've never said anything, but I think it's time you leveled with me."

"About what?" she asked, her eyes wide and questioning.

"Why you hate for me or any other man to touch you?"

"That's not true," she denied. "You've touched—"

"Sure, I've touched you, even kissed you, but you never respond, and you know it." He paused. "It's not just me, either. I've seen you react the same way when any other man innocently touches you, as I did now."

"Look, Rooney . . ."

"Who hurt you?"

Dana opened her mouth, then shut it, but she didn't take her eyes off Rooney. "You're imagining things."

"Am I?"

"Yes," she responded with steel in her tone.

"I don't think so, but we'll let it pass."

"I should hope so, as we . . . we have something to celebrate."

"You could've fooled me."

Dana flushed, then said in a cajoling tone. "Come on, Rooney, just continue to be my friend. Please?"

"Not to worry; I'll always be that."

She forced herself to reach for his hand and squeeze it. "Thanks," she whispered. Then, clearing her throat, she added, "*Issues* wants me for their Washington bureau chief."

"Why, that's great!"

"But first I have to prove myself—earn the position, so to speak."

Rooney waved a hand. "No sweat; you can do it."

"I'm sure I can, too."

"So where's the assignment? Not far, I hope."

"Charlottesville." Dana thought she might choke on that word when she spoke it. She almost did.

"Well, I'll be damned. I've been looking for a way to get you to finally visit my family. Voilà! The opportunity's been dropped in my lap."

Dana looked at him, confusion mirrored in her eyes.

"You've forgotten, haven't you?"

"Forgotten what?"

"That I'm from Charlottesville." His voice had a scolding edge to it.

Dana's confusion turned to dismay. Following through with this assignment suddenly took another twist. Since she would have to be in Charlottesville for several weeks, she saw no way to avoid meeting his family. It was one thing to have a casual relationship with him while they both lived in Richmond; it was another to be dragged into his family's stronghold.

She hated to admit it, but that thought made her uncomfortable. While she was proud of her accomplishments, she still felt inferior when faced with the Old South caste system so prevalent in Virginia. She knew she would never pass muster in the Tremaine family.

Rooney obviously misunderstood her reaction. "I didn't

mean to make you uncomfortable, but there's no reason to worry about anything. We Virginians don't have anything against Texans."

"But—"

"Is it *your* fault your parents died in a car wreck? Come on, Dana. My parents aren't trolls under a bridge. They'll love you!"

Dana knew better, but she kept a small smile on her face. Knowing the way the First Families of Virginia felt about their sons and daughters, she would definitely be in the line of fire.

"You're right," he laughed, switching the subject, "we do have something to celebrate."

"Rooney—"

"Humor me, just this once, okay?"

She nodded, lifting her champagne glass in a mock toast.

What had she done? In telling him about the assignment, she had all but committed herself to the job. Deep down she knew she'd been committed all along, only she hadn't admitted it until now. She would call Wade Langely. Dana swallowed the champagne along with her panic.

Everything was going to be just fine. She hadn't clawed her way this far for naught. The sky was the limit. She could handle whatever lay ahead. The past would not shackle her.

Or was she simply fooling herself?

Dana's stomach gave a twist just as the phone rang. Her thoughts interrupted, she reached over and grabbed the receiver.

"Dana!"

"April?"

"Yeah, it's me. Am I calling too early?"

"Heavens no. I wasn't asleep. Anyway, I thought you'd disappeared off the face of the earth—or that you'd crossed me off your friends' list!"

April laughed, a bubbly laughter that time hadn't changed. It soothed Dana's troubled mind like little else could.

"I've reserved all morning for us. I won't take no for an answer."

Dana responded with a chuckle of her own. "You haven't changed one bit. Still as bossy as ever."

"You got it. So, get your butt out of that bed and get a move on."

Seven

Dana studied her friend and decided that not only was her laughter the same, but very little else had changed, either. Though still on the plump side, her skin had few lines, and her dimples remained as noticeable as ever.

The only thing that had changed were the streaks of gray in April's brown hair, which she was running her fingers through now as she leaned sideways and stared at Dana.

"You look great. You haven't changed any that I can see."

Dana smiled. "I was just thinking the same thing about you."

"That's a lie. I'm fatter than ever." Though she spoke in a critical tone, April grinned, exposing the gap between her front teeth.

Dana couldn't help but remember the time April had told her that she'd never have it fixed because her favorite movie actress, Lauren Hutton, had a gap just like hers. The thought brought a smile to Dana's lips.

"What?" April demanded, an eyebrow raised.

"I was thinking about what you said about Lauren Hutton."

April rolled her eyes. "God, can you believe I had the gall to compare myself with *her?*"

"Yes, I can," Dana teased.

"Only now, I wish I had her figure rather than her teeth."

"Why? You have a wonderful husband who loves you the

way you are, who makes good money so you don't have to work anymore. And you have two delightful children. What more could you want?"

"Yeah, I guess you're right. But when I look at your willowy but well-endowed bod, I turn green with envy."

This time Dana rolled her eyes. "Oh *please.*"

"And I miss the job sometimes, too."

"That's crazy."

A silence followed while they sipped their coffee. When Dana had first arrived at her friend's house, a yellow two-story that had been refurbished, she had been given a tour. Though the interior was lovely, it couldn't compete with the outdoors.

From her chair on the deck, Dana looked around the small, well-kept lawn, stared at the huge weeping willow filled with chirping birds, and breathed in the scent of nearby flowers. At that moment, it was Dana who felt gut-wrenching envy. April had what she herself wanted but could never have.

"What are you thinking about?" April asked.

Dana gave her a bright smile. "Actually, I was envying you all this."

"Hell, and here I was envying you."

"You really miss being a journalist?"

April grinned. "Actually, I always thought of us as more investigative snoopers than journalists."

"Well, you're right. I was thinking this morning about how I enjoyed dodging Scud missiles, but I believe you enjoyed it as much as me."

"Not quite, but almost."

Dana didn't respond right off, content to feel the warm sun on her back while she thumbed through an album of the latest photos of April's family. It seemed that April had been her friend forever; they'd met and bonded in their teen years when working together on their high school newspaper. Still, there were things about her that she had never shared with April and never would.

Dana knew that April had been curious about her past, especially as April's life had always been an open book. But when she hadn't confided in her, April had stopped asking, though it hadn't affected their friendship.

"So what brings you back here? It's got to be some hot story. Right?"

Dana traced a finger around the top of her empty cup. "Right."

"In Charlottesville?" April laughed. "Lord a'mercy, I can't imagine anything or anyone who's hot in this hole."

"How about Dr. Yancy Granger?"

April sucked in her breath. "You gotta be kidding?"

"You know I'm not."

April's face turned serious.

"Surely you've heard that he's being considered for the Nobel Prize in medicine?"

"Probably. I guess it didn't make that much of an impression."

"Well, I'm here to find out if he's a worthy candidate."

"And *is* he?" April pressed.

"Hey, I just got here, remember? I guess I'll know in due time, especially if you can shed some light on the good doctor."

"Ah, so this isn't just a social call?"

Dana laughed. "You know the drill."

"Looking for some more Scuds, huh?"

"Right. And if I find them, I could land a plum job with another magazine—which, by the way, is just between us."

"So you're here on the sly?"

Dana flushed. "Sort of, and I'm not real keen about that either, but . . ."

"Hey, go for it, kid. If you don't, someone else will. All's fair in love and journalism."

"Love can be a bitch," Dana said.

"So, you're telling me things with Rooney aren't going too hot?"

"They're too hot for me . . . not hot enough for Rooney. I

don't know, April. I just don't feel, well, Rooney's a wonderful guy, but I don't love him. I mean, not in *that* way."

"He's handsome enough and—"

"And he wants me to meet his parents, here in Charlottesville. They're blue bloods, April. You know the type, and nobody's worse than Virginia's blue bloods. What am I supposed to say to them? 'Don't worry, folks. I don't love your son enough to marry him?' It'd kill Rooney."

"Maybe once you get this job and move to Washington, things will be better."

"Well, first I have to *get* the job."

"So what can I do to help?"

"Like I said, tell me everything you know about Yancy Granger—the good, the bad, and the ugly."

April laughed. "Okay, but first tell me what you already know."

Not much, except that his kisses made me wet, Dana thought; then she almost choked. When she cleared her throat, she drew a strange look from April.

"You all right?"

"Of course."

April reached for the carafe on the table and refilled Dana's empty cup. "Drink up. My coffee'll cure all ills."

"You got that right. I'm afraid it's going to grow hair on my chest."

They both laughed, then sobered. "Actually," Dana said, "the only thing I'm sure about besides his candidacy for the Nobel is that he's hellbent on getting a new women's hospital."

"Everyone knows about that."

"Does everyone know that he might have a malpractice suit slapped against him?"

April's eyes widened.

"Well, say something. Is that just gossip or is there some truth to it? You're an ex-reporter—you're bound to know the skinny."

"Unfortunately, I don't," April said. "But I hope there's no truth to it. The worst I've heard about Yancy Granger is that he likes the women."

Dana twisted in her chair and cleared her throat again. "Now why doesn't that surprise me?"

"Mmm, do I detect sarcasm?"

Dana smiled sheepishly. "Yeah, but don't pay any attention to it."

"And he's about as ambitious as anyone I've ever known."

"Which means he's not about to do anything to jeopardize his career?"

"Exactly."

"So I guess that goes for the malpractice suit as well."

"I'd say so, though I know he once had a drinking problem."

"Oh?"

April shrugged. "I don't know any juicy details, though. I only met him once, at a party, and he was drinking then, or appeared to be. He had a glass in his hand, and it wasn't empty."

"What about his family?"

"Everyone knows about the Grangers. They were steeped in Virginia blue blood. But when his parents died they left him with lots of debts. Still, at one time they had loads of it—old money. And once a blue blood, rich or poor, always a blue blood. But then you know that."

"Don't I though." Dana didn't bother to disguise the bitterness in her voice, which brought on a short silence.

"But I have a friend who knows him well," April said, her features once again animated. "And she thinks he's the most wonderful thing since sliced bread."

Dana's lips turned down in a scoffing manner.

"Well, she does. What can I say? Because of his work in fertility, she has two children. Before Granger, she went to several other doctors with no results. In fact," April added, "she's such a believer, she's spearheading the fund-raising committee to get money for the land."

"What's her name?"

"Alice Crenshaw."

Dana made a mental note of that. "Anything I should know about the committee? Is there any friction there?"

"I'm sure. There's a whole lot of ego among those five, with Vida Lou Dinwiddie's being the biggest."

"Who is she?"

"A piece of work."

"Other than that, who is she?"

"She's the chairwoman, and from what else I hear she's determined to have things her way."

"Which means?"

"I don't know, except the old broad has more money than anyone else in this town. When old man Dinwiddie passed on, gossip has it that he was riding her good and hard."

Dana's lips twitched. "In other words, she screwed him to death."

"That's about the size of it, and now word has it that she's balling her personal trainer."

"And you said there's nothing hot in this hole. No pun intended, of course."

They both laughed, even as Dana decided to check out Ms. Dinwiddie first thing. She would most likely be the one who could offer insight not only into the doctor himself but the entire project and its chance of success.

Dana looked at her watch. "I'd better run. It's almost time for you to pick up the kiddos."

"You could come with me, you know?"

"No, I can't. Oh—before I go, what about the land? If the money comes through, will UVA get it?"

"I assume so," April said, "since another blue blood owns it, which means it'll probably be named after him."

"And who might that 'him' be?"

"Old man Tremaine."

"Any relation to Rooney Tremaine?" Even though she'd asked, Dana knew the answer would be no.

"Yep. It's Rooney's old man, Shelby Tremaine."

Dana gave her an incredulous look. "*He* owns the land?"

"Yep. Does that mean something?"

Dana's lips were tight. "Not really." But it did. Rooney had failed to tell her that *un*small tidbit.

Why?

"You'll be making a big mistake."

Dr. Misty Granger stared at the man she'd been sleeping with for more than a year now, a building contractor with megabucks. Although Tony Browne didn't mind spending those bucks on her, Tony and money weren't enough. He wasn't the type to stay slim and trim, and judging from the pale frog's-belly color of his skin, he never worked with his men on the job site, either. Not even his money could hold her, for she earned a tremendous salary in her own right. No, Misty wanted more. Much more.

She wanted power, power that stemmed from her work. Most of all, she wanted recognition, something that so far in her career had eluded her. But dammit, Yancy was getting it—in spades—and that stuck in her craw.

"I don't care," Misty finally said in answer to Tony's blunt statement.

"Ah, babe, you know better than that. You do care. You'll just be getting yourself in a high snit for nothing."

They were in bed in his swanky apartment in Richmond; dawn had just broken through the skies. Misty had just returned from a research conference in Atlanta sponsored by the American Medical Association, and they'd made love throughout the night. She'd pinned her hopes on seeing Yancy instead, but he hadn't been there, which had deepened her frustration and anger.

"I'm in a snit all right, but it's not going to be for nothing. I'll assure you of that."

Tony grimaced, she noticed, but it did nothing to detract from his handsomeness. In fact, he was almost too pretty. No man should have such deep-set brown eyes, perfect features, beautiful teeth, and a winsome smile. His only imperfections were the burgeoning paunch around his waist—the result of too much alcohol and no exercise—and that dead-frog pallor. God, hadn't the man ever heard of a tanning bed?

At times, especially when they were in bed, naked, she couldn't help but compare his body with Yancy's. Even though she'd never known her ex to work out in a gym, he was solid muscle with only the barest amount of fat. She guessed genetics and his hectic lifestyle made that possible.

But she didn't want to think about Yancy now, while Tony was lacing his fingers through the curls between her thighs.

"Forget about him," he said in a cajoling yet strangled tone. "You . . . we don't need that arrogant s.o.b. You'll make your own mark in medical research."

"But Yancy's about to be—"

"Screw Yancy! You're intelligent in your own right; hell, you're brilliant . . . and a hell of a lot better-looking."

The palm of his hand replaced his fingers, and she moaned, her eyes on him. "Oh, Tony," she whispered.

"That's more like it, babe. Me. Tony Browne, that's all you need." He dipped his head, and his tongue surrounded a small nipple.

She moaned much louder when his hands and mouth brought her to another rousing orgasm, but it wasn't Tony she was thinking about—it was Yancy. Regardless of how Tony made her body feel, she had a score to settle with her ex, especially now, in light of what was happening.

Misty knew what she had to do.

Eight

Call him, Dana told herself. Make an appointment. Now was the time to make her move. If it had been anyone other than Yancy Granger, she would have already been sniffing for the kill.

Instead, she was dragging her heels—Dana Bivens, known throughout journalistic circles as an aggressive, in-your-face reporter. If her colleagues could see her now, they would taunt her, saying that she had lost her nerve. They would be right.

She laughed a hollow laugh. She'd been aggressive toward Dr. Granger, but not in the way that counted. Every time she thought about that hot, savage kiss they had exchanged, her stomach rebelled. Unfortunately, her stomach wasn't the only part of her body that reacted, which was at the heart of her problem. Okay, she had screwed things up. She acknowledged that. Now, she had to put behind her that entire episode and how it had affected her and go on, pretend it had never happened. She could do that; she was a master at pretense. She'd been pretending for the better part of her life.

So, back to square one: She had to confront him, and to start digging into his life, his past, his present. She had to get to know this man from the inside out.

Determined or not, she didn't think that would be an easy task, despite the way he had come on to her. He used his charm when necessary to get what he wanted, but instinct told her that underneath that charm was a hard, driven man who wouldn't like anyone poking into his business.

Too bad, she thought, her confidence gaining. He should have thought of that before he became such a public figure. She would contact the fundraising committee, beginning with the chairwoman, Vida Lou Dinwiddie. In fact, she'd already tried to reach the Mrs. Dinwiddie, but her housekeeper had told her that she was out of town and wasn't sure when she would return.

Before she had left April's house, she had gotten the names of the other committee members. She had called them and managed to make appointments with three out of the four, all scheduled for tomorrow.

Today, she intended to interview the woman who had filed the lawsuit against Yancy.

Dana paused in her thoughts, stretching her back as her stomach growled. She looked at her watch and saw that it was almost noon; she hadn't had anything except coffee. She decided that before she ate lunch, she would call Rooney, still miffed over the fact that he hadn't told her his father owned the proposed land site.

She had the phone in her hand when she heard the knock on her door. Thinking it was Mrs. Balch, Dana was loathe to answer. She liked the innkeeper, but once she started talking, it was hard to get her to stop. Dana didn't have time for idle chatter.

"Come in," she called, her conscience winning over her sound judgment.

"Bet you weren't expecting me."

Dana's eyes widened on Rooney Tremaine as he lounged just inside the door, a "gotcha" grin on his face.

"No, I wasn't, but I'm glad to see you."

Rooney blinked. "You are? Well, that's a switch. I don't recall you ever greeting me with this much enthusiasm."

"Trust me, I have an ulterior motive."

"Ah, I knew something had to be going on. But aren't you curious as to why I'm here?"

"As a matter of fact, I am. I was just about to call you."

"Wasn't by chance 'cause you missed me and couldn't live another moment without seeing me?"

Dana had to smile. When Rooney wanted to, he could be endearing at best and irritating at worst. Right now, she wanted to hug him and slug him. She did neither.

"So what's up?" he asked.

"Have you eaten?"

"Nope."

"Good. Come on, I'll treat you to lunch."

"I'll come, but it's my turn to pay, and if you argue, I won't go."

"Fine. Your treat."

Seated on the patio of the Chesapeake Bagel Company and enjoying chicken salad sandwiches with iced tea, Dana didn't waste any time or mince any words.

"Why didn't you tell me that your father owned that land?"

"You didn't ask."

"I shouldn't have had to."

Rooney took off his glasses, blew on each lens, then cleaned them with his napkin. Dana tried to curb her impatience. "You knew I was coming here to investigate Yancy Granger."

Rooney replaced his glasses and stared at her. "Right. But if you'll recall, about the time you told me that, we were interrupted. I had to be in court."

"I remember, but still—"

"Still nothing. I didn't *not* tell you on purpose. Anyway, why're you so upset?"

Why? Maybe because without the land, there would be no hospital.

"What difference does it make what my old man does with the land?" Rooney was asking.

"So tell me, is Daddy going to sell it?"

Rooney was silent for a moment. "Who knows, with him. If they raise enough money, then I guess he will."

"So money's the bottom line, not the town's best interest?"

Rooney's face turned red while his tone turned defensive. "I wouldn't say that, at least not entirely. I'll admit my old man likes money, says he wants to get a bundle and put me in politics. Now, is that a joke or what? But more than anything, he *loves* the land and isn't sure he wants to part with it. After all, that land's been in our family for generations. It's steeped in history; several small battles in the Civil War were fought on it."

"I see."

"Maybe you do, but there are more problems right now than the land."

Dana's journalistic instincts kicked in. "Such as . . . ?"

"The infamous Dr. Granger, for one."

Dana could barely control her excitement. "Really?"

"That's what I thought too."

"Stop talking in riddles and spit out what you know."

"He's the reason I'm in town." Rooney paused, his face softening. "And to see you, of course."

Ignoring the latter declaration, Dana asked, "Why? I mean, I don't get it. What do you have to do with Yancy Granger?"

"He's my client."

"Your client?" Dana knew that if she looked as dumb as she sounded, she was in big trouble.

"Yep. He's being sued for malpractice, and I'm handling the case." He grinned. "So guess what, darlin'? You're going to be seeing a lot of good ol' Roone, 'cause the good doctor has gone and gotten himself in a hornet's nest."

"Why you?" Dana managed to get out.

"Why not me?"

"For one, your father owns the land."

"So? It's not *my* land."

Though still dazed at this sudden twist, Dana asked, "So what's the malpractice suit about?"

"Granger allegedly operated on a pregnant woman while intoxicated, and the baby died."

"Oh my God."

"That's what I thought, too, just like my old man. He went

into orbit when I told him." Rooney scratched his head. "Isn't that a hell of a note."

"What?"

"A candidate for the Nobel Prize being hauled into court first on a civil suit, then possibly murder."

Dana was stunned. *Murder!*

The house looked like an average American home. Maybe just from the outside, Dana thought, trying to quiet her unexpected case of the jitters. Sitting in her Honda, Dana stared at the white picket fence covered with honeysuckle vines and wondered what kind of woman she would encounter. Heartbroken? Vindictive?

Still, Dana remained in her car, the dread increasing. This was one interview she wished she didn't have to keep.

She'd gone straight from the restaurant to the courthouse and looked at a copy of the lawsuit. She hadn't bothered to quiz Rooney any further, knowing that client confidentiality prohibited him from saying more. But the lawsuit was a matter of public record, and she'd found what she needed to know for now.

The petition was clear and simple: Dr. Yancy Granger was being sued for negligence, which meant that he fell below the standard of care in his duties. Since the suit was new, there were no additional papers on file.

The woman responsible for the suit, Mary Jefferies, lived in Front Royal, about a hundred miles up Interstate 81 from Charlottesville. Dana had called Ms. Jefferies and made an appointment.

Finally, she stepped out into the bright sunlight and made her way up the sidewalk. The door opened before she had a chance to knock. Dana found herself staring into the face of a woman who didn't look as if she were grieving over anything or anyone, much less the loss of a child.

Her cheeks and lips were redder than any fire engine Dana had ever seen. But it was the way she was dressed—in a shrunken T-shirt that highlighted her large breasts and a tight skirt that showed off her heavy thighs—that alerted Dana. Something was definitely amiss.

"Ms. Jefferies?"

"That's right," the woman said, noisily working on a wad of chewing gum. "You the newspaper lady?"

Dana nodded. "May I come in?"

"Sure." Mary Jefferies stepped aside and motioned for Dana to go first.

Once inside and seated on the edge of the couch, Dana surveyed the premises. Signs of neglect were much more obvious inside than out. The furniture was old and dilapidated, and the smell of stale tobacco hung in the air.

"Uh—this isn't going to take long, is it?" Ms. Jefferies asked.

"No, but if this is a bad time—"

"Nah, not really. I got a few minutes to spare." She smiled. "But I do have an appointment I gotta keep."

I just bet you do, Dana thought, getting her pad and pen ready. "So, what happened that night?"

"My baby died."

"I'm sorry."

Mary averted her eyes. "Yeah, me too."

"How did it happen?" Dana kept her tone soft, yet forceful. God, she hated having to ask these questions. They brought back so many memories. . . .

"You want something to drink?"

Dana shook her head and smiled. "No, thanks."

"For a second there, you turned kinda pale."

"I'm fine," Dana said quickly, mentally kicking herself for the personal reaction. "So again, in your words, what caused your baby's death?"

"I'm not really sure. That medical stuff's over my head."

"Please try," Dana urged.

"The doctor told me and my husband that I had some kind of poisoning." She stopped and rolled her eyes. "I never can remember that word."

"Toxemia."

"Yeah, that's it. Anyway, my body went into failure or something like that."

"And you're blaming the doctor?"

"Yeah, 'cause he was drunk and couldn't do what was needed to fix it. Not only that, but I'm told I can't have no more children. And boy is my old man mad, 'cause the kid was a boy."

"Do you have witnesses to prove that Dr. Granger had been drinking?"

"Sure do. Want their names?"

"Please."

Shortly thereafter, Dana returned to her car. She started the engine, then picked up her car phone, determined to find and then interview those witnesses. No such luck. One was out of the state and the other was unavailable until the following Friday.

When Dana pulled away from the curb, she looked in the rearview mirror. Mary Jefferies was standing at the door, watching her.

Dana frowned. Her first impression hadn't changed. If that woman was grieving over the loss of her child, she sure as hell had a strange way of showing it.

More puzzled than ever, Dana shook her head. Something was definitely out of sync.

"Hey, Doctor, wait up!"

Yancy stopped in midstride on the hospital parking lot and turned around. Ted Wilkins was grinning at him, stained teeth and all.

"What brings you to this hallowed ground?" Yancy asked.

"My wife's having a little outpatient surgery."

Ted was an insurance salesman whom Yancy had played golf with in several fund-raising tournaments.

"I hope everything'll be okay."

"Thanks," Ted said. "I'm sure it will. So, how's it going with you?"

Yancy shrugged. "Same old same old—work."

"I knew you hadn't been seen in public lately."

"Man, I stay covered up."

"Well, I hope we—you get that new hospital. Maybe this'll help."

Yancy watched as Ted reached into his pocket and pulled out a bulging envelope.

"What's that?"

"Two grand. In hard, cold cash." He held out the envelope.

"Are you crazy?" Yancy backed away.

"Go on, take it. Consider it my contribution to the hospital cause. I won it in Vegas, and if my wife gets her hands on it—" He shrugged.

"Hell, I appreciate it, Ted. Don't get me wrong. I just don't want to be responsible for cash."

"Aw, it's just money. Go on, take it, and be damn grateful you got it."

"Since you put it that way, I guess I can't refuse." He shook Ted's hand. " 'Thanks' seems kind of inadequate."

"Just send me a receipt when you get around to it." He grinned. "So my wife'll know what I did with it."

"No problem; and thanks again."

Yancy watched as Wilkins ambled off, then he got into his car and immediately called Carter Lipton, the committee's treasurer, who owned his own business.

After five rings, the answering machine picked up. Yancy pushed the End button on the phone. Dammit, he didn't want to talk to a machine, nor did he want to talk to Vida Lou, who would be the next logical person to give the money to.

Then he thought about Herman Green, who was also on the committee and whose office was nearby. Yancy called him.

"What can I do for you, Doctor?"

"Take some money off my hands," Yancy said, then explained.

"I'm about to take a little breather, but my secretary'll be here. Just come in and leave the money in my desk drawer."

"Your desk drawer? You sure?"

"Sure, I'm sure. Besides, I won't be gone that long. When I get back, I'll see that Lipton gets it."

"I hate to ask you, but would you mind sending Ted a quick receipt?"

"Sure. I'll have my secretary take care of that."

"Thanks. I'll owe you."

Yancy whistled all the way to Green's office.

Nine

The short but well-built man looked at the others seated at the small round table, then leaned back in his plush executive chair and smiled.

"Well, gentlemen," he said, "now that you're all here, we can get started."

At first, no one showed any enthusiasm, which caused Newton Anderson to frown. In fact, they looked downright bored—or was it anger he saw etched in their faces?

Dammit, he hoped he wasn't going to have trouble with these men. He'd handpicked them himself and knew that all three were wealthy, influential, and intelligent. Most of all, they were movers and shakers who could get things done. Or so he'd thought. At the moment, they looked as if they had one foot in the grave and the other on a banana peel. Hells bells!

Maybe their lethargy was due to the fact that he'd called this meeting in his office high above the city of Atlanta at seven o'clock on a Saturday morning. But he hadn't wanted to wait. He'd gotten up at four-thirty, run his five miles, an everyday ritual, then headed to his office eager to settle the pending business. Too, he'd left a "lady" in his bed, one he didn't want to keep waiting much longer. Just thinking about the things she had done to his body, and would continue to do, forced him suddenly to cross his legs.

That move seemed to awaken the deadbeats around the table.

"Jesus, Newton, why'd you get us here so early?"

"Now, Edwin, don't go gettin' your shorts in a wad." Which was like asking him not to breathe, Newton thought. If this banker had one fault, it was a nervous personality. Still, Edwin Minshew had a shitload of money, so that fault could be overlooked.

"Yeah, I'd like to know the same thing," Barton Engles chimed in, all the while pawing his right shirt pocket, which held a pack of cigarettes.

Newton winced, thinking of what Engles's office must smell like since he was a chain smoker. Stink hole or not, his was one of the most prestigious architectural firms in Atlanta.

"I wish to hell you'd let me smoke." This time Engles's voice came out in a whine. "Hell, at this hour I need the caffeine."

"Caffeine my ass, Engles," Winston Taylor said, the last of the three. He owned construction companies all over the world.

Newton smiled at his chosen ones; they were about to make him as rich as they were and at the same time fulfill another goal of his.

"You're just hooked on those damn things and you won't admit it," Taylor added. "There's coffee over there; go get some and forget about lighting up."

Engles glared at his friend, though he did get up and trudge to the coffee bar.

Once the architect was back in his seat, Newton leaned forward and was about to speak when Edwin Minshew fanned his hand across his face. "Damn, Newt, did you take a bath in your goddamn cologne? Hell, I almost think I'd rather smell Engles's smoke."

Everyone chuckled except Newton. He felt his face flush, then gave a condescending smile. "What can I say, guys. After

Sheryl gave me that last blow job, she insisted on rubbing me down with foo-foo juice."

"Get outta town," Taylor said in disgust.

"You're full of shit, Newton," Engles added. "But I'm with Minshew—take it a little easy on the smell-um-good from now on, okay?"

This time Newton's smile was plastic. "Okay, you've had your fun. Let's get down to business."

"We're listening," Taylor said. "This is your baby, so run with it."

"I think we have a good chance of acquiring the land."

"Now, tell me again where this land is," Minshew said.

"In Charlottesville, Virginia."

"And you still think that's the best location for our project?"

"No doubt about it," Newton said with authority. "Albemarle County is ripe for an explosion in growth. As most of you know, it not only has the UVA, but more and more tourists are drawn to its beauty. So you see, it's a gold mine on the ground." He grinned. "No pun intended."

That set off a round of chuckles.

"None taken," Engles finally said, slapping his pocket again.

"So why don't you just buy the land?" Taylor asked. "We trust you, or none of us would be here at this ungodly hour."

"It's not that simple," Newt said, frowning.

"Why? Hell, money's no problem. What we're short, any bank would loan the rest to us."

Newt massaged his clean-shaven chin. "There's another faction that wants the same tract of land."

"So just shoot them out of the tub with a higher bid."

"It's not that simple," Newt repeated, rocking in his chair, his eyes shifting from one to the other. "Actually, the reason I called this meeting is to bring you up to speed on what *I've* done on my own."

He had their full attention now.

"The other faction's a local group that wants the land for a small hospital just for women and their infertility problems. There's a clinic on the adjoining piece of property that will connect to the hospital."

"If the land's as valuable as you say, it would be a crime to waste it on another hospital. Anyway, the last thing that town needs is another goddamn hospital. As it is, the University Hospital's multiplying like cancer."

"My sentiments exactly," Newt said. "That's why I've already put a plan into action."

"So enlighten us," all three said at once.

"I'm moving to cover all our bets. The first step I've taken is against Yancy Granger, the primary doctor involved—the one who's slated to head the hospital. I've begun to discredit him."

"Is that necessary?" Engles asked.

"Absolutely. I've done my homework. This was all Granger's idea from the start. Without him and his supposed infertility expertise, there wouldn't be a need for the hospital."

"So what have you done?"

Newt gave them a satisfied smile. "Dr. Yancy Granger has been officially slapped with a malpractice suit for causing the death of a newborn." His smile broadened. "And the woman who filed the suit is one happy broad, mainly because she's been amply compensated."

"Ah, so the charge is a trumped-up one," Minshew said, rubbing dark stubble on his chin. "But does she have a chance to win? You know how hard it is to get doctors to rat on one another."

"No other doctor has to. The fuel for Granger's demise fell right into our lap. He was seen at a party the night of the emergency surgery with a drink in hand."

A short silence ensued.

"So you're saying he was drunk?" Engles asked.

"It doesn't matter," Newt said, his expression having grown dark. "We have two witnesses willing to testify that his drinks contained alcohol. So you see, we have Granger right where we want him—with his balls hanging out."

Taylor gave Newt a strange look. "Hell, the way you're gloating makes me think you have something personal against this guy."

"Just business, my friend, just business."

Only it wasn't just business, not by a long shot. But these men didn't have to know that he had his own private agenda. Still, he'd best be careful; either they were much more perceptive than he'd given them credit for or he'd let his facade slip. If the latter was the case, he wouldn't let it happen again.

It was going to be hard, though, to contain his excitement. He couldn't believe his good luck. Sometimes fact was stranger than fiction. Newton's mind suddenly jumped back a few years to the time when his first wife had wanted a child. She'd heard about Granger before he'd become famous and had insisted on going to him for tests. In the end, it had turned out that he, Newt, was shooting blanks and couldn't father a child.

Since the day Yancy Granger had paraded into his office and told him, he'd hated the man and vowed that no one humiliated Newton Anderson like that and got away with it.

Now he had a chance to get even with that son of a bitch, and he was going to run with it. Besides, when this deal went through, he'd have more money than he, or any of his mistresses, could ever spend.

"Newt?"

He thrust a hand through his dishwater-colored hair, then shook his head. "Sorry. The strategy is to ruin Granger's reputation long before the suit ever gets to trial. That way, we'll be assured of getting the land."

"In other words, if Granger's reputation gets smeared, then the townsfolk may not be so generous in loosening their purse strings." Winston fell silent, a faraway look in his eyes. "I like that."

"Good," Newt said with a smile. "And to add more fuel to

that fire, the owner of the land hates scandal; he's so steeped in that tradition bullshit that it's sickening."

"Which means he'll turn on the good doctor as well," Engles said.

Newt nodded. "And to sweeten the pie even more, the woman we paid off called and said she'd had a visit from an investigative reporter, doing an article on Yancy Granger."

Minshew chuckled. "Did she blab like a woman at a hen party?"

"No, she didn't have to. Apparently the reporter knew about it and was there to get the scoop."

"Sounds good to me," Engles said.

"Me too," Winston put in. "You have our blessing, Newt, so hang tight. There's nothing we like better than a good fight." He smiled. "Over the almighty dollar, that is."

"That's good to know," Newt said, "because that's just what it might turn out to be. But I intend to win, gentlemen. Make no mistake about it, that land *will* be ours."

Dana yawned, then took another sip of coffee. She couldn't seem to wake up this morning. But then it was Sunday, and she could afford to be lazy. Wrong. She should interview more people about Yancy Granger, but she suspected that the small-town folks frowned on having their privacy invaded, especially on the Sabbath.

Besides, she had promised to spend the afternoon and evening with Rooney. She'd picked up the phone to cancel their outing several times, but didn't have the heart to do so. She genuinely liked him and wished that was all he felt for her.

Dana reached for the *Washington Post.* She set her cup down, then scanned the headlines, ending up on the society page—something she enjoyed persuing, even though she hated to admit it.

The top item in the column jumped out at her.

* * *

WILL THERE BE A NEW MEMBER IN THE SPEAKERS HOUSE?

Rumor has it that the Speaker of the House, Clayton Crawford, and his young and lovely wife Gloria are trying to have a baby. And because that hasn't happened, she's consulting a renowned infertility specialist.

Any truth to these rumors, Congressman?

Dana's hand froze on the page as her heart began to race. *Yancy Granger!* He had to be the doctor referred to. So why hadn't she known about this? Dammit! If Nancy Simmons, the reporter for the society page, had found out about the congressman's wife, then she should have too. Anything concerning Yancy Granger was her job.

Suddenly Dana thought about the phone call Yancy had received in the restaurant the other night. The look on his face was unforgettable. But then he'd come right out and said he had a VIP waiting. She hadn't given that statement any thought, especially after the fiasco that followed. That kiss had blown everything important from her mind.

"Dammit!" she said again, this time out loud.

She'd have to confirm that Yancy was indeed Mrs. Clayton Crawford's doctor, then figure out what would be in it for him. Offhand, she could think of several things: money, prestige, notoriety, not to mention the fact that it would further endear him to the people of Charlottesville.

If he failed in his endeavor, however, it could backfire in his face. He could become the scapegoat. She could blame him for her inability to conceive.

Whichever way it went, the potential for a story was there. She had to act on it and soon.

Deciding that she was too keyed now to remain in her room, Dana dressed and drove into town. She'd grab a bite to eat at the same time she worked on her list of questions for Yancy Granger.

The smell of bread baking tickled her nose even before she

walked into her favorite café. She was about to sit down when her eyes wandered to the counter.

The only occupant met her gaze. "Hiya, Dana. Long time no see."

Dana gripped the back of the nearest chair while her blood iced over and her mind raced. Albert Ramsey, one of the most hated freelance journalists in the business, was smiling at her as though she were a long-lost friend. She abhorred him and his tactics. He'd stop at nothing to get a story. *Nothing.* He was the type who had such thick skin that you could stick needles in him and he'd never flinch. He had no feelings.

"What are you doing here, Ramsey?" she asked, the coldness she felt coming through her voice.

He placed a hand over his massive chest, but it was his face that made her wince, and not because of his huge acne-scarred skin. Rather, it was the contempt registered there—contempt he had for everything and everyone.

Another journalist had described Ramsey as someone who always looked as if he'd just stepped in a pile of dog crap. Dana couldn't have agreed more.

"Why, is that any way to speak to a friend?" he said.

"You're no friend of mine and never have been."

"My my, you must've gotten up on the wrong side of the bed this morning."

"What are you doing here?" she repeated, glaring at him.

"Well, the last time I checked, it was a free country." His drawl was insulting. "Besides, I could ask you the same thing."

"Stay away from me, Ramsey."

He laughed. "I could say the same to you. But since I'm in such a good mood, I'll answer your question. I'm here about a story, sweetheart."

Fear gripped Dana as the society page item jumped to mind. No way would she let that bastard beat her to any story on Yancy Granger. No way.

As though her thoughts were an open book, Ramsey

laughed. "Why, sweetheart, you look like someone just poked a hole in your boat."

Dana's lips tightened. "You wish, Ramsey. You wish."

Before she completely lost her composure and got into a verbal slinging match with this creep, she turned and walked out.

Ten

"Are you still mad at me?"

"I wasn't ever mad at you."

Rooney splayed a hand across his heart as if he were in pain. "Are you kidding? I felt the daggers right here." He banged on his chest.

Dana rolled her eyes. "Talk about overreacting."

They had just finished dinner in Charlottesville's most upscale restaurant, the one where she'd first met Yancy Granger. For the most part, the evening had been a pleasant one.

Up until the last minute, Dana had continued to dread the outing. But since she hadn't come up with a way to ease out gracefully, she had kept her commitment.

Besides, the prospect of spending the evening alone with her thoughts had not been enticing, since her mind was stuck on Yancy. Her decision to use that to her advantage, by questioning Rooney about his planned defense of Yancy, had increased her enthusiasm.

To further buoy her spirits, she'd chosen to dress for the occasion, knowing that Rooney would wear a shirt and tie. He always did, wherever he went. She had long ago accepted that as part of his aristocratic upbringing. For a moment she had even pictured his father taking his mother to bed in a tuxedo.

She had giggled at that image as she slipped into a simple,

short black dress, an Ann Taylor original. When she had met Rooney in the B&B parlor, he'd whistled.

Now, though, as he stared at her, he was very much the stiff professional. Despite his teasing, apparently he didn't understand her reasoning.

"I guess my mind was just boggled there for a time."

"You were justified, actually. I should've told you that my old man owned the land. I just didn't think. But as to the attorney agreement, you knew that shortly after I was hired."

"I know. It's just that both things together smack of such coincidence that I find it hard to swallow."

"So now that you do, it's safe to say that you'll pester me every chance you get to know what's going on."

Dana smiled. "If that's a question, you've already answered it."

He gave her an exasperated look. "Have you sunk your tenacious teeth into the doctor's business yet?"

"Not yet."

"From what I already know of him, he isn't going to like that."

Dana pursed her lips. "Sorry, but that's the way it is. In fact, I've already started."

"I know. Mary Jefferies told me you'd been to see her."

Dana cocked her head to one side. "So what do you think?"

"About what?"

Rooney appeared so innocent that for a moment she almost bought the charade. Then she shook her head. "Oh no you don't. You just admitted that I'd want to know everything you know."

"But I didn't say I'd tell you," Rooney responded with a grin. "You knew when you started this fishing expedition that you weren't going to get anything out of me."

"I know, it's privileged information."

"So why do you still try to worm it out of me?"

"Because I'm a reporter and here to do an in-depth story on your client, which means probing every aspect of his life. It's part of my job."

"And keeping my mouth shut is part of mine. But on the other hand, if you uncover something that you think I ought to know, then it's your obligation to tell me. I'd like to get the guy off."

"Without knowing or caring if he's innocent or guilty?"

If Rooney took offense to her statement, he didn't show it. He shrugged. "I try not to ask that question or worry about that."

"Spoken like a true attorney, which is one reason why our court system stinks."

Rooney raised an eyebrow. "My, I didn't know you had such strong feelings on the subject."

"Well, now you know," she replied in a heated tone.

Rooney grinned, only to have it wane suddenly as he peered beyond Dana's shoulder. "Well, well."

"Well, what?"

"I just spotted the subject of our conversation."

Dana struggled against the panic she felt rising within her, tried to let her common sense reassert itself. What was wrong with her? She should look on crossing paths with Yancy Granger as a stroke of luck.

Unfortunately, she didn't. Her insides were much too raw from their encounter. So he'd kissed her. So she'd liked that kiss far too much, to the extent that she could still taste it, taste him. So it had created an ache between her thighs. *So* get a life, that was what! She'd just have to get past this and move on. It wasn't the end of the world, nor would it stop her from doing her job.

Still, she wanted to leave, but pride kept her seated.

"Is he alone?" she forced herself to ask.

"No, but I can't tell who he's with. The woman's back is to us."

Unable to curb her curiosity and something else she refused to identify, Dana turned around. Though Yancy was across the room, he was in her direct line of vision. His head was bent, and he appeared to be studying the menu. Dana then looked at his companion, who definitely was not his ex-wife. The woman's face wasn't visible, but Dana could see her hair; it was blond, bleached. She appeared to be saying something to Yancy.

Dana switched her gaze back to Yancy as an unwanted twinge of jealousy darted through her. God, what had this man done to her to make her forget . . .

He chose that moment to close the menu and look up. Their eyes met. Dana fought to control her racing pulse as she noticed a disturbing glint in those stark blue eyes.

She tore her gaze away and turned back to Rooney, who asked, "I suppose you want to say something to him?"

That was the last thing Dana wanted to do, at least right now, but she wasn't about to admit that to Rooney. "Maybe later. I don't think this is an appropriate time."

"Why?"

"They're having dinner."

"About to have dinner, don't you mean?"

"Okay, if you want to split hairs, 'about to have dinner.' "

At her sharp tone, a mystified expression appeared on Rooney's face, just as the waiter arrived with the check. Rooney gave him a credit card, then leaned forward. "Like it or not, we have to stop at their table. Since it's on our way out, it'll be rude if we don't."

"Suit yourself."

"Anyway, now that I can see who he's with, I recognize her."

"Oh?"

"It's Vida Lou Dinwiddie, the committee chairwoman."

Dana's spirits perked up. "In that case, you're right. We do need to stop. She's at the top of my must-see list."

"I figured as much. And she's a good one to get to know. That woman has her finger in lots of pies in this town."

Dana was about to question him further about Ms. Dinwiddie, but at that moment the waiter returned. Rooney scrawled his name across the receipt, then looked at Dana. "Ready?"

"When you are."

"Let's go."

Dana realized that Yancy knew they were going to stop, because he rose before they reached his table. His companion's seat was empty.

"Tremaine," he said, shaking Rooney's outstretched hand.

An awkward silence followed as Yancy fixed his gaze on Dana, who forced her expression to show none of the violent emotions churning inside her. She couldn't help but notice the smell of his cologne mingled with the male scent of his body. And he looked sexy as hell, dressed casually in jeans, which showed off his long, well-muscled legs, and an off-white sport shirt that contrasted with his tan.

"So we meet again, Ms. Bivens," he finally said.

Her breath faltered as she said, "Hello, Doctor."

He never failed to disconcert her, even frighten her. Yet a stampede of wild horses couldn't have made her move.

As if he read her thoughts, his eyes held hers again before rolling away quickly. Too quickly. "Ah, here comes Vida Lou."

Dana didn't have to turn around to know that; she smelled the woman's strong perfume.

"Hello, Ms. Dinwiddie," Rooney said heartily, as if he was tired of being upstaged. "This is my friend Dana Bivens, whom I don't think you've met."

"That's right, I haven't." Vida Lou stepped in front of Dana.

Dana's smile froze as she looked into the face of her mother.

Eleven

After all those years, Dana stood eye to eye with the woman who had given her birth, the woman she had pretended was dead. Only she wasn't.

Dana wanted to run. She wanted to scream at the unfair blow she'd just received. Most of all, she wanted to slap the cold, contemptuous look off her mother's face. Yet she could only stand there and stare, unable to take her gaze off the woman who had cursed her from the day she'd been born to the day she'd walked out of the house.

"It's a pleasure, Ms. Bivens," Vida Lou said, following the brief silence.

Dana blinked. Even the voice was different. That once harsh, raucous tone had been replaced by a soft, southern drawl so fake that it made Dana want to throw up.

Pretense or not, the woman knew who Dana was; Vida Lou recognized her own flesh and blood. Dana's instincts told her that. But if her mother chose not to acknowledge that fact, that was fine with her. Dana didn't want anyone to know either. She hated the woman. God help her, but that was a truth she wasn't about to apologize for. Vida Lou, or whatever she called herself, might have given her life, but she was no mother and never would be.

"Likewise," Dana said into the uneasy silence.

"How's the fund-raising project going, Mrs. Dinwiddie?" Rooney asked with what looked like a constipated smile.

"Why, just great, Rooney." She returned his smile, placing a hand on his arm. "And do call me Vida Lou, please."

This time Dana thought she would throw up for sure. *Fake* was a mild word for what this woman was. Couldn't anyone else see through her charade?

"All right, Vida Lou," Rooney responded, his smile broadening, as if he were lapping up every word she said.

Dana turned away. And when she did, her gaze met Yancy's. His expression was bland, but there was something stirring in those blue eyes, only she didn't know what.

"So how's it going with you, Ms. Bivens?" he asked, his tone low and almost rough in its intensity.

His eyes had now moved to her lips. Dana forced herself not to react, though a flush of another kind flooded through her body. Damn him. Damn Vida Lou Dinwiddie. "Things could be better."

An eyebrow shot up. "How so?"

"You could make time for an interview."

In the silence that followed, Dana was aware that Vida Lou and Rooney had ceased their exchange and were listening to her and Yancy.

"An interview? With you?"

Dana realized she'd caught him off guard. Fantastic. Her smile was cool and professional. "Yes, with you. Remember the other night, I told you I was here to do an article—"

"You mean you two have already met?" Rooney interrupted, his eyes darting from one to the other.

Dana caught a peripheral glimpse of Vida Lou. Her smile was now as tight as her face. Dana hid a smile. Nothing had changed. Her mother had always insisted on being the center of attention and resented anyone who usurped her place.

"We have," Yancy said to Rooney, though he never took his eyes off Dana.

"So," Dana continued in a rush, "you're my subject, Dr. Granger."

"Yancy's why you're here?" Vida Lou asked, sounding both surprised and annoyed.

Dana hid another smile. Sounded like she'd gotten things stirred up, which couldn't have been better.

"That's right." She made herself look at her mother. "I'm in town to do an in-depth article on Dr. Granger. After all, he's big news since he's a candidate for the Nobel Prize."

"I see," Vida Lou said, turning her gaze to Yancy and holding it there.

"Well, Doctor, how about tomorrow?" Dana pressed.

Yancy's smile was mere formality. "Sorry, but tomorrow's out."

"The day after?"

"That's out too. But I'll tell you what—I'll get in touch with you."

Sure you will. "Better yet, Doctor, why don't I stay in touch with you." Dana paused. "I'm sure we can work something out."

"I wouldn't count on that, Ms. Bivens." His voice remained calm and controlled. "Right now, just finding time to sleep is tough."

She could have mentioned the fact that he'd found time to eat dinner with Vida Lou, but she didn't. She and Yancy had gotten off to a precarious start; she didn't want to provoke him to the point that she never got an interview.

"In fact, I think you'd best find another assignment," Yancy said with irritation.

My, my, what a change of heart. After that kiss, he'd been hot to see her again. Now that he'd learned she was here to interview him, he wanted nothing to do with her.

Why?

Arrogant, self-confident men like Yancy Granger usually craved the limelight, especially when they were being considered for a prestigious prize—unless they had something to hide. Maybe it was the pending lawsuit and the threat of another that made him skittish. Or perhaps he had other secrets.

"I don't think so, Doctor." Dana gave him a sugary smile. "I'll be in touch."

Rooney had a glum expression on his face. "What was that all about?"

"You'd best keep your eyes on the road, my friend, or we're going to end up wrapped around one of those telephone poles."

Rooney snorted, but faced forward, though Dana noticed his profile remained rigid.

"Why didn't you tell me you knew Granger?" His tone had a whine to it. "I felt like a fool."

Dana sighed, striving to hang on to her temper. She didn't want to take the frustrations warring inside her out on Rooney; but he was asking for it with his aggressive and possessive attitude.

"I can't imagine why."

"For starters, the way he looked at you, like—"

"You're imagining things," Dana said, cutting him off.

"Am I? I don't think so."

She let that pass. "I met him right after I arrived here, in that same restaurant, actually. But we didn't get a chance to talk because he got called to the hospital on an emergency."

"And you haven't seen him since?"

"Hey, what is this? You sound like you're jealous, which is ridiculous."

Rooney cut her another glance. "You know how I feel about you, Dana. And Granger's so—" He broke off, setting his jaw.

"Rooney, I thought we had an understanding about our relationship. I'm here to do a story, the most important one of my career." She heard the desperate note in her voice but couldn't help it. "I need your cooperation, not your criticism. And certainly not your paranoia."

"Sorry," he muttered. "It's just there's something about the man that makes me want to slug him."

Dana gave him an incredulous look. "And you're planning to defend him?"

"Nothing says I have to like him to do that."

Dana shook her head. "Men! And y'all think *we're* hard to figure out."

A short silence followed as Rooney turned his BMW into the drive at the inn. "Mind if I come in?" he asked.

Dana placed her hand on the door handle. "Another time, okay?" She softened her tone. "But thanks for a lovely evening."

"I'll call you," Rooney said in a hopeful tone.

She leaned over and kissed him on the cheek. "You're a good friend, Rooney. Thanks again for that."

With those words, she got out of the car, knowing that once she reached her room, sleep would elude her.

The woman lifted her breasts to his mouth. Newton Anderson's lips surrounded one distended nipple.

"Oh, God, Newt, you don't know what that does to me."

"I know what it does to me," he said, pulling away and reaching for her hand.

"For a small man, your cock is something, you know?"

"I'm glad you like it. It's hand-raised. For years it was the only toy I had."

"You gotta be kiddin'."

"Nope, but that's all history. I have you to play with it now."

"You got that right, honey."

"So show me how much you like it," he ground out, feeling himself harden again just from looking at her.

The tall, lissome woman climbed atop the advertising executive, her curly blond hair framing her youthful face. She smiled down at him as she rode him hard—as if she hadn't already ridden him twice within the last few hours.

"Oh, my God!" he cried as he emptied his seed into her.

Once she'd rolled off him, Newt stared up at the ceiling, thinking about the phone call he was expecting. To hell with that, he thought. He hoped it didn't come anytime soon. Business could wait, but his pecker couldn't.

Besides, a woman like the one next to him didn't come along very often, especially since his second wife kept such a tight rein on him and his money.

Thank God, her sister had croaked and she'd gone scurrying to Maine for the funeral. He hoped she stayed for at least a week. Regardless, he was about to boot her out of his life.

Once this sweetheart of a deal he was about to pull off became final, he could afford to pay his wife off and still live like one of those Third World oil rulers.

"I have to go, honey," she whispered in his ear, licking it at the same time. "I got a job, you know?"

Chills shot up Newton's spine just as the phone rang.

"Shit!" He reached for the receiver, knowing it was his secretary.

"It's your call from Virginia, sir. I wouldn't have bothered you, only—"

"It's okay. Put him through." A few seconds passed, then Newt asked, "What's the latest?"

He listened, nodding. "That's great. Keep up the good work. And keep in touch."

Hanging up the phone, Newt turned to his companion and whispered in *her* ear, "How would you like to take a trip to the Bahamas?"

She grinned, then laid a hand on his bare chest. "Just say when."

"Soon, honey, soon."

Newt pulled her down to him.

Sleep had indeed escaped her. Dana stood at the window and watched the first signs of dawn. She hadn't even bothered to take off her clothes. The only constructive thing she'd done since Rooney had dropped her off was to turn on a lamp. She'd been at the window for hours now.

The woman who now called herself Vida Lou Dinwiddie occupied every nook and cranny of Dana's thoughts. Even

Yancy Granger had been usurped. Fifteen years. It had been that long since she'd seen her mother. Yet she would have recognized her anywhere.

Still, her mother's metamorphosis was stunning, including the name. Dana almost smiled. *Vida Lou.* What a name. Where had her mother come up with that? It had to be straight out of a circus. It sounded so country, so un-blue blood. Suddenly the old adage came to mind: "You can't make a silk purse out of a sow's ear."

Her mother was definitely a sow's ear. She might have changed her name and her body, but nothing could erase that hard edge or that cold, brutal expression in her eyes, especially when she looked at Dana.

Every time she saw that look, Dana knew she'd had it. Her mother would walk with unhurried steps to the closet, take out a coathanger, and walk back to her daughter.

"How many times is it gonna take before you do like you're told?"

Dana remembered always cringing backward, her heart in her throat, often unable to speak.

"Answer me, damn you!"

Dana's chin would quiver as her eyes filled with hot tears. "But, Mamma, I did do what you told me to."

"Don't you dare argue with me. Just get them panties off and bend over that bed. Now!"

"Mamma, please, don't," Dana begged. "I'll be good."

"Do it!"

Suddenly Dana flinched, in the darkness, reliving the pain of the metal striping her bare skin as her mother hit her over and over again. Dana began to cry.

She didn't want to think about that terrifying time, nor did she want to think about her mother. But the memories, once awakened, kept on coming with paralyzing force. . . .

The beatings had been bad enough, but what had happened later, the day her mother had booted her out of the house, her belly swollen with child, had been the ultimate shame and humiliation. . . .

"Stop it!" Dana heard herself whisper.

Maybe it was the sound of her voice that jerked her out of the past. She didn't know or care. Whatever it was, she was grateful. Forcing her jellylike legs to move, she went into the bathroom and splashed cold water on her burning face.

She looked into the mirror and told herself to calm down, that her mother couldn't hurt her now. In fact, the reverse was true: She could hurt Vida Lou Dinwiddie more than the woman could hurt her. If she let it be known how brutally her mother had betrayed her years ago, Vida Lou would likely be run out of town on a rail.

As it stood, neither would gain anything by revealing their connection. Yet Vida Lou lived by her own code of conduct, not always guided by common sense. So would she take the chance on exposing her daughter, the daughter she denied and despised? No—unless that daughter became a threat.

Dana shivered, then turned away from the mirror. Underneath that fake charm beat the heart of an evil and vindictive woman who would stop at nothing to get what she wanted.

Hadn't she proved that fifteen years ago when she'd turned one of her boyfriends loose on Dana? Of course she had. Dana had the scars to prove it.

Suddenly Dana bit her lip to stop it from quivering. Power. That was what Vida Lou Dinwiddie wanted. No, Dana corrected herself. What her mother wanted more than anything was to be a legitimate blue blood Virginian. She would stop at nothing to attain that goal.

Vida Lou wouldn't let anyone get in her way, least of all her daughter. So, the answer was to avoid her, do her story, then get out of town.

Dana thought about how she'd convinced herself she need not fear the past. She'd been so confident that she wouldn't run into any old ghosts here in Charlottesville. Well, the joke was on her.

But her mother? God, she'd assumed that Clara Bivens would've left this area a long time ago, never to return.

Panic was sharp and sour in Dana's mouth, but she wouldn't

give in to it. She wouldn't let Vida Lou win, not this time. Fate had played an ugly, unexpected trick on her. But she would not whimper this time. She would deal with the viper that was her mother, only not now. Later. Her job, which was Dr. Yancy Granger, took precedence.

Twelve

"Hold all my calls, Inez. Unless it's Dr. Granger, of course."

Inez nodded at Vida Lou, then said in a subdued tone, "Yes, ma'am. Will there be anything else?"

"Yes. Bring me a pot of tea. And make sure the cream's fresh this time. If it isn't—" Vida Lou's voice trailed off, but the housekeeper got the message, because her face lost all its color, which was exactly what Vida Lou had intended.

Damn, it was hard to get competent help these days, Vida Lou told herself as she made her way upstairs to her office. She had another fund-raising gala to plan. She hoped this one would be much more successful than the last.

Vida Lou walked across the plush carpet and sat behind her desk. Her secretary was due to come in later. For now, though, she wanted to be alone, to think, to come up with a spectacular theme for this party. She refused to settle for anything less than an overflow crowd.

The money hadn't been pouring in as she'd expected. At first it had, but now it seemed the interest had waned a bit. Shelby Tremaine hadn't budged on his asking price, either, the bastard.

Vida Lou switched her thoughts from him to the list of ideas in front of her. She barely acknowledged Inez when she set the silver tea tray on the cart next to the cherrywood desk and scuttled out.

Picking up the cup, Vida Lou noticed that her hands were shaking. "Dammit!" She shouted, then set the cup down, fighting the urge to throw it across the room.

Pitching a hissy fit wouldn't help her accomplish her goal. Only patience and careful planning would do that. Her daughter's appearance in Charlottesville was what had her so pissed off.

Dammit, why had that kick in the teeth come now? It isn't fair, Vida Lou whined to herself. She'd never expected to see that idiot child again.

When she'd found out she was pregnant, she'd taken the end of a fly swatter and rammed it up with the sole intention of aborting. She had botched the procedure, but she hadn't realized that until it was too late. Because she'd been obese and stupid, she hadn't known she was still pregnant.

After she recovered from the shock of the baby's birth, she'd considered giving the brat up for adoption, but it had seemed too complicated a process and she hadn't known how to go about it. Besides, she had secretly hoped that the baby's father would marry her.

He hadn't. So, scared and ignorant, she'd kept Dana, which had been her big mistake—one that had now come back to haunt her.

Perspiration suddenly drenched Vida Lou's body and a sick feeling invaded her stomach. Not only did Dana's timing stink, but the reason for her being here added to the stench. She didn't want Dana sniffing around Yancy. He was *her* personal property. She couldn't stand the thought of anyone other than herself getting that close and personal, least of all her stunning daughter.

Vida Lou had to admit that Dana had indeed become a lovely young woman, though it galled her to do so, especially since her daughter would probably never have to go under a surgeon's knife to remain that way.

Blind rage, brought on by jealousy, ripped through Vida

Lou. She jumped up from her desk and paced the floor. But it wasn't just jealousy that turned her pace frantic. It was the damage Dana could do to her reputation and standing in the community.

If the secret she'd kept buried all these years ever surfaced . . . No! That wouldn't happen, Vida Lou assured herself, stopping in the middle of the room, her eyes narrowing. No one would ever find out who Dana was, because she would have to leave town ASAP. Vida Lou would see to that.

Suddenly she chuckled. She couldn't imagine why she'd even worried. She had enough power and money to perform miracles, if she so desired.

Dana Bivens was just another bug she'd have to step on to get where she was going.

Feeling better about the situation, Vida Lou thought about calling Tyson Peters, her personal trainer and stud. She smiled. Lord, what his big hands could do to her body. He'd pummel and massage until all the tension was gone, then he'd fuck her until her bones melted.

Yes, Tyson was good for her, as long as she paid him. But she didn't mind. She had to have a man, and since she couldn't have Yancy right now, Tyson would do. He wouldn't be in her life much longer anyway. Yancy would soon take his place.

Vida Lou placed her hand on the phone and flinched when it rang. She'd told Inez to hold all her calls. Damn that woman!

"Yes," Vida Lou snapped into the receiver.

"Vida, this is Lester."

Vida Lou downplayed her impatience. Lester Mayfield was on the fund-raising committee and one of the clinic's most avid supporters. Personally, she found both him and his wife repulsive. However, he had money and influence, which counted for everything.

"I hope you won't be upset with Inez. I insisted she put me through."

"That's all right. What is it?"

"I just wanted to confirm the meeting this evening."

"Is that all?" This time Vida Lou didn't bother to hide her impatience.

"Yes and no."

She heard the reluctance in his voice and immediately changed her tone. "I'm getting mixed signals here, Lester. What's going on?"

"I'm not sure. Call Yancy and ask him to be there, too."

With that, he hung up. Vida Lou stared at the receiver.

What the hell was that all about?

The instant the doors to the operating room swung open, Yancy dismissed everything from his mind except what he had to do. He was consumed by the clean, antiseptic odor that surrounded him and the patient before him. This was especially true today.

He had already performed two successful surgeries and was due to perform another one, which he anticipated would be equally as successful.

Now, though, he had a while before he had to be back on stage. He hoped to get some shut-eye.

"Good job, Doctor."

"Thanks, Rick," Yancy said, jerking off his surgical gloves.

Rick Cline, a fellow surgeon and one of Yancy's few champions, spoke in awe. "It's amazing to me how you continue to pull off the impossible."

"That's because I'm good."

Rick shook his head. "Add that to being a cocky sonofabitch, and I guess that's the secret."

Yancy laughed. "I'm outta here for now. See you later."

Back in his office, Yancy all but fell onto the couch. God, he was tired. His eyes and his stomach felt like they were on fire. It was a miracle he'd been able to do anything right in the OR.

Stress. That should have been his middle name. But until Dana Bivens had brought her tight ass to town, he'd been able to handle that stress, which was inherent in his job.

Lately, though, he'd been far too distracted, and that unnerved him. The last thing he wanted or needed was an ambitious reporter, no matter how sexually attractive, dogging him.

On the other hand, how could he turn down such an opportunity? If she was determined to do a human interest story, what harm could there be? It would be great publicity for him and the hospital.

Not so fast, Granger, he warned himself, his gut instinct waving a red flag. Human interest, my ass. *Snoop* was what she intended to do. He couldn't permit that.

Because he had never wanted the public to have access to a certain part of his past, he had shunned publicity. He preferred to keep his nightmares to himself. So to hell with Dana Bivens and her warm, wet lips and knock-'em-dead body. He had to look out for number one.

He would do whatever it took to protect his reputation as a doctor and as a man.

Dana sat among the pillows on the bed, the receiver cradled between her shoulder and ear. "Find out what you can, then get back to me, okay?"

"Will do."

"Oh, and Billy, be discreet."

"Hell, Dana, what do you take me for, an imbecile?"

"Of course not. It's just that—"

"I know, I know," Billy interrupted. "If anyone finds out about where you are and what you're doing, your goose is cooked."

In spite of her concern, Dana chuckled. "I guess that's as good a way as any to put it."

"Don't worry, sweetie, Billy'll take care of you. Have I ever failed you?"

"No, you haven't. And you know I'm eternally grateful."

"You've more than paid your dues."

"Thanks. I'll wait to hear."

Following that phone conversation, Dana continued to

smile for a few minutes. Thank heavens for Billy Barnes, a fellow reporter and friend who worked the Washington beat. They had met years ago and had remained firm friends.

She'd phoned Billy at home and asked him what he knew about the story on Congressman Clayton Crawford and his wife, Gloria. Billy had followed the congressman and done several articles on him. He had told her that he'd heard the same rumor but didn't know any of the particulars, namely the doctor involved.

Dana was keeping her fingers crossed that the doctor would indeed be Yancy Granger. *Issues* would be impressed.

She was about to walk out the door when April called.

"What's going on?" Dana asked in response to her friend's excited voice.

"A meeting that I bet you'd be interested in."

"You've got my undivided attention."

A few minutes later, Dana grabbed her briefcase and her purse and darted out the door.

With the exception of Vida Lou, all the committee members were there, in a room at the local community center. Dana stood outside the door, which had a glass partition, and surveyed the group. She had no idea what kind of reception she would receive, but she knew that if she wanted to meet the entire committee, now was her chance. Once Vida Lou arrived, Dana wouldn't be welcome.

If time and memory served her correctly, her mother would make it a point to be late so that she could make a grand entrance.

Dana pushed the door open and walked in, a warm, confident smile on her face. Three men and one woman stopped talking and stared at her.

"I hope you don't mind the intrusion. I'm Dana Bivens." She broadened her smile to encompass everyone. "I'm a journalist in town to do a story on Dr. Granger and the proposed hospital."

They all looked at one another as if they didn't know what

to say or do, though their expressions made it clear that they were pleased. Dana could almost see their minds clicking: publicity, exposure, money . . .

Then a tall man, with lean features and a crooked nose, stood and extended his hand. "I'm Herman Green."

Dana stepped forward and shook it.

"This is Lester Mayfield," Green added.

Dana then shook hands with a dark-haired, dark-eyed man with a distended belly that bespoke too much booze or food or both. "Mr. Mayfield."

"And I'm Carter Lipton, Ms. Bivens. What publication are you representing?"

Lipton was as trim as Mayfield was overweight, and the fact that he wore braces made him appear much more boyish than he actually was. "This story is for *Issues,*" she said humbly, though she saw their faces light up at the mention of the prestigious magazine.

"Hey, you guys, give it rest, will you?"

They all laughed, turning to the woman, who remained seated. Dana sensed that she could hold her own among the men. When standing, she would be close to six feet tall.

"You must be Alice Crenshaw, April's friend."

Alice smiled, which made her otherwise somber face come alive. Her brown eyes twinkled as she rose and shook Dana's hand. "That's right. She's already told me about you."

"Uh-oh." Dana laughed. "I don't know if that's good or bad."

"Oh, it's good," Alice said, sitting back down. "She thinks you're wonderful."

"That's a far cry from the truth, but it's nice to hear anyway."

Dana took the liberty of placing her briefcase on the table, then opening it and removing pad and pen. "Mind if I ask a few questions?"

They all shook their heads, then began to talk at once, which brought on another round of laughter. Dana couldn't have been more thrilled with their willingness to talk. She wrote quickly as they told her of their hopes for the infertility hospital and precisely what it would mean to the town.

Of course, not one word was mentioned about the impending lawsuit, which all were aware of, she knew. In fact, nothing was said about Yancy Granger that hinted of any impropriety.

"So, are you banking on Dr. Granger's reputation alone to bring in sufficient funds to pay for the land?" Dana asked, just as the door burst open.

Dana's breath caught as her mother came into the room, dressed like she'd just walked off the pages of *Vogue,* a superior smile on her face.

It was only after she saw Dana that her expression changed. "What are you doing here?" The bite in her tone was obvious.

Dana didn't so much as flinch, but Alice Crenshaw did. Not only that, but she gave Vida Lou a scolding look and said pointedly, "Vida Lou, this is Ms. Bivens, a reporter."

"We've met," Vida Lou said, but in a much more conciliatory tone.

Dana rose without any trouble, but smiling was another matter. Her face felt as if it were made of dry plaster and would crack if she smiled. But smile she did.

"Hello again, Mrs. Dinwiddie."

"We've been giving Ms. Bivens the lowdown on the hospital and Yancy," Alice continued.

"That's fine, but I'm afraid she'll have to leave for now. We have some important business to discuss." Vida paused, then faced Dana. "I'm sure you understand."

"Of course," Dana said, gathering her materials. "Thank you all for you openness and candor. I'm sure we'll meet again."

Dana had just stepped out into the hall when she glanced up and saw him rounding the corner. He saw her at the same time. They both pulled up short.

Dana swallowed hard as her startled eyes met his.

Yancy looked like he'd been through hell, she thought, appraising him, from the mussed, overlong hair that grazed his collar, to the deep lines in his face, to the rumpled white coat and the wired energy that seemed to fill it.

Her stomach suddenly knotted.

"What are you doing here?" he asked tightly.

"My job."

"Which is?"

"Learning all I can about you. But you know that."

"I don't recall giving you permission."

His mouth twisted and his eyes were cold. Nowhere in sight was that sexually charged charisma of the other night that promised all things to all women. Dana knew that if she hadn't been there to interview him, she would have had to fend him off.

What a hypocrite.

"But I'm assuming you will." Her tone was anything but antagonistic even though anger surged through her at his arrogant assumption that she was just another puppet on his string. "After all, good publicity's to your benefit."

Without warning, he reached out and circled her wrist, then bent down. "Don't play with me, Ms. Bivens. I guarantee you'll lose."

He let her go, then turned and walked into the meeting room.

"This had better be goddamn important, Vida Lou," Dana heard him say as she leaned against the wall for support. Something had to give. Her insides couldn't turn to mush every time she saw him. Such behavior was ridiculous and completely out of character.

She would have left had it not been for Vida Lou's next words: "It is important. We've got a problem on our hands."

Problem? Dana's journalist instincts kicked in.

"What kind of problem?" Yancy asked. Then everyone started talking at once, until Vida Lou rapped on the table.

Dana realized she shouldn't be eavesdropping, but she

made no move to leave. She stood still, though at war with her conscience, which told her to get the hell out of there. Yet her mind told her to stay.

Which one should she listen to?

Thirteen

Vida Lou stared at the group, her posture rigid. She couldn't say anything; her throat was constricted from the rage that gripped her.

"Vida Lou, what the hell?" Herman Green finally asked. "You look like you're about to have a stroke."

"Why was that reporter let in here?" Vida Lou demanded, hearing the tremor in her own voice and struggling to get control.

"That's water under the bridge, Vida Lou," Yancy said, sitting on one end of the long table, swinging a leg. "She was here and that's that. Besides, she's not your concern."

Vida Lou felt her blood pressure rising again. *Wasn't her concern!* How dare he talk to her like that? The last person she wanted snooping around the committee was Dana, but she had to be careful how she handled her daughter's presence in town and the entire situation.

Still, she'd remember Yancy's condescending attitude, and once she had his ring on her finger, she would make him pay. Until then, she had to mollycoddle him along with everyone else on the committee.

Idiots. That was all they were, small-minded, wanna-be big shots who thought they were better than everyone else, namely her. Oh, but how wrong they were. When she pulled off this land coup, they'd be bowing and kissing her feet.

"So what was so urgent that *I* had to be here?" Yancy pressed.

Vida Lou heard the impatience in his voice and knew that he was about to explode or, worse, walk out. "Actually, I don't know. This part of the meeting belongs to Lester."

She turned to Lester Mayfield, who she saw was suddenly fidgeting in his seat, causing his big belly to shake. All eyes followed her lead.

Lester cleared his throat, then placed a hand over his mouth, but not quickly enough. Vida Lou heard his belch, and turned away disgusted.

"Er . . . excuse me," he said, red-faced. Then he cleared his throat. "To make a long story short, my wife was approached at the grocery store by Ted Wilkins's wife, who said he never got a receipt for the contribution he made."

"You might as well go ahead and drop the other shoe," Alice said, mincing no words. "I feel it's coming."

Still red-faced, Lester said, "Well, Ted's wife was just wondering if the committee ever got the money." He looked helplessly at Vida Lou.

She shook her head. "I know nothing about this, except that it's dangerous to have even the slightest hint of wrongdoing concerning any funds."

"Come on," Yancy said, disgust lowering his voice. "Who pays attention to that kind of gossipy crap, especially when there's no truth to it."

"The people who contribute, that's who," Carter Lipton cut in, his face red now.

Lester rubbed his chin, then glared at Yancy. "Ted's wife said he gave the money to you, Doctor."

"That's right, he did." Yancy's tone now was smooth and bored. "And I took it to Herman's office and put it in his desk like he told me." He focused on Herman. "The man wants his receipt, so get off your dead butt and send it. End of gossip. End of story."

Herman shook his head. "Can't do that."

"Why not?" Vida Lou asked.

"I never got the money," Herman said, staring at Yancy.

For several seconds, silence filled the room—a silence so explosive that it seemed as if a bomb had been dropped.

Yancy surged to his feet. "What did you say?"

"When I got back to the office, the money wasn't in the drawer."

"Well, I sure as hell put it there!"

Vida Lou held up her hand, fearing she would have to referee soon, even though Yancy and Herman were friends.

"So why haven't you said something before now, Herman?"

Now it was Herman who was on the hotseat, though he seemed quite comfortable there. His demeanor was cool and calm. "I kept thinking the money would turn up."

"Dammit!" Yancy threw up his hands.

"How much money are we talking about here?" Alice asked in a soft but concerned tone.

"Two grand," Herman said. "At least that's what Yancy told me."

Yancy turned cold eyes on Herman. "Then you can bet your ass that's what it was."

"Did you count it?" Carter asked, scooting forward as if to get a better look at Yancy.

"Hell no, I didn't count it. Ted gave it to me in an envelope. I called Herman on my car phone, and he told me to take it to his office and put it in his desk drawer."

"Don't you think that was a pretty careless thing to do?" Carter asked. "I mean—"

"I know what the hell you mean." Yancy clenched his fists. "Maybe it wasn't the smartest thing to do, but at the time I had other things on my mind, like getting my ass back to work."

"Well, again, all I can say is that the money wasn't there."

"Then someone took it!" Yancy lashed back at Herman.

"What about his secretary?" Lester asked, sounding desperate. "Surely she can back you up, Yancy."

"She wasn't there either. I just assumed she was in the ladies' room." Yancy slashed the air with his hand. "The truth is, I didn't see a soul. I hold you responsible for this, Green!"

Herman jumped up, his eyes narrowed. "Now you wait just a minute!"

"Stop it!" Vida Lou said. "Both of you. Just calm down. No one's accusing anyone of anything." She faced Herman. "There has to be an explanation. Maybe someone in your office took it, like the maid. Is that possible?"

"Of course it's possible. Anything's possible. That's exactly why I didn't bring it to the committee's attention." Herman turned to Yancy. "Hey man, you're my friend; I know you put the money in the drawer. But since it wasn't there, I've been conducting an investigation on my own, thinking it'd turn up and I wouldn't have to even mention it."

"So have you turned up anything?" Alice asked, frowning.

Herman shook his head. "Not yet."

"Shit," Yancy muttered, his face blazing with anger.

Vida Lou was losing control, something she wouldn't tolerate. Everyone's anger was close to the boiling point. The entire group needed a reality check, Yancy most of all. If he exploded, there would be hell to pay. She could not allow them to leave the room until they were once again a cohesive group, working as a team to raise money.

Vida Lou was sure there was a logical explanation for the missing funds. She believed Yancy. He had no reason to keep the money. He might have been a lot of things—arrogant, self-centered, brazen, to name a few—but he was no thief. Besides, the entire hospital project meant everything to him. He wouldn't do anything to jeopardize it.

She also believed Herman Green. He was a deacon in the local Baptist church, and probably hadn't ever stolen anything in his life. Vida Lou wanted to laugh at the image that came to mind. Hell, she'd bet he didn't have enough balls to steal a piece of pussy from his own wife.

But the money *was* missing. That alone could undermine the committee and its work.

"Until this matter is settled, word of this cannot leave this room," Vida Lou said. "Understood?"

The others stared at one another. Yancy was the only one who spoke, his eyes on Herman. "Send Ted a receipt. Today. I'll put the money in the goddamn coffer myself."

"No you won't," Herman said. "It'll turn up. If it doesn't, then we'll go from there."

"Vida Lou's right, though," Alice said. "This is serious. Think what it could do to your reputation, Yancy. . . ." Her voice faded, but the message did not.

"That's my point, Alice," he replied. "Ted has to get that receipt or we're screwed. The townsfolk'll think they're turning their money over to a bunch of thieves."

"That's right." A line of sweat formed on Lester's upper lip as he crossed his pudgy hands over his stomach. "They have to have confidence in us to handle their money."

"No one's blaming you, Yancy," Carter said. "You know that. Nor are we blaming Herman."

Vida Lou stood. "While it's an unfortunate thing to have happened, it's not the end of the world or this committee. It's just a bump in the road." She focused on Yancy for a moment, who still looked as though he was itching to slug someone. "Again, we have to keep our mouths shut and make sure none of this leaves this room. Agreed?"

They all nodded, then shoved back their chairs and headed to the door.

"Yancy."

He stopped and turned around.

Vida Lou waited a moment, until they were alone. "I want to talk to you."

"Not now, okay?"

"Yes, now. I don't think you realize how serious this could be."

The cords in Yancy's neck tightened. "You're telling me that, and it's *my* ass in the sling?"

"That's not true and you know it. No one thinks you kept that money."

He closed the distance between them. When he glared down at her, she backed up and swallowed. When he was in one of these moods, he both excited and frightened her.

"They sure as hell don't think Herman kept it."

"Of course they don't, and you don't either."

"Well, someone sure as hell has sticky fingers, and I'd like to know who that someone is."

"I'm sure in time we'll find out."

"See what you can come up with. We depend on you to take care of the money and everything connected with it."

Vida Lou turned pale, except for her lips; they remained a gaudy red. "Are you saying this is somehow my fault?"

"No. What I'm saying is that hopefully you, with your magic touch, can clean up the crap before it starts stinking."

"You know I'll do what I can." She smiled confidently. "After Herman sends that receipt, I'm sure it'll die a natural death."

"God, I hope so."

He was at the door when she stopped him again. "What about her?"

"Her who?"

"That reporter, Dana Bivens. I believe that was her name."

Yancy's smile was mocking. "You know damn well that's her name."

Vida Lou hadn't planned on bringing up her daughter again, but she couldn't help herself. She didn't want Yancy talking to her. In light of what had taken place today, Dana's presence could up the ante considerably.

"Are you going to let her do her story on you?"

"Maybe." He shrugged. "Maybe not."

"I see."

Yancy laughed a hollow laugh. "I take it you don't approve."

"I didn't say that."

"Yes, you did." With that, he walked out the door.

Vida Lou dug her sharp nails into her palms, and bit down on her lower lip to keep from screaming in frustration.

Then her composure returned in full force. Patience; that was the key. And her best asset.

Fourteen

Yancy had never liked Richmond. It reminded him of every other big city he'd ever been in. Although parts of Richmond had maintained their southern charm, with old homes in elegant splendor, it was nonetheless an urban center with its share of violent crime and homeless people.

Maybe having to be there for such an unpleasant meeting was what pissed him off. It had taken two days to jostle his surgery and clinic schedules to free himself for this trip. The emergencies would be handled by his assistants and residents.

He hadn't been given any choice in the matter. Rooney Tremaine had insisted on meeting with him about the lawsuit on the attorney's home turf. So here he was, driving down a street in Richmond—an upscale one at that—his frustration rising as rain pounded his windshield so hard that he could barely see where he was going.

Finally spotting Rooney Tremaine's office complex, Yancy pulled into the parking lot. Seconds later he was inside the lobby, feeling as if he'd taken a shower with all his clothes on. Hell of a way to make an appearance, he thought, but really he didn't give a damn how he looked.

When Yancy walked into Rooney's front office, he saw the secretary's expressive eyes register disapproval, but all she said was, "Mr. Tremaine's expecting you, Doctor."

Yancy gave her a cursory smile before disappearing into Rooney's private office.

"Ah, Doctor, I'm glad to see you made it." Rooney came to his feet behind his massive desk.

"Me too."

Rooney frowned. "God, you're wet."

"No shit." Then, realizing he'd been rude, Yancy added, "It's okay. I'm okay." He forced a smile.

"Are you sure?" Rooney asked, his tone stiff.

"Yeah—that is, if you don't mind looking at a drowned rat."

Rooney's expression softened. "Actually, I've seen drowned rats that fared better."

"Maybe that's why your secretary looked at me the way she did."

"Ah, don't mind Pamela. She gets her nose out of joint real quick."

Now that the small talk had broken the ice, Yancy wanted to get down to business. He was eager to get the meeting over with and return to Charlottesville. The forecast promised more rain. Besides, attorney's offices made him nervous.

Rooney seemed to pick up on his mood. "You don't look happy to be here, Doctor."

"I'd rather be having a barium enema."

Rooney laughed. "I'd say that's real unhappy. But maybe this ordeal won't turn out to be that bad. So have a seat, and we'll get started."

In spite of his damp clothing, the plush chair felt good. Every bone in Yancy's body ached. He still couldn't remember when he'd last had a solid night's sleep.

"The way I see it," he said, "there's nothing to start. I'm innocent."

Rooney sat down, his mouth tightening. "I wish it were that simple."

"It is to me. Either you're innocent or you're guilty."

"Again, and unfortunately, that's not the way our system works."

Yancy shrugged, then looked around the room. The walls were cream colored and littered with paintings that he figured were extremely valuable. In addition, the forest green leather furniture and the plush carpet were obviously of the best quality. Yeah, if this office was anything to judge by, Rooney Tremaine was indeed one successful bastard.

But then his old man, Shelby Tremaine, was one rich bastard. He'd bet *Daddy* had had a lot to do with his only child's start at the top of his career.

"So, what's your advice?" Yancy finally asked. "How do we play out this scenario? But just so you'll know, I'm innocent. And you can take that to the bank."

Rooney sucked in one cheek and began gnawing on it. Yancy watched him for a minute, then turned away. When the silence continued, he got up and began pacing the floor, feeling like a caged animal.

"Please, Doctor, sit down."

Yancy paused in midstride just as Rooney shoved his glasses closer to the bridge of his nose. He really ought to get those damn things fitted, he thought.

"Can't," he snapped.

"Suit yourself, but at least stand still. God, are you ever *not* moving?"

"Nope."

"Tell me exactly what happened the night you operated on Mrs. Jefferies."

Yancy rubbed his chin as he looked hard at the attorney. "I made an appearance at a party, something I rarely do, only that one time I made an exception."

"But you did have something to drink?"

"Two Perriers with a twist of lime."

"Nothing stronger?"

"No, dammit!"

"Hey, calm down." Rooney smoothed his bold Countess Mara tie. "I'm on your side, remember?"

"Are you sure about that? My boss—"

Rooney smiled. "Boss? I didn't know you had a boss."

"Funny," Yancy said, his mouth turned down.

Rooney cleared his throat. "Sorry. Please, go on."

"The chief of staff was certain you wouldn't take the case."

Rooney's expression remained bland. "Why not?"

"Because your father owns the land the hospital wants. You got a problem with that, like some kind of conflict-of-interest crap?"

"Look, this is the second time that point has been raised."

Yancy was sure he knew who had raised it—Dana Bivens. After all, he'd seen her and Rooney having a cozy dinner that night in the restaurant, when he'd felt that pinch of jealousy in his gut. "So, what's your answer?" he finally asked.

"My answer is no. This lawsuit has no bearing on the land deal whatsoever. It's my father's land, not mine."

"Good. Now, can you make this fucking nightmare go away?"

"I'll give it my best shot. This is a thumbnail sketch of how things work. First off, you, as her doctor, must show a duty to your patient, which you did. Next, did you breach that duty? If so, they have to prove that."

"I told you, I didn't do anything wrong in that operating room," Yancy stressed. "I did everything possible to save that baby's life. But with the umbilical cord wrapped around its neck—"

He didn't want to relive that time; it hurt too much. When that baby had turned blue and stopped breathing, he'd wanted to die. And every time he thought about it, which was almost every day, he felt the same way. That loss was like an open sore that wouldn't heal.

"That's my point," Rooney was saying. "Her attorney has to prove by a preponderance of the evidence that you fell below the normal standard of care in dealing with her and the baby. And that's going to be near impossible, even though the woman is sticking to her story."

"So you've talked to her?"

"Yes."

Yancy grunted. "Could be a candidate for mother of the year award, right?"

"Not in this lifetime."

"I'm glad we agree on that."

"But there are witnesses, though I haven't taken their depositions yet."

"I bet I know who one of them is—that mangy-haired putz of a bartender."

"You're on target. Mrs. Jefferies said he swore that he fixed you a mixed drink."

"Well, he's a liar. It's obvious someone greased his paws."

"Any idea who that someone might be?"

Yancy sighed. "The list's too goddamn long."

"Well, don't worry. You just leave everything to me. That's what I'm getting paid to do."

"Then do it."

"I'll be in Charlottesville quite a bit during the next few weeks, so I'll keep in close touch." Rooney paused, smiling. "Dana Bivens is a special friend of mine. And since she's there to do a story on you, our paths will cross often; I'm sure."

So Rooney Tremaine *was* smitten with the lovely reporter. Again Yancy felt that pinch in his gut.

"Before you go, I'd like to get names of witnesses who will back you up."

"I was in a piss-poor mood that night," Yancy admitted. "I'm not sure I said five words to anyone."

"Well, you'd best think about those five words and who you might have said them to."

Yancy gave him a disgusted look.

Rooney shuffled through some papers, then looked back up at Yancy, his gaze piercing. "Tell me, Doctor, have you ever been sued before?"

"No."

By the time he reached his condo in Charlottesville, Yancy felt like he'd been put through a wringer. He'd kept the air-conditioner on max all the way home, yet he was perspiring heavily. It wasn't the climate that had him sweating—it was the inner churning he felt.

He had to get hold of himself; people's lives depended on him. His hands needed to be steady, his mind sharp, his heart distant.

He was a mess and he knew it. The lawsuit had his blood running cold, since his career and reputation were at stake. Nor could he ignore the missing money, which made him feel like kicking a dog. And he loved dogs. He couldn't forget his strong, ambivalent feelings for Dana Bivens, either.

"Shit!"

Yancy felt relieved when he spotted his driveway. He'd had enough of his paranoid thoughts. He had his sights set on a hot shower, then a dive between the sheets. He didn't know when he'd ever been more exhausted, both mentally and physically.

He unlocked his door, only to pull up short. He wasn't alone. Later, he realized that all the signs had been there but he hadn't noticed them until it was too late. What galled him most was that he hadn't seen her car. That was what he got for having his head up his ass. Or maybe she'd parked it out of sight.

"Vida Lou."

Her perfume gave her away, that cloying scent that smelled like honeysuckle and roses. His stomach rebelled along with his temper.

He turned, and there she was, her lips only inches from his.

"Hello, darling," Vida Lou whispered in a husky tone as she flung her arms around his neck.

He managed to twist his head just enough so that her wet, red lips landed on the side of his mouth instead of on it. The stripe of red lipstick looked like blood. He'd left one nightmare only to walk headfirst into another one.

"How did you get in here?" he asked, his breathing coming hard and fast.

She smiled and edged closer to him, a glint in her eye. "Oh,

I can be quite persuasive when I want to. And your manager is quite easy. Anyway, I couldn't wait to give you the good news."

"The money's been accounted for?"

"Unfortunately, no," Vida Lou replied, running her tongue between her lips.

"Then what are you talking about?"

"I got you off the hook, that's what. I gave Herman the money and told him to send that receipt and not say another word about it."

"You did *what?"* His tone was hard but controlled.

She placed a hand on her chest. "Why, I thought you'd be pleased."

"I appreciate the gesture, but this is my fight." Yancy took her arm and steered her toward the door. Only after she was on the porch did he say, "This has been a hell of a day. We'll talk later."

Vida Lou looked as if she would argue, but instead she smiled and ran one fingernail down his cheek.

Fifteen

The morning promised to be a full one. Dana intended to cover a lot of territory and to work nonstop. She awakened early, and while she was dressing she kept hearing that relentless ticking clock in the back of her mind. Time was of the essence, and she couldn't afford to squander any more of it. She needed to complete this investigation and get out of town.

She had thought she could handle the past, if the occasion arose, even return to where she'd been born and raised, perhaps even travel that highway where the accident had occurred. Maybe she could have, if she hadn't encountered her mother.

Now, every time she walked out of her room, she expected her mother to be waiting for her around a corner. Chills laced with panic would invade her until she realized that Vida Lou was nowhere around. At least not at that moment.

Now, as she finished dressing, Dana rehashed in her mind the conversation she had overheard outside the door of the committee meeting room.

She'd kept telling herself to leave, that she had no business listening in. Yet she had remained; the very nature of her job, if nothing else, told her that she had to stay put and get all the details.

Missing money. That was certainly a twist she hadn't expected. It had never entered her mind that Yancy Granger might take money intended for the hospital project. But someone had. Could it have been someone in Herman Green's office, as had been pointed out? That was the most logical explanation, but it wasn't the only one. Dana didn't know where her mind was going with this, but something didn't ring true about the entire scenario, just as Mrs. Jefferies and the lawsuit didn't ring true.

Both episodes had an underlying hint of overkill, which she intended to check out—not that she thought Yancy couldn't be guilty of any wrongdoing.

She'd already found that he had more flaws than a brown diamond. She refused to forget about those secrets she was sure were buried beneath his cocky facade, nor would she ignore his potential to explode at any given moment. She guessed that was what kept her frightened and fascinated and determined to pursue this story.

Her thoughts jumped back to her unexpected clash with Yancy in the hallway. *Animal magnetism* were the first words that came to mind. He reeked with it, and that fact alone should have sent her scurrying. Instead, she was in for the duration, for there was something about him that was both foreign and exciting to her. She didn't want that blazing attraction to fizzle, not yet.

And you're crazy as a bat, she told herself.

Admitting this was what settled her down and jolted her mind back to business.

The first thing on her agenda this morning was an interview with the bartender at the club where Yancy had been accused of drinking. Next, she would go to the University Hospital to talk with some of his co-workers, both doctors and nurses.

Dana had just finished her coffee when the phone rang. It was Billy Barnes, her reporter friend in D.C.

"Hiya, kid," he said in his forever upbeat mood. "How's it goin'?"

"Slow, which is my fault."

"That's hard to believe. You've never let any grass grow under your feet before."

Dana chuckled. "Well, at least it's interesting." She paused. "Billy, have you ever been involved in an investigation where you took one step forward, only to take two back?"

"Those situations are a bitch."

"That's where I am with Yancy Granger, or so it seems."

"Well, speaking of the doctor—and Congressman Crawford—here's the skinny: Crawford and his wife, Gloria, are definitely trying to have a baby. My sources have placed the couple in Charlottesville more than once. So, the doctor in question is most likely Yancy Granger."

"Which means that if he's successful in helping them, he's pulled off a real coup."

Billy laughed. "I can almost see the wheels turning in your mind. Where are you going with this?"

"I'm not sure, but you can bet there's something not quite kosher if that creep Albert Ramsey's in town. Something's brewing."

"I second that. So, go get 'em, kid, and let me know if there's anything else I can do."

"Thanks, Billy. I owe you one."

"Next time you're in D.C., you can buy me a steak."

"It's a date. See ya."

After she hung up, Dana continued to think about Billy's question. Where *was* she going with the congressman's story? She could understand the secrecy, the need for privacy, on Crawford's part. But what about Yancy? Wouldn't it benefit him to let it be known that he was helping a very influential, political couple attain their goal of having a family? That kind of publicity could add thousands to the project's coffers.

Unless?

Dana held her breath. Unless what? . . . Unless Yancy had a reason for keeping their liaison quiet. If there had been some greasing of palms on both sides, Yancy would not want that known.

But Dana did. As a member of the press, it was her duty to keep the public informed as to what their elected officials were up to. And if that involved an infamous doctor with sights on the Nobel Prize, then so be it.

With that thought in mind, Dana called the congressman's office.

"And who is calling, please?" the secretary asked in a polite but firm tone.

"Dana Bivens. I'm a reporter and I'd like to visit with Congressman Crawford to discuss Dr. Yancy Granger."

The silence that followed was almost deafening. Then Dana heard the woman's teeth click as if they were dentures. When she spoke again, her voice sounded like dripping icicles. "I'm sorry, but that's not possible. The congressman's schedule is full for the next several weeks."

"Thank you," Dana said. "I'll try again later."

The dial tone sounded in her ear. The "gotcha" game was becoming more intriguing by the day.

Smiling, Dana replaced the receiver.

"I appreciate your taking the time to see me, Doctor."

Carl Parker nodded, and a hint of a smile appeared on his ruddy-complexioned face, which was in concert with his red hair. "I don't have long, but what time I have is yours."

"Again, I appreciate that. I'll get right to the point. I'd like to talk to you about Dr. Granger."

"What about him?" Parker's tone took on a cautious edge.

"As I'm sure you know by now, Doctor, I'm doing a story on him and the proposed hospital. For starters, I'd like to know your opinion of Dr. Granger and what it's like to work with him."

Parker frowned and turned to face the window.

He wasn't going to talk. Dana squelched her cry of frustration. She had hoped he would be a "tell all" guy, as she'd heard that on several occasions he'd butted heads with Yancy. But apparently it wasn't going to work out that way.

Before coming to the hospital, Dana had stopped by the club where Yancy had been the night of the surgery. She'd had no trouble locating the bartender or getting him to talk.

"You damn right the doc was drinking," he said. "I oughta know. I mixed the drinks."

It took a great deal of effort for Dana to concentrate on what Fred Larkin said, as opposed to how he looked. The man needed a good scrubbing, from his greasy blond hair to his toes.

"You'll swear to that in court?" she asked, averting her gaze.

"Yep, just like I told that investigator from his lawyer's office."

So someone from Rooney's office had finally checked his story. She wondered just how Rooney planned to undermine this man's statement. But then maybe he was telling the truth. It was his word against Yancy's. If Yancy had been drinking, than he stood to lose everything. Somehow, though, she didn't believe that. He wanted that hospital too much to risk it.

So, if Fred Larkin had lied, what was his reason?

That question nagged at her now as she waited for Dr. Parker to answer what she'd asked him. But her patience was growing thin.

"Doctor?"

He swung around, his expression grim, "Sorry."

"Do you have anything to say?"

"Yeah, I got lots to say. I wouldn't throw water on the man if he were on fire, but I sure as hell might piss on 'im. If my crudity shocks you, I'm sorry." He shrugged. "But you asked."

"Care to tell me why you feel that way?"

"I think you already know the answer to that. He plays God with sickening arrogance, especially in the OR."

"Are you saying that he's not qualified to do his job?"

"No. It's the way he goes about that job that irks me."

"So you're saying that Dr. Granger's respected as a doctor, but despised as a man?"

"I guess that's about the size of it."

Dana stood and held out her hand. "Thank you again for seeing me and being so candid."

When Dana left Dr. Parker's office, she intended to interview one of the witnesses from the party that night. She made it as far as the front doors, only to turn around and walk back down the hall.

Why not? she asked herself, her heels clicking against the hard tile. Why not take this opportunity to interview the man himself? She'd put off doing it long enough.

She also had a personal agenda. Before she lost her nerve, Dana opened the door to the waiting room of Yancy's consulting office and crossed to the secretary behind the desk.

"Hello, I'm Dana Bivens."

"Ah, you're the reporter who's here to do a story on the doctor."

Dana smiled. "That I am. Is the doctor in?"

The woman hesitated. "Actually he is, but only for a few more minutes."

"I promise I won't keep him."

With that, Dana walked toward the closed door adjacent to the secretary's desk.

"Ma'am, you can't," she spluttered. "Please, wait—"

Dana ignored her, pausing only long enough to rap on the door before opening it and walking in. Later, when she'd looked back on that incident, she couldn't believe what she'd done.

"What the hell—"

Yancy's words seemed to jam in his throat when he swung around and saw her.

He was standing by the filing cabinet, dressed in dark slacks and his white doctor's coat, that errant strand of hair grazing his forehead.

For a moment Dana fought the urge to walk over and sweep that hair back into place. A frown drew her brows together.

"You," he said in a whispered tone, as if talking more to himself than to her.

His eyes were dark and intense, and she could see the film of moisture on his upper lip, which suddenly triggered memories of the night when he'd kissed her.

Her stomach hollowed and for a moment she couldn't say a word. Apparently he was having the same problem. In the heat of the moment, they simply stared at each other.

"What do you want?"

His tone was curt, yet there was a huskiness to it that she didn't miss. Nor did she miss the fact that his probing gaze was blatantly sensual. She struggled to regain the composure that had deserted her.

"What do you want?" he repeated.

She forced a smile. "You know very well what I want—an interview."

He opened his mouth to speak, but before he could say anything, she added, "But first there's something else I want."

It was obvious from his expression that he was both surprised and angry at having his space invaded. So why did he hesitate and give her the edge she needed?

Maybe it wasn't what she said but the way she said it that piqued his curiosity and made him ask in a civil tone, "And just what is that?"

"I'd like to become a patient here."

Yancy's jaw dropped.

Sixteen

"Don't look so shocked, Doctor. I didn't mean *your* patient."

Dana had managed somehow to get those words out, even though she was almost in a state of shock. This moment had played havoc with her mind since she'd arrived here; she'd never dreamed she would have the courage to go through with it.

"Uh, I didn't think you did," Yancy said at last. "Please, sit down."

The offer was so ordinary in such an unordinary situation that Dana wanted to laugh. But even that was impossible, as her confusion was far too deep. Until now, she'd had no intention of involving him or anyone associated with him in her personal life.

"Are you going to sit down?"

Only because her legs were beginning to tremble did she ease into the nearest chair.

"I'm ready to listen when you're ready to talk."

Another heavy silence fell between them, during which Dana found it hard to look at Yancy. But his eyes were so direct and compelling that she couldn't pull away. Besides, she had opened this can of worms. It was too late to close it. Or was it?

"Would you prefer I go to another clinic?" Dana couldn't

keep the husky tremor out of her voice or the color out of her face.

He pinned her with his gorgeous blue eyes. "Absolutely not."

Once he said that, Dana realized that *she* wanted to go somewhere else. Relief loosened something inside her. She stood. "Look, forget I—"

"Don't go."

She heard a matching tremor in his voice that made her heart turn over, which added to this insanity. She sensed that he was every bit as confused as she was.

Now she grappled with what to do, certain that the land mine she'd deliberately stepped on was about to blow up in her face.

"I—"

"Sit down, please."

She couldn't ignore the raspy plea.

"I can easily arrange for you to be examined by one of my colleagues. In fact, Dr. Conner is doing a fellowship in infertility this year and is seeing all of my patients for their initial visits."

He glanced at his watch. "That's exactly what he's doing now. He should be just about finished for the day. I'm sure he could squeeze you in."

Dana didn't respond. Examined now? This minute? She bit down on her lip to hold it steady. If she got so much as one tear in one eye, she thought she would die on the spot. Pride came to her rescue. Where was the strong, in-control woman who had jumped so many hurdles in her short lifetime?

"Do you want to discuss the problems you're having?"

Dana shook her head, feeling another surge of panic at the thought of discussing her most private fears. So much for the strong, in-control woman. She felt spineless. But she knew she was among the best gynecologist/obstetricians in the country. Could she afford to let this opportunity pass?

"Look, perhaps another time," she said at last. "Just forget I said anything, okay?"

"No, it's not okay. Dammit, Dana, I'm not letting you walk out of here until I get to the bottom of this."

"I'm not one of your residents, Doctor."

His expression turned fierce, yet his voice was gentle. "You started this, remember?"

"So it's my call to end it."

His sigh was as deep and intense as his scrutiny. "Suit yourself."

Dana walked to the door, placed her hand on the knob, then stopped, indecision rendering her motionless. She turned and looked at Yancy, who now had his back to her. She should go. She should leave this room, get in her car, and get as far from him, this hospital, and this town as she possibly could.

Dana closed her eyes for a moment, asking herself what would be worse—swallowing a portion of her pride or finding the answer to a question that had haunted her for a long time?

"I want to know if I'm normal," she blurted. "If I can get pregnant."

Yancy whipped back around, his eyes wide.

"Sorry." Dana's smile was lame. "To keep shocking you, that is."

His gaze flickered over her. "It takes a lot more than that to shock me. As for your concern, that's easy enough to check. Shall I call Dr. Conner?"

Dana licked her dry lips and said in a half-whisper, "All . . . right."

"When he's through," Yancy said, "he'll consult with me. Do you have a problem with that?"

"No," Dana said, looking him straight in the eye.

Yancy opened his mouth, then shut it. Dana knew he wanted to ask a million questions. She could almost see them swirling inside his head. But he refrained, as if sensing that the moment was too fragile, that *she* was too fragile. He was right; one wrong word and she would bolt.

Yancy punched the intercom button on his phone. "Nurse, please page Dr. Conner, then come in."

Seconds later, Dana's breath came in short, raspy spurts as a petite, gray-haired woman Dana judged to be in her late fifties crossed the threshold.

"Yes, sir?" Her eyes darted from Dana to Yancy, then back to Yancy.

"Laverne, this is Dana Bivens."

Yancy remained in his private office near the OR, sweat oozing out of every pore. But that was nothing new. When he came out of surgery, that was usually the case. However, he knew this agitation stemmed not from surgery but from Dana.

He was still taken aback by her request, regardless of the fact that she considered his staff the best in the country. The problem was that no matter what Dana did, it affected him. That woman, with her combination of innocence and steel, had him by the short and curlies and he couldn't shake himself loose.

If only she didn't arouse him physically the way she did. When he stared into those beautifully dilated eyes, looked at her lovely, shapely legs . . .

A resounding knock on his door broke his train of thought. He wiped beads of sweat off his brow. "It's open."

Dr. Winston Conner strode into the room. Yancy watched as he plopped his gangly body into a chair. He was destined to be an excellent specialist, Yancy thought. Not only did Conner have a sharp mind, but his bedside manner was perfect.

"Finished already?" Yancy asked.

"Yep. I'm here to report."

"By the way, thanks for coming to the rescue on such short notice."

Conner grinned, then shoved a large hand through his bright red hair, leaving it standing on end. "Hey, you don't have to thank me. I was up to my elbows in paperwork. I'd have done anything to get away from it."

"Only now you have to go back. I expect those reports on my desk today."

Conner grimaced, then said, "About Dana Bivens."

"I'm listening," Yancy said.

"As far as I'm concerned, the lady is okay. Actually, she's already *had* a baby."

Yancy was astounded.

Conner scratched his chin. "I wonder why she thinks she can't have another one."

That was what Yancy wanted to know.

"I tried to talk to her," Conner said, "but she didn't want to confide in me, so I let it drop."

Yancy forced his expression to remain blank, to show none of what he was thinking. But he was perplexed as hell. Just what was her angle? Why would she want an exam if she already knew she could get pregnant? Had she tried to conceive a second time and failed? As a doctor, he'd need to know more to determine a course of action.

"So where do we go from here?" Conner asked.

"I'll take over. Thanks for helping out."

"Anytime." Conner reached the door just as Laverne opened it.

"Ms. Bivens is dressed and ready," she said.

"Thanks," Yancy said, standing. "Tell her I'll be right there."

Inwardly, Yancy was a mess. He made sure, however, that none of that turmoil showed when he walked back into his consulting office and faced Dana.

She too seemed composed, but he knew better. She was just as big a mess as he was. He stared at her, always a mistake because he got sidetracked. She looked delectable. Her hair was in wild disarray; her eyes were deep and shadowed; her full lower lip trembled. Another jolt of lust shot through him.

She turned away and asked in a halting voice, "What did Dr. Conner tell you? Am I all right?"

"Seem to be. Everything looked fine," he said. "He did a Pap smear, of course."

Dana faced him again. "So he doesn't suspect any problems?"

"No." Yancy paused, searching for a way to ask his next question without further encroaching on her privacy. "Why didn't you tell me you'd had a child?"

She averted her eyes and took a deep breath. "Under the circumstances, I didn't think it was necessary."

"I see."

"So, am I free to go?"

"You were always free to go, Dana."

As if the pointed use of her name disconcerted her, she straightened, and when she spoke she sounded more like the confrontational journalist he knew her to be. "You're right, I was."

"How long has it been since you were examined?"

She hesitated. "A long time."

He wanted to get on his soapbox, to tell her how stupid, how careless, how *dangerous* it was to have neglected something so important. Though he sensed that she would tell him to mind his own business, he couldn't stop his next words. "What happened, Dana? What's this really about?"

"I told you, I wanted to see if I . . . I could have another child."

"Why did you think you couldn't?" He kept his voice as impersonal as possible. "Were there complications?"

Dana looked down at her hands, then back up, her face tormented. "Years ago, I was involved in a terrible automobile accident." She paused and ran her tongue across her lower lip, leaving a dewy sheen.

His body rose to the occasion and he cursed silently. "Go on," he said.

"I was pregnant at the time." She stopped again.

"What happened?" Yancy pressed.

"Some man took me to the hospital."

He felt the hairs at the back of his neck stand on end. "What man?"

The phone rang.

Yancy cursed. Dana flinched. But their dialogue was severed, the moment shattered. He reached for the receiver.

"What?" His tone was terse.

While Laverne talked on the other end of the line, he watched Dana, aching to ask her to repeat what she'd just told him. "I'm on my way," he said to the nurse.

Dana rose. "An emergency?"

"Always." He stood also. "Look, I gotta go."

"So do I." She walked to the door, then turned. "Thanks for—"

He batted the air. "It's okay."

"Oh—and don't think you're off the hook about the interview." She paused deliberately. "Because you're not."

She walked out and closed the door behind her. Yancy's face darkened as he hurried out the other door and up to the OR, his mind racing. Was it possible that she was the woman whom he—

Yancy slammed the door on that thought. Despite the similarities, Fate couldn't play that dirty a trick on him.

Seventeen

Dana munched on a piece of toast, but even smeared with peach jam, it tasted like cardboard. She shoved the plate aside and reached for her coffee. It didn't taste much better. She drank it anyway, needing the caffeine.

Setting the empty cup on the bedside table, she opened her laptop computer. She called up Yancy's file and stared at the information on the screen.

"Grrrh!" Frustrated, she realized that she was getting nowhere. She should be staring at Yancy Granger, not at a computer screen.

If Wade Langely at *Issues* knew that she hadn't yet done an in-depth interview with the doctor, he'd have a fit, and the chance of her getting that prestigious job would be nil. She wouldn't blame him.

With her computer still on her lap, Dana fell back against the pillows, having grave second thoughts. She shouldn't have given in and added another personal dimension to her and Yancy's relationship.

Tears threatened, but she refused to give in. It was too late to become emotional over what she'd done. But if she had it to do over again, would she? Yes. She had no regrets.

For years she had suppressed even thinking about another pregnancy; the one she'd gone through had been too traumatic. Yet there had been moments, usually at the most inopportune times, when the thought had hit her, crippling her with an intense longing.

She no longer had to suppress that longing. If Dr. Conner and Yancy proved to be right in their assessment—and she was confident they would be—there was no medical problem that would prevent her from getting pregnant again if she wanted to do so.

The fear that she could not was apparently psychological, but she'd wanted to be sure. That night there had been so much blood, so much blinding pain, so much fear. . . . Thanks to Yancy and Dr. Conner, at least one aspect of that fear had been quelled.

Now she could get on with her job. But was she fooling herself into thinking she could do an unbiased story on Yancy after what had taken place between them?

No. She was a professional. True, she had broken the rule and mixed her business and personal life, but she had no intention of ever doing it again.

So, what did she know about Yancy Granger? What facts could she report to Wade Langley if he were to call today?

Dana sat up straight and looked again at the screen. In front of her was the information on Yancy she had garnered to date. She read aloud:

"1. He has more enemies than he has champions.
2. He likes women.
3. He's arrogant and lords his power over everyone.
4. Two witnesses reported seeing him drink hard liquor at a party before performing emergency surgery.
5. A baby died in that surgery.
6. He's being sued for malpractice by the mother, who appears not to be grieving the loss of her child.
7. He's been implicated in money missing from the fund-raising coffers.

8. He's thought to be involved with Congressman Clayton Crawford and his wife in their efforts to have a child."

Dana fell silent for a moment. If the last point was indeed a fact, what, if anything, was the congressman promising him in return?

Reviewing these points out loud reinforced Dana's instinct that Yancy Granger would command a sensational story. And she had every intention of breaking that story.

She had gotten past her fascination with him. No more personal involvement. From now on, their dealings would be strictly business. She would concentrate on finagling that interview.

Though she didn't know how, as yet. But she *would* get it.

"I don't think I've ever heard you give a better lecture."

Yancy's lips twisted. "Is that a compliment, Brodie?"

"Ah, hell, Yancy, cut the sarcasm. I meant it."

Dr. Brodie Calhoun had just come into Yancy's private office following his lecture on a new infertility drug that had just been approved by the FDA.

"Okay, thanks," Yancy said, unused to such praise, especially from Brodie. Usually the chief of staff only came to Yancy's office to ream his ass for crossing the line and doing things "his way."

"You're welcome." Realizing that Yancy was uncomfortable, Brodie grinned. "Yep, you had those students eating out of your hand, and it was a damn good sight to see."

"Enough, Brodie. You've made your point. Besides, the last time I checked, UVA was a teaching hospital. I'm supposed to wow 'em."

"True, but lately it's only been on rare occasions that we get the infamous Dr. Granger to speak."

Yancy cut him an odd glance. "You're full of it today. What's going on?"

"Actually I'm feeling rather good." He slapped a leather

case down on Yancy's cluttered desk. "You really oughta clean this place up, you know." He frowned, which made him look fiercer than usual under his dark, heavy beard. "It looks like Beirut."

"Get lost, Calhoun."

"Is that any way to talk to your boss?"

"Yes. I have work to do, if you don't mind."

Brodie opened the case. "I have the final blueprints for the hospital."

Yancy's eyes lit. *Final* was the key word. He felt his adrenaline kick in. If ever he'd needed something uplifting, it was now. He'd been crawling on his belly ever since Dana Bivens had come to him seeking help.

"If we pull off this venture, a lot of other doctors and communities will be green with envy."

"I doubt that, but it sounds good."

"Always the cynic, huh, Granger."

"Whatever."

Brodie shook his head as he drew out the plans. "Take a look-see."

Yancy examined the blueprint, thinking what a marked improvement it was over the version Vida Lou had shown him. In fact, it was a masterpiece. Everything that he had asked for and more had been incorporated into the plan.

"So?"

Without looking up, Yancy said, "You're right—it's damned impressive."

"Now all we have to do is tie up the loose ends."

"Hell, Brodie, we don't even have the land yet."

Brodie rubbed his beard. "Don't worry, that's in the bag. Only thing, I'd like for Tremaine to come off his price a little."

"For the good of the community?" Yancy said with a smirk.

Brodie nodded. "I think he'll eventually accommodate us." He paused. "Speaking of the Tremaines, how did your interview go with Rooney?"

"Great. Like I told you, he's going to take the case."

"Well, I still think it's professional suicide on your part."

"Look, we've already had this conversation. Rooney says it's his old man's land, not his—which, despite what you think, does make a difference. Anyway, I need someone who can perform miracles, so I'm sticking with him."

Brodie frowned. "Can he make the lawsuit go away?"

"He says not to worry, he'll take care of it."

"Well, he'd better, if this project's going to fly."

Yancy glared at him. "Are you saying if this lawsuit gets nasty, the new hospital's in jeopardy?"

"That's exactly what I'm saying. It could take down the entire project."

"That's crazy!"

"It's not crazy. Hasn't it dawned on you that if the committee gets pissed off enough, they might renege on their donations?"

"That's not going to happen. Why, those old bastards want this specialty hospital almost as much as I do."

"Don't bet on that, not with what might come out in the lawsuit."

"I'm not guilty, for chrissake!"

"I know that, but there's a lot of people in this town who'd love for you to be guilty."

"That's their goddamn problem."

"No, it's yours. Need I keep stressing that it's imperative that your reputation and name remain intact and unsullied. If not, then they might get cold feet about forking over money for the land. And if we don't get the land . . ."

"Maybe old man Tremaine'll decide to give us the land."

"Your humor's sick."

"Maybe, but you need to lighten up. It's going to be all right. Rooney's going to make this all go away, because that Jefferies woman doesn't have a case."

"I still can't help but worry."

"Then go worry somewhere else," Yancy said in a tired voice. "I have work to do."

Brodie looked as though he wanted to argue, but he put the

plans back in his case and walked to the door. There, he turned and said, "By the way, talk to that reporter. It'll be a good PR move. I want to see a glowing story about Dr. Yancy Granger." He paused, his expression hardening. "That's an order."

Once the door closed behind Brodie, Yancy threw up his hands in frustration. Dana Bivens was the last person he wanted to talk to. Or was she? In truth, he wanted very much to see her, but not to talk.

He ached to touch her. From the moment he'd tasted those lips, felt her nipples poke into his chest, he'd wanted her. He still did, dammit!

He needed a good lay; that was his problem. He considered calling one of his old flames for a one-night fling. Maybe that would put out the fire in his groin.

To hell with that; he wasn't about to get involved with another woman. He'd made a grave error in his one-night stand with Vida Lou. With Dana, it would be far more than a one-nighter. He vowed not to touch her again.

Yancy raked an impatient hand through his hair. While he might not touch her, he guessed he did have to talk to her, but not for the reason Brodie had cited. He couldn't get their last conversation off his mind. If only that emergency hadn't interrupted them.

He knew his imagination was playing a mean trick on him, that Dana couldn't be that woman. Yet he couldn't ignore the similarities. And the age fit, he reminded himself, breaking out into a cold sweat.

Shit! If she was "that woman," he had to find out. Better the devil you knew . . .

Yancy stared at the phone. Should he call her? Did he have the guts? It didn't matter. Sooner or later he had to come to terms with Dana Bivens as a reporter. It might as well be now.

He looked up the number of the inn where she was staying and dialed it. Maybe she wouldn't be in her room, he told himself, hating what she did to him, hating what she *could* do to him.

The phone rang four times. He was about to hang up when he heard her say, "Hello," in a soft, sultry voice.

"Dana."

Her sharp intake of breath was a dead giveaway; she had recognized his voice. He identified himself anyway. "Yancy Granger."

"I was just about to call you."

Despite his determination to fight the physical effect she had on him, he felt that familiar tightening in his gut. "What about?"

"You know very well what about."

"The almighty interview, of course."

"Of course," she said in a mild, teasing tone, which only unsettled him more.

"How 'bout lunch?"

Silence.

"Are you still there?" By turning the tables, he'd caught her off guard.

"Yes, I'm still here." Her voice was stronger now, back to normal.

"Tomorrow?"

"That's fine with me."

He told her where to meet him, then hung up, all the while wondering if he really wanted to know that devil after all.

Eighteen

"Get dressed."

"Aw, Vida Lou baby, don't be that way."

Tyson Peters reached out a callused hand and rubbed her bare back.

She jerked away, then swung around and stabbed him with her eyes. "I said get dressed, then get out."

Tyson sighed before hauling his big body upright. But that was as far as he went. He stood beside the bed naked, his muscles bulging in all the right places. "What's with you?"

"I don't know what you mean." She did, but it wasn't any of his business.

"Sure you do. Instead of your personal trainer, I feel like your fast-fuck boy."

Vida Lou smiled, briefly. "That's all right, isn't it?" Her voice was silky smooth and deadly. "I mean, you're willing to be anything I want you to be?"

Tyson ran a hand through his shoulder-length blond hair and said, "Uh, you bet. Anything."

Vida Lou smiled again, though her eyes remained cold. "I'll call you soon for another training session and massage. Meanwhile, don't forget your little present." She winked at him.

He winked back before slipping into his gym shorts and

picking up an envelope on the desk. Vida Lou watched as he stuffed it into his pocket on his way out the door.

Vida Lou took a shower and got dressed. What a great start to the day, she told herself, spraying her clothes and hair with perfume. Although Tyson was great in the sack and would do anything she wanted, kinky or otherwise, he wasn't Yancy. But Yancy would come to his senses soon.

She peered at her desk calendar and saw that the next two hours were free. Still, she was glad she'd sent Tyson on his way. Once he finished servicing her, she always wanted him gone from her sight.

Later that afternoon she had a bridge game, then dinner that evening with a man from Richmond, a friend of her late husband, who'd hinted that he was interested in contributing to the hospital project.

She had wanted to ask the old geezer what he wanted in return, but she suspected she knew. Well, if it took a quick roll in the hay with him, so be it. At this point, Vida Lou was willing to do whatever it took to get the money for Shelby Tremaine's land.

This fund-raising business had consumed her life and Yancy's. She was growing weary of the work and his attitude. Something akin to panic rushed through her. She couldn't lose him. He was just fighting his feelings for her because he had so much on his mind. But once the land had been secured and the hospital was under construction, he'd turn to her in gratitude.

Commitment and marriage would follow. She was confident of that.

Reaching for the phone and her telephone/address book, Vida Lou walked onto the veranda and sat on the chaise longue. Although she dreaded speaking to Shelby Tremaine, she felt it was time to make him commit to the amount he wanted for that almighty tract of land.

He'd told the committee up front, "See how much you can raise, then we'll go from there."

That kind of fence straddling was no longer sufficient. She wanted an answer.

On the third ring, Shelby's wife, Anna Beth, answered, which surprised Vida Lou. Where was their housekeeper?

"Anna Beth, this is Vida Lou Dinwiddie."

"Why, Vida Lou," Anna said in her sweet, southern drawl. "How nice to hear from you."

I bet, Vida Lou thought, gripping the phone with a sweaty hand. She despised Shelby's wife, who was everything Vida Lou wanted to be. Just wait until she married Yancy Granger; no one would look down at her then.

"Is Shelby there?"

"No, he isn't. May I take a message?"

"When will he be back?"

Anna Beth hesitated, and Vida Lou knew that she was taken aback by her bluntness.

"Actually, I'm not sure. He's out of town looking at some Thoroughbreds."

"I see. Well, tell him I called and I'll get back to him."

"Is there anything I can help you with?"

"No, I don't think so," Vida Lou said. "It's your husband I need to talk to."

When she hung up, she knew she'd given Anna Beth food for thought, for she'd heard her sudden intake of breath. Vida Lou chuckled.

Since she couldn't meet with Shelby, she decided to take care of some unfinished business, something she should already have done.

Besides, she was in the mood for a good fight.

Dana was amazed that she was having lunch with Yancy. What was more amazing was that *he* had invited *her.* But she wasn't about to look a gift horse in the mouth.

She had chosen her outfit with care, finally settling on a lime green silk suit. After giving her hair that "trashy" look, she slipped on gold earrings.

Dana had told herself that it didn't matter how she looked,

that she wasn't trying to impress Yancy Granger with anything other than her journalistic skills. Still, she found herself scrutinizing every detail of her appearance.

Damn him and his effect on her, she thought, peering at her watch; she had thirty minutes to kill before she had to meet him. It was then that she heard a knock on her door. She wanted to say go away, but her manners surfaced.

"Come in, Mrs. Balch."

It wasn't the innkeeper who opened the door. The color drained from Dana's face as she stared at Vida Lou. "What are you doing here?"

Vida Lou strode into the room, slamming the door behind her.

"I don't remember inviting you in," Dana said, trying to control the anger building inside her.

"Yes, you did," Vida Lou responded, stopping in the middle of the room and turning around. "My, my, but aren't we dressed fit to kill."

"What are you doing here?" Dana repeated, her jaw clenched so hard that it hurt.

"I thought it was past time you and I had a talk."

"We have nothing to say to each other."

"I think we do."

"I don't want you here."

Vida Lou sat down on the corner of the bed. "Now, is that any way to talk to your mother?"

"You're no mother," Dana spat. "You're a whore."

Vida Lou's expression didn't change, other than a slight narrowing of her eyes. Nevertheless, that one tiny sign let Dana know that she'd struck a nerve.

"Tut-tut, the little mouse has finally developed sharp teeth."

"Go away, Vida Lou, or whatever the hell you call yourself now."

Now Vida Lou's face hardened, which accentuated the new lines forming around her eyes and mouth. Time for another face lift, Dana thought. Soon there wouldn't be any skin left to stretch. Dana couldn't help but smile.

"What's so funny?" Vida Lou demanded.

"I was just wondering when you were going to run out of skin to stretch."

"You little bitch. How dare you talk to me like that!"

"I dare do anything I want. You can't hurt me anymore, Mother dear."

"I wouldn't be too sure about that. You're on my turf now."

Dana lifted her chin. "That's fine with me. I'll take you on anywhere."

"Too bad you didn't have that kind of firepower in your mouth and belly when you were a child. I could've made a hell of a lot more money."

Dana slapped her, hard. It was as if her hand had developed a mind of its own. The sound of her palm striking her mother's cheek sounded like a gunshot.

For what seemed a long time but in reality was only a second, Vida Lou didn't respond. She sat there as if stunned.

Then suddenly she raised her hand to retaliate, only Dana was too quick. She jumped out of the way, dashed to the door, and opened it.

"Get out!" she cried. "Get out and don't ever come back!"

Vida Lou stormed toward Dana, who held her ground, refusing to show how scared she was, all the while envisioning her mother attacking her physically as she'd done so many times in the past.

"Now you listen to me, you hear?" Vida Lou hissed.

She was close enough for Dana to see the red whelp on her cheek. She hoped it hurt like hell, like she was hurting inside from the memories that her mother had dredged up.

"I want you out of this town!" Vida Lou screeched. "Today!"

"I'm not leaving until I finish my job." Dana clenched her fists. "You drove me away once before, but never again."

Vida Lou sneered. "We'll see about that."

"Oh, before you go, mind telling me if the missing money ever showed up?"

Vida Lou sucked in a harsh breath as her face twisted with rage. "You listened! I should've known you wouldn't leave."

"I learned that deceit from a master—you."

"If you live to be a hundred, you'll never be in my league. I can ruin you and your precious job, you know?"

Dana took a step backward, having seen that evil look far too often. Having struck her mother now heightened her fear. As a child she had dreamed of taking that bold move, had even played it out in her mind. But she'd never had the courage or the nerve before now.

"And I could return the favor, *you know?"*

Vida Lou's rage intensified, turning her face purple. "You'd best keep your mouth shut and mind your own goddamn business or you'll be sorry." She paused as if to let the warning sink in. "And you know how sorry I can make you."

That comment froze Dana's insides even before Vida Lou trailed a long, lacquered nail down one side of Dana's face.

Dana jerked her head back. "Don't you ever touch me again!"

"See that you don't do anything to make me."

"Go, dammit!" Dana opened the door wider.

Vida Lou walked out, only to turn back and look Dana up and down, a chilling smile on her face. "By the way, whatever happened to that brat you spawned?"

Nineteen

"Darling, what's wrong?"

Congressman Clayton Crawford sighed. "You're much too perceptive."

Gloria smiled and kissed him on the cheek. "I'm your wife. Of course I'm perceptive where you're concerned."

Clayton ran the back of his hand along her cheek before returning to his desk. He didn't sit, though. He looked at his wife and asked, "So, where're you off to this afternoon? Looking absolutely ravishing, I might add."

"I'm taking an interior designer out to the house."

Clayton frowned, making the premature wrinkles in his forehead more pronounced. "I know where you're heading with this, and I'm not sure it's a good idea." He tried to soften his words, but knew he'd failed by the pained look that crossed his wife's face.

"Why not? Is that what your sour mood's all about?"

"I wasn't aware I was in a sour mood."

"Well, *something's* wrong. Instead of telling me what it is, you tell me how nice I look, like I'm some housewife who's brain dead unless she's in the kitchen."

Clayton harrumphed. "You know better than that. Besides, since when have you ever been in the kitchen? Not since we've been married, as I recall."

"You're right, and there's a second verse to that: I'm not

going to be. As the wife of one of the most influential members of the House, I'm much too busy helping my husband handle his adoring constituents."

Clayton rolled his eyes, then drawled. "Give me a break here, darlin'."

"Only if you tell me what's bothering you. Since when don't we share everything?"

Clayton's expression clouded. When he caught an image of himself in the mirror, he grimaced.

He was not a handsome man. He wasn't even close to it, with his flat features and short, beefy frame. But what he lacked in looks, he made up for in enthusiasm and fire.

He loved this country, and he loved his job, though at times he got discouraged. Never, though, did he consider giving it up. He couldn't imagine doing anything else. In fact, he hoped to be the next president of the United States. He hadn't shared that secret dream even with his wife, whom he loved with all his heart.

"Clayton."

At the sound of her voice, he shook his head. "Sorry, I guess I was daydreaming."

"My point. You've been doing that for two days now, going off into a troubled world of your own." She took a breath. "You haven't heard anything about . . . the tests, have you?"

He heard the pain and fear in her voice and knew that he had to tell her. He went to her and folded her into his arms. She clung to him for a moment, then pulled away.

"That's it, isn't it? You've heard the results?"

Her tone had reached a higher pitch now, and he rushed to head off another crying jag. "No, honey, I haven't heard."

Her relief was so intense that she visibly sagged. "Then what is it?" she pressed. "If it's job related and you can't share it, then just tell me. I'll understand."

"I'm pretty sure someone's on to us."

Gloria gasped, her eyes widening in horror.

"Your reaction's exactly why I didn't say anything to you before."

"But it's making you crazy."

"I'm not crazy; I'm mad as hell."

"Tell me," she said in a dull voice.

"It's not the end of the world. It's just a minor glitch."

"Sure it is."

Clayton ignored her sarcasm. "Some reporter called and asked for an interview."

"So? That happens all the time."

"When Becky asked what she had in mind, the woman said she wanted to talk about Dr. Granger."

Gloria's face turned ashen, and she lifted a hand to her mouth as if to stifle a cry. Seconds later she said, "I can't believe this is happening. We've been so careful, so sneaky, so—" She broke off, her chin trembling.

"I'll take care of it, you hear?"

"If the media—"

"They won't." His tone brooked no argument. "I promise you that."

Gloria clutched at her stomach as she sank down on the leather love seat near his desk. "I don't care about me," she said, looking up at her husband. "It's you I'm worried about. You've got so much important legislation pending that if this gets out, it'll sidetrack—" She broke off again and bit down on her lower lip.

Clayton sat down beside her and reached for her hands, which were cold. "Stop it right now," he said. "Don't let that mind of yours conjure up something that's not going to happen."

"But it *has* happened. Our worst nightmare. You know how the damn media is."

"I know. That's another reason why I didn't say anything to you before."

"Which goes to show that you aren't very good at covering up your feelings."

Clayton brushed a tear from her cheek. "It's going to be all right. Trust me."

"Always." She was silent for a moment. "Why don't you

want me to see an interior decorator? Your attitude about that bothers me almost as much as this other thing."

Clayton rubbed her hands, trying to warm them. "I just don't want you to be disappointed, that's all."

"In other words if I get pregnant, only then I should think about fixing up a baby's room."

"Yeah, I guess that's what I'm saying."

They were quiet for a moment.

"You don't think it's going to happen, do you?" Gloria whispered, her green eyes brimming with fresh tears.

"Granger's supposed to be the best. If nothing's wrong with either of us, it'll happen. If not, then we'll go from there." He kissed her gently on the mouth. "But if it'll make you feel better, go ahead and talk to the decorator, 'cause I really think it's going to happen." Clayton smiled.

She hugged him before standing. He followed, walking her to the door.

"Try not to be late," she said. "Remember, the Domineys are dining with us tonight."

"I'll be on time." He touched her on the end of the nose. "Count on it."

The moment the door closed behind her, Clayton's expression turned bleak. He strode to his desk and punched the intercom button. "Tell Ed I want to see him."

Seconds later his aide, Ed Ubanks, came into the room.

"Sit down."

Ubanks paled, which seemed to make his large ears, now red, stand out even more. "Uh-oh, you're pissed."

"You're damn right I'm pissed. Some reporter called and wanted to have a heart-to-heart."

Ubanks shrugged. "So, that's good, isn't it?"

"Not in this case. She mentioned Dr. Yancy Granger."

"Oh shit."

"Her name is Dana Bivens. Find out who she is and what the hell she wants."

"I'll get right on it," Ubanks said, jumping up.

"While you're at it, find out the status of that grant in my subcommittee."

"The one for Granger's proposed hospital?"

"Yeah."

"I'll get back to you on both."

"The reporter gets top priority. There's too much at stake now to let her misconstrue things. What I'm doing with the grant is on the up and up, but the public could see it a different way. And that could blow me and my career sky high."

"Oh boy."

"Don't worry. No ambitious reporter's going to do to Gloria and me what the tabloids did to Chung and Povitch when they wanted to have a baby."

"So you want me to handle her—the reporter, I mean?"

"Not yet. First, find out who the hell this Dana Bivens is and what she's after. Then I'll decide the best course of action to take."

Dr. Misty Granger glared at the man in front of her.

"I'm not the enemy here, Misty."

"You couldn't prove it by me," she responded in a stinging tone.

Rayford Giles flushed and lowered his eyes as if he couldn't bear to look at her another second. Misty didn't care. He was her attorney; he was supposed to be on her side.

As if he could read her thoughts, Rayford looked at her again, his round, baby face back to its normal color. "For the last time, I am on your side."

"So check out my options concerning Yancy's work—*our* work."

"Then what?"

"Tell me if I have grounds to sue him."

"Sue him?" Rayford's tone was incredulous. "You've got to be kidding?"

"I'm not kidding." Misty's voice was hard and unrelenting. "During the early years of our marriage, I helped with some of the research he's getting all the credit for,"

"What this boils down to is money, isn't it?"

"Partly."

"If we pursue this crazy notion of yours, we've got to have more than your word to back up the claim."

Misty crossed her arms over her flat chest and stared out the window, the sights and sounds of downtown Richmond barely registering.

"Misty?"

She blinked. "What?"

"I've been your friend a long time. So—"

"Spare me the platitudes, Rayford. Just back me up."

He stiffened. "Are you sure there's not more to this than you're telling me?"

"I don't know what you mean."

"Yes, you do. Maybe you want Granger back, and this is your way of getting his attention."

Misty shook her head, which sent her chestnut hair swirling around her face. But it didn't hide the anger his remark brought on. "That's not true! I wouldn't have the bastard back if he got down on his knees and begged me."

"That bad, huh?"

"Worse." Her tone was bitter. "He's the most self-centered person I've ever known. But . . ."

"Go on."

"Never mind. It's not important."

"Look, why don't you think about this a little more. There's a good chance he won't win the Nobel. He's got damn stiff competition. But if he does, we'll go from there."

"I see I've wasted my time coming here."

"Dammit, Misty, you're—"

"Consider yourself fired."

Before he could reply, she added, "There's more than one way to skin a cat, you know."

Dana still looked ravishing, even though her lips were pale. At that moment, while the waiter poured their after-lunch coffee, Yancy wished he'd had the pleasure of eating her lipstick off, especially from that protruding bottom lip. Damn! Thoughts like that made both his groin and his mind ache.

Why the hell did this woman turn him on so?

They had met for lunch as he'd suggested. From the instant she'd come in and sat down at the table, he'd been out of sorts. Maybe that was because *she* was out of sorts. Something had happened, he'd swear to it. Her eyes had given her away; there had been a wildness about them, a combination of defiance and fear.

Perhaps she'd had a fight with her lover boy, Rooney Tremaine. He'd smirked at the thought.

Still, she had not lost her composure, which had stirred both his admiration and his curiosity. He would have given anything to know what smoldered behind those lovely eyes within that luscious body. But he'd never know—at least not about the body.

He sighed inwardly as he continued to observe her. Lunch had been pleasant enough, considering that they were both a bit on edge. But then, their relationship was an odd one. Dana Bivens was a stranger, yet he'd kissed her as a man and talked to her as a doctor. Despite that, the conversation over lunch had been impersonal.

Yancy figured that was about to end. Soon he'd get the old who-what-when-where routine. And more.

First, though, he had his own agenda, if he could pull it off.

"Lunch was delicious," she said. "Thank you."

"You're welcome. You didn't eat much, though."

She smiled politely and reached for her notepad. "I'm ready to get down to business, if you are."

"Mind if I go first?"

"Excuse me?"

"You never finished the story you started in my office. You were telling me about a man who took you to the hospital."

Dana's face lost its color. "I'd rather not go into that again."

"I know, but I want you to."

"Look—"

"It's okay. We could stretch it and say you're my patient."

The color flooded back into her face. “Not really,” she said flatly.

“So turnabout’s no longer fair play, huh?” he teased, hoping that she would relax and confide in him.

“In other words, if I don’t tell all, you won’t?”

He grinned.

She didn’t. “Do you always play hardball, Doctor, or is it just with me?”

“Sorry, that’s my personality—I’m just a sonofabitch.”

She smiled then, which made his groin stir. He gritted his teeth.

“Remember, you said that, I didn’t.”

“Yeah, right.” His tone was gruffer than he’d intended.

Dana’s expression grew serious. “I . . . I don’t really remember anything about the man other than what the ER doctor told me later.”

“Which was?”

“That whoever he was, he apparently didn’t want to be seen or heard from because he’d been drinking heavily. There was a strong odor of booze all over my blouse, only—”

She broke off again, and it was an effort for Yancy to curb his impatience. But curb it he did.

“Only what?” he asked, though he felt like he was about to explode.

“The blood work showed that *I* hadn’t had a drop to drink.”

He swallowed hard. “And the baby?”

For a moment Dana didn’t answer. When she finally did, her voice sounded fractured. “It died.”

Twenty

All the air seemed to have been sucked out of the restaurant. Yancy fought off a disabling sense of déjà vu as he sat there, motionless, feeling as if he'd been stabbed in the heart.

The accident that night on that rain-soaked road had been his dark, lonely secret for all these years. Now it was in his face again, in the cruelest way possible, in the flesh-and-blood woman who sat across from him.

Only *she* didn't know that.

He was the only one who had all the pieces to that puzzle. Averting his gaze, he stared out floor-to-ceiling windows. He hadn't been sure of the baby's fate, although he'd felt in his gut that it had died.

Suddenly he wished he hadn't eaten, for fear he'd vomit. No matter how many times he'd replayed that night, nothing changed. Oh, the pain had dulled somewhat, the stark reality of it, but the details remained.

The rational portion of his mind had told him he wasn't to blame for her baby's death. But he knew better. He could have saved the infant, *if* he'd had all his wits about him, *if* he hadn't been drinking. He felt as if a giant hand were squeezing the life out of his heart.

Realizing how lengthy the silence had grown, Yancy turned back to Dana, but it was an effort. Jesus, her eyes were filled with so much sadness and pain that it took his breath away.

"I'm sorry," he finally said, hearing the brusqueness in his tone but unable to control it.

Dana blinked then, which caused a tear to roll down her cheek. He fought the urge to reach out and lick that tear off her face.

She wiped it away, cleared her voice, and said, "Me too. But that was a long time ago. I've . . . gone on with my life."

But with scars, just like me. "It's still not clear to me why you thought you couldn't get pregnant again."

Though he felt terribly uncomfortable continuing this conversation, he had to ask, wanting to know what she'd been told by the OR doctor or whoever had taken care of her.

"My own paranoia, I suppose," she said.

"So it wasn't anything the doctor said to you?"

"Oh, he quoted some technical jargon."

"Which was?"

"Something about the placenta separating."

"That would be placental abruption." He went on to explain in layman's terms what that meant.

"That sounds familiar," she said when he finished, "but again, it really didn't register."

"All you were afraid of was that you'd done something terrible to your body?"

"Yes," Dana said, biting down on her lower lip, "and I was too scared or too ignorant or both to ask any questions."

"Do you feel better now?"

"Yes." She peered down at her hands.

He wished he did. "Since you and Rooney Tremaine are an item, you—"

Her head snapped up. "Who told you that?"

What had possessed him to take this conversation to an even more personal level? He felt like giving himself a royal kick in the butt.

"Tremaine told me."

"He had no right to say anything to you about our relationship."

It was clear that she was furious, which stirred mixed emotions inside Yancy. For his own good, he wanted to believe that she was crazy about Rooney and wild to marry him. On the other hand, the thought of any other man kissing those lips, touching her where *he* wanted to touch her . . .

Yancy rubbed his cold hands together. "All he said was that he'd be in town as much as possible because you were here. So, is there something between you two? Is that why you wanted to know if you could have a baby?"

Dana's eyes flashed. "That's none of your business."

He winced at that brutal truth. He didn't know when to quit. He was more out of line now than ever, but he couldn't seem to shut his mouth.

"You're right, it isn't." Yancy regrouped and forced a coolness into his voice, hoping it would calm her and put things back on an even keel. "So is there anything else about the accident and that night you want to tell me?"

"No."

"Not even how you feel about the man who—"

"Dumped me and ran off."

Yancy showed no emotion. "Yeah, him."

"I hold the bastard responsible for the death of my baby. And if our paths ever cross, I'll make him pay for what he did."

Yancy almost choked on the hot bile that surged up his throat. He was helpless against the emotions raging inside him. But he didn't let on. He couldn't.

It was the memory of this woman that had reshaped his career, that had made him the doctor he was today. Only now this same woman had the power to send that world toppling down around him.

That was why she must never learn that he was the one who had "dumped" her that night in a drunken stupor. As far as he knew, no one other than himself really knew what had happened.

That brought him little comfort. What if she did find out? After all, she was a reporter. If she discovered the truth, with the stroke of a pen she would destroy him and take pleasure in doing it.

"Enough about me," Dana said, interrupting his fearful thoughts. "I'm the reporter here, remember? I'm supposed to be interviewing you. Now, tell me something about yourself."

A chill ran through him, but he remained poker-faced. "Like what?"

"Oh, come on now, you've been interviewed a million times, I'm sure. You know the drill."

"Yeah, and that's what bothers me."

"You'll get over it."

"That's where you're wrong. I've never liked having anyone pry into my business."

"Even if it could help attain your goal?"

"You can honestly tell me that's what you're here for? I thought reporters' jobs were to uncover their subjects' dead bones."

He knew she caught the sarcasm in his tone because she flushed—a flush that started in her face and moved to the open V at the top of her blouse.

His eyes settled there unwittingly, watching her breasts move in concert with her breath. When he forced himself to look back up, their eyes met.

As if scrambling for composure, she said in a hurried tone, "I'm not letting you off the hook."

He looked away. If only their paths had never crossed and he didn't feel such a deep sorrow and responsibility for her loss. If only he didn't feel so sexually drawn to her. If only he hadn't gone crazy in that parking lot and kissed her.

But all those things had happened and couldn't be undone. He had no one to blame but himself.

"Maybe we should start with why you became a doctor," Dana said, clearing her throat as though that would somehow diffuse the tension between them. "Were you the star student in the biology lab, the one who loved to dissect frogs?"

"Yep. I couldn't wait to get there and pull those little suckers' legs right off their twitching bodies."

He managed to piss her off again. He saw it in the stiffening of her body and the angry set of her jaw.

Piss off time. "This isn't a joke, Doctor."

"Yes, it is."

"This is your show, remember?" Her voice shook.

"Oh, I remember, but I see now that it was a mistake. I don't see how probing into my life can help the project."

"From what I've heard, you *are* the project."

"That'd be nice, only it's not true."

"Why, such modesty." Her voice reeked with sarcasm.

"What can I say? It's part of my charm."

"Okay. Let's go back to when all that charm developed."

Yancy made a point of looking at his watch. "I don't think so. Time's up."

"You can't mean that."

"Oh, but I do."

"I'm not going to let you weasel out of this interview. You yourself said that turnabout's fair play."

"Surely you don't believe everything people say to you?"

"You can't do this!"

"I can do anything I please. And choosing not to give you an interview pleases me."

Yancy stood and tossed some money onto the table for their lunch. "I don't think the story's a good idea. I suggest you forget it."

Dana sat there choking on her fury. First Vida Lou, now *him.* At that moment she didn't know which one she hated more.

For a day that had started out to be so promising, it had gone downhill real fast, she thought, leaving the restaurant. She didn't need this. She didn't need any more setbacks. The conversation about her baby had ripped the scab off that old wound, leaving her bleeding emotionally once again.

She was fighting back the tears when she reached her car. It was then that she saw Yancy exit the parking lot.

Like hell she'd forget the story.

She watched as his BMW disappeared. "If you think you're going to get away with pitching that little fit, Doctor, you're dead wrong," she muttered, getting into her own car and pressing down hard on the accelerator.

Minutes later she heard a siren. Her heart lurched as she peered into her rearview mirror, thinking that it was an ambulance and she should get out of the way.

Wrong. It was a police car. And he was on her bumper. Her heart lurched again when he motioned for her to pull over.

"Oh, Lord," she whispered, maneuvering the car onto the shoulder of the road.

The officer appeared at her window. "Ma'am, is there any reason you were going fifty in a thirty zone?"

"No, sir."

"No emergency or anything?"

"No, sir."

"Your driver's license, please."

Red-faced, Dana scrambled for her wallet and handed him the license, which he took back to his police car. She couldn't believe she was about to get a speeding ticket. But considering the way her day had gone, it seemed par for the course.

The officer returned. "Ma'am, sign here, please."

She reached for the clipboard, and as she scribbled her name, she noticed the cost of the ticket—seventy-five dollars.

"I'd advise you to slow down, ma'am," the office drawled before tipping his hat and stepping back.

Furious, Dana could only nod. She was sure that Rooney could get the ticket thrown out, but since she had been speeding, she hated to ask him.

The next best thing, she decided, was to drop the matter where it belonged—in Dr. Yancy Granger's lap.

He'd pay for the ticket, one way or another.

Hubert Cox shifted the unlit cigar from one side of his mouth to the other. He hated that he couldn't smoke in his office anymore. Hell, he couldn't smoke anywhere in the building, and it was almost as bad on the street. Whenever he went outside and leaned against the building for a smoke, passersby either dodged him or stared at him like he was pond scum.

Now, as he chomped down harder on the soggy end of the cigar, he stared at the pile of work on his desk. He had to get it cleared in order to make a good impression on the boss, who was about to retire.

Hubert leaned back in his chair and smiled. He'd been the editor in chief at *Old Dominion* for twenty years. Now, finally, he had a chance to nab the coveted position of publisher—if he didn't screw up in the meantime. Ah, hell, he didn't have anything to worry about. He was a shoo-in, since Ned Amhurst, the present publisher, was going to recommend him to the board.

Still, Hubert couldn't quiet that niggling warning in the back of his mind that something would happen to stop him from reaching his goal.

Not only did he need the prestige that the elevated job would bring, he needed the financial security as well. He wanted to remarry, and that took money, especially since his lady friend was twenty years younger than he.

He smiled, his thoughts turning to her, then back to Ned's anticipated visit. The meeting was to be an informal one, Ned had said, just to make sure everything was in order for the board, so that no questions would come as a surprise.

Hubert appreciated his boss's support and concern. He left his desk and took a long look at himself in the full-length mirror on the back of his office door.

Not bad. His dyed black hair, plastered to his head, looked shiny. His blue and gray paisley tie matched both his hair and his shirt. He moved his gaze down to his waistline and gave a satisfied smile. Janis was responsible for the trimness there.

"Hubert?"

The sound of his name, followed by a knock, startled him. He stepped back, opened the door, and smiled. "Come in, Ned."

Hubert's smile faded as the publisher came in looking about as grim as the grim reaper. He was a tall, large man who always seemed to dwarf any room he was in. He also had a thatch of steel-gray hair that matched his steely demeanor. Hubert's insides knotted.

Ned didn't waste any time or words. "Hubert, we—*you* have a big problem."

Hubert barely stopped his mouth from gaping like a guppy's. What the hell had he done now? "Do you want to sit down?" He pointed to the most comfortable chair in his office.

Ned waved a hand. "No. This won't take long. But it might be a good idea if you sat down."

Hubert began to sweat. He could just see his promotion about to be flushed down the toilet.

"I don't understand."

Ned smiled without a fraction of humor. "Trust me, you will."

Twenty-one

Shelby Tremaine swigged down what was left of the Chivas Regal. The fact that it burned his stomach made no difference. He didn't give a damn if the stuff killed him. He had always liked his toddies, and he saw no reason to change—despite Anna Beth's constant nagging.

Thinking about his wife brought a frown to his face. Hell, just because she was a teetotaler didn't give her the right to preach to him. He should have become used to it by now, but he hadn't. In fact, he believed she'd gotten worse, having threatened to pour all his booze down the drain.

"If you so much as touch a drop, I'll break both of your arms," he'd told her.

She had sniffled and run out of the room, then hadn't spoken to him for days afterward. But she'd gotten the message. Shelby Tremaine was in charge of his family, always had been, always would be. He cared about Anna Beth, but she had her place.

And so would his son's wife, when he married.

He reached for the bottle on his desk, then remembered that Rooney was due to arrive at any moment.

Ah, his son. The delight of his life. Shelby smiled, thinking of the day Rooney was born. He'd thought his chest would burst with pride the first time he saw that tiny bald head nestled close to Anna Beth's breasts. Nothing had ever brought that kind of high to his life again.

He also remembered his wife's expression and the exact words she'd spoken: "Here's the son you've always wanted to carry on the Tremaine line."

Shelby hadn't realized it then, but Anna Beth had given him a message, which was that she'd done her duty as a wife and he shouldn't expect her to do it again.

She had never made love with him again. He hadn't cared, realizing after their honeymoon that she disliked sex. Yet the thought of divorcing her never entered his mind. Tremaines did not get divorced. His daddy had drilled into his head that whatever bed you made for yourself, you had to lie in it, no matter what.

Shelby had been true to his daddy, but not to his wife. He'd had his share of flings before he married Anna Beth and after as well. Even if his wife had liked sex, he doubted that he would've stayed faithful to her. He was a virile man whose sexual needs couldn't be met by any one woman. While he was sure that Anna knew about his indiscretions, she never let on, nor did he.

To the outside world, he and Anna Beth had the perfect marriage, which was the way it should be. Nothing—no incident or person—must blight the Tremaine name. He would kill before he'd let that happen. He'd preached the same lesson to Rooney, who so far had not disappointed him.

He had to make sure that didn't change.

That thought brought Shelby from his chair to the French doors, where he looked out as far as his eyes could see. Three passions in life kept his juices flowing: his son, politics, and his land.

The house and land had been in the family for generations, land where Civil War battles had been fought and crops had been grown and harvested. He'd made millions off it. Only because he had a chance to make more, and to further immortalize the Tremaine name, did he consider selling a chunk of it.

Shelby belched, then rubbed his paunchy waist, feeling the start of that burning in his gut. He wasn't surprised; every time he thought of giving up even an acre of his precious land, his stomach rebelled, booze or no booze.

But there was more to his rebellion than parting with the land. He didn't like what he'd been hearing. The thought of any type of scandal associated with him or his family was intolerable, which was one of the reasons he was so eager to talk to his son. He had plans for Rooney, and it was time he told him so.

He hadn't realized he was no longer alone until he heard his wife say, "My, but you're deep in thought."

Shelby wheeled around as Anna Beth walked into the room. She had indeed been a suitable wife in every way except in the bedroom. She was a damn good mother and still lovely to look at, with a heart-shaped face that bore scant testimony to her age. She had also maintained her trim figure, which complemented the designer dresses she wore with such poise and ease. She was a true southern lady, adoring her son and tolerating her husband.

Shelby couldn't help but smile.

"What's funny?"

"Nothing, dear."

Anna Beth gave him a puzzled look. "I thought Rooney would be here by now."

"You know how these kids are. They're never on time."

"Rooney's not a kid, Shelby, and he's *always* on time."

Shelby shrugged, then peered at his watch. "You did tell Marian to hold lunch, didn't you?"

"Of course." She paused, toying with her bottom lip. "Has Rooney mentioned anything to you about the case he's working on? I mean—"

"I know what you mean, Anna Beth. And yes, he has, but very little."

"Did I hear my name mentioned?"

They both swung around and smiled as Rooney came into the room. He bent down and kissed his mother on the cheek, then shook hands with his father.

"Hello, son."

"Oh, it's so good to see you!"

Rooney put his arms around his mother's shoulders. "Now, Mamma, I was just here the other day."

"I know, sweetheart, but before that, we've seen you so seldom."

Rooney touched the tip of her nose. "That's right, but my job keeps me hopping, Mamma, so don't go gettin' too spoiled, you hear? You know the only reason I've been here lately is that I have a client in town."

"I'm glad you brought that up," Shelby said.

Rooney stared at his father. "Why?"

"Anna Beth, would you mind leaving us alone for a minute." Shelby winked at her. "Men talk."

"Shelby—"

"It's okay, I won't keep him long." Though Shelby's tone was even, there was a hard note in it. "Now run along; we'll join you shortly."

Anna Beth looked as if she wanted to argue, but instead she stood on tiptoe and gave Rooney another kiss on the cheek. "Don't you let your daddy keep you away from me too long, you hear?"

"I won't, Mamma."

Once she left the room, Shelby turned to his son. "Want a drink?"

"No, thanks, Daddy."

"Well then, sit down and take the load off."

Rooney did as he was told, but kept his eyes on his daddy

as he poured himself a healthy drink. "What's up? Am I about to be put on the hotseat?"

"Of course not, son. I just wanted to know why you decided to defend Yancy Granger."

He shrugged. "His insurance company offered me a lot of money."

Shelby scoffed. "Only you don't need the money, and we both know that."

"Hey, what is this? Do you have a problem with my defending this man? After all, he's—"

"An arrogant, cocky sonofabitch," Shelby finished.

"But a damn good doctor."

"If that's the case, then why the hell can't he just do his job and stay out of trouble?"

"How do I know. I'm not his keeper, only his attorney."

"I want you to withdraw from the case. That kind of shit turns my stomach."

Rooney's eyebrows rose. "Does that mean you're not going to sell the land?"

"I didn't say that."

"Then what are you saying? That you don't like Yancy Granger?"

Shelby took a sip of his drink and felt an instant calm. He had to approach this situation with a delicate hand. While Rooney had always listened to him, the boy did have a mind of his own. Shelby didn't want to alienate him; nonetheless, he didn't want him having anything to do with the likes of Yancy Granger, who was a blue blood turned white trash with the morals of an alley cat. Shelby couldn't think of anything worse.

Hell, he didn't care if Granger had a loose zipper, but he did care that he wasn't discreet about it. Airing one's dirty laundry in public repulsed him.

"I'm saying that I don't want you involved in a case that you might lose."

"So you believe Granger's guilty?"

"I didn't say that." Shelby played his cards close to his chest. "I know he has a reputation for having sown more than his share of wild oats. Besides . . ."

"Besides what?" Rooney pressed.

"I don't want you involved in such a distasteful matter. I have big plans for you, son. You know that."

"Come on, Daddy, I'm not political material. I've told you that."

"I don't buy that malarkey for a second. Why, Virginia needs young men like you, so does this country. You'll make a great senator."

"Probably would, if I were interested."

"You will be."

Rooney rolled his eyes, which sent anger rushing through Shelby, but he managed to control it. Kids. They had no respect for family or tradition. But he wasn't about to give up. He intended his son to do exactly as he was told. Shelby had always gotten what he wanted, and he didn't see why that should change now.

"Daddy, let's not get into this again now, okay? Anyway, Mamma's waiting and—"

The phone at Shelby's elbow rang, cutting Rooney off. Shelby lifted the receiver, said, "Hello," then listened.

After a moment, he covered the mouthpiece. "I need to take this call, son. I'll join you and your mother in a minute."

Rooney left the room. Shelby frowned when he noticed that his son hadn't closed the door all the way.

"I'm sorry, go ahead," he said in a low voice.

Dana didn't have to wait. As soon as she identified herself to the chief of staff's secretary, she was told to go right in, that she was expected.

"Ms. Bivens, what a pleasure," Dr. Brodie Calhoun said, meeting her halfway, his hand extended.

Dana smiled at the burly man. "Thank you. I appreciate your taking the time to see me."

"No problem. Please, have a seat."

Dana sat down and glanced around the doctor's office. Though rather austere, it had a homey touch, with pictures of his wife and children occupying a prominent place on his desk. Also, there were fresh flowers on a table near the window.

"Before we get down to business," Brodie said, taking a seat behind his desk, "I'd like to take the opportunity to welcome you to Charlottesville. I hope you're enjoying your stay."

"I am." Dana saw no reason to tell him that she was originally from this area.

"I also want to extend an invitation to tour the hospital anytime you want to. Take pictures, whatever."

"I'll certainly take you up on that offer. Though not today."

Brodie leaned back in his chair. Dana almost winced as the springs gave a grunt of protest under his weight.

"Having you do a story on the proposed hospital and Dr. Granger is something that money can't buy. I want you to know how grateful I am."

"Too bad Dr. Granger doesn't feel that way."

Brodie's chair grunted again as he straightened. "What do you mean?"

"Dr. Granger has refused an interview."

Brodie cursed, then he flushed. "Sorry."

"That's all right. I've heard that word before."

Brodie gave her a quick, limp smile. "What exactly did Granger tell you?"

"In a nutshell, forget the story."

Dana hated being put in this position; she felt like a child tattling on someone. But Yancy had left her no alternative. She intended to do whatever was necessary to get that interview. If tattling to the chief of staff was what it took, then so be it.

"We'll just see about that," Brodie finally said, popping the knuckles on his right hand, then his left.

Again, Dana fought the urge to wince. "I was hoping you'd be on my side."

"You can rest assured I'm on your side, Ms. Bivens. You just leave Dr. Granger to me."

"Are you saying I'll get my interview?" Dana asked, standing.

"You're damn right. I'll see to it."

Twenty-two

"I'm surprised to see you back in town so soon."

The lines in Rooney's forehead deepened. "You shouldn't be."

"No, I guess not," Dana said, "especially since you have a client here."

"Yeah. One who says he doesn't have time to come to Richmond."

"Sounds like you don't believe him."

Rooney shrugged his slender shoulders. "It doesn't matter really, who comes where, just as long as I get the job done."

They had met at a new restaurant on the outskirts of town that had been highly recommended. So far, Dana hadn't been disappointed. Both the food and the service had been excellent, and the clientele upscale.

Maybe that was why she had a feeling that if she looked around, she would see Yancy staring at her.

She tensed inside. It seemed as if she had Yancy Granger on the brain, which kept her upset and irritated. His attitude about the interview still grated, but she felt confident that in the end she would win. She'd like to have been eavesdropping when Brodie Calhoun called Yancy into his office.

Her career hinged on Calhoun winning that battle.

"What's churning in that lovely head of yours?"

Dana blinked. "Sorry, I was just thinking about what all I have to do."

"So how's your work going?"

"So-so." Dana paused, then tilted her head. "What about yours?"

Rooney took a sip of his wine, then looked at her over the rim. "It won't work, you know, your fishing expedition."

"I don't know what you're talking about." Dana's tone was prim.

Rooney snorted. "Yeah, right."

"I know you can't discuss Yancy's case with me; we've already covered that territory. But you could tell me if you've managed to track down that second witness who was at the party."

"No, as a matter of fact, I haven't. I've called several times, but he's never in town."

"Don't you find that strange?" Dana asked.

"From the sound of your voice, you apparently do."

"Well, after talking to the bartender, I can't understand why this one's all of a sudden dodging us."

Rooney readjusted his glasses, then squinted. "Maybe he *is* out of town. Or maybe he decided he doesn't want to get involved after all."

"That's exactly what I'm thinking."

Rooney grinned. "So for the good of your story and for the defense of my client, I guess we'll both have to find that out, if and when we track him down."

"Oh, *I'll* track him down, all right," Dana said, after sipping her wine. "Make no mistake about that."

Rooney gave her a pensive stare. "You're really wrapped up in this Granger thing, aren't you?"

"It's my job, Rooney. Besides, you know what's at stake here."

His stare deepened. "Well, I for one am tired of Dr. Yancy Granger. If you don't mind, I'd like to talk about something else."

"Like what?" Dana asked in what she hoped was a light tone. She didn't like the glint in Rooney's eyes.

"Not what, but who." He paused, leaning forward. "Us. I'd like to talk about us."

An alarm signal went off inside Dana. "Rooney, you know there's no us. I—"

"Shhh." He grabbed her hand and held it. "For once, will you keep quiet and hear me out?"

Dana nodded, dreading what was to come.

"You know how I feel about you."

"Rooney—"

He squeezed her hand. "You said you'd hear me out, right?"

Again she nodded, but she couldn't look him in the eye.

"I want to marry you, Dana."

She forced her eyes to meet his. "Oh, Rooney, please. You know—"

"I know, you don't love me."

"Then why on earth would you want to marry me?"

"Because I'm crazy about you, and I think in time you might come to be crazy about me."

"Rooney, Rooney. You deserve better than that. You deserve someone who truly loves you."

"Hey, you let me be the judge of that. Right now, all I'm asking is that you think about it. Just don't say no right off the bat."

Dana couldn't respond. Her mind and heart were filled with turmoil.

"So you'll know, no matter what you decide, we'll always be friends. I just couldn't hold back my feelings any longer."

Tears pricked Dana's eyes, but her voice was firm. "I refuse to lead you on, Rooney, give you false hope."

"I know, and I respect that. But please just hold the thought; that's all I'm asking. I'm in no hurry."

Dana didn't say anything. Rooney had obviously made up his mind, and nothing she said at that point would have made any difference. Soon, though, she would have her say, and he *would* listen.

"May I get you more wine, ma'am? Sir?"

Neither one wanted more, but Dana was glad for the interruption, as it gave her a chance to change the subject.

Once they were alone, she forced a smile. "I'm sure your folks are enjoying having you so close to home."

"Especially Mother and Marian."

"Marian?"

Rooney chuckled. "She's our housekeeper, and does she ever love to cook." He patted his stomach. "If I don't watch it, I'll have a paunch."

"I doubt that."

"Just wait'll you taste her peach pie."

"I'll let you continue to have that privilege," Dana said in a light tone. She knew that he was hinting for her to visit his family home, and she refused to take the bait.

"I will, if I can put up with Daddy."

Dana was surprised. "I thought you two were close."

Rooney's face clouded. "I guess we are, only Daddy has a nose problem, and he's determined to keep it up my you-know-what."

Dana laughed at Rooney's choice of words. "Trust me, I'm familiar with the word *ass.*"

"I know. It's just that I hate being crude around you."

Her expression sobered. "Always the perfect gentleman."

"Do you find that offensive?"

"Of course not," Dana said, realizing they were again stepping into dangerous waters. She didn't want to hurt Rooney's feelings, yet it seemed that was destined to be the case no matter what she said or did.

"So what does he want you to do? Drop the Granger case?"

Rooney looked surprised. "How'd you know that?"

"I just guessed."

"You guessed right."

"Did he give you a reason?"

Rooney frowned bitterly. "Yeah. He doesn't want anything

to mess up my career. He wants me to go into politics. Imagine that."

"Are you kidding?"

"No, unfortunately, I'm not. He envisions me running for a seat in the U.S. Senate."

"Well, I think you'd make a great senator."

"Those are Shelby's exact words." Rooney's frown deepened. "But I don't want to be a senator. I want to do just what I'm doing—practice law."

"And defend people like Yancy Granger."

"That's right, only again Daddy doesn't think that's a good idea."

"He doesn't like your client." Dana said this as a flat statement of fact.

"That too, but it's the lawsuit that bothers him, especially as Granger's in line to be the head honcho at the new hospital."

"So he is going to sell them the land?"

"I hope so."

It wasn't so much what Rooney said that set off the alarm in her head again, but rather the way he said it. "What does that mean? You don't sound so sure." Dana held her breath.

Rooney swished what little wine was left in his glass. "I probably shouldn't tell you this, but I overheard Daddy talking on the phone to someone about the land."

Dana could barely contain her excitement. "You mean someone who isn't connected to the hospital?"

"Sounded like it."

"What did you hear, exactly?"

Again Rooney hesitated, as if he were at war with his conscience and his loyalty. "Daddy said something to the effect: 'So you're definitely interested in the property, then?' "

"Which implies there's another interested party."

Rooney didn't say anything, but he didn't have to. Dana felt like her mind might explode, like a stick of dynamite had been planted there. "If what you say is true, then things could get nasty."

"You're telling me," Rooney said, his expression bleak. "Come on, let's get out of here."

Dana didn't argue, as her mind was starting to explode for real. What did this latest turn of events mean?

Yancy was taking off his surgical scrubs and cap when Carl Parker strode into the OR. He didn't mince any words.

"Calhoun wants to see you."

"Hell, Parker, I guess I'm going to have to put you on my secretarial payroll. Seems like you spend all your time delivering me messages."

"Keep it up, Granger. One of these days, your mouth's going to overload your ass, and you'll be history."

"I wouldn't count on that." Yancy turned and walked out of the room.

He couldn't believe Brodie wanted to see him. Hell, he'd just seen him when he turned in his budget. Suddenly, Yancy remembered how much he'd asked for in equipment alone. But then, he'd been thinking about the new facility. What he'd ordered could be transferred.

Still, he knew how tight Calhoun was with money. Yancy smiled cynically. If he didn't know better, he'd swear the money was coming out of Brodie's own pocket.

A few minutes later, he walked into the chief's office and said, "Before you jump my ass about the budget, hear me out, okay?"

Brodie's face looked like it had been carved out of wood. "The budget has nothing to do with why I sent for you."

"Oh?"

"Sit down."

Yancy set his jaw. "I don't want to sit down."

"Sit down anyway."

"Dammit, Brodie, I have better things to do than scratch you every time you get an itch."

"That goes for me, too."

Yancy wrinkled his nose like there was a bad smell in the air. "What's happened this time?"

"As if you didn't know."

"I asked, didn't I?" Yancy was trying to hang on to his temper, but Brodie was making it damn hard.

"Dana Bivens came to see me."

"Ah, so that's who put that burr up your butt." He shouldn't have been surprised, but he was.

"Don't push it, Yancy."

"I can't believe she came to you; she has more guts than I gave her credit for. But more than that, I can't believe you let her put your nuts on a hotplate."

"That's not funny."

"Look, I just don't think the interview's a good idea. Anyway, it's my call."

"No, it isn't."

"Look, Brodie—"

"If you want the hospital, then get off your high horse or whatever the hell you're on concerning this woman and give her what she wants. I thought I made myself clear the first time I told you to cooperate with her."

"I don't want—"

"It's *not* negotiable," Brodie said in a testy tone.

Yancy shifted his gaze to the window, feeling his pulse jump in his throat. He tried to concentrate on how the sunlight bathed the trees in its warm glow. He couldn't. His mind was on what to do about Dana Bivens. The more he protested the article, the more attention he drew to himself. He was damned if he did and damned if he didn't. Either path he chose, he'd have to sidestep land mines all the way.

"What's in it for me?" he finally asked.

"What do you mean?" Brodie's face turned livid and tight. "Are you trying to get me to bribe you?"

"You're damn right."

"I ought to fire you, Granger."

"Yeah, you probably should, only you won't. So, do I get my budget?"

Brodie was trembling. "Get the hell out of here!"

"I knew you'd see it my way," Yancy said, grinning.

Once he was out in the hall, Yancy's smile disappeared. What the hell had he done? He'd just stepped on that first mine, he told himself, walking to his office.

Yet he knew Brodie was right in calling his hand. If he didn't cooperate, Dana would make it her business to find out why. If she ever got a sniff of his fear, she'd be like a shark that smelled blood. She would remain for the duration and the kill.

He sank onto the couch. He'd just have to bullshit his way through this nightmare and hope to hell he didn't say anything incriminating.

Most of all, he had to think of Dana Bivens as an ambitious reporter who could ruin him rather than as a desirable woman who could jumpstart his sexual battery.

He blew out a slow breath, then picked up the phone.

Twenty-three

Dana stood at the window of her room and watched the rain pelt against it. In the distance, lightning ripped across the sky with a vengeance. Shivering, she turned away. The storm wasn't supposed to last more than a few hours.

She hoped the forecast was right. She was depressed enough as it was. If she'd stared at the telephone once, she'd stared at it a hundred times. Why hadn't Brodie Calhoun called? Better, why hadn't *Yancy* called?

Had she put too much faith in Dr. Calhoun? Pinching the bridge of her nose, she paced the floor. He'd sounded so confident that he would get Yancy's full cooperation. Now she was beginning to think that Brodie was all bark and no bite. Damn!

No one controlled Yancy Granger. It was wishful thinking on her part to believe otherwise. He was a loose cannon who could explode at any moment, and probably would when he found out that the land sale might be in jeopardy. Dana's heart thumped against her chest. She still hadn't fully comprehended the fact that Shelby Tremaine might consider selling the property to anyone else.

From what she'd ascertained, he'd been a big backer of the university and everything connected with it. So why the change of heart now, if indeed there was one?

Money? Power? Control? These possibilities swirled

around in Dana's mind, yet none of them made any sense. Shelby had more money than he could ever spend. Or did he? Maybe he was living behind a facade as so many others did nowadays. Maybe he had the name but no longer the wealth that went with it.

No. She scrapped that thought, only to go back to it, as Shelby's love of politics jumped to mind. It seemed that anyone who entered the political arena never had enough money. Was that what Shelby was about? Did he need bigger bucks than he had to launch his son into politics?

Dana groaned aloud. Rooney. She couldn't bear to think about him, esepcially after he'd asked her to marry him. Besides, she was consumed with thoughts of Yancy Granger.

The phone rang, startling her out of her reverie. She answered it after the second ring, her heart beating hard in anticipation.

"Hello."

"Dana."

She frowned. "Hubert, is that you?"

"Of course, it's me. It hasn't been that long since you heard my voice."

It wasn't irritation Dana heard in his voice, but rather cold, hard anger. She pressed her lips together. Great, More trouble. She sat down on the bed. "What's wrong?"

"I thought you were on vacation."

A chill ran through her. "I am."

"Does Congressman Clayton Crawford ring any bells? Like ding-a-ling?"

Her stomach hollowed. "Yes, as a matter of fact."

"Well, he damn well shouldn't. You're *supposed* to be on vacation."

"But—"

"What the hell are you doing sticking your journalistic nose in the congressman's business? Who gave you that authority?"

Somehow, Dana remained unrattled. She didn't know how she pulled it off; inside she was trembling.

"You know Albert Ramsey, don't you?" she asked.

"What's that bastard got to do with this?" Hubert's tone was heavy with impatience.

Dana explained about having read the society page headlines concerning the congressman and his wife.

"So what?"

"The 'so what' is that it was the same day I ran into Albert. I figured he was here to get the story, which was like waving a red flag in front of my face. I—"

"Rip that goddamn flag up and forget you ever heard of Clayton Crawford."

"Hubert!"

"I mean it, Dana."

"What's going on? It's just another story about a politician."

"He's not just another politician. He wields a fucking lot of power on the Hill."

"Since when is any politician on sacred ground?"

"Since *I* said he was, that's when!"

Let it go, Dana, she warned herself. Let it go while you're ahead. As it was, she was treading on dangerous ground, balancing her present job at *Old Dominion* against a possible one at *Issues*. If she wasn't careful, she'd end up without either.

"Did the congressman call you?"

"It doesn't matter. Just do as you're told."

Dana's right temple began to pound. Hubert had never spoken to her like this, nor had she ever heard him pitch such a temper tantrum, which meant that the congressman or someone else had played hardball with Hubert's head.

"I didn't mean to get you into trouble."

"I'm sure you didn't. Just back off. Now. I don't want to have a pissing contest with you, Dana. I know how tenacious you are—that's what makes you good at your job. But this is not open for negotiation. Forget the job and just have a good time. Okay?"

"Okay, Hubert."

"Good. I'll see you soon." With that, he hung up.

Dana's trembling was visible now, and she clutched at her stomach. However, her stomach's upheaval wasn't from fear but from excitement. When she got that kind of reaction, she knew she was on to something big.

Apparently the congressman had more to protect than his personal privacy. Suddenly she was rabid to know. The story about this man had the potential to erupt like an angry volcano, turn into everything *Issues* wanted and more. Since she wasn't able to ask Crawford, she would go to the next best source. Yancy.

Somehow, she would worm it out of him.

"No, I can't come by tonight."

"Why not?"

Yancy fought the urge to lean over and bang his head against the desk. Yet when he spoke, his voice was low and calm. "If you could see my desk, Vida Lou, you wouldn't have to ask."

"Then let me come over and help you clear it."

Yancy forced a chuckle. "Even I don't know where to start."

"When *am* I going to see you?"

He heard the hard note in her tone, though she'd done a damn good job of masking it. "Well, we have another committee meeting next week, then the dance."

"That's not what I mean and you know it."

He changed the subject. "By the way, did you get your money out of the till?"

"No, I didn't." Her tone brooked no argument.

He ignored it. "Then get it. ASAP."

"Oh, for heaven's sake, it's no big deal. But if it'll make you feel better, you can give it back to me at the unveiling."

"Unveiling?"

"Surely you haven't forgotten we're having a private VIP party in the boardroom to show off a scale model of the hospital?"

"Yep, as a matter of fact I had."

"See you do need me," Vida Lou said, adding an intimate warmth to her voice.

"We *all* need you. You're the brains behind the project."

A long silence followed. Then: "You're seeing someone else, aren't you, Yancy?"

He felt a sudden surge of arousal thinking about his fixation with Dana Bivens. "No, Vida Lou," he lied, "I'm not."

"That's good to know."

"We'll talk later, okay?"

She chuckled. "We'll do more than talk."

The gloves had come off. Careful, Granger, he told himself, recalling Brodie's warning. Don't say something you'll regret. You'll get your day in court, only not now.

He heard the dial tone then and slammed the receiver back in its cradle. That crazy broad just wouldn't take no for an answer. The thought of touching her again made him sick.

Yancy walked outside to his car. A short time later he pulled into the small parking area of the B&B where Dana was staying. Twilight was fast approaching, and he took a moment to look at the trees surrounding the old colonial home. It reminded him of the one he'd grown up in.

He got out of his car. Maybe when he saw her again, he'd be immune to her, wouldn't give a damn. Either way, he had to give this interview so that she would go away.

Each day she remained in Charlottesville, the more dangerous she became. Two women, and both were driving him crazy! Right now, he preferred Vida Lou's grief. She was only a possessive irritant, while Dana was a smoldering bomb.

He knew she was there because he'd parked beside her car. Inside, Mrs. Balch directed him to Dana's room. He knocked on her door.

"Coming," she called out in her husky voice.

By the time she opened the door, his jaws were so rigid he expected to hear his teeth snap in two.

"You!"

He didn't know if she actually spoke the word aloud or if she mouthed it. It didn't matter; he still couldn't have responded. He was too caught up in the picture she presented standing there with her untamed hair, wild eyes, and pouty lips. But it was the way she was dressed, in shorts and a tank top, that made his blood pound.

"What—"

"What am I doing here? Is that what you were about to ask?"

She licked that bottom lip, leaving it moist. "Yes."

"I thought you wanted to interview me," he said, inwardly crumbling like an idiot.

"I do," she said, then gave a shaky laugh.

"Well?"

"Well what?"

"Let's go to it."

"Where are we going?"

"To talk."

She didn't move.

"You'd best get the lead out. This is your last chance."

"But . . . I don't understand."

He buried his hands in his hair. "Neither do I, but let's get the hell out of here anyway."

Twenty-four

Damn! Her hands were shaking so hard that she had trouble buttoning her slacks. She glanced one last time in the mirror. Her hair—well, there was no hope for it. It was as frenzied as she was.

Excitement and surprise—that's what had her in such a tizzy. The fact that he'd looked so good leaning against the doorjamb didn't figure into it, Dana told herself. Yet she couldn't have helped seeing the way his shirt clung to his lean, sculpted torso and the way his legs seemed to go on forever under his jeans.

For a second, she had wondered what it would be like to touch those hard thighs, to . . .

Dana rushed out of the bathroom. She couldn't blow this chance; she had to get as much information out of him as possible. She didn't intend to waste a second by giving in to the unwanted and foreign emotions this man stirred in her.

"You didn't have to change," he said as she came back into the room, his eyes moving over her.

There was something in that look that brought an uneasy tingling to Dana's skin. She knew what it was: He was thinking about that fiery kiss. Though they hadn't spoken of it again, it hovered between them, teasing, tantalizing, mocking.

But that had been just a fluke, something that wouldn't be repeated, she reminded herself, feeling her confidence return.

Besides, kiss or no kiss, he didn't like her any more than she liked him. Under these circumstances, dislike was a healthy emotion, as long as it didn't interfere with her getting the information she wanted from him.

"I feel better in slacks," she finally said in what she hoped was a matter-of-fact tone.

He shrugged. "Let's go."

Once they were in the car, she glanced at him sideways and realized her heart was still beating faster than it should be. "Do you have a specific place in mind?"

"Yeah, but if you—"

"No," she said, cutting him off. "Wherever you take me is fine."

He threw her a quick look, his lips curved in amusement. "Are you sure about that?"

She knew he was toying with her, so she forced a dazzling smile. "Maybe I should've said 'within reason.' "

"You ought to smile more often, you know."

Dana grappled to come to grips with that unexpected statement. "So should you." She ignored the slight tremor in her voice and hoped he would, too.

"I guess maybe you could chalk that up to our incompatible personalities." He paused. "Or maybe the problem is we're *too* compatible."

He deliberately soaked those words in intimacy, which made her blush. Was he flirting with her? If so, what was the point? Did he hope to throw her off balance, to disconcert her? It probably amused him to undermine her with his charm.

"You're imagining things, Doctor." Her voice was like silk.

Ha gave her another disturbing glance. "Am I?"

A frown marred her forehead. Damn him and his innuendos. She was beginning to feel the pressure; the force of his nearness was grating on her nerves. Yancy Granger had more sides to him than a chameleon.

"I hope you like Mexican food," he said into the silence.

"It's one of my favorites."

"Good. A buddy of mine owns this place. Now mind you, it's not fancy, and it's off the beaten track. Not too many college kids know about it."

"Which means it'll be quiet and we shouldn't have any problem conducting our interview."

Yancy suddenly pulled into a parking lot where a gaudy red sign was blinking. He shut off the engine, then turned to her and said with a mocking smile, "Give it a rest, okay? I want you to enjoy the meal."

"Only after the interview is over." She knew she sounded as uptight as she felt, but she couldn't help it.

"Right," he said flatly.

Once they were inside, Dana paused and looked around. It was more a café than a restaurant, and not a fancy one at that. The table and chairs appeared rickety and the floor was uneven.

It was clean, though, and the food smelled delicious. What it wasn't was quiet. The jukebox in the corner was going full blast, and a large party took up several tables nearby. They were having a whooping good time.

She felt Yancy's eyes on her as he placed his hand lightly in the middle of her back. The heat from his body, so close to hers, was achingly real. She wished he would move that hand.

"Looks like I screwed up," he said, peering down at her.

She stepped away. "It is rather noisy."

"You want to go somewhere else?"

"The food smells awfully good."

He chuckled. "I was thinking the same thing. Let's eat, then take it from there."

They found a booth as far from the noisy party as possible and sat across from each other. She made no attempt to pull out her notebook, knowing it would be impossible to carry on a serious conversation. Having decided that, some of the pressure seemed to ease. She planned to enjoy dinner.

Yancy introduced her to his friend, the owner, an overweight, jovial man who took their orders. Moments later, a young waitress with a mouthful of braces brought their drinks.

"Mmm, this is good," Dana said, taking a sip of her red wine.

"Enjoy."

"I hate to drink alone, though," she said, fishing.

He didn't bite. "Sorry. I don't drink."

"Not at all?"

"Nope. Iced tea's my drink of choice."

She raised her eyebrows. "I guess that's a good thing, since you're a doctor." She should have let that statement slide until later, but the words just slipped out.

He gave her a piercing look but didn't say anything. Nevertheless she felt a sudden undercurrent that remained with them through their Mexican dinners and coffee afterward.

"Doctor?"

Dana and Yancy both swung around and stared at a woman who, in spite of a scar down her right cheek, was lovely. But it was the smile on her face, and the way she was looking at Yancy, that highlighted that loveliness. Dana found herself holding her breath.

Yancy stood and held out his hand. "Hello, Sara."

"I hope you don't mind my interrupting." Her tone was apologetic as her eyes darted to Dana, then back to Yancy.

"Of course not. I'm glad to see you, especially since you're looking so well."

"Only because of you," Sara said, her voice filled with adoration.

Obviously embarrassed, Yancy glanced at Dana and said, "This is Sara Mullins, a patient of mine. Sara, Dana Bivens."

"Hi, Sara," Dana said with a sincere smile, though curiosity gnawed at her.

Sara smiled, then returned her gaze to Yancy. "I want to thank you again for what you did."

"Please, Sara, you don't have to keep thanking me."

"Yes, I do, Doctor." Her voice broke. "I wouldn't be alive today if it weren't for your generosity and skill."

Dana could see Yancy growing more uncomfortable by the second. Still, he handled himself well, she thought. In fact, she was seeing yet another side of this multifaceted man—a tender and compassionate one.

"So how are Howard and the kids?" he asked.

Sara nodded to her left, then beamed. "They're just fine. We're celebrating the youngest's birthday."

"That's great." Yancy squeezed her hand again. "You tell 'em all I said hello, and I'll see you in my office soon."

"Thanks," she said, then hurried off.

The moment Yancy was seated, Dana asked, "What was that all about?"

"Nothing."

An incredulous expression crossed her face. "You expect me to believe that? She looked as though she could've eaten you with a spoon."

He shot her an irritated look.

"So did you save her life?" Dana pressed.

"I guess so."

"What did she mean about you being generous?"

"God, you don't miss a thing, do you?"

"I'm a reporter, remember?"

"I remember."

"So?"

"A prowler broke into their house one night and beat the living shit out of her. Her insides were badly mangled. At the time, her husband was out of work."

"You didn't charge her?"

"No, goddammit, I didn't charge her. Okay?"

"Ah, so the doctor does have a heart after all."

"How the hell would you know what I have?"

"I don't," she said, not changing her tone, "only I'm about to find out, aren't I?"

"Let's get the hell out of here."

Dana didn't budge. "Where to?"

"Your place or mine?"

"Uh, the parlor at the inn probably won't be occupied."

* * *

Silence surrounded them as they sat on opposite ends of the couch, each holding a cup of hazelnut-flavored coffee. As she had guessed, they'd found the parlor empty. In fact, the entire house seemed vacant, although Dana knew that Mrs. Balch was in her room off the kitchen.

She put down her cup and reached for her notebook.

"I guess you've got your guns loaded and ready to fire," he said.

"Excuse me?" She had heard what he said, but she'd been paying more attention to watching him sip his coffee than to what he was saying. She'd been thinking that he did indeed have perfect surgeon's hands—slender, steady, and strong. She wondered if the rest of his body had those qualities.

"You don't need excusing. You heard me, so take your best shot."

He was back to his superior, hard self, she thought. She should have known that his civility of a while ago was too good to last. Yet in a way she was relieved; she could deal with his anger. What she couldn't deal with were his sexual innuendos and the way they affected her.

"I plan to," she said. Then she softened her tone. "Look, this isn't going to be as bad as going to the dentist."

His lips curled into a half-smile. "Is that a promise?"

God, she wished he wouldn't smile. It was nearly lethal. "Sorry, no promises."

"I didn't think so."

"So, let's start at the beginning."

"Let's not."

Dana's impatience flared anew, but she curbed it. "Suppose you just start talking, then."

"Okay. Why did you make such a big deal out of the fact that I don't drink? I'm sure you were trying to make a point."

His question blindsided her. "Maybe I was at that." She paused. "I know about the malpractice lawsuit."

The words hovered in the air between them.

"What else do you know?"

"I know about the missing money debacle."

His face turned the color of concrete as he gave her a long look, blatantly staring at her breasts, as if determined to make her sorry she'd broached that subject.

"Ah, so you *have* been snooping, as in listening outside closed doors."

She let the sarcasm slide. "What I want to know is, are you guilty of the first and involved in the second?"

"I don't figure either is any of your business."

"Why aren't I surprised you'd say that?"

Though he rose to his feet in a relaxed fashion, Dana knew he was wired to the max.

"What the hell else do you know?" he demanded, towering over her.

She stood, but kept her distance. "What else do you have to tell me?"

He laughed bitterly. "What you really want to talk about is that elephant in the living room."

"If you have nothing to hide, then you won't mind talking about it."

"You're a real piece of work, lady."

"Thank you. Now, I also know you're somehow involved with Congressman Crawford."

A deadly hush fell over the room as anger spasmed his jaw. "I don't know where the hell you got your information, but you'd best forget it."

"You can't have it all your way." Her eyes blazed. "You've got to give me something."

"I don't have to give you shit, if it means compromising my job."

"Why are you giving me such a hard time? If there isn't an elephant in your living room, then why don't you just answer my questions?"

"I've got a better suggestion," he said, slowly closing the distance between them. "Why don't you stop while you're ahead. Take your pad and your pen and your prissy butt back where you came from."

"Why you bastard!" Dana raised her hand, intending to slap his face, but he was too quick.

He caught her wrist in midair, pulled her roughly against him, and held her prisoner under his hot, hungry mouth.

Blood pounded through her body and she clung to him as his lips devoured hers, his tongue thrusting deep into her mouth. She felt a shudder run through him, followed by a deep groan and the softening of his lips. That was when she pulled back and stared at him, stunned.

"Next time I won't stop with just a kiss."

With that he turned and walked out. Dana stood motionless, her heart in her throat and heat between her thighs.

Twenty-five

Time was wasting. That clock in the back of Dana's mind was beginning to tick louder. She needed to gather her thoughts, assemble the information on the controversial Dr. Granger, and get it on paper. Yet she continued to indulge herself, as if she had all the time in the world.

Perhaps spring fever had struck. The sweet smell of honeysuckle drifted through the open French doors. She had rarely taken a moment to appreciate her private porch, which gave her access to a tiny courtyard.

Dana leaned against one side of the door and watched as a robin redbreast flapped his wings, then fluttered in and out of the water in the birdbath. He appeared to be having such innocent fun. With a melancholy smile, she walked back to the antique secretary that served as her desk.

She sat down and peered at her watch. Ten o'clock. Her fingers should have been clicking across the keyboard of her laptop computer, but her mind was in too much of a turmoil to concentrate. However, she had placed a call to Wade Langely at *Issues* and left word for him to call her back.

Dana stared outside again, thinking how gorgeous the day was, how it was made for a picnic in the woods, followed by long hours of making love. . . .

Sour juices rose up her throat. Dana coughed to keep from choking, then took several deep breaths. Her mind continued to betray her. She had never had thoughts like that before, had never had any desire for a man to touch her in an intimate way, though she'd managed to cover that aversion over the years so as not to offend anyone. Still, Rooney had seen through that facade.

Yancy hadn't.

She knew why. Regardless of the consequences, Yancy took what he wanted. And as he'd said, he wanted more. Was that the reason she was dragging her feet? Or was it because of her own passionate attraction to him?

No. Absolutely not. Even as she denied the charge, the memory of his hot mouth pressed against hers made her body weak. She sank onto the side of the bed, facing the brutal truth. She ached to feel Yancy's hands on her flesh, ached to know what it would be like to have him inside her, to be on fire with desire, to *climax*. . . .

Dana jumped up and ran outside onto the porch, furious and shocked at her thoughts. She folded her arms across her chest and squeezed. The last thing she needed was to get involved with that egotistical, philandering man.

She and Yancy had nothing personal in common, nothing that counted. His unrefined and unrepentant nature, coupled with his blue blood insolence, was a turn-off. Too, he was an accomplished womanizer with a reputation, which made him seem dangerous.

Ambition was their only similarity. She was determined to rise to the top of her profession, while he was determined to remain at the top of his.

The ringing phone sounded far away, only it wasn't. She darted back inside and snatched up the receiver. "Hello."

"Ms. Bivens."

At first she didn't recognize the male voice. She had expected the caller to be Wade Langely, only it wasn't. Still, she'd heard this voice before, only she couldn't pinpoint it.

"Yes," she said, a question in her tone.

"Brodie Calhoun."

"Oh, Doctor, how nice to hear from you." She would bet

anything he was checking to see if Yancy had cooperated with her. Just wait until she filled his ear.

He chuckled. "You sound surprised."

"Actually, I am."

"First off, I'd like to know if—"

"No, he didn't."

A short silence ensued, during which Dana could almost see the wheels turning in Calhoun's mind.

"Look, Ms. Bivens—"

"It's all right, really, I can handle Dr. Granger. I intend to finish this story, with or without his cooperation."

Brodie gave a loud sigh. "Sometimes I could choke him. I swear I could."

Dana had to smile. "He seems to have that effect on most people."

"Maybe you'll get another chance sooner than you thought," he continued, his voice having brightened. "We're having a private unveiling of the proposed hospital site in the boardroom this evening. I thought you might like to see it. The committee members will be there, along with others who've helped our cause."

"Thank you, Doctor. I'd love to come."

"See you then."

While she dreaded the thought of being in the same room with Vida Lou and Yancy, she couldn't pass up another chance to visit with the committee members.

She wondered if any of them was aware that Shelby Tremaine might have had a change of heart about the land. She had almost mentioned it to Yancy, but something had kept her mum. She smiled. If nothing else, this get-together would be interesting.

The phone rang again, startling her.

"Hello."

"Dana, is that you?"

Wade Langely. "Yes, sir."

"I'm glad you called. I was about to call you for a progress report. How's it going?"

"I'm making headway," Dana hedged.

"That sounds rather generic."

She laughed. "I'm working a lot of angles, though none have come together."

"You still think there's the potential for an explosive story there?"

"Without a doubt."

Dana then explained that someone else might be interested in acquiring the land in question, which would be equivalent to setting off a bomb. "I'd check on it myself, but I don't have the contacts—"

"Don't worry about that. I'll get Tim Garrison right on it. He'll get back to you."

"Thanks," Dana said, "And thanks for calling."

The room was abuzz. Dana paused just inside the large doors and looked around at the plush surroundings: long mahogany table, high-backed chairs, expensive paintings, to mention a few.

It was when her eyes found her mother that she froze. Vida Lou was talking to one of the committee members, Lester Mayfield, as if holding court.

Despite the savage emotions her mother evoked in her, Dana refused to budge. Vida Lou was dressed in a lavender linen suit that Dana figured cost a bundle. But it was more than the expensive clothes that held her attention. From where she stood, Dana couldn't see so much as one wrinkle in her mother's face or in her hair.

She'd never before seen anyone whose face and hair appeared as if they'd been starched, then ironed into place. Hysterical laughter bubbled inside her just as her eyes met Vida Lou's.

Moments later, Vida Lou stood in front of her. "What the hell are you doing here?" she hissed through her fake smile.

"I was invited." Dana's voice remained calm and controlled.

Vida Lou's expression turned to ice. "Well, you're not welcome."

"Don't start something you can't finish, Vida Lou."

Her features took on a pinched look, as if she were in pain. "You're no match for me, you little bitch. And don't say I didn't warn you."

Vida Lou walked off then, and Dana felt herself collapse inside.

"I'm glad to see you made it."

Dana almost jumped at the unexpected voice. She smiled into Brodie Calhoun's dark eyes. "I'm glad to be here."

"Come on, let's get you something to drink, then I'll show you the exhibit." He paused. "Afterward, I promise not to monopolize you. I know you want to mingle."

"Mind if I take a picture?"

"I'd be disppointed if you didn't."

A minute later, the committee members stood in front of the display. Others were gathered around as well. Dr. Calhoun introduced her to the ones she didn't know. She spoke a cordial word to each, then focused her attention on the model.

"Well?"

"It's . . . it's—" She broke off.

Brodie's laugh seemed to come from the bottom of his belly. "That's the reaction I love—speechless."

Dana had to admit that she was more than impressed with the miniature layout of the proposed hospital. If it became a reality, it would indeed put Charlottesville *and* Yancy Granger on the map. Not necessarily in that order, either.

"You're like a kid with a new toy, aren't you?" she asked.

"Worse," Brodie admitted with another chuckle.

Yancy chose that moment to make his entrance. Ah, she thought, so the doctor has arrived, expecting to receive his homage.

That catty thought brought an immediate flush to Dana's face. She looked down at her glass of wine so that the chief of staff wouldn't notice her discomfort.

Don't let him rattle you, she told herself. He's just a man

who puts his pants on one leg at a time. Just keep telling yourself that you're immune to him.

"So is the land ready for construction?" she asked, plastering a smile on her face.

She knew the answer, but she was curious to see if anyone else had an inkling that Shelby Tremaine might sell to another buyer.

"Not yet, but it soon will be," Brodie said. "It's just a matter of raising a little more money. It'll happen. The Tremaines are with us one hundred percent.

Then why doesn't he just give you the land? Dana wanted to ask.

"Feel free to do whatever." Brodie squeezed her elbow. "I'll see you later."

Left alone, Dana snapped several pictures, then leaned closer to the lifelike replica. She didn't have to turn around to know that he was behind her, nor did he have to say anything. She smelled his cologne and felt the heat of his body—a potent combination.

"You're still pissed, aren't you?"

She swung around. "What do you think?"

"Well," he said in a husky drawl, "I think you're lovelier than any woman has a right to be."

The silence that followed seemed as physical as if he'd touched her. Another flush stained her face, only this one was scalding in its intensity. He was too close, and his bold stare was turning her inside out.

"You've got your nerve." She thought her lips might crack, she held them so rigid.

"I know. But you still want that interview—"

"Dr. Granger!"

The loud voice stopped his words. Yancy spun around, but not before Dana had peered beyond his shoulder.

Albert Ramsey stood inside the room, his grin as wide as the acne pits on his cheeks. "What can you tell me about Congressman Crawford, Doctor?"

The room suddenly turned into a funeral parlor.

"Who the hell are you?" Yancy demanded, striding up to Ramsey.

"I'm a reporter, that's who. And I know about you and the congressman." Ramsey's eyes swept the room, and he preened as if he loved being center stage. "So why don't you be a good boy and fess up."

Yancy turned back to Dana and said in a tone that sounded lethal. "Is this your way of paying me back, talking to that sonofabitch?"

"Are you crazy?" Dana cried. "I—"

He looked her up and down, his eyes like ice. "Save it!"

"Come on, Doctor, isn't it true that Crawford promised to scratch your back if you—"

Yancy slammed his fist into Ramsey's nose. The sound of crushing bone could be heard all over the room.

Dana winced, and shocked gasps rippled throughout the room.

"You'll be sorry for this, you bastard!" Ramsey whimpered, struggling to his feet.

"Not as sorry as you're going to be if you don't take that camera and get the hell out of my face!"

Twenty-six

Newton Anderson belched.

He looked around to see if anyone had heard him, which made him feel like a fool because he was the only one in his office. He belched again, then grimaced. His dietary sins had caught up with him.

"Damn!" he muttered, then opened the drawer in front of him and scrambled for his bottle of Tums. He popped two in his mouth and crunched down on them. He needed immediate relief. His entire belly, from his breast to his groin, was on fire, thanks to the jalapeno peppers he'd eaten last night.

He couldn't believe he'd let that bimbette hand-feed him those nachos along with countless bottles of beer. Afterward, he'd been so drunk and sick that he'd been tempted to tell her to get the hell away and leave him alone. But he hadn't. Like an idiot, he'd let her climb on top of him and ride till they both were drained.

The instant she'd shut the door behind her, he'd raced into the bathroom and lost everything inside him. He'd had to look down to make sure he still had his toenails.

Now Newt counted the minutes until the Tums worked. He had three important meetings scheduled today, two pertaining to his work and the other pertaining to his pet project. He glanced at his watch, noting that his "hand-picked" partners were due any minute. Each had pledged to commit a certain amount of money; he couldn't help but worry about that. What if they had changed their minds? What if they didn't put their money where their mouths were?

His stomach rebelled again. He hated that he always looked on the dark side of things, but he had to be prepared if his plans took an unexpected twist today. Those nachos weren't the only reason for his aggravated gut. Fear that something would go wrong was the main contributor.

Dammit, he wouldn't let this venture fail.

The phone rang. It was too early for his secretary to have arrived, so he answered it himself.

"Anderson here," he snapped.

Only after he'd listened for a few seconds did his demeanor change. He smiled, and his gut unclenched.

"Why, we couldn't have asked for anything better, not even if we'd planned it."

The man on the other end chuckled. "I thought you'd get a kick out of this latest development."

"Well, you just keep me posted, you hear? Even though this was none of our doing, we're the clear winners. Hell, I feel better than an old maid's dream."

"I thought you'd feel that way." The caller paused. "Oh, speaking of money, a portion of mine is due. You haven't forgotten that, have you?"

Anderson frowned. "I don't go back on my word. You'll get your money."

He had just slammed the phone down when the door opened and the other men walked in. Anderson leaned back in his chair and grinned. "Have a seat, gentlemen."

Edwin Minshew, the banker, gave Anderson a strange look. "My, but aren't we in a good mood. Someone ring your bell last night?"

"Last night and this morning, my friend. Only there were two different ringers."

Barton Engles slapped the air with his hand. "Cut the double-talk and get to the point."

Newton waited until the third man, Winston Taylor, was seated. "I'm talking about a call I just got from our man."

"So don't keep us in suspense," Minshew urged.

"Well, it seems that the good doctor just strengthened our case twofold." Newt grinned. "He belted a reporter in the chops in front of some VIPs. Just imagine how the city fathers, especially Shelby Tremaine, are going to view that."

They all laughed.

"With our good fortune in mind," Newt continued, "I'd like to know that each of you is ready with the money you committed to. We have to make our move soon."

"Especially now that Dr. Granger's stepped in another pile of crap." Engles gave the thumbs-up sign.

Newt laughed. "I couldn't have said it better myself."

Dana hadn't been able to stand her own company a moment longer. She had replayed that incident in the boardroom until she was mentally exhausted. One minute she wanted to lash out at Yancy for thinking she'd have anything to do with the likes of Albert Ramsey. The next minute she wanted to shake his hand, congratulate him for putting his fist in Ramsey's obnoxious mouth.

The latter hadn't lasted long. When she recalled the contempt she'd seen in his eyes and the accusation he'd flung at her, she wanted to claw his eyes out.

Who did he think he was? She took as much professional pride in her work as he did in his. Just because she had mentioned the congressman to him didn't mean that she'd blabbed it to anyone else. He hadn't even given her the benefit of the doubt.

It was thoughts like these that had driven her to seek April's company. She found her friend at home alone, baking cookies for a school function.

April was delighted to see her, despite Dana's sour mood. She poured two glasses of mint iced tea and hustled her friend to the table in the breakfast room.

Then, with an eyebrow cocked, April asked, "So what's he done now?"

"How'd you know?"

"I have great hunches."

"He has all the characteristics I loathe in a man." Dana's eyes sparked. "He's opinionated, conceited—"

"Whoa! What on earth happened?"

Dana told her.

"I wish I'd been there."

"No, you don't."

"So are you guilty as charged?"

Dana gave her an incredulous look. "April! Surely you don't think I'd do such a thing."

"Oh, for Pete's sake, can't you take a joke?"

Dana didn't say anything, just sipped the cool drink, finding that it helped calm her nerves. She hated to dump all this on her friend, but she hadn't known what else to do. She felt as if everything was tumbling down on her and she couldn't stop the avalanche.

"You know what I think?" April asked.

Dana was still somewhat miffed. "What if I say it doesn't matter?"

"I'll tell you anyway."

She laughed. "I figured as much. So, tell me."

"I think you owe him an explanation." April held up her hands. "Before you go berserk, hear me out. I didn't say an apology, but an explanation. They're two different things, you know."

Dana was silent.

"Look, just think about it for a minute."

"That's all I've done since yesterday."

"I didn't mean that. What I'm trying to say is that in his place, wouldn't you have thought the same thing?"

"No."

April made an unladylike noise. "Oh, come on. You had just thrown the congressman in his face, which already had him ticked off, right?"

"Right," Dana answered reluctantly.

"Well, then here comes this little turd who gets in his face with a camera and a notebook and demands to know virtually the same thing you hit him with."

"So?"

April looked exasperated. "So, it's only logical that Yancy Granger would make the assumption that you and Ramsey were in bed together on this one."

"I'm going to let that 'bed' business pass but only because you're my friend."

April giggled. "You know what I mean."

"I know, but I didn't say one word to that creep Ramsey, and for Yancy to think I did, makes me see red."

"Then tell him. Have it out with him. Get it off your chest."

"He won't see me."

"You're joking?"

"Nope. He's been jerking my string about an interview ever since I first approached him, and I haven't gotten one yet."

"I guess he doesn't want to talk to you."

"So maybe *you* ought to talk to him." There was a hint of a smile on Dana's lips.

"Hell, I'd like to do more than talk." April giggled. "Seriously, though, you can't dodge this bullet forever. Besides, I've never known you to back down from a challenge." She leaned forward. "Don't let him get by with it. Do whatever it takes to get that story."

Dana thought for a moment, then jumped up and gave her friend a hug. "Thanks!"

"What—where are you going?" April spluttered.

Yancy stared at his skinned knuckles and knew that he should feel remorse. He didn't. If he had it to do all over again, he'd hit the slimy bastard even harder.

Immediately after the reporter had slunk out the door, still sniveling, still threatening, no one had said a word, not even Brodie. But then, Yancy hadn't given them much of a chance. He'd gone straight to his office and put through a call to Congressman Crawford, hoping it wasn't too late for damage control. After he'd explained what had happened, the congressman had told him about Dana's call.

"I don't know how she found out," Yancy said, feeling sick, "or that idiot Ramsey."

"I'm not blaming you. In my business this shit happens. Still, I'm going to do everything in my power to protect my privacy."

"So will I, Congressman, so will I."

He had just gotten off the phone with Crawford when Brodie Calhoun stormed in, his face twisted in a scowl.

"What you did in there wasn't smart."

"Don't start." Yancy's tone was weary. "I'm not in the mood."

" 'Not in the mood.' " Brodie gave a sardonic laugh. "No, but you were apparently in a mood to screw up this project."

"What the hell was I supposed to do?"

"Not resort to violence, that's for sure," Brodie hammered on, his breathing labored and his face red.

"You'd better calm down before you have a heart attack."

Brodie slammed his fist down on Yancy's desk. "You owe every member of that committee an apology and you'd damn well better give them one."

Yancy didn't so much as flinch. "That's not going to happen."

"I wouldn't bet on that. Your attitude and your conduct have always stunk, but lately the smell is even too ripe for me. Get it together, Granger; I'm warning you. No one wants a loaded cannon running the show."

That conversation had taken place yesterday. Today, Yancy's mood was even darker. He closed his eyes, but he continued to see only Dana's face.

She was driving him mad, from both desire and fear. He didn't know which was stronger. At the moment, he suspected his desire for her would win hands down. Therein lay the danger.

He had to stay away from her, only he couldn't. Until he

gave her what she wanted, she would not go away. Yet to go anywhere near her was suicidal.

He couldn't get past the shock on her face after he'd flung his accusation at her. Was she innocent? Had he misjudged her? It didn't matter. He still had to deal with her.

Fed up with his thoughts, Yancy opened his eyes. That was when he felt arms circle his upper body from behind. He stiffened, not having realized he wasn't alone.

"I thought you might need some consoling," Vida Lou cooed, her lips grazing his neck.

Repulsed, he fought to control the urge to lash out at her. At all costs, he had to maintain his cool. "It's been a long two days."

She softened her voice, then her eyes. "What if I'm here to make you feel better?"

"I'd say that's not likely. I've never known you and Brodie not to think alike, especially where this project's concerned."

"Well, you're right about that. And you were rather naughty yesterday."

"I'm not a child, Vida Lou."

"Then stop acting like one. I'm trying to treat you like the man who gave me the best fuck I've ever had."

Yancy shuddered inwardly. "This is not a good time," he said, blowing out a breath. "I'm really beat."

"How much longer are you going to play this silly little game?"

The venom was back in her voice, but he pretended not to hear it. He still had to play Brodie's game. "I told you, I'm no good to anyone."

"That's unacceptable." She walked up and ran a long fingernail down his cheek.

Yancy forced himself to stand still. It was all he could do not to slap her hand away.

"Now's not the time to cross me or get too big for your britches."

Before he realized her intention, she reached up, pinched

his jaw between the fingers of one hand, pulled his head down, and kissed him hard on the lips.

Then she pulled back and with a Cheshire cat smile on her face said, "I'll be in touch."

The instant the door closed behind her, Yancy wiped the back of his hand across his mouth. Jesus! He couldn't bear the thought that Vida Lou had kissed him, especially after he'd tasted the sweetness of Dana's lips.

He groaned; the tension was taking its toll on him. Dana had changed him. He'd become a wreck emotionally, physically, and sexually. He couldn't let her go on doing this to him.

Brodie was right; he had to get his head back on straight before it was too late. He wanted her, but she was forbidden fruit. End of story.

Only when she left town would he again find peace. Though he loathed what he was about to do, he knew he had no choice.

Twenty-seven

The setting was perfect. The steaks were on the top rack of the grill, slow cooking; the salad was in the fridge, chilling; dessert was on the cabinet, waiting. The only thing Yancy hadn't done was set the table. Hell, they could eat on the deck, on the picnic table—*if she came.*

Of course she would come, he told himself; he was going to pick her up. But what if she wasn't at the inn? He'd find her. He'd do whatever it took to bring this fiasco to an end. Meanwhile, he had devised a plan he could live with. He would tell her harmless stuff to satisfy her curiosity about him, then encourage her to focus on the land and hospital.

It was so simple. If he'd been thinking with his big head instead of the little head, the story would have already been written and she'd be out of his life.

Still, he knew that when he saw her, he'd have to tread carefully. She only had to come near him to arouse him. But he would not touch her again. No way. He couldn't afford to flirt with disaster anymore, especially now that he'd seen who she really was and realized that she could ruin him.

Suddenly Yancy slapped his forehead as it dawned on him what he'd forgotten—wine. Well, she'd just have to drink iced tea. He grabbed his car keys and was heading for the back door when the doorbell chimed.

He froze. Vida Lou? Ignore it, he told himself. If he didn't answer, she'd go away. But she would have seen his car. Rehearsing what he would say to her, Yancy stormed to the front door and yanked it open.

It wasn't Vida Lou who stood there; it was Dana. He tried not to show his surprise, but he knew he'd failed. He felt the color in his face go from tan to pasty white, and for a moment he was actually tongue-tied.

"I hate for someone to show up unannounced at my door, don't you?"

God, that raspy voice, slightly uncertain now, grated on his insides, scraping him raw. A feeling of dread worked its way up his spine. "It depends on who that someone is."

Their eyes met and held.

"Uh, come on in," he said finally, stepping back.

She hesitated, peering up at him through her lovely, smoky eyes that looked more blue today than gray. "Are you sure?"

"I'm more than sure." His own voice sounded husky now, but he couldn't help it.

Dana walked past him into the living room of his condo. He hung behind and watched, thinking how enticing she looked in her jeans and an orange linen jacket. As usual, the snug jeans did marvelous things for her long, slender legs, and the color of the jacket made her hair look darker and lovelier.

As if she realized she was getting the once-over, she swung around. That was when he noticed how her white stretch-knit top hugged her breasts and tiny waist before disappearing beneath her leather belt.

He shifted his gaze just as she wrinkled her nose and said, "Something smells good."

"Steaks."

She looked contrite. "Oh—were you expecting company?"

"I was hopeful, anyway."

"I . . . don't understand," she said, looking as uncomfortable as he felt.

He laughed, hoping to put them both at ease. "No, I guess you don't. I have a confession to make." He joined her in the middle of the room, though careful to keep the correct amount of distance. "Actually, I was expecting you."

"Me?"

"Yeah. One of those steaks on the grill is for you."

"But—"

"I know, it's crazy. The truth is, I was about to drive to your place and invite you to dinner."

"You're lying."

"Swear to God, I'm not."

"But why?" Her face clouded. "After that scene in the—"

"That's why I cooked dinner for you. I was out of line."

She angled her head, which caused the lingering shadows of twilight to play across her features. "Is that an apology?"

"As close to one as you're going to get," he said, giving her a half-smile, though he was concentrating on *her* lips.

She licked them, then shook her head as if she couldn't believe what was happening.

"So what's *your* story?" he asked.

"You mean why did I show up at your door?"

"Yeah."

"Looks like we both had the same idea, only different motives. I wanted you to know that I don't deal from the bottom of the deck, despite what you might think."

"So you really didn't tell that slimeball about Congressman Crawford?"

Dana's chin jutted. "Absolutely not. I try my best to avoid Ramsey at all cost."

"Sounds like a good idea."

"Do you believe me?"

"Yes."

"Is that all? I mean—"

"I know what you mean. And no, I'm not going to confide in you about Clayton Crawford."

"Ooo-kaaay. But you *are* going to confide in me about other things without snapping?"

"I think that can be arranged."

She nodded but didn't say anything as their eyes locked again.

Dana was too close to him. He could smell her perfume, smell the electric sexuality that was so much a part of her, that had aroused him the first time he'd seen her in that restaurant.

A jolt of fear suddenly charged through him, so strong that he blurted, "I hope you're hungry."

"I could eat."

A short time later they were seated on the deck, staring at empty plates.

"I'm miserable," Dana said, leaning back in the cushioned chair and rubbing her stomach. "I don't know when I've eaten so much."

"Be glad you did. Cooking's not something that comes easy to me."

She looked skeptical. "I don't believe that for a minute. You're just fishing for a compliment."

"Maybe," he said with a smile, amazed that they were actually carrying on a conversation like civilized adults. So far, so good. "I do like to cook, only I don't ever have time to play Martha Stewart."

Dana laughed. "I can understand that." She took a sip of her iced tea. "So tell me, what really made you decide to be a doctor?"

Yancy eased back in his padded wrought-iron chair. "Like you said, I had a fixation with frogs. I really enjoyed pulling those little buggers' legs off."

"I'm serious!"

"My granddaddy was a doctor. I guess maybe his influence rubbed off on me."

"What about your parents? How did they feel?"

"They didn't give a shit. They were too busy jet-setting around the world."

"They're dead now," she said cautiously.

"Yeah, so I shouldn't speak ill of the dead."

She gave him a strange look. "I gather you didn't get along with them."

He laughed bitterly. "You could say that."

"Care to elaborate?"

"No."

Aware that arguing would be futile, she switched the subject. "I'm curious as to why you chose the field of infertility. There had to be a reason."

You. You're the reason, he wanted to say, but he couldn't. Those were words he would take to his grave. "I'm not sure. I knew I wanted to specialize in something. At the time, that seemed such an untapped field. And there was so much desperation there."

"You're right about that," she said, biting down on her lower lip.

A silence fell between them. Yancy took a deep breath and tried to concentrate on how lovely the evening was instead of how lovely *she* was. A cricket chirped nearby and the scent of the flowers surrounding his deck drifted on the air. There wasn't a cloud in the sky. There were no stars yet, but soon they would start winking down from the heavens.

"Your Pap smear came back fine. As far as the other . . ."

She knew he'd deliberately shocked her with his blunt, unexpected statement. Yet she covered it well by looking him in the eye and asking, "So what are you saying?"

"I'm saying that the only way you'll know for sure if you can get pregnant is to try."

"Well, that's not likely to happen."

She spoke in a light tone, but he knew he'd thrown her another curve. Her hand shook as she lifted her glass to her mouth. He watched her lips circle the rim, and for a moment was mesmerized, feeling that fever return to his libido.

"You don't much like men, do you?"

Her breath expelled in a rush, but again she rallied, not about to let him get the better of her in this game they were playing.

"I like men just fine."

"But only from a distance, right?"

"My career's my top priority at the moment." Her tone was

stiff. "There's no time for a home and children. There probably never will be."

"So why all the concern? It still doesn't make sense to me."

"It's not supposed to."

She sounded rational, as though they were discussing the weather. But her lips were tight, and he sensed that now she was hanging on to her temper only because she wanted the interview.

Still, he couldn't let it go. "Your wanting to know if you can get pregnant doesn't jibe with not having time for a home and children."

Dana turned white, then red. "Look, we've veered off the track here. I'm not here to discuss me."

"Is it because you're afraid?" His voice was low and probing.

"No." She looked away.

His gut told him she was lying—that she would love to have a baby; otherwise she wouldn't have taken such a bold step in coming to his clinic for help. She *was* afraid; he was convinced of it.

Hell, he didn't blame her, after what she'd been through. God, if only he hadn't been involved. But what about the slimeball who'd gotten her pregnant? He was probably some stud who wanted to make whoopee but didn't want the responsibility that went along with it.

Had that devastating experience ruined her for a normal relationship with a man? He hoped not, for underneath that fear simmered a hot, untapped passion. He knew because he'd been on the receiving end of it. When he'd kissed her and her tongue had meshed with his . . .

Feeling his jeans tighten, Yancy stood with such abruptness that her eyes widened.

"Sorry," he said, "but it's getting late, and knowing you we have a lot more territory to cover."

"You're right, we do." He could hear the relief in her voice as she stood, then added, "But first let's clean up this mess."

"Leave it; I'll do it tomorrow."

She shook her head. "I wouldn't dream of leaving you in the lurch after such a delicious meal. That's the least I can do."

"Suit yourself, but I'll help."

She smiled, and he tore his gaze away.

A few minutes later they were in the kitchen, working as a team. He rinsed the plates; she placed them in the dishwasher.

"I like your condo," she said, following a short, tense silence.

Dammit, she was too close. Again. Her scent was slamming into his gut like heat off concrete on a hot summer day. Yet there was something more than sex involved; he felt an unexplainable ache, a need to hold her, to tell her he was . . .

"You're about to scrub the flower off that plate, you know."

Her confused, husky voice brought him back to reality. He handed her the plate and watched as she bent over. That was when he saw the tops of her creamy breasts.

He drew in his breath and held it.

He knew she heard him, for her head came up and her lips parted.

"Dana."

She opened her mouth as if to speak; no words came out. But then her eyes got to him, pleading with him not to touch her.

"Let's forget the dishes and do the interview now," she whispered, continuing to gaze up at him. "Where do we start?"

He reached for her and pulled her slowly toward him. "How 'bout I start with your lips and work my way down?"

Twenty-eight

His lips came down hard on hers. Dana moaned. Even if she had wanted to, she couldn't have stopped him. The explosive pressure of his touch sent all sanity out of her mind and heart.

She only wanted to feel and then greedily indulge in what was happening to her body—something wild and wonderful.

"Oh God, Dana," Yancy whispered, his breath coming hard and fast.

"Don't stop, please."

"Never," he whispered, sinking his lips onto hers again, sliding his tongue into her mouth, exploring at will. But it was when her nipples hardened like pebbles and pressed into his chest that he lost control.

Despite her halfhearted moans of protest, he thrust her away just long enough to loosen her top and pull it off over her head, as though starving for her nipples.

When he tongued one and then the other, she moaned louder, feeling as if she'd been set on fire.

"You . . . they taste so good," he murmured thickly, kneading her breasts into fullness while he continued to suck and lick her nipples.

There was no time now for anything except the surging of blood, the frantic need to satisfy the lust that had been building between them since they'd met.

Yancy unbuckled her belt, unsnapped her jeans, and shoved them all the way down. Then with unsteady hands and a curse, he unzipped his.

"Let's go to bed," he ground out, reaching for her again.

"No!" she cried. "Let's stay here."

The urgency in his eyes hadn't lessened, yet he hesitated. "I don't want to hurt you."

Dana shook her head. "Please, you won't."

He backed her against the wall then, and she gasped, her eyes widening. Lifting her arms high, he plundered her mouth, drawing her bottom lip between his, sucking on it, then moving to her cheeks, her eyes, back down to her throat.

"Oh Yancy!" she cried under the sweet/savage attack, clutching at him, even as his hand found its way between her thighs.

Unknowingly, she spread them, letting his fingers roam at will. Only when he caressed her at entry did she lunge forward, the aching heat spreading to her mind, almost melting it.

"You're perfect, so wet, so ready," he whispered against her lips, gently easing one finger into her.

"Ohhh!" she cried, unable to understand how he could make her feel this way, remove her deepest fears as easily as sand blowing in the wind.

He entered her unexpectedly, and she gasped, but only because she felt so sweetly filled. Her hips opened to receive him as he cupped her buttocks and lifted her off the floor, thrusting himself deeper into her.

That erotic, unexpected motion sent her blood pressure skyrocketing as her eyes widened in disbelief. Her mind couldn't cope; her body had no such problem. It reveled in the feel of him inside her. Then suddenly she stiffened in exquisite agony and experienced her first orgasm, unaware of the soft moaning sounds that escaped her lips.

"Wrap your legs around me!"

The guttural urgency in Yancy's voice sent her into action. Closing her eyes, Dana straddled his hips and began the rhythmic movement, no longer in control of how much or how little she gave. She could only echo his groans of gratification.

Dana was frenzied with passion. She sank her teeth into his neck and tasted not only cologne mixed with body sweat, but something that was far more potent. It was as if she could smell that masculine need, as if it oozed from his pores.

Fully penetrated by this big man, the pleasure spiraled and she shuddered once more, moving her hips wildly against him. Her head lolled from side to side until it fell onto his shoulder, which she began to lick and nibble.

Yancy groaned, shivering, then lowered his head and once again wrapped his lips around one hard, distended nipple. She felt as if she couldn't stand any more, and cried silently, having never before experienced anything like the pleasure rippling through her body.

And still it didn't end. More delight pelted her. Then with a cry that rose from her heart, she withered, breathless, clinging to him in utter exhaustion.

She was aware of nothing except Yancy and the joy, the miracle, he had given her. He'd awakened her to something so wonderful, so powerful, so consuming that she knew she would never be the same.

She knew too that the feeling wasn't just from the joining of their bodies, but from the caring, the sweetness of it all.

"Yancy, I . . ."

Though he stopped her words with his kiss, he couldn't stop her from reaching down, cupping him, and squeezing until he thrust one last time, spilling into her, uttering a sound she had never heard before.

Then, sinking in her own newfound bliss, she echoed his final cry.

Dana couldn't remember how or when they got into bed. She only knew they were there, their bodies entwined as one. She didn't regret one moment of what had happened; their coming together had been inevitable. In truth, she'd known that from the first moment she'd laid eyes on him.

What would happen next was anyone's guess. She didn't want to think about that now. She only wanted to savor the moment, savor the fact that she had never known what it was like to make love to a man, to have a man make love to her.

"Hi."

She turned and stared into his eyes, shimmering in the moonlit darkness. "Hi yourself."

"Are you all right?"

"I'm wonderful . . . I'm better than wonderful." Her tone was soft and husky.

"You're not sorry, then? We did get a little carried away, you know."

"I know, but I'm not sorry—not for one minute."

"So what happens next?" he asked, his eyes darkening.

"We talk?"

He sighed, then kissed the tip of her nose. "An interview in bed, huh?"

"Hey, I'll take it anywhere I can get it."

"Okay."

" 'Okay,' just like that?"

"Right now," he drawled, "I'd say you got me where you want me." He took her hand and placed it on him.

"Again?" she said in a breathless tone, then removed her hand.

"It's all your fault," he teased.

"So tell me something about yourself," she said in an uneven voice. "What were you like as a child?"

"Lonely. And belligerent. I think I spent my entire childhood feeling angry. The sad part about it, I didn't know why I felt that way or what to do about it."

"Probably because of your relationship with your parents."

"I guess so. I'm sure I must've sensed I was in their way, not to mention getting on their nerves. If it hadn't been for my grandfather, I'd have been up shit creek without the proverbial paddle." Yancy furrowed his forehead. "But hell, I survived, and hopefully I've dropped that baggage."

"What about your marriage?" Her tone was tentative as she wandered onto that precarious ground. She expected the old Yancy to resurface and dodge that bullet, maybe snap at her in the process.

He sighed and stared at the ceiling for the longest time. She began to think he wasn't going to answer her. Then he said, "It was a total wash from the get-go. She was ambitious, greedy, and self-centered. But then, so was I."

And still are, she almost added. Though she had made love with him, she was not about to fool herself into thinking he was a different person. He had simply shown her another side of himself.

She tried not to think about that sexual marathon they had just indulged in, but she couldn't help it. Suddenly her mind roared in agony. He had somehow found the secret combination to her body and had used it to unlock her emotions, and so easily, too.

"Which made for one helluva bad marriage," he added, interrupting her thoughts.

"Is . . . that when you started drinking?"

She felt him stiffen. "How did you know?"

"Instinct, I guess. That and the lawsuit."

"Dammit, Dana, that baby's death wasn't my fault. I wasn't drinking that night. Hell, I told you I haven't drunk in years."

"Do you know of anyone who might want the hospital project to fail?"

He gave her an incredulous look. "Why would you ask a thing like that?"

"There's something about the lawsuit that bothers me."

"You're saying that someone's deliberately trying to malign me in order to thwart the plans for the hospital?" He shook his head. "That's bull."

"I'm not saying that. I just raised the possibility, that's all."

They were quiet for a moment, then Yancy asked, "What about you? Do you think I'm guilty of malpractice?"

"No."

"And the missing campaign funds? Do you think I took that money?"

"No."

"Thanks," he muttered, clearly uncomfortable with having to ask those question.

"But again, that could be just another ploy to discredit you."

"Do you know something you're not telling me?"

"No," she lied. She didn't think that this was the right time or place to drop Rooney's bombshell about the land. When Yancy found out, he'd go ballistic. She didn't want to be around. More than that, she didn't want his anger to spoil this special time, a time she knew would never be repeated.

"Well, you can bet I'll beat that lawsuit, and I'll find out who took that goddamn money."

"Speaking of money," she said with care, "you'd think Shelby Tremaine, with all his millions, would just donate the land."

"No way. The more he has, the more he wants. He'll hold out for top dollar."

"That's too bad."

"You know, I'm tired of talking." His tone had grown thick.

Her pulse quickened. "Why is that?"

"Because I have something else in mind."

"What?"

"Come here and find out," he whispered, gathering her close.

Hours later, a hand slid between her legs and began to probe, ever so gently.

"Are you awake?"

"Sort of."

"Are you sore?"

"A little."

"I'm sorry; I shouldn't have made love to you that second time."

Dana chuckled. "What about the third and fourth?"

"Okay, so where you're concerned, I'm a greedy bastard."

"Stop apologizing. I've already told you I'm not sorry, and I don't want you to be either."

He kept his hand between her legs, basking in the warmth he felt there, even as he cursed the fact that he was hard again.

"That first time, in the kitchen, I felt like I was making love to a virgin, not to someone who'd been pregnant."

Dana didn't say anything. Instead, she shifted her gaze.

He propped himself up on an elbow, leaned over, and drew her chin back around so that she was looking up at him. That was when he saw her eyes; they were lined with tears.

"Dana, don't cry."

She sniffed. "It's all right. When it comes to the pleasures of making love, I am—was a virgin."

"Want to tell me what happened?"

"No," she said in a small voice, followed by a shudder.

"I didn't want to confide in you, either. I didn't want to let my skeletons out of the closet, but I did. It's too late for any hedging now, for either of us. What's happened between us can't be undone. It's not just your body I want to know, but your mind as well."

God help him, he was speaking the truth. By making love to her, by continuing to see her, he might as well sign his own death certificate. Yet he didn't know if he could *not* see her again.

"It's . . . just that it's so painful," she whispered, her pulse throbbing in her throat.

He could see the pain in her face, making her appear fragile, breakable. It tore at his heart. At a loss for words, he bent down and kissed her nipple.

She buried her fingers in his thick hair. "I love it when you kiss me there. It makes me tingle all over."

"And I love to kiss you there. I love to kiss you all over." He lifted his head. "But go on, finish your story. I didn't mean to sidetrack you."

"It's so ugly."

"It won't be the first one I've heard."

"You think your childhood was the pits? You don't have any idea. I lived in hell."

"With your parents?"

Her face remained grave. "I didn't have a family. My daddy took off before I was born, or so my mother said."

"Was that so bad?"

"Yes, it was." Her voice broke. "Because he left me with her." Held-back tears now trickled down her cheek.

"Shh, it's okay. Don't cry."

"My mother was nothing but a whore; she had one live-in boyfriend after another."

"They didn't bother you, though, right?"

"Wrong."

"What happened?" His voice sounded dead. He didn't want to know, but he *had* to know.

"One . . . one of her boyfriends raped me."

"Godamighty. So what did your mother do?"

"Said it was my fault."

The answer cut through him like the lash of a whip. He muttered a violent curse.

"After she found out I was carrying his child, she kicked me out."

"Sweet Jesus!"

"The night I had the wreck, I was on my way to a preacher's family to live there until the baby was born." Her voice broke again. "But as you know, I never made it."

Yancy felt his heart crack a little more as he reached for her and held her so tight he feared he might crush her bones. "No wonder you're afraid of men," he whispered, more to himself than to her.

She clung to him.

"What about counseling?"

"My friend's daddy was a preacher, and though he was wonderful and helped me a lot, he was never able to get me past the desire to kill that bastard who . . . who hurt me."

"Believe me, if I ever got the chance, he'd rue the day he was born."

"I'm sure he would," she said, sunken-eyed now.

"I'm the first man who's touched you since you were—" He couldn't go on. The monstrous word wouldn't come.

"Yes."

"Sweet Jesus," he said again. "And your mother? Tell me that bitch isn't still alive."

Dana pulled back and looked up at him, her lips quivering. "Oh, she's alive all right, and living here in Charlottesville."

"What?"

"Vida Lou Dinwiddie's my mother."

Twenty-nine

Her stomach rebelled. Her heart palpitated. She drew in deep, gulping breaths of air. She gripped the steering wheel. She slammed her fist on the dash. Nothing helped. The pain and fury continued to wash through her in waves.

Vida Lou didn't remember the last time she'd been so angry. How *dare* he? How dare Yancy Granger betray her like this? Tears of rage filled her eyes, even as she watched Dana, looking disheveled and sleepy, unlock her dew-covered car and get inside.

The knife twisted deeper in her belly. Her daughter, of all people. The thought was so repugnant to Vida Lou that she feared she couldn't endure the pressure, that she couldn't stop herself from screaming out loud.

She pounded on the steering wheel with both hands, pretending it was Dana's and Yancy's heads she was pummeling. She didn't realize she'd broken a nail down to the quick until she noticed drops of blood in her lap.

"Shit, shit, shit!" she cried.

That didn't calm her. No amount of cursing or physical violence lessened her pain and fury.

Yancy and Dana! Her eyes followed Dana's car as it pulled away from the curb. The evidence had socked her—pow, right in the kisser. How had she not seen it coming? How had she been so blindsided?

Her lover had fucked her daughter!

Hysterical laughter rose to the back of her throat, almost choking her. She couldn't accept that. She wouldn't accept that. Maybe it wasn't true, she told herself, her mind grasping for any sense of relief. Maybe she'd read too much into Dana's presence at his condo.

Who was she kidding?

Dana had come to his place and they had fucked. End of story. But when had their liaison started?

Vida Lou couldn't say what had made her get into the car and drive to Yancy's condo in the middle of the night. Tyson had spent the early part of it with her, then she had dismissed him like a speck of lint. Still, she hadn't been able to sleep. She'd taken two pills, but they hadn't worked.

As she looked back, she realized that she had fought those pills because she hadn't wanted to go to sleep. She had been thinking of Yancy, aching for him, having fantasies of going to his place and crawling naked under his covers.

She knew Yancy had been avoiding her. As long as he was slighting other women as well, Vida Lou could live with that. She had chalked up his distance to overwork, to exhaustion. Yet his hands-off policy had rankled more with each passing day, and she had begun to suspect that he was flat out avoiding her. That was when she'd started to rethink their situation.

However, when she'd accused him of seeing someone else, he'd denied it. And she'd believed him!

"You fool!" she cried, hatred poisoning her system like an infected sore.

She should have known he wasn't doing without pussy. He was no different from any other man. But her daughter? God! Again, the thought of Yancy putting his big cock inside Dana made her crazy.

Apparently Yancy still didn't realize that he belonged to her, Vida Lou, and that no whoring daughter of hers was going to have him. No more dallying around; the bitch had to go.

She would pay, though. Vida Lou would see to that.

* * *

Dana couldn't believe all that had happened in just two weeks' time. Yet she didn't have the information necessary to conclude her story on Yancy Granger. There were too many loose ends, too many questions without answers. Without those factors resolved, she couldn't deliver the sensational article *Issues* expected from her.

Dana glanced at her watch. Rooney was in town again and had asked her to join him for lunch. She had agreed, mainly because she hadn't wanted to be alone. Besides, Rooney wouldn't take no for an answer.

She should be walking out the door right now. Only she didn't move, her thoughts switching back to Yancy. Had it only been two days since they'd made love?

Her face flamed. Was that really what they had done? Despite the hot, raw passion that had flared between them, she clung to the fact that they had indeed made love. Even now she craved the feel of him inside her. Her nipples under her blouse were hard and distended, a testimony to that desire.

Dana sank onto the bed, suddenly weak-kneed and trembling. She couldn't continue to think like this and still function in a normal fashion. Yancy Granger was a cad, pure and simple. He had no intention of becoming involved with any woman. She was just one in a long line of many.

Still, she wasn't sorry for what had happened. That heady time in Yancy's arms had gone a long way toward healing her. It had proved that she wasn't different from other women, that she wasn't a freak because she'd been raped. She was indeed a whole woman.

Before Yancy, she hadn't known if she could ever let a man touch her in an intimate way. She hadn't known if the scars were too deep, if the damage to her body and soul was irreparable.

Yancy had answered those questions. She could enjoy sex, but not with just any man. The idea of anyone other than Yancy touching her was repugnant.

Dana smiled suddenly, thinking of how tender, how kind

he'd been—until she'd told him that her mother was Vida Lou. She could not forget the look of utter disbelief that had drained his face of all blood, leaving him looking like a cadaver.

"Damn that bitch!" He had stopped, sounding as if he were choking to death.

"I shouldn't have told you," she'd said, "considering she's your friend—"

"She's never been my friend!"

"But she is working on your behalf for the hospital, and nothing must interfere with that." Dana had grabbed his arm. "Promise me you won't say anything. She's *my* problem, not yours."

Before he could answer, the phone had rung, summoning him to the hospital. She had left while he was in the shower, and she hadn't talked to or seen him since.

Now she wondered if he would call. Did she want him to? While the sex had been explosive and left her aching for more, she couldn't get past the fact that she had told him things she had never told another living soul—her deepest, darkest secrets: that she had been violated and who her mother was.

The instant those words had left her mouth, she had regretted them. She had no right involving Yancy in that part of her personal life. She had done so in the heated moment of passion, which made her regret it all the more.

She didn't want anyone feeling sorry for her, least of all Yancy Granger.

Unable to deal with these tumultuous thoughts another second, Dana lunged off the bed, grabbed her purse, and left the room.

"You promised."

"No, I didn't promise any such thing, Rooney. So stop whining."

"You did promise, and I'm not whining."

Dana set her coffee cup down and counted to ten. They had

eaten a delicious meal, during which Rooney had entertained her with some of his off-the-wall courtroom experiences. But then he had asked her to do what she'd dreaded the most.

"Okay, so you didn't promise," he said with a sheepish look. "But please come with me anyway. What can it hurt? I swear we'll only be gone a little while."

He had invited her, or rather insisted, that she go with him to his family's estate. They were expecting him for a visit and he didn't want to go alone. She had known this moment was coming. After all, he had told her in Richmond that he wanted her to meet them, so she shouldn't have been surprised.

Still, she'd been opposed to it then, and that hadn't changed.

"Rooney, look at me," Dana said, her tone soft.

"Don't say it."

"I have to. I can't marry you. You have to know that."

He set his jaw. "And *you* have to know that I'm not giving up."

"As long as you know where I stand."

"I do, but that doesn't change anything. I want you to come with me to my parents'." His grin was cajoling. "As a friend?"

"Oh, all right." She massaged her temples, hoping to ward off a headache. "No wonder you're such a good lawyer."

Rooney grinned as his chest expanded.

Thirty minutes later he guided his BMW up the circular driveway, stopping in front of the sidewalk that led to the huge front door of the antebellum home.

"It's beautiful," Dana said, awed.

"Yeah, I guess it is at that. Come on, let's get this over with."

"Shame on you. They're your parents."

Once inside the house, Dana stopped, forcing Rooney to do the same. She had seen some lovely homes during her days as a journalist, but this one was in a class by itself.

Greeting her were dual staircases and a high-ceiling entry

that allowed her to see the plush great room at the back of the house.

"Hi, darlin'."

Both Dana and Rooney swung to their right. A middle-aged woman was walking toward them, a smile on her lovely face. Rooney's mother looked just as Dana had expected—elegant in every way, from the top of her perfectly coiffured hair, to her designer dress, to her beautifully manicured nails.

"Hello, Mamma." Rooney gave her a peck on the cheek. "This is a friend of mine, Dana Bivens."

"Welcome to our home, Ms. Bevins."

"Please, call me Dana."

Anna Beth smiled. "Dana it is, if you'll call me Anna Beth."

"Ah, son, 'bout time you got here."

Dana switched her attention to the man who could have passed for Rooney's twin were it not for the steel-gray hair and potbelly, the latter a result of too much booze, Dana suspected.

"Daddy, this is Dana Bivens."

He took her hand as his green eyes looked her up and down. Dana sensed that Rooney's mother had liked her on sight. Not so with *Daddy.* She knew Shelby Tremaine disliked her on sight, which was fine with her since the feeling was mutual. All her life she'd dealt with men like him, who thought they were better than women and most other men.

"Let's go into the solarium," Anna Beth said. "It's such a lovely day. If you'll excuse me, I'll have Marian bring us some refreshments."

The solarium, Dana saw, was next to the kitchen, which obviously served as an informal family gathering place.

"Tell me a little about yourself," Shelby said, once they were all seated and the refreshments had been served.

"Daddy, for heaven's sake, can't you let her at least drink her tea and eat one of Marian's fudge squares before you grill her?"

Although his tone was light with amusement, Dana caught Rooney's underlying embarrassment.

She gave Shelby a cool smile. "It's all right. I don't mind. Actually, there's nothing to tell. I'm also a southerner, having been born and raised in Texas."

Rooney winked at Dana. "I should've warned you that Daddy and others around here swear that Texas was never part of the South."

"Now, son, I think that's a bit of an exaggeration." Shelby took a sip of his iced tea and frowned. "God, I'd forgotten how awful this stuff tastes." He turned toward the door and yelled, "Marian, bring me a bottle from my study."

Anna Beth gave him a disapproving look, which, Dana noticed, Shelby deliberately disregarded.

"I suppose your parents are still there?" he asked, focusing his attention back on Dana.

Shelby's question seemed harmless enough, but Dana knew better. He was prying, trying to decide if she was good enough for his son.

Before she could say anything, however, Rooney cut in. "Actually, they're dead. They were killed in a plane crash."

Thirty

She had created that fantasy background years ago. To date, she had never used it to advance her career, as it was more a social fib than an outright lie. Still, it made her uncomfortable to tell it anymore. And she was mortified now that Rooney had blurted it out, even though Shelby's condescending attitude had brought it on.

"Oh, you poor dear," Anna Beth said. "I'm so sorry."

Dana felt terrible. "It was a long time ago."

"Any siblings?" Shelby asked, after filling a glass with a generous amount of scotch.

"No, I was an only child." At least that much was true.

"So what brings you to our fair city?"

"She's a reporter, Daddy," Rooney cut in, winking at Dana again, trying to put her at ease.

"A reporter, huh?"

"That's right." Dana's response was as cool as her smile.

"Actually, she's in town to do a story on Yancy Granger and the new hospital."

Shelby seemed taken aback. Good, Dana thought, surprised that he'd been caught unawares. She had figured that this man knew everything that went on. Maybe the old codger wasn't as smart as he thought he was. Or maybe that booze was taking its toll.

"Now, that's interesting," Shelby said, scratching his chin.

Anna Beth touched Dana's hand and smiled. "I think that's nice, dear. Dr. Granger deserves all the recognition he can get. I think it's wonderful that he's a candidate for the Nobel Prize."

"Me too, Mamma." Rooney's tone was indulgent as he looked at her.

"So what's your spin on things so far, Ms. Bivens?" Shelby asked in another of his condescending drawls.

"I think the facility will be good for the town."

"I'm glad you feel that way. That's exactly my sentiments."

"Now, that surprises me, Mr. Tremaine."

His eyes narrowed, and his tone grew cautious. "How so?"

"With that attitude, I would've thought you'd just donate the land. I was wondering why you haven't."

The veins in Shelby's neck bunched and he stood quickly. "That's none of your goddamn business, little lady!"

Rooney lunged to his feet, and Anna Beth gasped.

Shelby ignored both, pinning Dana with his eyes as though she were under a microscope. "Tremaines don't discuss their business with outsiders."

He walked to the door. The silence that followed his exit soon became tense.

At last Rooney coughed. His mother, clearly mortified, said, "Please forgive my husband's rudeness."

"It's all right, Mamma." Rooney spoke as though he were talking to a child. "Why don't you go up and lie down."

"Well, I do have a headache." She gave Dana a lame smile. "Would you excuse me, my dear?"

"Of course. It was a pleasure to meet you."

Anna Beth leaned over and kissed Dana on the cheek. "Do come again, you hear?"

Not in this lifetime, Dana thought. "Thank you, I will."

"Sorry about that," Rooney said once they were alone.

"It's not your fault. I shouldn't have said anything, only he—"

"I know: You're a reporter and it's your job to go for the jugular."

Dana didn't say anything. She just wanted to get out of there. As if reading her thoughts, Rooney grasped her arm.

They had reached the front door when Shelby reappeared. "Son, I'd like a word with you."

Rooney swung around. "Not now."

"Yes, now."

He shrugged, then said to Dana, "I won't be long."

She watched as Rooney followed his daddy back to the solarium. She then looked around for a powder room, which she found on her left. It was after she'd walked out that she noticed the room next to it. Shelby's study. And the door was open. Dana stopped.

Should she? No, of course she shouldn't. But then—why not? She'd been accused of having Teflon balls before; why not use them now?

Her heart pounding, she walked into the room. What if she got caught? She shoved that thought aside and looked around.

She had no idea what she was looking for, even as her eyes focused on his desk. A Waterford paperweight in the shape of a magnolia blossom caught her attention, not only because it was unusual and lovely but because under it was a piece of paper with a name and number printed on it.

Maybe they were important, maybe not. Nevertheless, Dana committed them both to memory, then hurried out the door, her heart still pounding.

Rooney stared at his father. "Okay, have your say and get it over with." His tone was resigned.

"Now is that anyway to talk to your old man?"

"Don't start, Daddy. Maybe she did step out of line, but I happen to like her."

"She's nothing but a goddamn snoopy reporter."

"I said, I happen to like her."

"Just as long as 'like' is as far as it goes."

"I love her." Rooney paused. "And I've asked her to marry me."

Shelby's face turned ashen, and when he spoke, his voice shook. "What did *she* say?"

"She said no, but I haven't given up, not by a long shot."

"Dammit, Rooney—"

Rooney turned, then waved his hand over his shoulder. "See you, Dad. I don't want to discuss this or keep her waiting."

"Don't you dare walk out on me!" Shelby screeched.

Rooney kept on walking.

"You don't look so good," Dana said as he joined her in the car. "What was that all about?"

"I bet you can guess."

"Me." Dana's tone was flat.

"Righto."

"Was it about the land?"

"That triggered his tirade, I'm sure."

"Are you upset with me?"

"No, but I don't want you saying anything to anyone else right now. You haven't, have you?"

"No."

"I know he'll do the right thing by the hospital."

"What else did he say?" Dana asked.

"Not much, because I told him to mind his own business."

"Do you think he will?"

Rooney's lips twitched. "Of course not."

Dana pitched her purse onto the bed and sat down. She couldn't stay put; she was too fidgety as she continued to mull over her visit with Rooney's family. Boy, had she struck a nerve when she asked Shelby about the land. Because he had jumped so fast and hard on the defensive, she suspected he was sincerely considering a double-cross.

Money. She held firm that that was Shelby's motive. But didn't he know he couldn't force Rooney to do something he didn't want to do, such as go into politics? Maybe he truly didn't, Dana thought bitterly. People like Shelby

Tremaine thought they could browbeat anyone into doing what they wanted at any time.

She wondered if he'd ever butted heads with Yancy Granger. That brought a smile to Dana's lips. Talk about an explosion—if that ever came about, she'd love to see it. When Yancy found out what the old man was up to, there would be hell to pay.

Suddenly recalling the name and number she'd found in Shelby's office, she picked up the phone and called Washington. A few moments later she was put through to her contact at *Issues,* Tim Garrison.

Dana identified herself, then said, "I have a name and number that you might want to check out, which may or may not have anything to do with the pending land sale."

"Ah, this has to be mental telepathy."

"Why is that?" Dana asked.

"I was about to call you."

She sat a little straighter. "Really?"

"Is the name you have by any chance Anderson?"

"Yes." Dana's palms turned clammy. "Do you know who that is?"

"Sure do. A man by the name of Newton Anderson has gotten some money men together. They call themselves the Anderson group."

"What do they have to do with the Tremaine land?"

"A lot. They want it for a theme park and are prepared to pay megabucks for it."

Dana was flabbergasted. A theme park, in place of the hospital? God, that certainly upped the stakes.

Thirty-one

Shelby Tremaine laced his coffee with scotch, then took a sip and smiled. Although it burned from his throat to his stomach, it felt damn good. Manna from heaven.

He sighed, leaned back in his desk chair, and peered out the window. Too bad he wasn't in the mood to enjoy the glorious morning. For all he cared, the huge orange ball rising in the east might as well have been a mound of mud. At the moment, he could fight a tiger with a switch and win.

Marry her, his ass. Shelby burped, then tried to ignore the bitter taste that permeated his mouth. He'd be cold in his grave before Rooney ever married the likes of Dana Bivens. He'd seen working women like her before, going after men like Rooney. Poor white trash—that's all they were.

It had been two days since he'd brought her to the house. During that time he'd been in a hellish mood. He'd made Anna Beth cry more than once. But hell, it didn't take much to make her cry anyway. Besides, who gave a damn? He didn't, not when it came to Rooney. No little twit with a sharp tongue and tight ass was going to thwart his plans for his son. Rooney just didn't know it yet, but he *would* become a politician.

All Rooney needed were a couple of sensational cases under his belt and lots of money behind him and he'd be on his way to the top of the political ladder. The cases were a bit of a problem, Shelby conceded, but the money wasn't.

He smiled. Soon he'd have that kind of money, and he would use it to boost Rooney into a power seat in the Senate.

That was why he would continue to listen to that other faction whisper those sweet promises in his ear.

Meanwhile, he had to do something about Dana Bivens, which wouldn't be easy. First, Rooney was thinking with his dick instead of his head, and second, the Bivens broad was no pushover. She might be poor white trash, but she covered it well.

She hadn't hesitated to stand up to him, either; he had to admire that. In fact, she'd won round one, which in the scheme of things didn't mean shit. She would get taken down a notch. Her kind always weighed in short when it counted. She might appear urbane, but she lacked the old-line polish required for the wife of Rooney Tremaine.

Shelby smirked, taking another drink of his doctored coffee. *Texas.* He didn't believe that cock-and-bull story, although he didn't know why. But it didn't matter. She wasn't the woman for his son. Rooney would marry a Virginia blue blood like himself and have fine children to carry on the Tremaine line.

Dana Bivens would just have to crawl back into the hole she came out of.

Deciding he'd messed around long enough, he reached for the phone.

After the seventh ring, a woman's voice came on the line.

"Let me speak to Howard."

"He's asleep," she responded, her tone petulant.

"I don't give a fuck what he's doing. Tell him it's Shelby Tremaine."

The line went silent for a moment.

"Sorry about that, Mr. Tremaine. Uh—Mary Jane didn't know who you were."

"Put your pecker in your pants," Shelby said without mincing words. "I have a job for you. I want you to find out all you can about a woman named Dana Bivens. She's a reporter based in Richmond."

"When do you need the info?"

Shelby looked at his watch. "Two hours?"

"You shittin' me?"

"I might shit on you," Shelby said coldly, "but I'm not shitting you."

"I'll get on that ASAP, sir."

Shelby slammed down the phone, then walked to his wet bar and fixed himself another concoction, only stronger.

He might as well relax, he told himself. Knowing that prick of a PI, it would be longer than two hours before he'd receive his call.

He was right. He had just finished eating an early dinner with Anna Beth when Marian came into the dining room.

"There's a call for you, sir. A Mr. Howard Donovan."

He tossed his napkin onto the table. "I'll take it in my study."

His wife's eyes followed him, a worried look in them. "Don't forget we're going—"

"Not now, Anna Beth!"

In his study, he picked up the phone. "Let's hear it."

Howard Donovan talked.

Shelby Tremaine cursed.

No doubt about it, now he *was* certifiable. He needed to be in a padded cell. He couldn't keep his hands off her or his dick in his pants. He just had to have her. When she had leaned over and he'd gotten a glimpse of the tops of those creamy breasts, he'd lost what little control he'd had.

He slapped his forehead with the palm of his hand, as if to knock some sense into his head. Of course, it was too late.

If there was ever a woman he should *not* have made love to, it was Dana Bivens. And the mind-boggling fact that she was Vida Lou's daughter had turned that night of torrid passion into a full-blown crisis. Yancy felt sick with regret. Was his life destined to be a long series of regrets? He'd thought that when he made the choice to become a doctor, to turn tragedy into triumph, he'd have no more regrets.

He laughed bitterly. So much for his dream world. If Vida Lou ever found out that he'd slept with another woman, much less her daughter, for chrissake, her vengeance would know no end. She would ruin him, no matter what the cost.

Yancy couldn't believe that fate had played such a nasty trick on him. How the hell could he have become involved with mother *and* daughter? One, he'd die before he touched again; the other, he'd die if he didn't touch her again.

He knew he had to leave Dana alone, only he didn't know if he could. Each time he saw her, she reduced him to a puddle of jelly. Now, wasn't that sick?

Yet he couldn't stop thinking about what it would be like to wake up every morning for the rest of his life with Dana beside him, watch her belly swell with his children. . . .

Shit, was he out of his mind? Even if he wanted to settle down, which he didn't, a future with her was out of the question, unless he told her who he was. And if he did that, he wouldn't have a snowball's chance in hell with her. She would never forgive him. Hadn't she told him that if she ever found the guy who deserted her that night, she'd exact her pound of flesh?

Right now, though, he wasn't worried about Dana finding out who he was. No one had seen him that night; no one knew what he'd done. What worried him was Dana being anywhere around her mother.

The thought of what Vida Lou had done to her own daughter turned his stomach. He'd like nothing better than to make Vida Lou pay for turning her boyfriend loose on Dana.

Dana raped! Thinking about some filthy pervert entering her room, climbing on her, tearing her flesh . . .

For a moment Yancy's rage was so blind, so consuming, that he lost control. He banged his fists down on the kitchen table, sending the sugar bowl flying across the room. When it landed on the floor and shattered, the sound was like an explosion.

Tormented though he was, vindictive though he felt, he couldn't say or do anything. His hands were tied. He wasn't Dana's knight in shining armor. That image brought on another round of bitter laughter. He was anything but that.

Dana had to fight her own battles, handle her mother in her own way. Besides, if he tried to interfere, she'd tell him to butt out in a minute.

Hell, he had no idea how she might react to him in the stark light of day. Having had time away from him, she might now be blaming herself for their passionate liaison.

Yancy broke out in a cold sweat, though the early morning was warm. Unable to contain his restlessness another second, he reached for the newspaper. Instead of perusing the front page, he dropped the entire paper, then his cutoffs, and walked into the shower.

Even there, with the hot needles of water pelting his skin, he found no relief from his tortured thoughts.

He switched the water to cold and flinched, then cursed.

Did his obsession stem from guilt? Perhaps he wanted to make it up to her for leaving her that night. Or was it more? Had he fallen in love for the first time in his life?

Oh God, no! He didn't want to be in love. He didn't want to be burdened with that sickening need. He'd learned as a child not to need anyone. Need was synonymous with pain and heartache. He had needed his parents, only to have them betray him, first in life, then in death.

Still, he hadn't answered the one question that plagued him now and would continue to plague him. Even knowing the threat she represented to his peace of mind and his career, would he stay away from her?

Ah, to hell with it, Yancy told himself, climbing out of the shower. He had a hellish day facing him in surgery. He needed to get his act together.

A few minutes later he was dressed and sitting at the table, a cup of coffee in hand. He had about five minutes to look at the paper.

Halfway down the front page, Yancy's eyes froze.

MONEY MISSING FROM CLINIC-FUND COFFERS

It didn't get better. Underneath that jarring caption, the article detailed the rumor that some money had been stolen. . . .

He couldn't bear to read another word of that garbage. Red-hot fury blasted through him. Standing, he grabbed the front page and wadded it up until it was no bigger than a spitball.

He didn't know who was responsible for leaking that to the press, but he was sure as hell going to find out.

"I can't imagine what we have to talk about, Mrs. Dinwiddie."

Vida Lou gave Rooney Tremaine a silky smile and said, "Oh, I'm not so sure about that."

He shrugged. "Well, I will say you know the way to a man's heart. I don't know when I've had better fried peach pies."

She had invited him for lunch, and as luck would have it, the weather had turned out perfect so they had dined on the veranda.

"Actually, that's my cook's specialty," Vida Lou said, thinking that Yancy also liked those pies. Then, ignoring the pain the thought of him brought her, she went on, "I must give Anna Beth the recipe or—" She paused. "Or should I give it to Dana Bivens?"

Rooney looked taken aback. "Dana? How did—" Then, as if he realized he'd stepped into her trap, his look switched to one of haughty anger.

"How did I know about you two? Let's just say I have my sources."

"I'm sure you do," he said tersely, "just like my father."

"Now now," Vida Lou said, patting his hand, "don't be upset. You know you do the same thing in your line of work."

"Only you don't work, Mrs. Dinwiddie. And what's my love life to you?"

"I don't want to see you get hurt."

"Hurt? What the hell does that mean? And since when are you my keeper?"

Vida Lou laughed another silky laugh. "Oh dear me, is that what you think? Well, that's not it at all. Actually, my concern is for Dr. Granger and the hospital." She gave him what she hoped he would interpret as a discreet smile. "You know, with the pending lawsuit and all."

"You're wasting your time. I can't discuss the lawsuit with you."

"I don't expect you to. What I do expect is that you keep your reporter girlfriend away from Yancy Granger."

"I can't do that. He's why she's in Charlottesville. And even if I could, why should I?"

"What if I told you that the story's not the only thing she's after?"

"Are you . . . you saying," Rooney spluttered, "that Dana and Yancy are . . ."

"That's exactly what I'm saying."

"I don't believe that for a second," he snapped. "But even if it's true, what business is it of yours?"

Vida Lou smiled. "Let's just say I don't think it's wise for Dr. Granger to be any more distracted than he already is—not until your daddy sells the land and the hospital construction begins, that is."

"I see." Rooney's tone was stiff.

"Oh dear boy, I do hope so. Yancy's like a son to me. I do so want his dream to come true." She cocked her head and studied Rooney. "Can I count on you for help?"

Rooney stood, his face dark. "If what you say is true, then yeah, you can count on me."

"Do I have your word that this little tête-à-tête will remain just between the two of us?"

"You have my word." Again Rooney's tone was terse. "Now, if you'll excuse me, I have to go."

"Of course, I understand," she said, a conspiratorial smile on her face.

She watched as Rooney strode across the lawn. When he

was out of sight, she lifted a full glass of wine to her lips and drank it all at one time.

She didn't stop there. She refilled the glass, then drained it again. She was in control. It was about time everyone in this damn town knew it.

No one fucked over Vida Lou Dinwiddie and got away with it.

Thirty-two

Dana's fingers burned up the keyboard. She was on a roll, organizing her notes, everything she had learned about Yancy thus far—good, bad, and indifferent.

Then her mind jumped to the hospital and the land. She hadn't yet come to grips with the staggering notion that Shelby Tremaine might sell the land to a theme-park group. If he did, what would be the town's reaction? She knew what the hospital's would be.

Dana had held on to the thought that greed was Shelby's motivation, but it still didn't make sense, as he apparently had more money than he could ever spend. Deciding it was time to stop speculating and find out the truth, she called Tim Garrison again and asked him to run a check on Shelby Tremaine's finances.

"That shouldn't take long," Tim said. "I'll get back to you as soon as I can."

"Thanks, Tim," she said, hanging up, her mind still conjuring up questions to which she had no answers.

The specialty hospital was what drove Yancy, what he seemed to want above all else. And Vida Lou—it seemed the project had become her life's blood. Knowing how her mother's mind worked, Dana figured that Vida Lou saw it as a sure way to get herself inducted into the blue-blood hall of fame.

Two strong personalities with two strong goals were bound to clash with this latest twist of events, along with various others such as Brodie Calhoun. No doubt, things would get nasty if Shelby reneged.

As far as she knew, she and Rooney were the only two who were privy to Shelby's intention. Nothing would have pleased her more than to blow the whistle on him, not only because she disliked the man himself but because of the gritty edge it would add to her story. But she couldn't betray Rooney's confidence, at least not now.

Besides, why should she air Shelby's dirty laundry; he should be the one to break the news to Yancy and the committee. And reap the consequences, she reminded herself.

The phone rang, making her jump. My, but she was skittish. If it was Yancy . . . She bit down on her lower lip. She wanted it to be, yet she didn't.

With her head feeling like it was in a vise, she answered the phone.

"Dana."

It was Hubert Cox, her boss at *Old Dominion.* The bottom dropped out of her stomach as their last conversation rushed to the front of her mind.

"Yes," she said, hearing the trepidation in her voice and hating it.

"I know what you're up to. I didn't when I called you before. I'll admit you had the wool pulled over my eyes."

Dana's mouth went dry. She knew now why his voice had sounded odd; it shook from suppressed fury.

"Hubert—"

"I know what you're going to say—that you can explain, right?"

"Something like that."

"I'm not sure I want to hear anything you have to say."

"So what's the bottom line here, Hubert?"

"I suggest you stop playing with me. You were never in Charlottesville for a vacation. That was a crock of crap you fed me. You're working on a story about Dr. Yancy Granger for *Issues*.

"All right, I'll admit that."

"Look, you got caught with your hand in the cookie jar. But if you're willing to take it out, I guess I could pretend this never happened." Hubert paused. "I don't want to lose you, but—"

"But what?"

"I refuse to let you play *OD* against *Issues*."

"It's not that easy, Hubert. I'm committed to doing more than just a story here."

"Then you leave me no choice."

"What are you saying?"

"You're fired."

Dana sucked in her breath, then let it out. "Just like that?"

"Just like that. I'll have your desk cleaned out and your things shipped to your house."

"Hubert—"

"Goodbye, Dana."

She sat holding the receiver long after the dial tone started buzzing in her ear. Finally she pulled herself out of that daze and walked outside. The wind whipped around her, moving the trees and the clouds at a rapid clip. She wrapped her arms around herself. She felt cold and devastated.

Just like that, she was out of a job; and that could turn out to be permanent if she didn't pull off this story and get the job at *Issues*. For a moment, an almost paralyzing panic held her motionless, then she forced herself to calm down and look at the situation rationally.

This had been a gamble from the onset; she had known that. There had been no guarantees. The new job hinged on her ability to pull off this article. Maybe she hadn't been totally honest with *OD*, but still it was her vacation time. And she didn't know any journalist who wouldn't have jumped at the same chance. She hadn't yet taken a dime from *Issues*, nor would she have until she resigned from *Old Dominion*.

Still, telling Hubert should've been her call—not someone

else's—which made her furious. So who *was* the culprit? Whoever it was had done it on purpose. But why?

Revenge? Or was it meant to be a scare tactic? Did the malefactor think she would grovel to get her job back and promise to leave town, thus dropping her investigation into Yancy? If that ploy worked, would the guilty party stop there? Or would that person go further and see that *Issues* didn't hire her either?

Vida Lou was the first person who came to mind. She had been determined to force Dana out of town from the get-go. Shelby Tremaine was another strong possibility. He hadn't liked her, hadn't thought she was good enough for his son.

She couldn't overlook Congressman Clayton Crawford, either. She had stirred up a potential hornet's nest with him. Another person she never wanted to think about pushed to the top of her mental list—Albert Ramsey. That lowlife would stop at nothing to taint her reputation.

The last name that flashed to mind almost sent Dana to her knees. Yancy. Suddenly she felt totally defenseless against the ugliness of it all. Was this *Yancy's* way of trying to get rid of her? If so, what was he afraid of? It wasn't the lawsuit or the missing money; he'd made it plain that he was innocent on both counts.

Yet he had fought her asking personal questions at every turn. Did he indeed have an elephant in the closet? Had she been wrong about him on both levels—business and personal?

No! her heart cried; it couldn't have been Yancy. Despite his faults, and Lord knew he had plenty, deception was not one of them. She had to believe that what they had shared counted for something.

Fool! What made her think he hadn't just been using her? That night of passion could've been a sham to get her off guard before the kick in the teeth. But then, she had already set herself up for that possibility. So why was she so outraged now? Because she cared, dammit!

Thank God, she was only in lust, not in love.

Unable to sustain the continuous blows from those thoughts, Dana returned to her computer, forcing her mind back to the article. It was of paramount importance now that she was no longer officially employed.

Dana's fingers froze on the keys as she felt the unexpected prick of tears in her eyes. She gave her head a savage shake when what she wanted to do was lay it on the desk and sob. She had promised herself a long time ago that she would keep a tight rein on her emotions no matter how deep the wound. That kind of crying jag was for the fainthearted and she was no longer that. Still, she was about as low as she could get.

If only she could be sure that Yancy hadn't been behind her getting fired, for no other reason than vindictiveness. Surely he didn't think she would turn tail and run? She figured him to be a better judge of character than that. She *knew* him to be.

The phone rang again; she snatched it up as if it were a lifeline.

"Hello."

"Hi, friend."

"Hi yourself." Dana smiled. "What have you been up to?"

April chuckled. "Herding kids, what else? How 'bout you?"

"Not much." For a second Dana was tempted to tell her that she'd just been fired, but she couldn't bring herself to say anything. The wound was too raw, the panic still hovering.

"You mean you don't know? Haven't you seen the paper?"

"I don't think it's come yet. Suppose you tell me."

"The proverbial shit has hit the proverbial fan," April said, talking ninety miles an hour. "Someone ratted about the missing money to the paper."

"Oh my God."

"It gets worse. They don't come right out and implicate Dr. Granger, but they beat the bush to death."

"You're kidding?"

"Swear on my daughter's head, I'm not."

Dana groaned. "What a mess."

"Look, just go get your paper. I gotta run now. We'll talk later."

"All right. Thanks."

Dana didn't have to read the paper. She knew what it would say. She rubbed her suddenly throbbing temples, wondering what was going through Yancy's mind, wondering if he blamed her.

Suddenly, Dana started to laugh.

She didn't trust him, yet here she was thinking he didn't trust her. And she had slept with him. God! She'd come here just to do a story on a doctor, someone she didn't know.

How had things gone so haywire?

"I want to know who opened their big mouth?"

Vida Lou placed a hand on Yancy, who sat beside her. He gave her a hard stare and shifted his position. He saw her face turn pale and knew that his gesture had not only embarrassed her but pissed her off.

He didn't care. He didn't care about anything at the moment, except nailing the bastard who'd leaked that story to the paper.

Since it all revolved around Herman Green, Yancy had called him and told him he was coming to his office. Apparently Herman had then called Vida Lou for backup—or maybe she'd just shown up on her own. Either way, he didn't give a rat's ass.

"Hey, calm down," Herman was saying, his crooked nose seeming more out of joint than ever. "We'll be rushing you up to the hospital with cardiac arrest."

"Funny."

Herman sighed. "Look, I know we have a problem, but losing your cool isn't going to solve it."

"Herman's right, Yancy," Vida Lou put in.

"I don't lose my cool; it's my temper that's in jeopardy. Besides, it's easy for the two of you to offer advice, but it's me, goddammit, who's on the hotseat."

Vida Lou's fuchsia-colored lips tightened. "Not for long, I

promise. I think I know who's responsible for this little fiasco."

Both men stared at her. But it was Herman who said, "One of those reporters, right?"

"Not Dana Bivens." Yancy spoke before he thought. He sensed rather than saw Vida Lou stiffen. What he did see was the hard glint that appeared in her eyes. *Careful, Granger.*

"I'm not so sure about that," Herman said.

"Me either," Vida Lou said, her tone pointed.

Yancy lifted his shoulders in what he hoped was a nonchalant fashion. "Hell, you might be right. Maybe it was her," he lied, "but it's that sniveling bastard Albert Ramsey who gets my vote."

"You're probably right," Herman said, "especially after the way you decked him."

Yancy stood abruptly. "It doesn't matter who blabbed. We were afraid of this and now it's happened. It's how we fix the damage that counts."

"I'll take care of it," Vida Lou said with a smile at Yancy. "I always do, don't I?"

Yancy ached to put that insufferable bitch in her place once and for all. But he couldn't, for more reasons than one. Not only was this the wrong time and place, but Vida Lou continued to be the major artery to the hospital's success, and she wouldn't want him playing watchdog.

"So do you feel better now?" Herman asked.

Yancy glared at him. "No, dammit, I don't. I hold you responsible for this, Herman."

"That's absurd and you know it. I'm still convinced one of the cleaning crew helped themselves to that money, only I haven't been able to prove it."

"In the meantime, I'm hanging out to dry?"

"How the hell did I know someone was going to say something to the press?" Herman's tone was huffy.

"Okay, you two, cool it," Vida Lou ordered. "No telling how the paper got wind of the story. Ted Wilkins or his wife—either one could've blabbed to the wrong person. Or like I said, it was probably one of those reporters. My point is, it doesn't matter. We have to clean up the mess."

"How?" Yancy snapped.

She smiled, then touched his arm again, the look in her eyes daring him to pull away. He didn't.

"You let me worry about that. Nothing is going to sink this project. I'll get a retraction; you wait and see."

"Fine. I'm going to the hospital."

"Stay cool, you hear?" Herman said to his back.

Yancy swung around. "Why don't you stop worrying about me and find out who the hell took that money."

Anger darkened Herman's eyes, and he would have responded, only Yancy had already walked out.

Ten minutes later, Yancy was in his office at the clinic, where he had a full patient schedule. Later, he had to return to the hospital for a lecture on in vitro fertilization to a class of residents.

He placed his hand on the phone, only to pause. What was there about this whole scenario that stunk? Herman Green's lackadaisical attitude for one. Another was his ability to look Yancy in the eye when he discussed the missing money. Then there was the fact that he'd gotten huffy.

So? Yancy had gotten huffy, too.

Maybe the problem was with him and not Herman. Maybe he was just overreacting. Hell, he'd admit that Dana had him mixed up and distracted. Still, something wasn't right. He couldn't put his finger on it, but he felt it in his gut.

Dana's loaded comment about someone possibly wanting to malign him was partly responsible for his paranoia.

Lifting the phone, he punched out a number. He had an idea.

Thirty-three

"Rooney, I'm sorry, I can't. Not right now, anyway."

"Why?"

His tone had an obstinate, possessive note that rankled.

"I have an appointment, that's why."

"Can't you make an exception? I'm only going to be in town for a little while, just long enough to see my client and my parents."

Her heart skipped a beat. She knew that client was Yancy.

"We'll get together next time," Dana said. "I promise."

Such a long silence followed that for a minute Dana thought he'd hung up on her. "Rooney, are you still there?"

"Yes," he said, his tone frosty.

Dana curbed her impatience. "Hey, what's the deal here? You know I have a job to do." Especially now, since I'm technically unemployed, she almost added.

"Yeah, but is that all you're doing?"

It wasn't so much what he said—it was that, too—but more, it was how he said it. Bitter sarcasm underlay each word.

"What's that supposed to mean?" Now Dana couldn't keep the sarcasm out of her voice. Yet she was puzzled as well. "What are you getting at?"

"Nothing. Forget it."

"Noooo, we won't forget it. You opened this can of worms, so let's just let them all crawl out."

Another silence.

"Rooney, you started this."

"All right. Have you been seeing Yancy Granger?"

"Of course," she said with irritation. "If I'm doing a story on him, how could I not see him?"

"I don't mean like that."

"What do you mean, then?"

"You know, on a personal basis."

Feeling like she'd been punched in the stomach, Dana sucked in her breath. Apparently that sound was enough to confirm Rooney's worst fears.

"Dammit, Dana, that's about the stupidest—"

She scrambled to regroup. "Who told you that?"

"It doesn't matter. What matters is whether it's true or not. But I think I already have that answer."

"The answer is that it's none of your business." Her jaw ached from being clenched so hard.

"Okay, Dana, have it your own way. If it's true and you are sleeping with him, you're nuts. That man uses women like—" Rooney broke off in a splutter. "And to think, you flinched every time I touched you. I—"

"Time out! You've had your say. I care about you, Rooney. We have a friendship I don't want to lose, but I won't have you meddling in my personal business."

"Dammit, I asked you to marry me."

She heard the pain in his voice and hated that she had hurt him. "I know that, and I told you I wouldn't."

"That you did."

"Look, let's hang up now, okay? Call me next time you're in town, and we'll get together then."

"So are you mad at me?"

"A little, but I'll get over it." Dana tried to infuse a little humor into her voice, but she wasn't sure she had pulled it off.

"All right, I'll see you later."

When she replaced the receiver, Dana massaged her stomach, still feeling the effect of that verbal blow. How had Rooney found out that she'd slept with Yancy? She detested the thought of her personal business being bandied about.

Who else knew? And why would anyone care? Dana shivered with a fear she couldn't identify, which made things worse.

Shoving those thoughts to the back of her mind, she returned to business. In an anonymous phone call, she had finally found the last witness at home. When Rooney called just now, she'd been about to walk out the door.

Upset or not, she couldn't let this opportunity pass.

"Ah, so you have company, Mr. Hemphill," Dana mused, taking her camera off the seat beside her and clicking several pictures of the two men.

She didn't know why she thought the photos might prove useful. Instinct, she suspected. Actually it was more than that; pictures had served as a backup in more than one of her investigations. One never knew.

She put down the camera, got out, and walked across the street. She decided that the overweight, red-haired man with the ruddy skin was Tommy J. Hemphill, her man, as he hadn't budged from the rickety front porch while talking to the other man.

Dana then concentrated on Tommy J.'s visitor, noting that he was not only well but expensively dressed. Pin-striped suit, polished shoes, the whole nine yards, she thought, not to mention his styled hair and manicured good looks.

He didn't seem the type who would be friends with Mr. Hemphill.

Dana didn't have a clue what she was going to say or do. Her instincts would guide her. When she opened the crooked gate and walked inside the yard, she spotted an old, mangy-looking mutt curled under the steps. He lifted his eyes, looked her up and down, then buried his head back in his paws.

No threat there, Dana thought, relieved.

"Tommy J. Hemphill?" she asked with a smile and an outstretched hand.

He seemed not only taken aback by her direct approach but dazzled as well. He grinned. "That's me."

"How are you today?"

"Can't complain." His grin widened, which allowed her an up-close and personal view of his mouth. She winced. Every tooth in his head was rotten. Only one front tooth was intact.

Dana swallowed, having gotten a whiff of the odor that went along with the rotten teeth.

"I'm Dana Bivens." She turned then to the other man and held out her hand. "And you're . . . ?"

His hesitation was only minuscule as his eyes appraised her. He obviously liked what he saw. "Clyde Danforth," he said, smiling.

"You selling vacuum cleaners or something?" Tommy J. asked, squinting at her.

She was about to answer when Clyde Danforth said, "I have to go, Tommy J. I'll be in touch."

"Sure thing, Mr. Danforth."

They watched in silence until he'd gotten in his car and driven off.

"Look, if you're selling them—"

"I'm not," Dana said. "Actually, I'm a reporter."

His demeanor changed; suspicion replaced admiration. "A reporter. Now look here, I don't talk to no—"

"I'm quite harmless, you know," Dana said with another bright smile.

"Well, maybe you are at that." He winked. "Wanna come inside? My old lady ain't home."

"No, I'm fine right here."

"So, what can I do for you?"

"I understand you were at a party several weeks ago."

"Lady, I'm at a lot of them shindigs around town. When it comes to cleanin' and fixin' things these rich people mess up and break, I'm the best." He paused. "Uh, I didn't mean no respect, if you're one of them."

"Believe me, I'm not," Dana assured him.

He sort of smiled. "Why are you asking about that party, then?"

"Did you see a doctor there? Yancy Granger?"

Tommy J.'s face underwent yet another change; it turned rigid. "Why you wanna know?"

"I understand you said he'd been drinking that night. Now, how would you have known that?"

" 'Cause I saw him, that's how."

"How do you know it was a glass of liquor he was holding?"

" 'Cause I watched the bartender mix it for him."

Liar. "What about your work? How did you have time to spy on the guests?"

He clenched his fist and stepped forward. Dana stepped back.

"Look, lady, I ain't no slave," he spat. "I can stop and rest when I want to. Anyway, what's it to you?"

"Do you know a man by the name of Newton Anderson?"

He didn't so much as blink. "Nope."

"Never heard of him?"

"Nope. Now, if it's all the same to you, I gotta go. The missus'll be along any minute now. She might not like it if you was here. Understand?"

Both his tone and his face were menacing now. "Oh, I understand. Thank you for the info."

He didn't say anything, but Dana felt his eyes bore into her backside all the way to her car. Goosebumps covered her skin.

She still had those goosebumps when she walked into her room at the inn. After pitching her purse onto the bed, she phoned Tim Garrison.

"Please be in," she said aloud, staring up, watching as the sunlight painted patterns on the ceiling.

"Tim here."

"Hi. It's Dana Bivens."

"What can I do for you?"

"When we discussed the Newton Anderson group the other day, I didn't get all the names involved. Was one of them by chance Clyde Danforth?"

"No."

"Damn. I'd hoped I was on to something, but I'm not surprised I wasn't. When I mentioned Anderson's name to that creep I talked to, he looked blank as an empty sheet of paper."

"You might be."

Distracted, Dana shook her head. "What?"

"On to something, like you said."

She straightened. "You know who that man is?"

"Yep. He's Newton Anderson's private attorney."

Gotcha! She had caught the rotten-toothed bastard lying red-handed, just like the bartender and the woman who was bringing the suit. From the way it appeared, the Anderson group had bought them all off. There was no telling how much money Anderson's attorney had given those phony witnesses to malign Yancy, which was synonymous with maligning the hospital project.

Unfortunately, Dana hadn't seen any money change hands. But the fact that Mr. Danforth had been there spoke volumes. Besides, it wasn't up to her to prove anything; that was Yancy and Rooney's job.

"Dana?"

"Oh . . . I'm still here, Tim. Look, thanks a mil for the help. I'll be back in touch soon."

She didn't even hear his response, her mind was clamoring so. What should she do with this incriminating information? Should she hold on to it and see how the scenario played out?

What she wanted to do was tell Yancy. She felt it was time that he saw the dirty hand he was being dealt. But was that her obligation, her call? No, not really. Besides, she had no hard evidence, only circumstantial.

She wanted to see Yancy: That was the bottom line. This information provided her with the excuse to do so. She hated herself for that weakness. But more than that, she hated herself for caring.

"Not half bad."

Vida Lou liked the sound of her fake voice almost as much as she liked the look of her tucked body. Standing naked in front of the wall-to-wall mirrors in her bathroom, she dug into the jar with her fingers and massaged more of the scented goo into her stomach.

She couldn't relax for one second; she felt driven to use these firming gels and lotions every night. She had convinced herself that by performing this ritual religiously, she wouldn't have to go back under the plastic surgeon's knife.

She wouldn't hesitate, though, if she saw a sag anywhere. Her fingers moved from her concave stomach up to her full breasts. She rubbed them long and hard, until the nipples were turgid, reminding her of plump, ripe raspberries.

She wondered if they had tasted like that to Yancy. Or what if Dana's had—

"No!" Vida Lou cried; then she snatched the jar of cream and threw it against the mirror.

She didn't know what made her cover her face and jump back, but after that she couldn't seem to move; she could only stand there and stare, a glint in her eyes and an odd smile on her face.

"Miz Dinwiddie? Are you all right?"

"Go away, Inez."

"But Miz—"

"Leave me alone!" she screamed.

The maid never responded. Vida Lou heard her maid scurry off, then she sank slowly onto the vanity chair, where her mind went into vindictive overdrive.

Dana could *not* have what was hers. After calling her daughter's boss, she had hoped that Dana would hightail it back to Richmond and beg for her job back. But no, she was still here, sniffing around Yancy.

Vida Lou's face twisted into a mask of hatred. She hadn't wanted to resort to another tactic, certainly a more dangerous one. But if necessary, she would.

The high cost, in the end, would be worth it.

Thirty-four

Dana wiped one sweaty palm down the side of her jumpsuit and took a deep breath. Had she completely gone off the deep end? Probably. But she wouldn't think about that now, standing on the steps of Yancy's condo at midnight.

She had been restless, unable to sleep—that was the best excuse she'd come up with, lame as it was. And then she had rationalized that Shelby Tremaine's underhanded dealings had pushed her into action, had made her realize that she must tell Yancy after all.

But the truth was that the need to see Yancy wouldn't go away; it was too strong. She yearned not only to see him again but to touch him, to have him reignite that fire inside her, a fire that continued to smolder.

She rang the doorbell and tried to ignore the butterflies in her stomach. *Loosen up,* she told herself, only she couldn't. She had made some brazen moves in her life, but this one topped them all.

"Go away. No one's home."

For a moment the terse statement rocked her, then Dana smiled. No one except Yancy Granger could pull a stunt like that and get by with it. But she could be just as stubborn.

She pressed the doorbell again. Harder.

"Shit!"

Though he muttered the word, she still heard it, so she figured he was nearer than he'd let on.

"Who is it?" he snapped.

"Dana." Her voice was tight.

He jerked the door open. "What the hell?"

He looked wild. No, Dana thought, he looked ill. His eyes were bloodshot and the lines around them were deep; his hair was mussed and in need of a trim; his shoulders were stooped as if it were too much effort to hold them up.

"I—I'm sorry," she stammered, feeling more like a fool by the second.

Yancy's eyes were unreadable, even though she could see them in the light from the lamp behind him in the living room.

"I'm not," he said bluntly, yet his tone was surprisingly gentle.

"I . . . should go."

The next few seconds seemed to crawl by as they stared at each other.

"Please don't go. Look, it's been a hell of a day. I was in surgery nonstop and I'm bone weary."

"That's the more reason why I should go."

His eyes seemed to drink her in. "That's the more reason why you should stay."

"Why do we always end up arguing?" She forced a lightness to her tone, hoping to diffuse the building tension.

"You tell me."

"Aren't you the least bit curious why I'm here on your doorstep at midnight?"

"Okay. Why are you here?"

"Would you believe me if I said I had something important to tell you?"

He stared down at her, his eyes dark. "No."

"I really did come to talk." Even as she said this, her eyes were fixed on his bare chest, which she had covered with kisses. She averted her gaze.

"Dana."

The husky appeal in his voice drew her eyes back to his. "I

thought you might be at the hospital, in your bed there," she said inanely.

"I'd like to be in bed, all right," Yancy said in a hoarse whisper, "with you."

He grabbed her then, hauled her into his arms and shoved the door shut with his bare foot.

"Oh, Yancy!" she cried, feeling him nuzzle her neck.

"God, I needed you."

"Aren't you too tired? I mean—"

Why was she trying to discourage him? Wasn't this the reason she had come? She had lived for this moment, craved it. So why couldn't she relax now, let him do the things to her body that only he could do?

As if he read her mind, he whispered, "Let me love you."

His mouth, hot and demanding, found hers.

"This is insane, you know," she said between kisses.

"Maybe, but I can't stop. Can you?"

"No."

His mouth closed over hers, his tongue thrusting inside. She sagged against him; what little resistance she had managed to hold on to leaked out like water from a broken faucet.

A hand found her zipper and eased it down; that hand then found a bare breast and surrounded it, bringing it to burgeoning fullness.

"Feel me; I'm so hot."

"Me too."

He cupped her buttocks and pulled her against him. "Hot, so hot," he groaned, his voice thick with urgency.

"Take me now!" she cried.

"No, not this time."

Without letting her go, he backed her to his bedroom.

The fiery, explosive atmosphere heightened when Yancy discarded her clothes, then his.

"I thought maybe I'd imagined how perfect you were." He swallowed. "Only I didn't. God, what you do to me."

"You do the same to me," she murmured.

He bent his head to her upturned breasts, sucking her nipples until she moaned and dug her hands into his hair.

"Oh yes, yes!"

Her hands were all over him then, tracing the muscles in his neck, his back, his shoulders.

"Touch me," he said in a strangled tone.

Her soft-tipped fingers moved between his thighs, caressing and squeezing. "Oh, Dana, I can't—"

"Yes, you can," she whispered.

Then, to his astonishment, she began rubbing against him, scorching him with her heat. Blood thundered to his head and a shudder rippled through him.

"Ohhh!" he cried.

The anticipation was nowhere near as exquisite as the actual experience. He felt himself sinking into a pit of sexual obliteration that he never wanted to crawl out of. Yet he held himself back, not wanting to come without her. He felt a need, a compulsion to bring her to that same brink, to reacquaint himself with every succulent part of her body before he took her again.

"Stop," he pleaded, covering her hand.

She blinked. "It's okay, if—"

"No, it isn't okay." He eased her backward onto the bed, then drew her to the edge and spread her legs.

She stared up at him, her eyes wide and questioning, as he knelt before her, positioned her thighs over his shoulders, and opened her.

"Yancy!"

"Relax," he urged, knowing that all this was foreign to her, this kind of lovemaking between a man and a woman. "I'm not going to hurt you. It's going to feel wonderful."

She nodded as he tasted her with his tongue.

She bucked as she cried out, "Oh my God!" She clutched at his hair while her hips bucked higher, as if begging for his tongue to spear deeper.

He felt the clenching of her muscles, the inner tightening;

then she began to shake, moaning, almost sobbing as his tongue continued to penetrate her flesh.

It was when she reached down and grasped his hardness that he rose and plunged into her.

"Oh, Yancy!" she gasped.

Her thighs were like a vise around him. Yet he was able to move her up while still inside her, and then flip-flop their positions.

"Oh!"

Despite her shocked cry, she buried her fingers in the hair on his chest and stared into his eyes.

He didn't think he'd ever seen anyone so beautiful as when she bent over and covered his neck and face with light kisses.

He began to move then, his back arched, his penis moving high inside her. There was nothing more he wanted in that moment than to go wild, to lose control, to erupt inside her, to reduce her to a mass of hot putty.

But he wanted to prolong the ecstasy for both of them as long as he could. He wanted this moment never to end.

"I want to watch you when you come."

"Only if I can watch you too."

He felt her shudder and her breath escape on a hiss as he thrusted deeper, faster.

"Let it go!" he begged, just as her thigh and stomach muscles tightened and his mouth latched on to a nipple.

She lurched against him and then nothing mattered except that sweet/savage give-and-take between them.

And yet it was not enough.

"Good Lord, woman, how many more of these things are you going to eat?"

"Until I get full."

"Hell, I've had one to your ten."

"I'll have you know I've only eaten five little pancakes and two strips of bacon."

"Is that all? I could've sworn it was twice that much."

"That's how many you've had, Bubba."

"Better watch that 'Bubba' shit; it'll get you in trouble."

Dana grinned at Yancy as he stood in front of the stove with nothing on but his boxer shorts. She'd had to force him to put those on.

"Surely you're not going to the kitchen naked?" she had asked thirty minutes earlier, her eyes soaking up his lean, muscular body despite having just sampled every inch of it.

He had turned at the door, an eyebrow cocked. "Pray tell, why not?"

"Because you're going to cook."

"So?"

"So . . . you know."

His lips twitched. "No, I don't know. Suppose you tell me what's the proper kitchen attire for three A.M."

"I don't know, but something!"

He laughed outright. "So my flipping flapjacks naked doesn't appeal to you, huh?" He sobered suddenly and that glint jumped into his eyes. "Or maybe it appeals to you too much."

Dana colored.

"Gotcha!"

She picked up a pillow and threw it at him. "You're awful."

"Don't you mean insatiable?"

"That too."

The glint returned, and he started back toward her. She held out her hand. "Whoa!"

He stopped.

"You promised you'd feed me." She struggled to her knees, dressed in one of his T-shirts. "I'm starving."

"Well, you should be, after the workout you gave me."

He was teasing her now, and her color deepened.

"Okay, I'll be good. I'll even put on some skivvies, if it'll keep your hands off me."

"You wish!"

That conversation had taken place thirty minutes ago, and now Yancy was cooking the last batch of pancakes.

"I hope those are for you," she said. "I'm stuffed."

"So am I."

"Then toss 'em and I'll clean up."

"Nope, just keep your seat, ma'am." He paused, leaned against the cabinet, and added, "We have to talk."

Dana looked down, then back up. "I know."

"When you first got here you said you had something important to tell me. Were you serious?"

Dana didn't know what to say. She'd been afraid this moment would come.

"You were serious." His tone was flat.

"Yes, I was—but I'm not sure I should say anything."

"Why?"

"It's not really my place."

"Let me be the judge of that."

She didn't say anything.

"I'm not budging until you tell me what's lurking behind those big eyes of yours."

"It's not funny, Yancy."

"So, it's not funny. But I'm still not going to let you off the hook, especially if it concerns us."

"It doesn't."

"Spit it out."

"It's about the land."

During the few seconds that followed, a pin could have fallen on the floor and they would have heard it.

"What about the land?"

"There's a chance Shelby's going to sell it to someone else."

Yancy looked as though she'd picked up a brick and hit him between the eyes.

Thirty-five

Dana made a trail through his chest hairs with one finger, all the while peering into his eyes, eyes so blue they never failed to fascinate her. She kept thinking that because they were so clear, she should be able to read everything that went on behind them. Still, she knew better. No one got behind the scenes in Yancy's head.

Once he had told her in that hard, deadly tone of his how he would handle Shelby if he didn't hold up his end of the bargain, Dana had cajoled him back into bed. It hadn't been easy. Yancy's body had been like a tight wire, ready to snap at any moment.

He hadn't uncoiled, even after she'd told him what little she knew about the prospective theme park.

"I'll see that bastard in hell first," he kept saying over and over.

Her touching him now was the catalyst she'd hoped would calm him. Yancy trapped that finger, brought it to his lips, and sucked.

"Ohhh," she whimpered, warmth pooling between her thighs.

"Like that, huh?"

"Too much. It makes me—"

He smiled. "Go ahead. Say it."

"No."

"Chicken." He proceeded to make clucking sounds.

"Okay, so I'm horny." Dana wrinkled her nose. "Are you satisfied?"

"For now." He chuckled, then the chuckle turned into a sober grimace and he fell silent.

Dana knew that his thoughts had gone back to Shelby and the land debacle. She swallowed a deep sigh, almost wishing she hadn't said anything. Not only had she tainted this precious time, but she had involved herself in the quagmire.

"I've never made love to another woman like I've made love to you."

His out-of-the-blue words sent another shaft of heat to that sensitive spot inside Dana. "Not even your wife?" Her voice didn't sound normal.

"Not even my wife."

They were silent for a few moments, then Yancy said, "You do crazy things to me, walk around inside my head all the time."

"Yancy, I—"

"I know. Me either. This is heavy stuff and we're not ready for it." His voice deepened. "But I can't stop seeing you."

"I feel the same way, only—"

"Only you have your job to do."

"Speaking of job, did you know I got fired?"

Yancy bolted upright and shot her an incredulous look. "Fired? You?"

She had her answer. No one could fake that kind of response.

"Yes, and it's because I wouldn't back off doing the story on you and return to Richmond."

"Hell, you're not making any sense. I thought your magazine sent you here."

Dana avoided his direct gaze. "Not exactly."

"What does that mean?"

"It means that the magazine I worked for didn't send me on this assignment."

"Am I missing something here?"

"It's rather complicated." She explained, then, about how she'd come to be in Charlottesville and what had transpired since.

"So now the shit's hit the fan."

"I refuse to look at it like that."

"I hope to hell you don't think I was the one who called your boss."

"I considered it, but now I know you didn't."

"Thanks for that much, anyway." He fell quiet again, then said, "So this *Issues* job is the chance of a lifetime?"

"Yes."

"But only if you nail the story about me?"

"Yes. I kind of like the idea of a girl from the wrong side of the tracks writing one of the most sensational stories of the year."

"I see."

A smile tampered with Dana's lips. "Not if your expression's anything to judge by. You look like I just shoved you in front of a firing squad."

"That's what I feel like." He shook his head and smiled. "But then that's what happens when you deal with a lady who has Teflon balls."

Dana made a strangled sound. "How did you know that—"

"Someone else has already said that about you?" he finished for her.

"Yes," she said primly.

"I take the Fifth."

"Now who's the chicken?"

"It was just a wild guess, okay? So, have you reached a conclusion? Do you think I deserve the Nobel Prize?"

"Do *you*?" Dana teased, but he didn't respond in kind.

"I'm serious."

"I haven't finished my investigation," she said with complete honesty. "If you'll recall, I haven't had a whole lot of co-operation."

"Touché"

"So when can I watch you perform surgery?"

"You want to do that?" He seemed surprised.

"Of course. I also want to sit in on a lecture and see your lab."

He tapped her on the nose. "I have no problem with any of that."

"You don't?"

"My work's not off limits. It's *me*, Dana; it's who I am." He shifted his gaze. "And it's all I have—all I'll ever have."

You could have me, too, she added to herself.

"So what's your gut feeling about all this?" he pressed.

"I'm on your side."

"Then you still believe that I'm not guilty of malpractice, and that I had nothing to do with the missing money?"

"Yes and yes. I'm convinced they're trumped-up charges." She told him then about visiting the third witness and encountering Newton Anderson's attorney.

"I'm inclined to agree with you. But it's ludicrous to think that throwing smut on me will nix the project."

"Apparently someone doesn't think so. I'm sure those witnesses were paid to lie."

"If you're right, then Shelby's playing into their hands. Just wait till I get my hands on that greedy son of a bitch."

"And I think whoever's behind the malpractice suit is behind the missing funds, too," Dana said. "Someone leaked that story to the paper, and it sure wasn't me."

"What about that fag Ramsey?"

"I doubt he'd have the nerve, especially after you nearly tore his head off."

Yancy suddenly looked pensive. "Then that leaves Herman Green—and he's on the committee."

"What makes you suspect him, other than the fact that the money came up missing from his office?"

"Hell, I don't know. Maybe I was just looking for a scapegoat. Anyway, I was so steamed I charged into Green's office demanding to know if he'd had anything to do with that crap in the paper."

"How'd he react?"

"Weird. I couldn't put my finger on it, but something was wrong." Yancy paused. "In fact, my gut instinct was working overtime to the extent that I called a private detective friend and asked him to check Green out."

"And?"

"Haven't heard back from him yet."

"Are you thinking Green might've actually taken that money himself?"

"It sounds crazy, I know, but something sure as hell happened to it. And Green does keep fiddle-fartin' around about finding the culprit."

"If you're right, he would almost have to be in cahoots with that Anderson group."

"If that proves to be the case, I'll break the bastard like a matchstick."

"But why would he do such a thing? Why him?"

"Maybe he needs money. Maybe they promised him a gravy position. Who the hell knows. I'll just have to wait till my buddy calls."

"Meanwhile?"

"I have to tell Vida Lou."

Dana's stomach knotted, but she didn't let it show. "I figured as much."

"Look, I hate it when I have to mention her around you. I—"

"Don't . . . don't apologize. Just because I despise her, doesn't mean she isn't doing a good job with the hospital. You have to give the devil its due."

"Still, she's—"

"I don't want to talk about her."

"No, I guess you don't, and neither do I."

Another silence ensued.

"Are you going to confront Shelby?"

"You bet. I'm going to force that s.o.b. to look me in the eye and tell me he's *not* going to sell us the land."

"How do you think that'll affect your professional relationship with Rooney?"

"Like I've always said, not in the least. He can't afford to take sides, unless it's mine, even if the situation gets sticky."

"What do you mean by sticky?"

"Getting rough with his old man."

"Like how? You wouldn't actually hit him, would you?"

"No. But I'd make him wish I had."

"It was Rooney who told me about the theme-park faction's interest in the land. He asked me not—"

"He won't hear it from me."

"He'll figure out where you heard it, but it doesn't matter. It's something that can't be kept secret for long."

Yancy balled his fists. "I'm not going to let that land slip through my fingers. Besides, if Shelby reneges, there are a lot of other people who would go for his jugular."

"After meeting Shelby Tremaine, somehow I don't think that would bother him."

"We'll see about that."

"I guess we will at that," Dana said, knowing that she'd have to admit to Rooney that she'd broken her promise and told Yancy what Shelby was considering.

"Have I told you that I'm glad you're on my side?"

"No, as a matter of fact you haven't."

Yancy's eyes brightened. "Then I guess I'd best remedy that."

"And just how do you plan to do that, Doctor?"

"It's already been taken care of." He looked down.

Her eyes followed his, then she blushed and looked up.

"Honey, all you have to do is come anywhere near me." His

voice turned low and raspy. "Go ahead, look at it. See how much I want you."

Dana not only lowered her eyes, she reached out and took that distended part of him in her hand. It felt like warm velvet as she caressed it.

"Oh, God, that feels so good." He closed his eyes. "I wish you never had to stop."

"When . . . when you touched me there—" She couldn't go on.

"You mean here?" He placed his hand on her.

Her heart palpitated so that she could only nod.

"What about it?" he asked in a thick tone.

"Do you . . . touch all your women—" The words were too agonizing to say.

He said it for her. "With my mouth? God, no. And just so you'll know, since you came to town, there haven't been any other women."

"Oh, Yancy." For no apparent reason, tears sprang to her eyes.

"Dana," he said in a thicker voice, "I wanted to show you all the pleasures that a man and woman can share. Before, you knew only the pain."

Her throat was so full she couldn't say another word. So she did the next best thing. She leaned over and placed her lips on his. It was a deep, gentle kiss that spawned an aching groan that seemed to come from deep inside him.

Then, without conscious thought, Dana lowered her head and began nibbling her way down his stomach. He fell back against the pillows as her tongue reached his thighs and she touched him there.

He groaned again, then raised himself onto his elbows, his eyes dark with passion. "You don't have to, you know."

"I want to," she whispered, lowering her head again, fire churning through her as her mouth surrounded him, sinking all the way to the root, her fingers cupping him.

"Ah, more, ohh, please."

Afterward, he grabbed her, then both went over the edge fused in body and spirit.

The country club grounds and terrace-side restaurant were teeming with people. Yancy swore as he made his way toward Vida Lou.

She occupied a table off to one side. He guessed he should be thankful for small favors. He wasn't. He didn't want to be here, but for the time being he had no choice.

Not for much longer, though, he promised himself. As soon as this fund-raising came to an end, she'd be history. Even now, when he looked at her, he wanted to vomit. He longed to confront her about what she had done to Dana; that gnawed at him day and night.

Also, her obsessive attraction to him was driving him around the bend. Nothing he said or did seemed to get through to her. Was he going to have to pay for that one night of lost sanity for the rest of his life?

He gave another silent curse as he reached her table and sat down.

Vida Lou smiled at him. Again he fought the urge to throw up, comparing her man-made perfection to Dana's natural beauty. But he had initiated this meeting and had to see it through.

"I'm so glad you called," she said in her most intimate voice. "I knew you would."

Yancy's mouth tightened along with his gut, but he let that pass. He hadn't come here to pick a fight. He'd come with a different purpose.

"What would you like to eat?"

"Nothing, thanks. I'm not hungry."

"Of course you're hungry." She lifted her hand and beckoned the waiter.

"Read my lips, Vida Lou. I'm not hungry."

She turned pale, but he had to admire her; she didn't lose her cool. "Then why did you come?"

"To talk."

"Oh, Yancy, I don't want to fight with you," she purred. "I was hoping you'd stop by the house tonight."

"That's not going to happen and you know it."

"No, I don't know it," she said in a heated voice. "You belong to me."

A dark stain crept up Yancy's face.

"And don't you forget it! You've been bought and paid for."

Jesus! This sick bitch must never find out about him and Dana. That was all he could think about.

"Look, I have something I think you should know, if you don't already."

"What is it?"

Vida Lou sounded disinterested, Yancy noted, thinking her conceit knew no bounds. She honestly thought he had made this appointment because he wanted to see her. If he hadn't despised her, he might have pitied her.

"Shelby Tremaine's up to something," he said at last.

That got her attention. "Oh?"

"Word has it he's talking to a company who wants to buy our land and put a theme park on it."

"Why, that's absurd! He can't do that!"

"He can do anything he damn well pleases."

"Who told you about this?" she demanded.

"It doesn't matter. What matters is whether it's true or not. Before I called you, I tried to see Shelby, but he's out of town."

"You stay away from him."

Yancy's sigh was as deep as his patience was shallow. He leaned forward and lowered his voice. "Don't tell me what to do."

"If you want that hospital you'll do exactly as I say. Keep out of this. I'll handle Shelby Tremaine."

"Fine. Have it your own way, for now. But if you fail—"

"I won't."

"Good. Now that we've settled that, I'll shove off."

Vida Lou stood at the same time he did and came around the table. "I haven't told you goodbye yet, darling."

Before Yancy could react, she reached up, pulled his head down, and kissed him hard on the mouth.

Thirty-six

Time was no longer a ticking bomb inside her, but Dana still felt pressure. She suspected that the feeling of rush-rush-rush to make a deadline, to be the first in the gate with a hot story, stemmed from the job itself. Every journalist who was worth her salt worked on a deadline, internal or external.

Besides, she needed to know if she had the job at *Issues*, which wouldn't be decided until she completed this story and turned it in. While she felt confident in her ability, one never knew. She couldn't take anything for granted.

However, her job wasn't the only reason for the pressure. She hadn't forgotten about that snake Albert Ramsey, though she would like to think that Yancy had succeeded in sending him back into the hole he'd crawled out of. Still, as she went about her business, she always looked over her shoulder.

But the strongest vein of pressure was Yancy, or rather her personal compulsion to bring her affair with him to a close or to a commitment.

Did she love him? This morning, two days after that second marathon night of hot lovemaking, she faced that question and answered it. She didn't hesitate. Yes, she had fallen in love.

But did he love her? She knew he wanted her. But love? She didn't know if a man like Yancy was capable of loving anyone with the passion with which he loved himself and his work.

Dana sighed, knowing that if she gave in to it, despair would render her useless. She didn't want to love this volatile man. She didn't want to love *any* man. After the trauma in her past, she'd felt that miracle would escape her. But now she realized that she had been blindsided; that what had started out as an adversarial relationship had turned into something so unique that she was still reeling from its impact.

She moved her right shoulder suddenly as if she had a crick. The gesture was only barely enough to pull her back to the moment at hand. She didn't have the luxury of dallying. She was due at the hospital to observe Yancy in surgery. Excitement leaped through her at the thought.

He had told her yesterday, following the tour of the hospital and his lectures, that he had a complicated hysterectomy scheduled the next day in addition to two artificial inseminations. He had suggested that would be a good time for her to observe.

Yesterday had been so fascinating that she couldn't imagine what today would bring. She had listened to his talk on the subject of in vitro fertilization and had been fascinated, not only with what he was saying but with the man himself.

Every time she watched him gesture or point with those beautiful surgeon's hands, she thought of how they felt on her body, how they had healed her.

On one occasion their eyes had met, and for a second it had seemed as if they were the only ones in the room. Feeling heat flood her face, Dana had broken that contact before anyone became the wiser.

Now, dressed and with notebook in hand, she was about to walk out the door when she remembered that she hadn't talked to Tim Garrison about Shelby Tremaine. She figured she wouldn't learn anything earth-shattering, yet she had to cover all bases.

She peered at her watch and saw that she had a few minutes

to spare before she was due in the surgical gallery. She dashed to the phone and dialed Tim's direct number at *Issues.*

"Gosh, I must be living right," she said when he picked up. "This is twice in a row I've caught you in your office."

"Hi, Dana. What can I do for you?"

"It's what you should've already done that I'm calling about."

"Oh, right—Shelby Remaine's financial records."

"Well?"

"I've got 'em somewhere here in this mess."

She heard him shuffling through papers and forced herself to stifle her impatience.

"Ah, here it is."

"Anything?"

"Nah, not really, except that the old fart has more money than anyone ought to be allowed to have and draw Social Security."

"So he *is* loaded?"

"That's an understatement."

"Then why would he even be tempted to let the theme park have that land instead of the hospital? It's obvious it's not for the money."

"Not necessarily."

Dana was confused. "But you just said—"

"I know, but here's the kicker. He's set up a huge political trust fund in his son's name. Apparently, he has big plans for him."

"I know he does. So what you're intimating is that maybe the Anderson group is promising to add to that coffer?"

"And maybe support in other ways too. 'You scratch my back, I'll scratch yours' sort of thing."

"Mmm, that's certainly food for thought. Thanks for helping out again, Tim. I'll be in touch."

She scurried out of the B&B then, making it in record time to the hospital and into the gallery. A smiling Brodie Calhoun met her at the door. "Ah, Ms. Bivens, it's good to see you again."

Brodie then introduced her to Nurse Myers, the woman next to him, and to some of Yancy's residents. "They're here to take in everything he says and does," Dr. Calhoun said in a pointed fashion. "Right, ladies and gentlemen?"

They all shifted from one foot to the other and said in unison, "Yes, sir."

Dana hid a smile as Brodie winked at her. The students seemed as nervous as she was. Yet, while she'd never witnessed any type of surgery, she was looking forward to it. She expected it to be an experience she'd never forget. More than that, she would see Yancy in his element, see him as she never had before.

The doors opened and Yancy walked in, gowned, gloved, and masked, ready to go.

As if he sensed she was there, his eyes lifted toward her. She smiled. Although he showed no outward sign of having seen her, she knew that he had. But then she was promptly forgotten, as was everyone else. His entire mind and body now belonged to the woman on the table.

Still, for a moment there, when their eyes had met, Dana had felt an emotion she'd never felt before, a premonition, maybe, that she was something more to Yancy than just a good lay, that the future held something special for them.

That thought was heady stuff, more so than what was about to take place in the surgical arena. But she wouldn't think about that now. She'd save it for later so as to savor the possibilities.

"Nervous?"

Brodie's eyes were on her; his were twinkling.

"No, actually I'm not," she said with confidence.

"So the sight of blood doesn't bother you?"

"Heavens no."

"That's great, because with that attitude you can really appreciate this man's talents." Calhoun shook his head. "Personally, he's a mess, but professionally, he's the best."

"That seems to be the consensus," Dana responded, knowing that he was right.

"Here we go," Brodie said, close to her ear. "Relax, listen, and watch."

"Ladies and gentlemen, welcome aboard," Yancy said, accepting the scalpel the nurse handed him.

He then explained the procedure he was about to undertake. Much of the technical jargon was over Dana's head, but she didn't care. At this point, everything he said and did was mesmerizing, whether she understood it or not.

"Now," Yancy continued through his microphone, "I'm going to make the incision."

Dana rose and stood on tiptoe to get a better view as Yancy placed the knife against the flesh on the woman's stomach and slowly split the skin.

"So far so good, huh?" Brodie asked, standing alongside her.

Dana couldn't answer. Her eyes were glued to the blood flowing out around the knife.

"Ms. Bivens?"

She heard Brodie's voice again, but this time it sounded like it came from afar. She felt hot, then she felt cold, then she felt sick. Then the room spun.

"Ms. Bivens, are you all right?"

She was frozen, numbed into immobility.

"Ms. Bivens!"

Dana heard and felt nothing else. A black void opened its arms to catch her.

"She's okay, Yancy. She just fainted, for chrissake! Trust me on that."

Yancy stared down at Dana, who was lying on the couch in his office. His stomach lurched as he noted that the only visible color on her lovely face was black, from her thick lashes fanned against her cheeks. He scowled up at Brodie. "What the hell happened?"

"I told you she—"

"I'm fine, Yancy."

His gaze shot back to Dana, whose eyes were open now

and staring up at him. Lines scored his face as he tried to smile.

"You gave us a scare."

"I'm fine, really."

She looked anything but fine, Yancy thought. She looked like a fragile piece of China that should be handled only with tender, loving care.

"That's your happy ass," he said more to himself than to her. "You're a long way from being fine."

Brodie rolled his eyes. "Yancy, I checked her before I brought her in here."

"Will you leave us alone?" Yancy asked.

Brodie shrugged. "Sure." Then, to Dana: "You hang in there, okay?"

She gave him a lame smile. "Thanks, and I'm sorry I made such a nuisance of myself."

Once they were alone, Dana struggled to sit up. Yancy helped her. "You sure you're up to this?"

"Yancy . . ."

"Okay, okay. Maybe I'm overreacting. But when I saw you keel over, I almost lost it."

"No, you didn't. You would never have done anything to endanger your patient's life just because some idiot in the gallery fainted."

Her teasing words unlocked his senses so totally that he wanted to grab her and kiss her. He held back and said in a hoarse voice, "Only you're not just any idiot."

"I'm not?" Her voice had a slight quiver.

"No, dammit, you're not."

She placed a hand on his arm. "Why does that make you mad?"

This time he couldn't stop himself. He leaned over and kissed her hard on the lips. Then he pulled back and peered deep into her eyes. "Because I'm a bastard, that's why."

Dana frowned. "Are you trying to tell me something?"

He grinned. "Right now, I'm ordering you to take that delicious tush of yours to my place and put it to bed."

"I will not! I told you, I feel all right." She paused. "Maybe a bit embarrassed—"

"You're not the first to keel over at the sight of blood."

"I know, but I was looking forward to watching and so sure I could handle it."

"There's always another time."

Her face paled.

"See why I want you to do as I say. Even when I mentioned the *b* word, you almost bought it again. So humor me, okay?"

"All right. I'll rest for a little while." Dana traced her tongue across her bottom lip. "Only on one condition, though."

He couldn't take his eyes off that tongue that had . . . Swallowing hard, he said in a gruff tone, "What's that?"

"You'll join me later."

His pulse quickened. "Count on it. As soon as I can."

Once she was gone, Yancy leaned against the door and took a deep breath. But that breath wasn't easy to come by. His lungs and stomach—all were on fire.

He was in love. When she had fainted, it had hit him with all the subtlety of a boulder crashing down on his head. A coldness swept over him, and he was frozen to the spot. Shit! Talk about having his nuts in a meat grinder.

"Doctor?"

He jumped forward like he'd been shot. "Yes?"

"Your next appointment is here."

Yancy pulled a handkerchief out of the pocket of his surgical greens. He mopped his face, then ran his fingers through his hair. By the time he opened the door, he had a rigid hold on his emotions. "Congressman, you and Gloria come in."

They shook hands, then Yancy gestured for them to have a seat.

"Let's get straight to it, Doctor," Clayton Crawford said, after he and his wife were seated on the couch.

Yancy walked to his desk and perched on one edge. "All right."

"What do you suggest we do next?"

"I'd like to try one more drug, then artificially inseminate Gloria one more time."

"But we've tried it three times, Doctor," Gloria said in a soft but strident voice

"I know, but I told you from the start that AI sometimes isn't effective the first few times. So before we discuss plan B, I think we should give it another chance."

The couple looked at each other, then back at Yancy. "It's your call," the congressman said. "We'll do whatever you say."

"Good. We'll order the drug and get started."

Gloria nodded, though Yancy could see that she was far from enthused. Times like this, when he saw the pain and the frustration in a patient's eyes, it tore at his gut.

This woman wanted a baby as badly as anyone he'd ever seen. He felt that desperation and was determined to do all he could to help her attain her goal.

"Look, Clayton, before you go, I want to tell you how sorry I am about that leak to the press."

"I don't blame you. Anyway, I should've expected it."

"I did what I could."

"You mean you put the muzzle on someone's mouth?"

Yancy smiled, though with no humor. "Something like that."

"You're my kind of man, Doctor. Ever thought about going into politics?"

"I'll take that as a compliment, but no and no thanks."

Crawford stood and shook Yancy's hand. "I haven't forgotten about that grant I promised you."

Yancy felt a choking sensation in his throat. Here comes the *chomp-chomp,* he told himself.

"You get that land, and I'll still do my best to see that you get that grant to build the hospital, goddamn nosy reporters or not."

"What about a baby?"

Although Clayton's features blanched, he didn't hesitate. "Baby or no baby."

For a second Yancy didn't know what to say. He wasn't used to anyone doing him any favors.

"Thanks is all that's needed, you know."

"Then thanks, Congressman. Thanks a hell of a lot."

After Clayton and Gloria had gone, Yancy sank into his desk chair, almost choking with frustration. Now that the money looked to be forthcoming, Shelby Tremaine was acting like an ass.

Yancy clenched a fist and pounded it into the palm of his other hand. Regardless of what Vida Lou said, it was time for him to face the old man and find out exactly what was going on.

Then he groaned, suddenly remembering Dana, naked and waiting at his condo.

Thirty-seven

Dana was mortified. She lay on Yancy's bed and stared at the ceiling, still unable to believe she had fainted. But then, she'd never been in an operating room, nor had she ever seen anyone's stomach slit open.

She shivered as a wave of nausea threatened to send her scrambling for the bathroom. She took several deep breaths, which helped calm her. She couldn't stop thinking that she was the laughingstock of the hospital, the entire staff whispering and snickering about her.

A fine doctor's wife she'd make.

Oh God, where had that thought come from? Another surge of nausea forced her to think about something else, like when she went on staff at *Issues.*

Exciting as that prospect was, it didn't push thoughts of Yancy and his return from her mind. She glanced at the clock and figured she didn't have much longer to wait.

Breathless with anticipation, she got up and headed for the bathroom. She had just shed her robe and was about to climb into the shower when the phone rang. Should she answer it? What if it was Yancy? She crossed her fingers that it wasn't him telling her that he'd been delayed.

Without grabbing a towel, she raced back into the bedroom and grabbed the receiver.

"Hello."

"Dana, are you all right?"

Hearing his deep-voiced concern, she eased down onto the side of the bed. "I'm okay," she said, though the breathlessness remained in her voice.

"You don't sound okay." He chuckled. "It's funny now, only it wasn't earlier."

In spite of herself, she smiled. "Okay, go ahead and laugh. I know how ridiculous I must've—"

"Hey, stop beating up on yourself. It's not every day that you watch someone take a knife and—"

"Oh pleeeze!" She felt her stomach do another somersault.

His chuckle deepened. "Some strong belly you have."

"Don't have, you mean. I just have to work on that part of my anatomy." She liked this type of bantering, something they so rarely did. Still, she knew he hadn't called just to chat.

"I don't think so."

She shook her head, forcing herself back to what he was saying. "Don't think so what?"

"That you should do anything to that part of your anatomy." Then his voice turned low and husky. "It's perfect the way it is, especially that delectable belly button that my tongue—"

"Yancy!"

"What?" His tone was as innocent as it was seductive.

Heat flooded through Dana, and she squirmed on the bed. "You shouldn't talk like that."

"You're right, I shouldn't. It makes me horny as hell. In fact I'm so hard right now I'm about to explode."

"I can take care of that," she said softly, then was amazed by her boldness. If someone had told her that she would ever say such things to a man—and over the phone of all places—she would not have believed it.

He groaned. "I know you can, honey, but I can't make it. That's why I'm calling."

"Oh, Yancy."

"I know. I want to see you so bad I can hardly stand it."

"There's no chance for later?"

"Surgery's so goddamn backed up that I won't be through until early morning. Too, I have a critically ill patient that I'm afraid to leave."

"I understand."

"I knew you would."

"Well, I guess I'll go take my shower now."

Another groan sounded through the line. "Are you naked?"

"Yes."

"God, I'm dying." His voice sounded as thick as if he'd been drinking.

"I know. Me too."

He cursed. "Look, I'll call you later. Meanwhile, don't stop thinking about me."

As if she could, she told herself, replacing the receiver, though she still didn't move. Her thoughts were running rampant, imagining them together in the shower, something they had not yet experienced.

His hands would be all over her, soaping her where she loved to be touched. She could visualize his eyes on her, studying her, while her legs parted, and she held his hand there. She wanted that so much that she ached.

She forced herself to get up and shower. She was in and out in record time.

Once she was dressed, Dana had no choice but to leave. Besides, she needed something in her stomach, and Yancy's refrigerator and cabinets were bare.

After gazing with longing at the empty bed and thinking about what might have been, she turned the lights off and walked out.

Food.

A filet couldn't have tasted any better than the chicken soup and crackers. She had just finished scraping the bowl when she heard the tap on the door.

Yancy! He had come after all. Smiling she raced to the door and jerked it open.

"Hello, daughter dear."

Dana's gut instinct was to slam the door in her mother's face. But she knew Vida Lou wouldn't go away. Instead, she'd make a ruckus until Dana complied with her wishes.

"What do you want?" she demanded, clutching the doorknob.

Vida Lou gave her a murderous look. "Let me in."

"No. You're not welcome. Don't you get it?"

"I'll make a scene. And I'm sure you don't want that." Vida Lou didn't raise her voice or even change her tone, but Dana knew she meant every word she said.

She stepped aside and let Vida Lou pass. Once Vida Lou was in the middle of the room, she stopped and swung around. Dana almost choked when she saw the smile on her mother's face. If she hadn't known better, she would've sworn that smile was sincere.

"What do you want?" Dana asked again.

Vida Lou craned her neck, as if surveying the room. "By the way, you never told me what happened to your brat. Where is it?"

"My brat, as you refer to it, is dead."

"My my, but aren't we acting like a prickly pear."

Dana glared at her, though her chest was aching terribly.

"Oh, all right," Vida Lou said, her false smile intact. "But you really must learn to relax. That stern look on your face is going to cause wrinkles before your time."

"I'm going to count to three, and if you're—"

"I think you've made a wise choice in Rooney Tremaine."

At first Dana was so taken aback that she was speechless. She opened her mouth, then closed it.

"I see I've surprised you, my dear."

"I'm not 'your dear.' I never have been and never will be."

"Just a slip of the tongue. But no matter." Vida Lou flapped her hand in the air, then lifted her chin in a haughty fashion. "I know how Rooney Tremaine feels about you, and I do think he'd make you an excellent husband."

"You don't know a damn thing about Rooney and me!"

"That's where you're wrong."

"How dare you interfere in my business?"

"Rooney's absolutely crazy about you and wants to marry you. And he's got scads of money, which—"

"Get out!" Dana was shaking all over; even her teeth were chattering.

"I will, but only after I've had my say." Vida Lou smiled again.

"No. Get out now!" Seething inside, Dana walked toward Vida Lou. "And if you know what's good for you, you'll stay out. Who I marry is *my* business and has nothing to do with you."

That faked concern disappeared, and Vida Lou's true colors showed. Her face turned ugly, then she laughed. "Don't say I didn't warn you."

"Get out of this room and out of my life!" Dana was almost yelling now, but she didn't care. The thought of this woman being anywhere near her made her physically ill. Vida Lou's mere presence was synonymous with evil.

A strange light appeared in Vida Lou's eyes, and her voice sounded odd. "Just because he's slept with you doesn't mean he wants you."

Dana froze. Clearly, Vida Lou was referring to Yancy. But how had she known? Or was she simply fishing? What business was it of hers anyway? More puzzling, why would she even care?

"I don't know who you're talking about," Dana lied.

Vida Lou laughed coarsely. "Oh yes you do, but I'll humor you anyway. I'm talking about Yancy."

"So what?"

"So what? I'll tell you so what. If you think he cares about you, you're wrong."

Dana's lips tightened. "Since when did you become an authority on Yancy's personal business?"

"Quite some time ago, actually."

"Are you saying he cares about you?" Dana laughed outright. "If you think that, then you really should seek professional help."

"For sooth and for shame, he really has been a bad boy."

"What the hell are you talking about?"

"Why, child, I'm talking about us—Yancy and me."

Dana laughed again, only now she felt as if thumbtacks were being jabbed into her head. "You're crazy! There's no Yancy and you. Except as chairwoman for the fund-raising drive, he wouldn't give you the time of day." Dana stomped to the door and pointedly held it open. "Anyway, my relationship with Yancy is none of your business."

Vida Lou didn't move. She just stood there with that evil grin on her lips and looked Dana up and down. "Oh, but it *is* my business. Yancy Granger belongs to me." She tapped her breast with a long fingernail. "Me! Understood?"

"In your dreams, maybe." Dana's voice was flat, colorless.

Vida Lou stared into space for a moment. "I see I'm going to have to take matters into my own hands."

"One last time, get out."

"I'm leaving, but I'm going to tell you one more time: Stay away from Yancy. He belongs to me."

"Go to hell!"

Vida Lou's expression didn't change. "That's where you're about to go, my dear. You see, Yancy's *my* lover."

Thirty-eight

Newton Anderson smiled at the man whose hand he had just shaken. "It's a real pleasure, Mr. Tremaine."

Shelby nodded. "Same here."

Newt introduced the other three men on the committee, then said to their guest, "Please, have a seat. Can I get you anything to drink?"

Shelby raised his hand as he eased into a plush chair. "Let's just get down to business, shall we?"

"Suits us fine." Newt could barely contain his excitement. Although he hadn't been able to get a firm commitment out of Shelby Tremaine over the phone, he had pinned high hopes on consummating the deal when Tremaine had agreed to meet with him and his partners.

Now they were face to face, and Newt could almost taste the success the old man's presence would bring. But then one never knew. He'd learned long ago not to count his chickens before they hatched.

Shelby Tremaine was one crafty bastard, and money-hungry to boot.

"So, do we have a deal, Mr. Tremaine?"

Yancy took off his white coat. Thank God, the workday was over. What a day it had been, too. Both his patient and surgery load had been unusually heavy. He was dog tired. Not too tired, however, to see Dana.

Adrenaline pumped through him just thinking about her. Yet a day never passed that he didn't fear she would find out who he was. Then he would quickly remind himself that that was not going to happen, unless he chose to tell her himself. In time, he would. Hopefully, by then she'd be so in love . . .

Love! There was that word again. He kept thinking that if he ignored it, it would run its course like a virus and go away. Dammit, he hadn't meant to fall in love, but he had. So what did that mean? Marriage? Home? Kids? Suddenly Yancy felt so weak that he had to sit down.

He'd been the marriage route once and swore he never would again. Hell, with his schedule, his devotion to his work, his foul temper, he'd make a lousy husband. He'd *made* a lousy husband. That was why he would never make that mistake again. But he knew Dana wouldn't live with him out of wedlock. Anyway, she deserved better than that. She deserved a man who would put her first, love her above all else—most of all, above his career.

Could he do that? Could he change? Could he put her first? Since he'd become a doctor, committed himself to healing others, he'd become the most selfish human on earth.

Once he got the land and the hospital, maybe that would change. Maybe he could do something for himself, as in live a normal life, eat normal food, sleep normal hours, have a normal personality. What scared him was that he didn't know if he was capable of normalcy.

The need to right that old wrong, to make up for past mistakes, was the fuel that drove him, that made him who he was. He hadn't wanted to change. He'd been content with himself the way he was.

Then Dana had come along. God, who'd ever thought that the one woman who had set him on this course would reappear in his life? The fact that he'd fallen in love with her had to be fate. Yet here he was thinking about tempting that fate and giving her up, the best thing that had ever happened to him.

No way could he let Dana walk out of his life.

Yancy rubbed his throbbing left temple and was about to head home when the phone rang. He almost didn't answer it; then, thinking it might be Dana, he picked it up. "Granger."

"Hey, Yance my man, it's me."

Yancy recognized his private investigator friend, James Ellis, because of his slight lisp and his deep, drawling voice. "I was wondering if I was ever going to hear back from you."

Actually, he hadn't been wondering at all. But he should've been. Instead of dwelling on Dana and his perpetual hard-on for her, he should have been thinking about his career, which was teetering on the brink of disaster. If the lawsuit went to trial, he was in very hot water; the missing money could add more fuel to the fire.

And he couldn't forget about Vida Lou and the claws that she'd sunk into him. But had he been thinking about any of those disasters? Hell no.

"Hey, old buddy, you still there?"

"Yeah, James, I'm here. Got anything for me?"

"Sure do."

A few minutes later, Yancy slammed down the receiver, only to pick it up again and punch in another number.

"This is Dr. Yancy Granger," he said to the woman on the other end of the line. "Is Rooney in?"

"No, sir."

"Tell him to get in touch with me. I need to talk to him ASAP."

Yancy hung up and walked out the door. He had an appointment that wouldn't keep.

"I'm sorry, but Mr. Green's tied up at the moment."

"He'll see me. Tell 'im Yancy Granger's here."

The secretary smiled, but her attention seemed focused on the pen in her hand. "Actually, he's on the phone. But I'll tell him you're here."

"Don't bother. I'll tell him myself." Yancy headed toward the heavy closed door adjacent to her desk.

"You can't—"

Yancy didn't hear the rest of her words as he had opened the door and was already across the threshold. Herman Green was behind his cherrywood desk, his feet propped on it. When he looked up and saw his visitor, he yanked his feet off the desk and sprang forward in his chair.

Yancy stood in the middle of the room and waited.

"Look," Herman said into the receiver, "I gotta go. I'll talk to you later."

He rose and held out a hand, a smile on his face. "Why, Yancy, what a surprise."

Yancy folded his arms across his chest and appraised Herman, thinking how pale his lean features were, which in turn highlighted his crooked nose.

"Yeah, I bet it's a surprise." Sarcasm twisted Yancy's full lips.

"Uh, is something wrong?"

Yancy stroked the side of his chin as if he had all the time in the world. "Oh, you could say that."

At Yancy's cool, even tone, Herman's face turned whiter. "What's going on? I . . . I don't understand."

"I think you do."

"Look, I feel like a drink. How 'bout you?"

Herman's voice had a touch of panic in it now, Yancy noted. Good; he hoped the little weasel was pissing in his pants. "No, thanks. What I feel like is ripping your goddamn head off."

Herman stopped in midstride and swung around, his eyes wide in his gaunt face. "What the hell's going on?"

"You set me up."

"I don't know what you're talking about."

Yancy's eyes smoldered with fury. "Don't you give me that sanctimonious shit. I know you're part of that scheme up to your dick and then some."

"I thought we were friends, and friends don't—"

"This is not about being friends, goddammit! This is about underhanded business dealings."

"Again, I don't—"

"Bullshit. I know what you did. And I know what they paid you. What I don't know is *why.*" Yancy stepped closer to Herman, who backed up, fear changing his expression once again.

"I . . . I—" Herman's voice seemed to dry up in his throat.

"You'd best stop stammering and start talking before I kick your ass all around this room," Yancy said in that same deadly but unruffled tone.

"You wouldn't lay a hand on me."

Yancy inched closer. "Wanna bet?"

Herman's Adam's apple bobbed up and down as Yancy inched still closer, his face hard and his fists doubled.

"Okay, okay." Herman's voice sounded thin and pinched. "I needed the money."

"Why?"

"My mother."

Those two words stopped Yancy. "Your mother? Shit, Herman, you can do better than that."

"It's the truth; swear to God." His voice was in the squeaky range now. "My mother's a gambling fanatic. She lives at the racetracks. She . . . she got in over her head and went to a loan shark." Herman wiped sweat off his brow with the back of his hand. "I had to help her."

"By stealing money and blaming it on me?" Yancy sneered.

"There wasn't any other way." His Adam's apple gave another convulsive jump. "I had exhausted every other avenue of help. So . . . so when I was approached by this group that wanted the land for a theme park, I agreed to help them."

"Help them ruin me through public outrage and humiliation, ergo deep-sixing the project." Yancy's reply came in a strained growl.

"You've got to understand, I had no choice," Herman cried. "She's my mother. You would've done the same thing."

"That's where you're wrong. I ought to beat you till you

can't stand up. But you're not worth the effort, you miserable piece of shit."

"What . . . what are you going to do?"

Yancy coughed to cover his laugh. "Oh, it's not what I'm going to do; it's what *you're* going to do."

"I—I can't pay the money back." Herman's eyes were pools of misery and fear. "I don't have it."

"I don't give a rat's ass about the money. What I do give a rat's ass about is my reputation. So you're going to go to the paper and spill your yellow guts, tell them what you did."

"I can't. I'll be ruined. I have a business to think about, a family."

Yancy suddenly reached out and jerked Herman up by his tie until they were nose to nose. "You should've thought about all that before you jumped in bed with those double-dealing scumbags."

"Please!" Herman begged.

"In the morning, Green. Be at the newspaper office in the morning. Got it?"

Herman shook his head, and his teeth rattled. "And if I don't?"

Yancy dropped him so quickly that he lost his balance and fell against his desk. "I think you're smart enough to figure that out for yourself." He leaned over, straightened Herman's tie, then patted his cheek. "You have a good evening, you hear?"

By the time Yancy got home, his rage had cooled somewhat.

If ever he needed Dana's arms around him, her soothing touch, it was now.

She didn't stop to consider what she was doing or what she would say. She just knew she had to confront him, had to hear his side of the story. But in her heart of hearts, she knew that Yancy had betrayed her.

Dana made it to the top step before her feet faltered. She couldn't do this. She couldn't hear him admit . . .

Suddenly feeling dizzy, she took deep breaths, forcing air through her lungs. What if her mother had lied? What if she had imagined Yancy in her bed? After all, Vida Lou was an accomplished liar, had been all her life.

No. Not this time. Vida Lou had been telling the truth; Dana was sure of it. She pushed the doorbell and waited. When he finally opened the door and saw who it was, his eyes sparkled and his lips broke into a smile.

"Dana! Thank God!"

She drew back and punched him in the face.

Yancy's head snapped back, his eyes widening in shock.

"How dare you!" she spat.

"Sweet Jesus, Dana, have you lost your mind?"

She pushed past him. "You damn right I've lost my mind. Otherwise I'd never have gone anywhere near you."

"What are you talking about? What happened?"

She laughed. "Oh, that's rich."

"Goddammit, I can't read your mind!"

"Vida Lou!" she yelled. "That's what's going on."

During the silence that followed, he turned green, then red, then white.

"How—"

"How did I know you've been fucking her?" Dana had never said that word before in her life. But that other side of herself, the dark side, had finally surfaced.

"Dana, please, I can—"

"Explain?" Her laughter had all the warmth of ice. "Oh, I just bet you can."

He muttered a few choice words.

"Is that all you have to say?"

"You damn well know it isn't, only—"

"Don't bother." Her jaws ached from clenching them. "It's too late for the 'onlys' and the 'buts.' I just came by to tell you to go to hell."

"Whatever she told you, it's a lie."

"Are you saying you never slept with her?"

Yancy rubbed the back of his neck, then looked at her

through tortured eyes. "No, I'm not telling you that. I did sleep with her, but only once, and that was before you came to town."

"You expect me to believe that?" Her eyes flashed.

"Yes, dammit, I do. It's the truth. I've never touched her since and don't intend to."

"That's not what she said."

"And you believe her?"

Dana didn't say anything. She wanted to walk out, not to listen to any explanation from him. But she couldn't seem to move. Her legs felt like lead.

"It's the truth. I swear it. Look, where I'm concerned, she's gone crazy. She's developed some sort of fatal attraction for me. What did she tell you, that we're having an affair, that I'm nuts about her? It's all lies. Once the project's in the bag, I never intend to see her again."

"Maybe you should."

"You don't mean that. I love—"

"Don't you dare say that to me, you bastard! You don't know the meaning of that word."

"Dana, Dana, Dana, don't let her win. Don't let her do this to you, to us."

"Don't let *her?* What about you? You're the one who fucked her." That word again.

"And I'll regret that the rest of my life, too," he said in a tight whisper.

"Sure you will."

Suddenly he grabbed her arm. She peered down at the strong hand that had had free access to her body, that had touched her in places and in ways that had melted her insides, had melted her heart. Only now to break it.

Dana raised her head. "Let go of me."

"Don't do this," Yancy pleaded, dropping his hand. "We can get past this, start over."

"I could never trust you again."

"You don't mean that."

"Nor could I ever forgive you."

He winced as if she had hit him again. "This is what she wants, to drive a wedge between us. I'm begging you, don't let her get away with it."

Dana looked at him through hate-filled eyes. "It's too late, Yancy. As far as I'm concerned, the two of you belong together, in hell."

Thirty-nine

At least something was working to her advantage. Vida Lou wanted to call on Shelby Tremaine but hadn't been sure it would work out. The key had been Anna Beth. She hadn't wanted Mrs. Tremaine to be at home. She had gotten her wish.

Vida Lou took one last look at herself in the mirror, only to change her expression instantly. God, she had been frowning. She couldn't afford that luxury, couldn't afford one more wrinkle or . . . She shut down that thought. No more scalpels for her.

When her skin looked smooth again, Vida Lou nodded her approval. She looked her best, which was imperative. The times she had run into Shelby at the country club or at a restaurant, he'd ignored her. That snub had never failed to rankle. He wouldn't have that option tonight, especially since his wife wouldn't be clinging to his arm.

The thought of Shelby's slow-witted wife almost brought on another frown. How Shelby put up with the likes of her, Vida Lou could not phantom. The few times she'd been around her, it was obvious Anna Beth's elevator didn't go all the way to the top.

But then she was a Virginia blue blood, Vida Lou reminded herself, feeling that old resentment come to the surface. Ah, to hell with that mousy bitch. Vida Lou had more important items on her agenda. She was just glad that fate had played into her hands and sent the lady of the house out of town.

Even at that, Shelby had insisted he wouldn't see her until late evening, under the cover of darkness, as though he was ashamed to be seen with her. He'd pay for that, too, Vida Lou told herself.

She smiled into the mirror, then leaned forward, flicking off a speck of mascara that had caked on the end of a false eyelash. Then she pulled back. Yes indeed, she had outdone herself. The melon-colored silk dress was perfect. The color, along with her gold jewelry, enhanced the creamy tones in her hair and skin.

Yeah, she'd knock old Shelby's eyes out. She laughed. Maybe "scratch them out" was closer to the truth. Deciding she had preened long enough, Vida Lou sprayed herself with her most expensive cologne, picked up her purse, and walked out of her room.

She wished she were going to meet Yancy. That piercing thought stopped her in her tracks. For a moment she clung to the banister, crippled by anger. How could he prefer Dana to her? How *could* he?

He didn't, not really. Vida Lou assured herself. He was just confused and in a dither over the mess surrounding the hospital project. It wouldn't be long now before he came to his senses. She was about to see to that.

Besides, she was Yancy's savior. Vida Lou straightened her shoulders. Soon he'd be begging her to make love to him.

With that joyous notion, Vida Lou's thoughts switched back to Shelby. "Here I come, you old bastard. It's nut-cuttin' time."

Fifteen minutes later, Vida Lou's driver eased the limousine up the circular drive to the front of the Tremaine maision. Vida Lou gripped the door handle, hating the idea of getting out and hating the idea of *not* getting out.

She had never backed down from a battle, and she didn't intend to start now. But she guessed that next to her daughter, she hated Shelby Tremaine more than she'd ever hated anyone. Therein lay the danger. She mustn't lose her cool; there was too much at stake. This meeting was more than a battle; it was a war—a war she couldn't afford to lose, for more reasons than Yancy Granger.

Time had run out for Shelby Tremaine. She was prepared to bring him to his knees, if need be.

"Madame?"

Albert had the car door open and was looking at her with curiosity. Without saying a word, Vida Lou got out and walked up to the enormous front door, forcing herself to take slow, unhurried steps.

She only had to ring once before the housekeeper responded. "Good evening, Mrs. Dinwiddie. Mr. Tremaine's expecting you."

Vida Lou nodded, then followed the woman along the foyer toward what she figured was Shelby's study. Though her house was equally as palatial, there was a distinct difference. This one spoke of dignity and elegance, which lit another slow burn inside Vida Lou. No matter how much money she had, it was that goddamn bloodline that she lacked.

Still, she would have the last laugh. She owed Shelby Tremaine big time, and today was the beginning of that payback—if he didn't heel, that is.

When she walked into the room, he was standing in front of the fireplace, drink in hand. His gaze settled on her as he took a long pull on his drink.

Vida Lou closed the door and came farther into the room, her heels sinking into the plush carpet.

"I hope this won't take long," Shelby said in a bored tone.

Vida Lou smiled. "It won't."

"So?" Shelby's stare was pointed.

"Are you sure you're in any condition to hear what I have to say?"

"If you mean am I drunk, the answer is no. But I wish to hell I was. Then I wouldn't have to listen to you."

"Just so you'll know, your insults are falling on deaf ears."

He sneered with contempt. "You're lucky I agreed to see you."

"I don't think luck had anything to do with it. If you hadn't, I would've cornered you at the country club, much to your displeasure."

"You bitch."

Vida Lou laughed. "That's right, but then we've always known that. It's kinda been our little secreet."

"What do you want?"

"I think you know."

"It's my land," Shelby said with blunt force, "which gives me the right to do as I see fit with it."

"You promised it to the committee. I won't tolerate your going back on your word."

"*You* won't tolerate? That's a hoot." He took another swig of scotch. "You don't have a damn thing to say about it."

"I know what you're up to."

"Really? And just what is that?"

"I know about the theme park, Shelby; the Anderson group."

She knew she had blindsided him. His face turned ashen as he seemed to grope for a comeback. "How—"

"How did I know? It doesn't matter, now, does it?" She smiled a saccharin smile. "What matters is that I *know.*"

"So what? It's still my land, and I can sell it to whom I damn well please."

"No, you can't, unless . . ." Vida Lou deliberately let her words fade.

"Unless what?"

"I think you know the answer without my spelling it out."

Shelby looked her up and down, that contempt of a moment ago having turned into hatred. "Don't forget who you're talking to. Remember, I know the gutter you crawled out of."

Vida Lou ached to slap his face, but she knew he'd just slap her back. Besides, she intended to catch this rat with sweet-tasting poison.

"And your threats don't mean a damn thing to me," he

added. "You're just full of shit, like you've always been. If you blab, you'll just be hurting yourself."

Vida Lou closed the distance between them, her breath quickening. "I gave you credit for having more sense than you're showing. But then maybe you don't. Maybe over the years your brain's become pickled, or maybe it's just stuffed so far up your ass you can't think straight."

There was no mistaking the savagery in his face. "You still don't get it, do you? What makes you think I'll listen to you now any more than I did years ago? Again, I'll sell that land to whom I fucking well please. Anyway, I know your motive and it's not the project."

Vida Lou's eyes flashed fire. "You don't know anything about me!"

"I know you're a sow's ear, Vida Lou, always have been, always will be. And if you think for a second that a Granger would *ever* do more than tickle your mattress, you're sorely mistaken. Gentlemen may take their pleasure where they find it, but their *wives* are never chosen at random."

"Why, you—!" Vida Lou couldn't stop herself. She smacked his fleshy cheek.

He slapped her back. She reeled against the assault, but stood her ground as they glared at each other.

Finally, Shelby broke the silence, first with a loud belch, then with more insults. "And while we're at it, stay the hell away from my son. I know what you're up to there, and your little scheme won't work. Rooney'll never marry beneath him."

Vida Lou laughed. "Shelby, Shelby, you're so full of yourself that you're blinded by it."

"I'm warning you on both accounts. You'll be sorry—"

"No, you're the one who'll be sorry." Vida Lou then leaned over and kissed him on the lips.

His head rocked back, then forward. "Don't you ever do that again!"

"Tut-tut. Don't get yourself all stirred. There was a time when you—"

"Shut your filthy mouth."

She laughed again. "All right, I'll shut it, but only on one condition. If you want me to take our little secret to the grave, and keep your family as pure as driven snow, then you'll forget about that theme park and keep your bargain with the hospital." She paused so her words would have time to soak in. "Is that understood?"

"If you so much as say a word, I'll kill you. I swear I will."

"No you won't."

Shelby grabbed her arm and jerked her forward. "I'm going to call your bluff, you bitch!" He shoved her back. "Now get the hell out of my sight before I puke all over your fancy whore's get-up!"

A man lurked in the shadows next to the windows. He hadn't meant to eavesdrop, but the car in the drive had piqued his curiosity, and he'd followed the voices. Now, with his head drumming, he hurried back to his car and drove off into the inky blackness.

"You look like you just buried your last friend."

"Maybe I did."

Rooney leaned forward and took one of Dana's limp hands in his. She wanted to withdraw it, yet she didn't. Having him here as a close and loving friend was a soothing balm. Of course, he didn't know that her heart was broken, that she was bleeding on the inside. She couldn't tell him, either.

Still, he knew that something was wrong. He had come by to see her during tea time at the inn. Since all the other guests were out and about, they had the parlor to themselves.

"You want to tell me what's wrong? Is it your job, the fact that you were fired?"

"No." Dana made herself smile to soften her bluntness.

"All right. But remember, I have big ears just made for listening."

"Thanks, Rooney. You're such a dear friend."

"But that's all I'm ever going to be, right?"

Dana squeezed his hand. "Yes, it is, and you might as well accept that." She forced another smile. "I'm sure your folks'll be pleased, especially your daddy."

Rooney lunged to his feet, his expression turning belligerent. "Forget my daddy. I don't care what he thinks about you or anyone else I consider a friend. He can go to hell."

"Rooney!"

"I mean it."

"No, you don't. Despite what you say, you love him. And I'm sure he has your best interests at heart."

Rooney smirked. "You mean *his* best interests. He wants me to be a goddamn politician. Can't you just see me in Washington?"

"As a matter of fact I can. I think you'd be excellent in politics. You're honest and smart and—"

"Boring."

Dana shook her head. "You're not boring."

"Well, it doesn't matter, at least not now. So far, I've managed to put him off and stick to law, which is one reason why I stopped by to see you."

"Oh?"

"Yeah. Because of you, Yancy Granger's off the hook."

At the mention of his name, Dana's heart cracked a little more. She turned away so that Rooney wouldn't see the pain she knew was reflected in her eyes.

"How's that?" she heard herself ask.

"You really don't know?"

"If you're fishing, you're wasting your time."

"Sorry, it's just that I can't get used to you and—"

He broke off, and Dana didn't say anything that would prompt him to continue along that line.

"Anyway," he went on, "Yancy asked me to thank you for him."

Fury choked off Dana's response.

"What I don't get is why he didn't thank you himself. I mean—"

"I know what you mean. I'd rather not discuss it, if you don't mind."

Rooney's brow furrowed. "Suit yourself. Still, he said I should thank you for him; that if it hadn't been for you he wouldn't have suspected there was a conspiracy to malign his name. He said he would never have gone to Herman Green and confronted him."

"What did Herman say?" Dana told herself she shouldn't care, that she didn't want to know anything more about Yancy. But God help her, she did.

Rooney told her about Herman's mother and her gambling debt. When he finished, Dana just shook her head. "I can't imagine such a thing."

"Me either. Anyway, as I said, Yancy's giving you all the credit for getting the lawsuit dismissed, especially after you caught that third witness redhanded with Anderson's attorney."

"That was a coup, I'll admit."

"And because of that, I'm in the process of filing charges on Yancy's behalf—for suborning perjury and initiating a false lawsuit." Rooney grinned. "Who knows, I might even toss in libel and slander charges as well."

"So it looks like Yancy's in the driver's seat, and the Anderson group is finished."

"Absolutely. Especially when the paper prints Green's story."

"I wish I could've seen that exchange between him and Yancy."

"No, you don't. I'm sure it was uglier than when Yancy punched that reporter."

"What about the land? Is your daddy going to sell it to the hospital?"

Rooney shrugged. "I'm still not privy to his business dealings."

Dana didn't say anything, wishing she could just run away from all the pain and heartache that had settled in every bone in her body. But she couldn't. Not yet. She still had *her* pound of flesh to exact.

"I guess you'll be wrapping up your story and heading to D.C., huh?" Rooney asked.

"I guess. Let's just hope the story earns me that job."

"Are you kidding? What with all that's gone on, you'll have one juicy article."

"We'll see," Dana said in a faraway tone.

Rooney stared at her a moment longer. "It's time I got back to Richmond."

Dana kissed him on the cheek. "I'll be in touch."

Once he was gone, she went back to her room, closed the door, and gave in to the tears that had jammed her throat.

Forty

"You're pregnant, Mrs. Howling."

The petite, blue-eyed woman blinked, then her mouth fell open in astonishment. "I am? Are you sure?"

For the first time in weeks, Yancy's smile was sincere. "Yes, I'm sure. You're six weeks, to be exact."

"Oh, my God! I can't believe it, after all this time."

"Well, it's true. Now all you and your husband have to do is celebrate!"

"Oh, my God, Charlie!" She laughed out loud. "He's—he's not going to believe me." Her excitement suddenly dimmed. "Maybe you should tell him, Dr. Granger."

"Oh no, this is your party. No one else should be invited." He smiled again. "Go home, Mrs. Howling, and do what women do when they have something wonderful to share."

Mrs. Howling turned red. "Like dress in the slinky gown and heels?"

"That sounds like a winner to me."

"Oh, Doctor, what can I say? I—" She broke off, tears flooding her eyes.

"You don't have to say anything. Your pregnancy is all the thanks I need."

She nodded, then walked to the door.

"See an obstetrician sometime this week, though," he called after her.

She turned around, grinning. "I wouldn't miss that for the world."

Once she was gone, Yancy's good humor fled. A little of the warmth lingered around his heart, but he knew it wouldn't last. Since Dana had stormed out of his life, he'd been cold, inside and out.

Only his work and his patients had kept him sane. Turning, he stared at the phone. He wished he had the guts to call her.

Dammit, it wasn't fair. He loved her! He wanted to marry her. First, though, he had to tell her the truth, which would be the hardest thing he'd ever had to do. He didn't know if the words would come. That was a sin he wasn't sure love would overcome.

He hadn't asked Dana how she knew about him and Vida Lou. He knew: Vida Lou had told her. Damn that woman. He had known all along she would burn him, and now she had done it.

But *defeat* was not in his vocabulary. He'd get Dana back. He would. And somehow he'd find the strength to tell her the truth.

Right now, though, he had never felt so lost and alone. He compared that feeling with lying in the desert while buzzards circled his carcass, nipping at his flesh.

"What's got your goat today, Doctor?"

Yancy hadn't realized he was no longer alone. Mrs. Howling hadn't pulled the door all the way closed, making it easy for someone to invade his space. That someone was Brodie Calhoun.

"You should be riding high," Brodie added when Yancy remained silent.

"Why's that?" Yancy asked, though he was thoroughly disinterested.

A bushy eyebrow lifted. "Apparently you haven't seen the paper."

"Nope. I've been here all night."

"And you bloody well look it, too. You're going to crash, start making mistakes, if you don't slow down."

"Not in your lifetime, Brodie. You might not want me to marry your sister, and I wouldn't blame you. But if it came to operating on her, then you'd want me. So back off."

Brodie sighed. "Okay, you've made your point."

They were silent for a moment, then Brodie said, "Green spilled his guts. I can't believe he took that money, even if it was to pay off his mother's gambling debts. Anyway, you've been exonerated—on the front page."

"Good."

"Is that all you can say?"

"What more is there? I knew I hadn't done anything wrong."

"I understand the lawsuit's been nipped in the bud as well."

"Yeah, I got out of that one still kicking, too." Yancy paused. "I take it you don't know the truth behind that money debacle or the lawsuit?"

"What do you mean?"

"Green took that money all right, but only for the sole purpose of maligning me."

"What?"

"The lawsuit was for the same purpose."

"I'm getting a bad feeling in the pit of my stomach," Brodie said.

Yancy had hoped that Brodie would hear the rumor, so that he wouldn't have to tell him the bad news. But it looked like that nasty task had been dumped on his shoulders.

"A group of businessmen in Atlanta known as the Anderson group mapped out a strategy to publicly crucify me in hopes of derailing the hospital project."

"But why?"

"They're hot to get the land for a theme park."

"A theme park!" Brodie practically fell into the nearest chair, his face looking like wax.

"Ain't that some shit."

"Surely Shelby Tremaine told them what they could do with that idea? He promised *us* that land."

"Promises are broken every day."

"Has Tremaine lost his mind?" The veins in Brodie's neck were standing out and his breathing was labored.

"You'd best get hold of yourself," Yancy warned, growing concerned for the chief of staff.

"Tell me this is a nightmare."

"I wish the hell I could."

The muscles in Brodie's neck bunched into knots. "I know he wants Rooney-boy to someday be president, which would take a shitload of money, but to sell us out is something I never even thought about."

"If it's any consolation, it was a kick in my gut as well."

"What about Vida Lou? Can't she do something?"

"She told me to let her handle him."

"Well, I'll tell you right now—that bastard better keep his word to us or I'll make him wish he had."

Yancy smirked. "Good luck."

"You're a lot of help. Why I would've thought *you'd* be there knocking Tremaine's door down. After all, you're the driving force behind this project." He paused and scrutinized Yancy. "Something's not quite kosher here. Something's really got your goat."

"And you want to know what it is."

"Damn straight I do. I'm entitled."

"That's where you're wrong. It's *none* of your business."

"It's that reporter, isn't it? That Bivens woman."

Yancy's eyes narrowed. "Don't push it, Brodie."

"You forget who you're talking to here. You'd best start thinking with your brain instead of your dick or you're going to mess everything up."

"So what do you suggest?"

"Talk to Vida Lou. Make sure she's talked to Shelby. *You* talk to Shelby. Hell, we all need to talk to the bastard."

"You ought to hear yourself ranting. You're beginning to sound like me."

"God forbid."

"The s.o.b.'s never liked me," Yancy said, "but I'll see what I can do."

"You'd better. If he takes the park offer, then the project goes under like a sinking ship." Brodie gave him a thumbs-down.

"That ship you're talking about is my lifelong dream."

"Then you get off your ass and get in touch with Vida Lou."

With that, Brodie turned and strode out of the room.

Yancy stood behind his desk, his thoughts and feelings in greater turmoil than ever. He'd rather be shot then talk to her, but he had no choice. He'd do whatever it took to get that land—except sleep with Vida Lou.

He'd sacrificed his soul to the devil once; he wouldn't do it again.

Right now, though, he had another call to make.

It rang four times before she answered. He fought for enough breath to speak. "Dana, I—"

Click.

He cursed as he slammed the receiver down. He wouldn't give up. He would plead his case again and again until she gave him another chance.

He might lose the hospital; but if he lost Dana, he'd just as soon check out of the whole fucking world.

Dana sat staring at the sheets of paper in her lap. She couldn't read the words that she'd typed into the computer, then printed. Her eyes were filled with tears. She dabbed at them with a tissue.

She didn't regret hanging up on him. When she'd heard his voice, blind panic had set in. Besides, what good would it have done to talk to him? What more could be said?

He had crushed her heart when he'd admitted sleeping with her mother. Even now that thought turned Dana's stomach. She was hellbent on bringing him to his knees just as he'd done to her.

Staving off a wave of fresh tears, she blinked, then peered at the words again. The story was damn good, she had to admit.

Her gut reaction had been to get back at him through the article, to ruin him. But could she do that? Could she penalize him because of a flaw in his character, a flaw that really only affected her?

No. His work had to stand. And so did hers. No matter how much she might want to, she couldn't compromise *her* work for a personal vendetta.

Dana pitched the papers aside and stared into space, her pulse still pounding from hearing his voice on the phone. Despite what he had done, despite the pain he had brought her, she still loved him.

Could she give him another chance? After all, he had told her he hadn't touched her mother but once, and not at all since he'd been with her.

God, she wanted to relent. She wanted to see him, to touch him, to have him touch her. But she had made too many mistakes in her life to make another one now, perhaps the biggest one of all.

Dana stared at the phone. What would it hurt to talk to him? To listen? She could always walk away a second time.

"Just do it," she hissed, reaching for the phone.

A knock on the door stopped her. Sudden exhilaration leaped through her like a flame. Was it Yancy?

She smoothed her hair and glanced in the mirror to make sure her mascara hadn't run. Then she walked to the door, only to hesitate again.

"Who is it?" she said in a small voice.

"Dana Bivens?"

She didn't know whether she wanted to cry with disappointment or laugh with relief. It wasn't Yancy, but rather a woman, someone whose voice she didn't recognize.

"Yes."

"I'm Misty Granger. May I come in?"

Yancy's *ex?* Both annoyed and curious, Dana opened the door.

The woman, with her slinky, model-like body, seemed to glide across the threshold. When she turned, Dana was again struck by her beauty and by the fact that someone so lovely had chosen to bury herself in a medical lab. She was also struck by a pinch of jealousy; after all, Misty had been Yancy's wife.

"What can I do for you?" Dana asked in a guarded tone.

"I know something about Yancy that would be worthy of your article," she said without hesitation.

Dana didn't bother to ask how she knew who she was and that she was doing a story on Yancy. The grapevine in Charlottesville was alive and flourishing.

"By 'something,' do you mean dirt?"

Misty seemed taken aback. "You don't pull any punches, do you?"

"No."

"Okay, I guess that's as good a word as any. If you're willing to use it, not only will it add a sensational slant to your story, but it'll damn sure guarantee your future as a reporter."

"That's promising a lot, Ms. Granger." It was all Dana could do to say those last two words.

Misty flipped a strand of hair in a dramatic gesture. "Are you interested?"

"What's in it for you?"

"Revenge."

"For what?" Dana asked.

"He won't recognize my contribution to his work, so I'm not going to get anything."

"Ah, you think part of the credit belongs to you?"

"I don't think; I know. I'm morally entitled to my share of the money if he wins the Nobel, as well as my share of the limelight."

Dana didn't believe that Misty Granger was entitled to either. Her motivation stemmed from vindictive jealousy, which was written on her face and which underlined every word she spoke. Too many people had confirmed that what Yancy had achieved had been on his own skill and merit.

Yet Dana couldn't quell the urge to hear the skeleton in Yancy's closet.

"So, do you want to know, or not?"

"I'm listening."

"My husband was involved in an accident a little over fifteen years ago now. A car accident. At the time he was a resident in medical school."

Icy ripples danced up and down Dana's spine, but she ignored them. "Go on."

"The woman he hit was pregnant, but because he was drunk, he couldn't do what was necessary to help her or the child."

Dana's hand went to her heart. "What . . . what did he do?"

"He took them to a hospital, left them in the OR hallway on a gurney, and disappeared."

For a moment, Dana thought she might faint, but then sheer willpower and fury kept her upright. "Did he tell you this?"

Misty's smile was malicious. "He damn sure did. Only he doesn't remember having bared his soul, you can bet on that. He was too wiped out."

"So—" Dana choked. "So he has no idea anyone knows his little secret?"

"None whatsoever."

"Thank you for telling me."

"So you're going to use it, huh?"

Dana somehow made it to the door and opened it. "Goodbye, Ms. Granger."

"But—"

"Goodbye," Dana repeated with force.

"I'm going, but you sure as hell better use this juice or I'll go to the paper myself. That s.o.b. owes me!"

Dana barely heard the door close. She sank to the floor, too devastated, too sick to move. "Ohmigodohmigod!"

Not you, Yancy. Oh, please, not you! How could it have been you? How could you have done such a thing?

The answer was obvious. He had been drunk and feared for his career.

"Ohmigodohmigod!"

She had thought his betrayal with her mother was the worst thing he could have done to her. But that pain was nothing compared to the pain that stabbed her now. To think she had considered giving him another chance.

Leaning over, she crossed her arms over her stomach and rocked. And rocked some more.

Forty-one

"Please! Oh my God—hurry!"

"Calm down, ma'am," the 911 dispatcher said. "Tell me what's wrong."

"Fire! There's a fire!"

"Where? Give me the address." Again that calm, soothing voice.

"Uh—it's—" The caller, struggled for breath. "It's the Tremaine mansion on Abbey Road. God, please hurry! It's burning!"

"Who are you, ma'am?"

"A neighbor!"

"Please, give me your name."

"Oh my God! Hurry!"

Sirens screamed in the silent night.

Dana bolted upright, her eyes wild, terror building inside her. She hated that sound; she had heard it often as a child when one of her mother's boyfriends would get overzealous and use her as a punching bag. An ambulance would come and take her mother away.

Dana shivered, though the night was warm. Tossing back the light sheet, she went out onto the screened porch.

The sirens continued. She couldn't tell if they were fire trucks or ambulances or both. She hoped that no one was seriously hurt, though she suspected from the number of vehicles that whatever was happening, the situation was grave.

She shivered again, thinking she should return to bed. It was three o'clock in the morning and she hadn't slept a wink. But then she hadn't had a decent night's sleep since Misty Granger had come calling three days ago.

Her exhaustion was boundless. She couldn't think or behave in a rational manner, so she just remained in her room, only drifting to the kitchen to grab a bite, which she then had to force down.

After Misty Granger had gone, Dana's frantic reaction had been to jump in the car, drive to the hospital like a woman possessed, and confront Yancy. She hadn't, of course. She hadn't had the strength. For hours she had remained on the floor, rocking back and forth, her low moans eventually rising to shrieks of fury.

To think she had bared her soul to him, told him all about the incident. Through it all he had never let on, had never once given the slightest hint that he was the one who had dumped her on that gurney and run.

No doubt Misty had told the truth. Even so, Dana found it hard to comprehend. It sounded like something made up, off the pages of a novel. Yet if she had read something like that in a book, she would have found it too implausible, too coincidental to have happened.

But it had happened, all right. She had run head-on into her worst nightmare. If the culprit had been anyone other than Yancy, she would've been ecstatic, for she had wanted to confront the chickenshit who had taken the easy way out and saved his drunken hide.

Dana still intended to confront him, only now he happened to be the man she loved. *Did love.* She stifled another cry that threatened to erupt; she refused to wallow in self-pity any longer.

When she had taken on this assignment, she had been sure that there were no old ghosts lurking around corners to haunt her. Obviously mistaken, she had no recourse now but to take action. She would leave this town and never look back—but only after she had settled the score with Yancy.

First, though, she had to put the finishing touches on the story, holding steadfast to her journalistic principles and keeping her pathetic personal life out of it. Her work was all she had left.

It wouldn't be long before a decision was made about the land, which was key to completing the article. As for Yancy winning the Nobel Prize, that wouldn't be determined for some time. No way would she be around for that announcement. A follow-up story would have to suffice.

The only person she would miss was April. During these past few grief-stricken days, she had spoken once to her friend.

"Hey, kid," April had said, "I just wanted to see if you'd left town without calling."

Dana had tried to muster some enthusiasm but had failed miserably. "I've just been busy."

"You sound like you're—I don't know—sick, maybe."

"I have felt better."

"Anything I can do?"

"No. I'm okay," Dana lied.

"I have some info that might be of interest to you, if you don't already know it, that is."

"What?"

"You remember Alice Crenshaw? She's on the committee."

"Of course."

"Well, she told me they've finally reached their goal and can now pay Shelby Tremaine what he's asking for the land."

If he hasn't already sold it, Dana thought. Then, out loud: "That's great, and I didn't know that. But I'm glad it's worked out."

April sighed. "It almost didn't. Alice was terrified that all that upheaval about Dr. Granger was going to torpedo their entire effort. Thank heavens that all got straightened out." She paused. "I understand you had a big hand in proving his innocence."

"Let's just say I did my job."

"You sure you're okay? For someone who should be riding high, you sound awfully down in the dumps."

"I've just been working real hard to finish the story." Again Dana stretched the truth, but it couldn't be helped. This was one battle she had to fight alone.

April talked a while longer, then rang off.

That conversation had taken place this morning, ending with Dana half-promising to come to dinner before she left town.

Now, as another chill ran through her body, Dana walked back into her room and looked at the rumpled sheets, knowing that she should try to get some sleep. Eyeing the glass of water on the nightstand and the bottle of Tylenol beside it, she swallowed two, then crawled back into bed.

Still, it was hours before she fell asleep.

"We interrupt our regular programming with this news bulletin."

Dana was in the bathroom the following morning, brushing her teeth, when she heard the newswoman's rather high-pitched voice. Dana's head was splitting so she didn't pay much attention, until she heard the word *fire.*

She froze.

"Channel 8 has just learned that a fire destroyed a portion of the Tremaine mansion early this morning. The owner, Shelby Tremaine, is believed to have been burned to death in that fire.

"The charred remains of his body were found in the study. At this point the police don't know . . ."

The woman's voice droned on, but Dana was no longer listening. She had heard enough.

Shelby Tremaine, dead! That wasn't possible! Then she relived all that commotion she'd heard during the night.

"Oh no, no!" she cried, spitting out the toothpaste and clutching the cold porcelain sink.

Rooney! She should be with him. And Anna Beth. Was she all right? The anchorwoman hadn't mentioned her. Or had she? If Rooney had lost both his parents . . .

She had to get to him. He would need her, *expect her.* Galvanized into action, Dana slapped on her makeup and jumped into her clothes.

She drove as fast as she could, but still it was past nine o'clock when she arrived at the estate. Chaos reigned supreme. She ended up parking far down the drive, then running up to the house.

"I'm sorry, ma'am, but that's as far as you can go," an officer said, just as she'd managed to push her way through the crush of police and media vehicles. "This is a crime scene."

"Look, please, I'm a reporter." Dana fumbled in her purse for her credentials. "But more than that, the son of the deceased is a close friend."

"I'm sorry, ma'am, on both counts, but I can't let you through. I have my orders." He gestured toward the other newshounds. "You'll have to stay on this side of the yellow tape just like them."

"But—"

"Dana! Thank God!"

She looked up; Rooney had just walked out onto the porch. "It's all right, officer. Let her through."

Dana ducked under the tape and ran toward Rooney, who met her halfway. Only he wasn't alone. Yancy was in his shadow.

Dana stopped in her tracks, her eyes daring from one man to the other. Rooney reached out and pulled her into his arms.

"Oh, God, Dana, I'm so glad you came." His voice cracked.

Dana clung to him, yet she couldn't stop her gaze from drifting to Yancy. For a moment the world seemed to tilt as his eyes trapped hers and held them.

"Hello, Dana," he said, his voice low and rough.

Dammit, it wasn't fair. She didn't want to see him like this, unprepared. As always, his presence was so strong, it almost knocked her feet out from under her. Yet he also looked as if he'd been caught unawares, showing a combination of weariness and shock. In fact, he looked downright haggard.

She hardened her heart against feeling any sympathy for him. He deserved whatever hell he was going through. But then, he didn't know what hell was, yet. But he would when he found out she knew his dirty little secret.

Her eyes narrowed with cold contempt and she turned away, but not before she'd seen the look of despair and pain that crossed Yancy's face.

"Oh, Rooney, I'm so sorry," she said, giving him her undivided attention.

"He's . . . he's dead, Dana. Daddy's dead."

"I know, and again I'm so sorry. I just heard it on the news and came as quickly as I could."

"Rooney, I'm going," Yancy cut in, his mouth stretched in a grim line. "The housekeeper's resting now. But if you need me, don't hesitate to call."

"Thanks for taking care of Marian," Rooney said. "I'll be in touch."

Dana ignored Yancy as he pushed his way through the reporters, several of them sticking cameras and microphones in his face, which he shoved aside.

"Come on," Rooney said, "let's go inside where we can talk."

"When did you get here?"

"I'm not sure. I've lost all sense of time."

Rooney didn't say any more until they were seated on the couch in the parlor, shut off from all the commotion.

"What happened?" Dana asked, taking his hands in hers.

Rooney looked at her through glazed eyes. "I don't know that, either. Marian called me screaming that the house was on fire."

"Your mother—where is she?"

"At my aunt's in Richmond, thank God. Or at least, she was. She's on her way home now. My aunt's driving her."

"How did it happen? I mean—"

"I expect I'll find that out shortly. I haven't talked to the officer in charge yet because I had to see about Marian. When I arrived, she was hysterical. That's when I called Yancy."

"Thank God the fire department got here in time to save the rest of the house. It looks as if only the study burned."

"That's right. It's—"

A knock on the door interrupted him. Rooney stood and said, "Come in."

They both looked on as a man of medium height and weight, with a black mole on the left side of his jaw, walked into the parlor.

"I'm Detective Boyd Fairchild. You must be Rooney Tremaine."

"Right." Rooney shook his hand. "This is my friend, Dana Bivens."

Fairchild nodded in her direction, then turned back to Rooney. "May I sit down?"

"Uh, of course." Rooney was clearly flustered. "Sorry."

The detective cleared his throat. "First, let me offer my condolences, Mr. Tremaine. Your father was a well-liked and well-respected man in this town."

"Thank you."

Rooney's voice was shaky, and Dana reached for his hand.

"Do you have any idea who would want your father dead?"

Rooney snapped his head back. "What makes you think someone did?"

"Under suspicious circumstances such as this, we always assume the worst—foul play."

Rooney looked at Dana, shock draining his face of color. "You mean the fire might not have been an accident?"

"There's always that possibility," Fairchild said, fingering the black mole on his face as though it were a hickey. Dana tried not to watch, but she couldn't seem to help it.

"Then that would mean that he was murdered." Rooney blinked. "I—" His voice broke, and he turned and stared at

Dana as though he were sinking in quicksand and she was his lifeline.

"And the fire was set to cover it up," Fairchild added in a sober tone.

"Jesus!" Rooney said, seemingly more to himself than to anyone else.

Dana bit down on her lower lip to keep it from trembling, while squeezing Rooney's hand harder.

"Of course, we'll know the exact cause of death when the autopsy is completed," the detective said. "Meanwhile, have you thought of anyone who might want to harm your father?"

Rooney remained silent for a long time. Then he said in a strained voice, "I did hear him arguing with someone several nights ago."

The detective visibly perked up. "Were you here, in the house?"

"No, not at the time. Actually I was outside, about to come in. I had driven in from Richmond. But when I heard voices, I stopped and listened because they were yelling at each other."

"Did you recognize the other voice?"

Rooney hesitated, an uneasy look on his face.

"Go on," Fairchild encouraged.

"It was Vida Lou Dinwiddie," Rooney muttered.

Dana blinked, then bit down on her lip harder, until she tasted blood.

"Do you think that argument could've led to his death?"

"Hell, I don't know. She was fighting mad, I can tell you that."

"So what were they arguing about?"

"She was ordering him to sell the land to the hospital."

"Was there an 'or else' attached to that order?" Fairchild asked.

"I guess you could say that. But there was something else besides the land that had them at each other's throats, only they never said outright what it was."

"Well then, I guess I'd best have a talk with Mrs. Dinwiddie, see if she has an alibi for last night." He stood. "I'll be in touch."

Dana and Rooney didn't say anything even after they were alone. Dana's mind was spinning.

Could she add murder to her mother's repertoire of sins?

Forty-two

"Hey, Nesbit, do you have the forensic report on Tremaine yet?"

"Nah, not yet."

"Then get it, dammit!"

"I'll see if it's ready. That's all I can do."

Detective Boyd Fairchild muttered a foul word, then pulled at a hair embedded in his mole. He should've known that if he wanted something done around there, he'd have to do it himself.

Once the report came down, he planned to pay Mrs. Vida Lou Dinwiddie a visit. First, though, he had to have his guns loaded; he smiled—and no pun intended, he told himself. Then the smile left, as there was nothing to smile about when it came to murder—any murder. But the fact that this victim was one of Charlottesville's leading citizens had elevated the intensity of the investigation.

His chief had already called him in and told him to clear this case up pronto, no excuses.

Now, he couldn't even get the goddamn report.

"I've got it!"

Miracles do happen, Boyd thought sarcastically, as he watched his partner, Ralph Nesbit, hurry into his office, a grin brightening his flat face. He used to tease Nesbit about having been a prizefighter, but Nesbit swore he'd never had a pair of boxing gloves on in his life. Boyd then decided that the Lord must have given Ralph that mug on purpose; he never mentioned boxing again.

"Have you looked at it?" Boyd asked.

"Yep, and you were right on target. It was murder. He was whacked on the head. That's what killed him."

Boyd reached for the report, read through it, then stood with such force that his chair slammed back against the wall. He did not even notice the racket. "Come on, let's pay Ms. Dinwiddie a call."

Nesbit grinned again. "Oh boy, this oughta be interesting."

Fifteen minutes later the detectives stood at the front door of the Dinwiddie mansion, only moments later to be escorted into the living room.

"Mrs. Dinwiddie will be with you in a moment," the housekeeper said, then disappeared.

Nesbit looked around, then whistled under his breath. "Man, this is some joint. No wonder she wanted old man Dinwiddie. But he should've been smarter. I heard she rode 'im into an early grave."

Boyd threw his partner a look. "We can only hope he thought it was worth it."

"Good morning, gentlemen."

Boyd swung around and watched as Vida Lou Dinwiddie seemed to glide into the room like a queen heading for her throne. He wanted to throw up, but first he wanted to wipe that holier-than-thou look off her plastic face.

Hell, if she wasn't guilty, he was going to be damn disappointed. The thought of her kind suffering the humility of prison life did his heart good.

"Hello, ma'am," Nesbit said, then introduced himself. "This is my partner, Boyd Fairchild."

She extended her hand, and Boyd took it, but he didn't want to. For some reason, he was loath to touch this woman.

"What can I do for you gentlemen?"

Boyd cut to the chase. "We're here about Shelby Tremaine."

"Isn't that a shame about what happened to him!"

"I understand you two had a violent argument a few days before his death."

Vida Lou raised her eyebrows. "I wouldn't exactly call our conversation violent, Detective—?"

"Fairchild," Boyd said in a mocking tone, knowing that she knew damn good and well what his name was. A little intimidation factor, or so she thought. Well, she thought wrong. Two could do this tango.

"Well, Detective Fairchild, I can't deny I visited Shelby about a pending business deal." She smiled coolly. "As I'm sure you know, he owned the land that's the proposed site for a new hospital."

"I'm aware of all that, Mrs. Dinwiddie," Boyd said, "but we have an eyewitness who says your visit was not congenial."

"A witness, you said?"

The broad didn't so much as blink, Boyd noticed. Instead, she acted as surprised as a kid on Christmas morning.

"That's right, ma'am," Nesbit put in.

"And who might that witness be?"

"Rooney Tremaine," Boyd said, watching for her reaction.

Still nothing. She stood as prim and poised as ever, which Boyd knew was a facade. Yet he had to tread carefully. She might not have any class, but she sure had money and influence.

"Apparently, he was arriving home," Boyd added, "and stopped outside when he heard the loud voices."

"I won't deny our discussion might've been heated at times."

"And just exactly what were you discussing?"

"I told you, the sale of the land."

"Isn't it true that you were angry because Mr. Tremaine was negotiating with someone else?"

"Yes, I was angry, but that doesn't mean I killed him."

"I don't remember accusing you of that," Boyd said.

"Oh come now, detective, that's why you're here, isn't it?"

"I'm here to find out where you were the night Mr. Tremaine was killed and his study set on fire."

Vida Lou gave him her trademark smile. "I'm sorry to disappoint you, but as the old saying goes, you're barking up the wrong tree. I'm not your culprit; I have an alibi."

"Oh?"

"I was with a friend that evening and night."

"Does that friend have a name?" Boyd asked.

"Tyson Peters. You can find him at the Live Well Fitness Club. But if you don't mind, I'd like to ask that you be discreet in your dealings with him."

Boyd almost busted his gut, holding back a laugh. She would never be able to live it down if her blue-blood cronies found out she was balling a young stud. "I can't make any promises, ma'am."

"Will there be anything else, detective?" Vida Lou asked, the haughtiness back in her tone.

"No, ma'am, not at this time." Boyd looked her up and down. "We'll see ourselves out."

Once they were in the car, Nesbit scratched his head as he stared at his superior. "God, that woman's got icicles in her veins."

"Shit!" Boyd hit the steering wheel.

"What?"

"What? You idiot, don't you know what? There goes our one and only suspect."

"You really think her alibi'll hold up?"

"Get real, Nesbit. Of course it'll hold up. She either paid that guy off with money or got him off in bed. I just want to make sure she doesn't screw us, too."

"So are we going to talk to this stud duck?"

"You bet your ass we are, but it'll be a waste of time. Mr. stud duck, as you called him, is not about to give up his free ride."

"So does that mean we're giving up on Mrs. Dinwiddie?"

"You crazy? Course not. We're going to stick closer to her than ticks on a dog's back."

"Sounds good to me," Nesbit said. "But that woman gave me the willies."

Brodie Calhoun strode into Yancy's office and plopped down in the nearest chair.

"I don't think I heard you knock," Yancy said.

"When it rains, it damn well pours."

"If all you're going to do is bellyache, then you've come to the wrong place."

Brodie gave Yancy a dirty look. "It's all right for you to whine, but no one else has that privilege, huh?"

Yancy sighed and threw down his pencil. He might as well forget trying to work; it was futile. He just couldn't concentrate.

"I still can't believe it. Everything's gone to hell in a handbasket."

"Now that the son of a bitch is dead, maybe all isn't lost," Yancy said.

Brodie scratched his chin as he frowned. "Don't speak ill of the dead."

"Why the hell not? He tried to fuck us over."

"Do you think he would've sold the land to that company?" Brodie asked.

"How do you know he didn't?"

"I don't. That's why I'm such a nutcase."

Yancy tapped his pencil on the desk and looked off into space.

"I just have to believe that he didn't."

"Don't count on it," Yancy said, "especially if big bucks were dangled in front of his eyes."

A moody silence fell between them.

"Let's just say for our sanity's sake that he didn't sell to the Anderson gang," Brodie said. "Now that he's dead, what happens next?"

"The best we can hope for is that Anna Beth or Rooney or both will honor the deal he made with us, but there's no guarantee."

"So do you think Vida Lou had anything to do with his murder?" Brodie asked, changing the subject.

"How the hell should I know?"

Only Yancy did know. If anyone was capable of murder, it was that bitch, he told himself. As long as he drew breath, he'd never forget the pain she had inflicted on Dana, her own flesh and blood. One of these days he expected her to get her comeuppance for her sins. Maybe that day was finally here. After all, no one got out of this life without paying. He ought to know; he was paying big time.

"Word has it that the cops are questioning her," Brodie added.

"If she did do it, I hope to hell they nail her."

"We've got another problem—Dana Bivens," Brodie said. "No telling how she's going to slant her story now."

"I guess we'll just have to wait and see, won't we?"

"Dammit, man, for someone whose lifelong dream is about to go down the tubes, you sure don't act concerned."

"What do you suggest I do, Brodie? Threaten her?"

"I don't give a damn what you do. Just do something, even if it's wrong. If an underhanded deal hasn't been struck, Anna Beth might be so repulsed over all that's gone on, she'll decide to keep the land." Brodie stood and edged back toward the door. "That's why I'm going to talk to her and Rooney. And *you* should talk to Dana Bivens.

"If *she* makes the hospital, the town—*you*—look bad, it can't help our cause." Brodie paused, but not for long. "And how 'bout Clayton Crawford? What if he decides to withdraw his grant? Ever thought about that?"

"Yes."

"I rest my case."

"Only because you ran out of breath," Yancy muttered.

Brodie threw Yancy an I-give-up look, then marched out the door.

As glad as he was to be rid of Brodie, Yancy's mood didn't improve. Dana filled his mind. He had seen her at Shelby's funeral, but only from a distance. He'd wanted to approach her, only he hadn't. But his eyes had soaked her up, thinking how gorgeous she looked in her simple black suit.

It had hit him then, like another brick between the eyes, how much he missed her, how much he loved her. That was why he had to see her again, to tell her who he was and to beg for her forgiveness.

He didn't care about anything else, least of all the article.

"Sir?"

Yancy's hand stopped in midair as he was about to knock on Dana's door. He turned to face the innkeeper.

"Are you looking for Ms. Bivens?"

"Yes, I am."

"She's not here."

"Do you have any idea when she'll be back?"

"She won't."

His mouth went dry. "How do you know? I mean—"

"She checked out this morning. Said she was going back to Richmond."

A feeling of dread worked its way up his spine. "Did she leave any messages?" he asked with no hope.

"No, sir, not a one."

"Thank you," Yancy said, turning and walking out the door, choking on pain that was as bitter as gall.

In the comfort of her rented home, in her favorite chair, Dana read the article one last time. Then she looked up and stared into space. She hadn't planned on returning to Richmond so soon, but after seeing Yancy at Shelby's funeral, she knew she had to get away from him.

She had wanted to finish the article without the threat of him showing up on her door. And now that it was complete, she would turn it in to Wade Langely at *Issues,*—but not before she made one last trip to Charlottesville.

Dana couldn't wait to see Yancy's face when he read what she'd written. Thanks to Misty Granger, she had what she needed to bring Yancy to his knees. So as not to be usurped,

Dana had called Misty to make sure there was no objection to her using the information she had so generously provided.

Both Yancy and Vida Lou were about to get what they deserved, too—swift and sure justice.

Suddenly Dana winced, then rubbed her stomach. That queasy feeling again. Her ulcer. It hadn't acted up in a long time. However, the last few days it had gone ballistic.

She had relented and called her doctor, who had renewed her prescription for Zantac but only after she agreed to have some blood work done. He'd also exacted a promise that she would return for more tests.

Her objections and excuses had fallen on deaf ears. He had insisted, telling her that he would have his nurse call with the time and day. Dana rubbed her stomach again. Maybe the tests weren't such a bad idea after all. When she confronted Yancy, she wanted to be at her best.

The phone rang. She jumped, then stared at it, fearing it might be Yancy. *And hoping it was.*

Angry with herself, she grabbed the receiver. "Hello."

"Dana, this is Dr. Pinner."

Her heart took a dive. Why was the *doctor* calling her? "Do I have cancer?" she blurted.

He chuckled. "No, you don't have cancer."

"Then what's wrong with me?"

"Nothing. You're pregnant."

Forty-three

"Shit fire and save the matches!"

"What'sa matter, honey?"

Newton Anderson glared at the woman who lay naked in the bed beside him. He'd thought she was dead to the world, having humped her relentlessly throughout the night. Apparently, his violent outburst had been louder than he'd intended.

"Nothing. Go back to sleep—or better still, get your butt up and outta here."

"Aw, you don't mean that." She reached over and ran her hands through his chest hairs, not stopping until she reached his penis. The instant she touched it, it sprang to life. He slapped her hand away. His body might crave more of her, but his mind did not. He had to think.

"Get out," he said, filling the silence. "Now."

Even though her brain was not her greatest asset, the harsh note in his voice wasn't lost on her. She gave him a nasty look, then scrambled up and slipped into her clothes, which lay strewn across the floor near the bed.

"Why are you so mean to me?"

Her petulant tone grated on Newt's nerves. "Shut the fuck up and leave before I kick your broad butt out, literally."

She glared at him one last time before dashing out of the bedroom. He heard the door close behind her and breathed a sigh of relief. Women like her were a dime a dozen. If he never saw her again, it wouldn't faze him.

What would faze him was *not* getting that land in Charlottesville. With palsied fingers he took a cigarette out of the pack on the nightstand.

After taking several deep puffs, he felt his insides settle down. Before, they'd been hopping around like a bunch of damn jumping beans. He puffed for a while, then crushed the cigarette in the ashtray. It looked like his best-laid plans had gone down the toilet. He'd thought he and his cronies had covered every base, that they were a shoo-in to get that prime land.

Why the hell did old man Tremaine have to go and get himself bumped off? Newt still couldn't believe it. As to who had done it and why, it didn't matter anymore. What mattered was that he get his hands on it.

Herman Green, the wimpy bastard, had caved in when pressure had been put on him and admitted taking a bribe. He'd thought the man was stronger than that or he wouldn't have approached him. But after delving into every committee member's background, with the exception of Vida Lou Dinwiddie, Green had been the most vulnerable.

He hadn't let Green get by with his duplicity, though. He'd called his hand.

"I want back every cent I've paid you," Newt had told him on the phone.

"But . . . I don't have it. I used it to pay off my mother's gambling debt."

"I don't give a damn if you ate it, I still want all of it back."

"Please, Mr. Anderson—"

Newt had visualized him sitting there sweating like a field hand.

"Stop your goddamn whining and just send me the money, or you'll be sorry."

He had then slammed the phone down. Two days later, he had received the money.

Green hadn't been the only kink in his plan. That nosy

bitch of a journalist had exposed the lawsuit for the fake it was. Having walked in on the conversation between his attorney and one of the witnesses had been the first hard strike.

Dana Bivens had either been on to them beforehand or she'd been one lucky broad. Either way, she'd launched the first missile, and Rooney Tremaine's firepower had finished them off.

And now Dr. Yancy Granger, or so it seemed, had been vindicated in the eyes of the committee and the public. They were once again behind the project one hundred percent. According to Rooney, the good doctor was now going to sue him.

Let him sue me, Newt told himself. He could beat that in court or settle out of court. Either way, a venture that had seemed so cut and dry in the beginning had turned into a fucking zoo.

"Shit fire!" he muttered again.

Newt reached for another cigarette, only to toss it to the floor. He didn't need nicotine; he needed a goddamn miracle.

But maybe all was not lost. Maybe he was about to be handed that miracle, if his attorney knew how best to use the explosive information they had uncovered. He wasn't going to celebrate until the deal was in the bag.

Still, the Tremaine family would be insane if they didn't take his offer, Newt reminded himself, tossing back the sheet and making his way to the liquor cabinet. But then neither Rooney Tremaine nor his mother liked him, which didn't bode well.

After pouring himself a generous amount of bourbon, he leaned back and gulped it down in one swallow. He then held on to the cabinet as a burning sensation rocked his body. Moments later, however, he felt calm and in total command.

Booze was like sex; it was the nectar of rejuvenation. He was ready to fight again, even though he knew that Rooney Tremaine was no fool. Then caution again interceded and damped his newfound enthusiasm. Rooney Tremaine, just like his old man, was a blue blood. Hopefully, though, he wouldn't let that lineage crap stand in the way.

But just in case, and to sweeten the pie, Newt had ordered his attorney to double the offer. Who in his right mind would turn down that kind of money? In addition, his sources had told him that Anna Beth Tremaine was so distraught that she was leaving all decisions to her offspring.

Newt had to believe that Rooney was his old man's son when it came to the almighty dollar. He peered at his watch. His attorney had been in touch with Rooney and should be calling anytime now.

As if mental telepathy was at work, the phone rang. He grabbed it on the second ring. "This had better be good!"

A *baby*!

She was going to have a baby. Yancy's baby.

It had been two days since Dana had talked with the doctor, since her life had been turned upside down once again. At first she'd been too stunned to take it in. Then reality had slowly begun to sink in.

The only way you'll know if you can get pregnant is to try. She remembered Yancy's words as though he had just whispered them in her ear. She had scoffed at him, assuring him that wasn't going to happen.

Famous last words.

In spite of the blow that news had dealt her, she wasn't sorry. She wanted this baby, even though it was Yancy's. God, what a strange turn of events, Dana thought as she finished packing.

She sat down on the side of her bed. The entire scenario was unbelievably bizarre. The man whom she held responsible for the death of her first child had now given her a second one.

Dana rubbed her still-flat stomach as tears flooded her eyes. Yancy would never know about this child. He didn't deserve to know. What he did deserve was exposure. She had already talked with Wade Langely at *Issues,* told him her article was almost ready and promised that it would indeed be sensational.

"Something told me you wouldn't let us down."

That was the closest he had come to assuring her that she had the job. If she thought about the possibility of *not* getting it, she would panic. She had no one else to depend on or to help her, except Rooney, and she would never impose on him, especially now that she was carrying another man's child.

Since his daddy's death she had seen Rooney often. However, she hadn't told him her news. Though he and Shelby hadn't been close, his death had had a profound effect on him.

Suddenly realizing that time was slipping away, Dana hurried to get dressed. If she wanted to be in Charlottesville before dark, she'd best get a move on.

She was untying her robe when the doorbell sounded. She steeled herself for the worst possible scenario. Every time the phone or the doorbell rang, she feared it might be Yancy. So far he'd left her alone, having obviously gotten the message that she wanted him to stay out of her life.

She walked into the living room, to the door. "Who is it?"

"Rooney."

She felt instantaneous relief.

"I hope you don't mind the intrusion," he said when she stepped aside and gestured for him to enter.

"Of course not, though I am about to leave." She pointed toward the sofa. "But for you I can always spare a few minutes." She smiled, hoping to put him at ease.

It didn't work. Rooney remained still and miserable-looking. Dana's sympathy went out to him once again. He'd lost weight that he couldn't afford to lose, and there were lines in his face that hadn't been there before.

"You need to talk, don't you?" she said, watching as he sat down on the sofa.

"In the worst way, but I don't want to keep you from leaving. Where are you going, if you don't mind my asking?"

"To Charlottesville." She sat down beside him.

"You won't believe this, but that's one of the reasons I stopped by. I was going to try to talk you into going with *me.*"

"Why? I mean—"

Rooney stood, jamming his hands down into the pockets of his designer suit. "Vida Lou's throwing a party tonight."

Dana gasped. "And you're going?"

"They haven't proved she killed my father as yet. She had an airtight alibi that Fairchild hasn't been able to crack."

"And you believe her?"

"Don't you?"

Dana looked away. "It doesn't matter what I believe."

"Well, the police are still keeping an eye on her. Detective Fairchild told me that."

"Did they ever find out exactly what killed Shelby?" Dana's tone was soft.

Rooney sat back down, a white line forming around his mouth. "A blow to the head. They think the weapon was that Waterford paperweight he kept on his desk."

Dana remembered that paperweight well, as Newton Anderson's name and number had been under it that day she'd invaded Shelby's study.

"It's the only thing missing from the room that we've been able to determine." He shook his head. "Fire is so damn destructive."

Dana grasped his hand. "I hate all of this for you. I wish there was something I could do."

"You can. You can come with me to Vida Lou's celebration shindig."

What's she celebrating—her engagement to Yancy? She choked back those words and lowered her head.

"Dana."

She looked back at him. "I'm sorry, Rooney, but I can't go."

"I sold the land to the committee."

"Ah, so that's what the celebration's all about." Dana guessed that Yancy and Vida Lou were ecstatic, having gotten exactly what they wanted.

"I imagine Vida Lou'll pull out all the stops."

"I think in the end your father would have come through for the hospital."

"I don't." Rooney paused. "Daddy was almost broke."

Dana opened her mouth but no words came out.

"I know. I was speechless myself at first. Came to find out he made some bad investments, but doctored the books so that no one would know."

"My God, I'm shocked."

"So you see, all that talk about my going into politics was a smokescreen." Rooney's lips twisted. "He wanted that money from the theme-park group to get his own butt out of trouble."

"Which is all the more reason why you should've taken the money."

"Not from that scumbag Anderson—not after what he tried to do to Yancy and the hospital. I still have my pride."

"So does Anderson know he's lost the deal?"

Rooney smiled for real. "Oh, you bet he knows. I told his attorney yesterday, then picked up the phone and sealed the deal with the committee."

"What about your mother?"

"She won't do without; I'll see to that."

"I'm glad you've made peace with yourself, Rooney. But I still can't go with you."

"Please, Dana. I don't want to go either, but I feel like I have to. Brodie Calhoun told me they were presenting me with some kind of gift—as if I give a damn. But I don't want to go alone."

"Rooney—"

"Please."

"You don't understand." Dana sighed. "I'm pregnant."

Silence. Then he exhaled with seemingly enough force to shake the walls. "Is it—"

"Yes, it's Yancy's."

Rooney gulped. "Does he know?"

"No."

"Are you going to tell him?"

"No."

"Then will you marry me?"

Dana gave his hand a hard squeeze. "Oh, Rooney, that's about the nicest thing you could've said to me, a real tribute to our friendship, but I couldn't do that to you."

"I wouldn't mind."

"But I would. You deserve better than my leftovers."

He flinched. "All right, Dana. I'll respect your decision. I understand now why you won't go."

On second thought, why not go? Dana asked herself, her mind shifting gears. She was returning to Charlottesville for the sole purpose of confronting Yancy, wasn't she? That confrontation might as well take place at a party.

"All right."

"All right what?" Rooney looked confused.

"I've changed my mind. I'll go. Help yourself to a drink while I get dressed."

Thirty minutes later, she looked at herself in the mirror and was pleased with what she saw. She walked to the door, then stopped. Should she? Yes. Absolutely.

She hurried back to her desk.

Forty-four

The Dinwiddie mansion was ablaze with lights both inside and out. The elite of Charlottesville were there in their finery, celebrating with music, food, and drink.

Yancy, standing alone in a corner of the room, away from the crowd, eyed the back door. No one would miss him if he took a hike, he told himself, the temptation growing. Hell, he hated parties; he hated crowds, too, except in the OR, which was where he should be at the moment.

But Brodie Calhoun had railroaded him into this fiasco.

"This is as much your night as it is Rooney Tremaine's," the chief of staff had said. "So put your ass in a tux and get over there."

Yancy hadn't put his ass in a tux, but he *had* come, which he now regretted. Sighing, he turned back to face the room, then gave a start. Vida Lou was within touching distance. He cringed within.

She laid a hand on his sleeve and smiled. "Well, how do you feel?"

"You really don't want to know," Yancy said, pointedly staring at her hand.

She flushed, then removed it, but not before he saw the flash of venom in her eyes. "What's got you so uptight? Whatever it is, I bet I can fix it." Her voice was gushy sweet.

Yancy didn't say anything, wishing she would just disappear. He couldn't stand the sight of her, much less her touch.

What he couldn't understand was how she remained free. He'd thought that by now she would be behind bars, without bail, charged with first-degree murder. He was convinced that she was not only capable of killing Shelby but that she had. Too damn bad the cops hadn't been able to prove it.

"Why are you so quiet?" Vida Lou asked. "This is your night, too. And now that we've got the land secured, don't you think it's time you and I had a little chat about our future?"

"You still don't get it, do you? We don't have a future, Vida Lou."

The atmosphere turned tense and heavy, and the venom returned to her eyes. "I did all this for you, for us," she hissed. "Now that it's over, I won't let you throw me aside like an old worn-out shoe."

"I didn't ask you to do anything, and you know it," he lashed back. "It was all your idea."

"Only because I thought you cared about me."

"Well, you thought wrong. Stay away from me, Vida Lou. Do you hear? Just stay the fuck away."

He walked off, unable to endure another second in her company. But he felt her eyes bore into his back, felt their heat strip his skin.

He wound his way through the throng of people, who all slapped him on the back and congratulated him. Hell, what did I do? he wanted to ask, but he didn't. They were enjoying themselves. Just because he felt like canned shit wasn't any reason to take it out on these people, who had done their best to make his dream come true.

His dream. He stopped in midstride. His dream had come true or at least part of it. Thanks to Rooney and to Clayton Crawford, who had ramrodded the promised grant through Congress, the plans for the new hospital could now go forward.

So why wasn't he on top of the fucking world?

Dana. He missed her so much that it was like an oozing sore in his gut that nothing could heal, short of Dana herself. He walked up to the bartender and ordered a Seven-up with a twist of lime. While he waited, his gaze wandered to the door.

That was when he saw her. He straightened as his heart leaped into his throat, almost choking him. Then he blinked, certain his eyes were playing a trick on him. They weren't. She was here, in the flesh, and Rooney Tremaine was next to her, his hand wrapped around her upper arm.

Crippling jealousy shot through Yancy, so crippling that for a moment he couldn't move.

"Doctor, your drink."

"Oh, thanks," he said, reaching for the glass, though never taking his eyes off Dana. What was she doing here, in Vida Lou's house? His mind scrambled for answers that wouldn't come.

They didn't matter, really. She was here and that was all that counted. Now he had the chance to talk to her, to do what he'd wanted to do when he'd sought her out at the inn, which seemed like a lifetime ago.

He knew that while confessing the truth would benefit him personally, it would cost him professionally. But he loved her, and even if she damned him and his career to hell, he still had to confess. He'd kept that ugly secret long enough.

She looked ravishing, he thought, his mouth feeling full of cotton as he watched her move deeper into the crowd. She had on another black dress, this one seeming shorter, tighter, and slinkier than the one she'd worn before. On her, that fit looked just right and sexy as hell.

In fact, everything about her was sexy, starting with the mussed black hair, to the diamond studs in her ears, to the black hose and heels.

His groin tightening, he drifted toward her.

When Dana saw him coming, a wild fury filled her chest. She had known he would be here. After all, that's why she had come. Still, seeing him in the flesh proved to be a greater jolt than she could have imagined.

She looked at him, and his steps seemed to falter as their eyes met, then held.

"Rooney, would you excuse me a moment?"

"Are you sure?" he asked, anxiously.

"I'm sure. I'll be all right."

He didn't look convinced, but he went off to join the party.

Dana focused her attention back on Yancy, who was now perilously close. Her heart knocked against her rib cage. He looked tired, but good, wearing a double-breasted suit and a paisley tie.

For a millisecond she ached to rush into his arms and beg him to love her, to protect her and their baby forever. But that burst of insanity was short-lived, as her deep-seated hatred reasserted itself.

He had betrayed her. Twice.

"Hello, Dana."

He didn't sound like himself, she thought. His voice was rough, with a note of uncertainty in it. She was glad; she didn't want this to be any easier for him than it was for her.

"Can we talk?"

A glint jumped into his eyes, and his mouth took on a sensual slant. "I'd like nothing better."

"Let's go outside, on the veranda."

He nodded, then let her go ahead of him. Thank God, he hadn't touched her. Had he done so, she wasn't sure she could have borne it.

At any other time Dana would've taken delight in the lovely evening. The stars were out in force, and the moon looked like a huge ivory crescent. And the flowers—their scents were heady as they drifted through the air.

However, the beauty escaped her. The only thing she was cognizant of was the cloying heat. And Yancy.

She moved to the railing, leaned against it for support, then faced him. His eyes were narrowed on her, and for the longest time they didn't say a word.

"Dana, I—"

She held up her hand. "I'm not interested in anything you have to say."

She saw his pupils contract with shock. "I see."

"No, I don't think you see at all."

"Apparently not," he said in a sudden, defeated tone.

She wouldn't let him get to her. She *wouldn't.* "I know who you are, Yancy."

Silence beat around them while she watched him closely, the starlight providing her that privilege. She wanted to watch him squirm, to see his reaction when she plunged that verbal knife deeper into his heart.

"And just who am I?" he asked in a hoarse tone.

Even though he asked, he knew. She could see it in his face and hear it in his voice.

"You're the drunken yellowbelly who deserted my baby and me."

He looked like she'd taken that knife and gutted him. He grasped the railing, his knuckles turning white.

"How—"

"How did I know?" Dana's smile was filled with bitterness. "Your ex, that's how. You went home that night and spilled your drunken guts to her."

He appeared now as if all the life had been sucked out of him. "I was going to tell you myself."

She laughed mockingly. "Sure you were."

"Oh, Dana," he said in a tormented, shaky voice. "I'm sorry, so sorry."

Heat suddenly surrounded them like a fiery furnace.

"You're going to be a lot sorrier when I get through with you."

"Do what you have to do." His voice now was thin and tight. "But just so you'll know, it's because of that night, that mistake, that I dedicated myself to my profession."

She shook her head, fighting the urge to cover her ears. She didn't want to hear those words. Yet he kept on talking.

"Still, I deserve to be punished, and who more fitting than you, the one person I hurt so terribly, and love so much."

Stop it! Dana wanted to scream. She didn't want him to tell her he loved her. She didn't want him to say that he was sorry. What she wanted him to do was burn in hell with her mother.

"Dana."

She ignored the pleading in his tone, ignored the pain in his eyes. Instead she jerked open her purse, pulled out the article, and dropped it at his feet.

"You're pathetic," she whispered, then turned and walked away.

Dammit, she should have followed them. She'd had every intention of doing that, but then she'd gotten sidetracked by an unruly, drunken guest.

Vida Lou had disentangled herself, found her chauffeur, and said, "Get rid of him. If you have to, toss him out on his ear."

While that problem was being handled, Dana and Yancy had disappeared outside. Now Vida Lou hesitated. Would anyone notice if she eased outside herself? Hell, what did she care? This was her house, her shindig. She could do as she damn well pleased.

Too bad no one else thought that. Even though her home teemed with people, she'd been treated for the most part as an outsider, as if she had some dreadful, infectious disease. The small-minded idiots thought she was guilty of Shelby's murder.

That damn detective was responsible; he'd kept snooping around for weeks now. The local paper hadn't helped either. The headlines had given the gossipmongers more to sink their teeth into.

But she'd had the last laugh. Her alibi had checked out, and now Detective Boyd Fairchild was eating crow.

Yet it galled her that these people would enjoy her hospitality, only to then shun her as their equal. But her day to gloat was coming. When she married Yancy Granger, they would accept her as one of them.

That was why she had to put a stop to Dana and Yancy's affair once and for all.

Pulling her thoughts back to the moment at hand, she saw Dana scurry back in through the French doors, a dazed look on her face. She paused for a second, then headed for the stairs.

Where the hell did she think she was going?

Vida Lou followed, and watched as Dana raced up the stairs. When she reached the landing, she turned and opened the door on her right. Vida Lou looked on as her bedroom swallowed Dana.

She smiled, envisioning her daughter's dismay when she realized where she was.

Now Vida Lou inched her way up the stairs and saw that Dana had failed to shut the door all the way. She could see her daughter standing by the window, her back hunched as if she was crying.

Easing the door open a bit more, Vida Lou entered the room. She stood quietly for a moment, then said, "He's mine, you know. I *won't* let you have him."

Forty-five

Dana swung around, a chill shooting down her spine. She blinked back her tears; that was when she saw the strange, almost demented look on her mother's face.

"Excuse me," Dana said, stalling for time, that uneasy feeling of long ago running through her.

"What's this polite 'excuse me' shit," Vida Lou spat. "You heard me. *Yancy's mine.*"

Her eyes turned into slits, and a smile stretched her lips to their limit. It was that smile that sent another chill through Dana, one of cold fear.

"You're welcome to him."

"Liar."

Dana shifted her gaze, then asked, "What do you want?" She made sure her voice masked that fear.

Vida Lou laughed. "I just told you what I want—Yancy."

"And I told you he's all yours. So now that that's settled, I'll get out of your room."

"No, you won't."

Dana halted. It wasn't so much what Vida Lou said but the way she said it. Underneath those rather innocent words lay a dark threat.

"Look, if you're expecting me to say I'm sorry—"

"Sorry," Vida Lou lashed out. "You're sorry, all right, through and through." Her gaze, hot with disgust and hate, seemed to peel Dana. "Why I didn't ram that fly swatter up me again and get rid of you is beyond me."

Dana blanched and her stomach churned. Still, she would not show it. Even though Vida Lou had obviously lost control, Dana refused to back down.

"Well, you didn't, so you might as well get over it." Dana straightened. "When I used to go to bed at night, I'd have nightmares about you, so terrified of you that I'd shake and cry like a baby."

"And the only way I could shut you up was to send one of my, uh, friends in your room."

Vida Lou's tone was so matter-of-fact that she could've been talking about the weather. If Dana had ever wanted to do bodily harm to another person, it was at that moment. But that was what Vida Lou wanted, and Dana wouldn't give her that satisfaction, nor would she stoop to her sick level.

"And long after I was grown," Dana continued, "I'd have those same nightmares." She paused and stepped closer. "But no longer. You're just a pathetic old woman chasing after a younger man who doesn't give a damn about you. Actually, you're to be pitied."

"Why you little bitch! No one talks to me like that and gets away with it, least of all you. I'll—"

It was then that Dana noticed it. "Oh no!"

Those words stopped Vida Lou cold. Following Dana's eyes, she whipped around.

"It *was* you," Dana whispered, not bothering to mask her terror. "You killed Shelby Tremaine!"

The Waterford paperweight. *The suspected murder weapon.* It was on Vida Lou's bureau, as if it were a trophy that she was proud of, that she wanted to display.

Vida Lou shrugged. "The bastard had it coming. He wasn't going to sell us the land, you know."

She was talking as if to herself, like an insane person, Dana realized. Then Vida Lou threw back her head and laughed, a bone-chilling laugh.

But when she focused on Dana once again, the laughter

was gone. Her face radiated evil. "You want to know another reason why I bashed his skull in?"

"Oh God, Vida Lou, you need help." Dana's fear intensified as she edged around her mother, trying to get to the door.

Vida Lou made every step she made. "He gave me money for an abortion, only I fooled him. I didn't get one."

"You're talking crazy," Dana said, desperate to get out of the room.

"And it worked, too," Vida Lou went on in a low, methodical voice, as though Dana hadn't said a word. "I threatened him with a paternity suit, and he paid me a hundred grand."

Dana backed over the threshold, then inched to the top of the stairs.

Vida Lou stalked her. "But that soon ran out, and I needed more. That was when I took you, *his* brat, to his house—"

Dana's body turned rigid. "What did you say?" Her voice was a shallow half-whisper.

"I said you're Shelby Tremaine's brat. He was your daddy. And after he saw you, the bastard beat the shit out of me, then told me if I ever brought you anywhere near him again, I'd be sorrier."

"Did he know who . . . who I was?" Somehow Dana managed to get those words through her bloodless lips.

"He knew all right, but only after he hired a private detective. That's when he threatened me again. I couldn't let him get by with that. I had to stop him before he ruined me."

Don't faint! You can't faint! Dana told herself, grabbing the top of the banister and clinging for dear life. Yet the world spun for a moment while her mind rebelled.

No! If Shelby had been her father, then Rooney . . .

"Rooney!" Dana cried out. "You tried to get me to marry my—my half-brother! How could—" She couldn't go on. She was going to be sick.

"That's right, dear. I couldn't think of a sweeter justice than to screw up Shelby's precious blue-blood genes." She smiled that evil smile again. "When my lover would fuck me, I'd often get off thinking about the kind of monster child you and Rooney might spawn."

"God, you're sick! I'm going to turn you in so that you can't hurt—"

"You'll do no such thing, you bitch!" Vida Lou grabbed Dana's arm.

Dana struggled to get loose. "Let go of me!"

"Never!"

Desperate, Dana raised her hand to strike her mother.

She never got the chance.

As if she saw the blow coming, Vida Lou hissed, "Oh no you don't!" Then she pushed Dana.

Dana screamed as her body tumbled down the stairs. The agony finally came to an end when she reached the bottom.

My baby!

Dammit! Why can't they leave me alone? Yancy wondered, watching Brodie make his way across the grounds toward him.

"Hey, get your sorry ass in there, man. They're clamoring for you to make a speech."

"No can do."

Brodie stopped near him and leaned against a tree. "Why?"

"Look, you know that's not my thing. Just tell them I'm in a pissy mood. They'll understand that."

"You're always in a pissy mood." Brodie's tone was sour. "But I was hoping that now that we had the land cinched you'd lighten up a little. You know, give the lesser of us a break."

"I'm not giving any goddamn speech."

"Okay. I don't think anyone really expected you to anyway."

They were quiet for a moment while the crickets chirped and the wind whined through the trees.

"You want to tell me what's eating you up?"

"No."

"I saw you and Dana Bivens head out here a moment ago."

"So?"

"So did she do a hatchet job on you, or what?"

"Probably."

"That's just great. You piss her off, and she writes an unflattering article about you and this hospital."

Yancy didn't say anything. What was there to say? The article would indeed crucify him. But he couldn't tell Brodie why, not during his moment of triumph, maybe not ever. He'd know soon enough that his chief surgeon's career was over.

Still, he wasn't bellyaching. He deserved what he was about to get. By running away that night, then purging himself to his ex-wife, he'd sealed his fate. Anyway, it didn't matter. He had lost Dana, and right now he couldn't get past that.

"Look, old buddy," Brodie said at last, "I'll leave you to your miserable self. Maybe we can talk tomorrow."

"Maybe."

Yancy watched Brodie saunter off, only to sink back into his misery. He could now do what he'd longed to do earlier—just disappear into the night. No one would care, except Vida Lou. On second thought, maybe she wouldn't care anymore either. Maybe he'd finally gotten through to her when he'd told her to leave him the fuck alone.

He didn't know how much plainer he could have made his thoughts than that. Yet his eyes were drawn back to the lights and the noise inside. Dana was still in there.

He had to see her one last time.

Cursing, he headed for the house. Once inside, Yancy made his way through a group of laughing guests, searching all the time for a glimpse of Dana.

He reached the foyer. That was when he heard the commotion. At first he couldn't identify the sound. Then he heard the horrified cry. He swung around and looked toward the stairs.

"No!" he yelled.

He was too late; it happened so fast. Before he could even move, Dana's body lay at his feet.

Instantly, they were surrounded by others. Ignoring their

screams, their shocked gasps, Yancy bent over Dana, who lay there, deathly white.

"Oh God, please no," he whispered, checking the pulse at her neck. Thank God, she was still breathing.

"Call 911!" someone cried out behind him.

"Dana, can you hear me?" Yancy heard the pleading in his voice, the panic, even though as a doctor he knew he had to keep a cool head.

"Shit, Yancy," Brodie said, kneeling beside him. "What the hell—"

"She fell down the goddamn stairs!" Yancy said. What he didn't say was that out of the corner of his eye he'd gotten a glimpse of Vida Lou.

"Christ!" Brodie muttered.

"Dana!" Yancy hovered over her, touched her face. "Can you hear me?"

Her eyes fluttered.

Yancy looked up, fighting back tears of thanksgiving. He moved his hands over her then, gently, feeling for broken bones. That was when he saw it.

Blood. Pooled between her legs.

Where was that goddamn ambulance! Fighting to maintain his professional demeanor, Yancy whispered, "Hang on, help is on the way."

Dana opened her eyes again. She clutched at his shirt.

He bent closer. "Shh, don't try to talk."

"I . . ." Her eyes fluttered again, and she fell silent.

Yancy thought his heart would split in two. If she died . . .

"Please." Dana clutched at his shirt again.

"Please what, love?" He covered her hand over his heart.

She licked her lips as though trying to find enough saliva to speak. "Save our baby."

Our baby! Yancy's mind went wild. Baby? His baby? Their baby? She was carrying their baby? That thought was so mind-boggling that he couldn't comprehend it.

Then reality hit him with a vengeance. He had thought he

only had *her* life hanging in the balance. Now, he had two. If she lived and her baby didn't . . .

He wouldn't think about that now. Nor would he think about this being his fault. Yet he couldn't turn off his mind. If he hadn't slept with Vida Lou, would this have happened? Had Vida Lou pushed Dana because of him?

"The ambulance is here, Yancy!" Brodie said. "Move aside, everyone. Let them through!"

"You and the baby are going to be all right," Yancy whispered, for Dana's ears alone. "I promise."

He followed the gurney, praying that he could keep that promise.

Forty-six

Dana would never forget the look on his face. She had been in pain and shock, but the memory of Yancy bending over her, calling her name, terror in his voice and love in his eyes, would remain with her forever.

That was when she'd realized she still loved him and would love him always. She'd also known that he would do everything in his power to save their baby, and he had done so.

Leaning close to her ear after she'd been wheeled out of surgery, he had whispered, "So far so good. You didn't lose our baby."

She had given him a weak smile as she touched her stomach.

That had been two days ago, and while Yancy had been in and out of her room almost hourly, he had always been accompanied by other doctors.

As soon as she had come to grips with what had happened, she'd known they would have their healing time together. His caressing gaze told her that every time he looked at her.

He had discouraged her from having any visitors, but she'd insisted on seeing April, who had sat with her much of that first day. She'd also spoken briefly with Detective Fairchild, telling him everything her mother had told her.

But talking had been difficult. She'd been diagnosed with a

slight concussion and had multiple bruises. But miraculously, she and her baby had been spared serious injury.

For now.

Dana's heart rebelled against the fact that she might still lose her baby. She closed her eyes tight against the horror of it all. But no matter how hard she tried, she couldn't erase those images from her mind: the murder weapon, Vida Lou's confession, the feel of that hand on her back, then the push.

If Vida Lou had succeeded in her mission . . .

Swallowing around that terrifying thought, Dana opened her eyes and stared at what should have been a typical, stark hospital room. It wasn't. Flowers were everywhere, giving it the look and smell of a florist's shop. Most of them had come from Yancy, though April and the hospital personnel had contributed their share.

Dana heard the tap on the door and was relieved. She'd stood her own company long enough. "Come in," she called, hoping it was Yancy.

It was Yancy, but he was accompanied by Boyd Fairchild, the detective.

"I wasn't sure whether or not to let him in again," Yancy said without preamble.

"But after he heard my news," the detective put in, "he thought maybe you'd best see me after all."

Dana gestured with her arm, then winced, which caused Yancy's eyes to darken. "You okay?" he asked, his voice gruff.

"I'm fine." Their eyes met, and they might as well have been the only two in the room.

Detective Fairchild shifted his feet, breaking the spell.

"It's about my mo—Vida Lou, isn't it?" Dana asked.

Fairchild nodded, then sat in the chair close to her bed. "I thought you'd like to know that we recovered the murder weapon; it was exactly where you said it was. Even at that, she pleaded innocent."

"Innocent, my ass," Yancy mumbled, leaning against the wall.

Dana gasped. "But how can she say that when she confessed to me?"

"It's her word against yours."

"Do you think she's sane?" Dana asked.

"She's being evaluated now. And yes, I think she's sane and capable of standing trial. Of course, she's hired the best criminal attorney money can buy."

"If she gets off—" A shudder went through Dana.

"I intend to do all I can to make sure Mrs. Dinwiddie is put away for life," the detective said in a hard tone. Then he rose.

Dana held out her hand, and this time she didn't wince. "Thank you."

"Good luck," Fairchild added, taking her hand briefly. "I understand you're going to have a baby." His face turned red. "I hope everything works out for you."

Dana's eyes turned soft. "Thank you again."

"I'll be in touch."

When he left, Yancy snapped his fingers. "Damn, I forgot. Rooney's waiting outside."

Dana sucked in her breath.

"Don't you want to see him?"

"Of course I want to see him."

"He's been about to have a shit fit to get into this room, only I—" Yancy broke off, his mouth stretched into a thin line.

"I wouldn't be too worried about Rooney anymore if I were you."

"Why?"

Dana hesitated, then blurted, "Because he's my half-brother,"

"What?"

"Shelby Tremaine was my father."

"My God, Dana."

"And to think she encouraged him to marry me." Dana's chin quivered. "I'm more convinced than ever that she's sick."

"A vicious fuckin' lunatic is what she is. And I hope she fries."

"Rooney doesn't know."

"Jesus."

"Will you stay while I tell him? I have no idea how he's going to react."

"I'll do anything you want." Yancy's eyes and voice spoke volumes. "But then, you already know that."

Rooney chose that moment to open the door and poke his head in. "Yoo-hoo! Y'all forget about me?"

Dana smiled. "Come in here. I'm so glad to see you."

Rooney waltzed in, his arms loaded with flowers. "Uh-oh, guess you didn't need these."

"Of course I need them." Dana smiled. "Just find a free spot for them."

He did, then turned to face Yancy. "So how's the patient, Doc?"

"Okay, as long as she stays parked in the bed."

"I'm toeing the line, believe me," Dana said, her tone upbeat. Then it sobered. "Rooney, please, sit down. I have something I have to . . . to tell you."

"This sounds serious. I guess you two are getting hitched, is that it?"

Silence filled the room.

"We haven't talked about that yet," Yancy said finally, his eyes delving into Dana's.

She felt her face grow warm as she focused on Rooney. "What I have to say has to do with you and me."

Rooney's eyebrows lifted. "Us? How's that?"

"This is really hard." Dana took a deep breath. "I don't know quite how to say this, except to just come right out and say it."

"Hey, it's okay. Whatever it is."

"You're . . . we're half-brother and -sister."

Rooney stared at her in stunned disbelief. "How—" He gulped, then slammed his mouth shut.

"Vida Lou's my mother," Dana murmured, then waited for

that bombshell to settle in before continuing. "I'm so sorry I led you to believe that my parents were killed. Somehow, after the upbringing I had, it was easy to go along with that story." Dana paused and looked at Yancy for support. He gave her a reassuring nod. "I meant no harm, Rooney, really I didn't. At the time, I think it was the only way I could cope."

"So you're saying that my old man and your mother—" Again he stopped, the words seeming to dry up.

"That's exactly what I'm saying. When Vida Lou told me that Shelby was my . . . father, I felt the same way. I know it's true; even Vida Lou couldn't have made up anything that bizarre."

"I had no idea they'd ever known each other until this committee was set up."

Rooney looked green, and Dana ached for him. But there wasn't anything she could do to soften the blow. They were on the receiving end of the sins of their parents, and it was hell.

"Apparently Shelby and Vida Lou had an affair a long time ago. She got pregnant and tried to give herself an abortion, but she botched it. Then she tried to blackmail him. That worked for a while, but eventually Shelby put a stop to it. From the way she talked, he beat her up. She never forgave him for me or for the beating."

"Holy damn." Rooney shook his head.

"So how . . . how do you feel about having a sister?"

Still looking somewhat shellshocked, Rooney said, "I've always hated being an only child."

Dana gave a nervous laugh. "Well then, brother dear, come give me a hug, only not too hard."

When they broke apart, Dana asked, "What about your mother? How—"

Rooney waved his hand. "She'll go bonkers at first. But later, after she calms down, she'll be okay. She likes you, and she's always wanted a daughter." He grinned. "Now, she has one."

"Oh, Rooney, that sounds so wonderful."

"Look, I'd best be shoving off."

"Are you sure you're all right with all of this?"

Rooney toyed with his glasses. "I guess I'll need some time to myself to come to grips with this. But I'll see you again soon."

"I hope so." Dana looked at Yancy. "It seems I'm going to be here awhile."

"That she is," Yancy said.

"See y'all later, then."

Once Rooney was gone, Dana suddenly felt weepy. She tried to blink back the tears but couldn't. Yancy crossed to the bed and eased down beside her, where he simply held her. Neither said a word for the longest time.

Then Dana said, "That was much harder and much easier than I'd anticipated, if that makes sense."

"It makes perfect sense. If anyone's due a good cry, it's you."

"Tell me about the baby."

"What more do you want to know?"

"Nothing really, except I still can't quite believe you actually tacked my cervix together."

"Well, I did. Because of that, hopefully you'll carry our baby to full term. But like I told you, it isn't going to be a piece of cake. You're going to have to be virtually bedridden for about six weeks."

"That's no problem."

"Are you sure?"

"I want this baby, Yancy." Her tone was fierce.

"Do you want me too?"

That softly spoken question packed such an emotional wallop that Dana pulled back and stared at his grave face.

"Yes," she said with sweet strength.

"Before you were hurt, you weren't going to tell me, were you?" His voice was thick with pain.

"No." This time her voice was weak with shame.

"God, Dana, how could you have kept that from me?"

"Because I wanted to make you pay for what you did."

"There hasn't been a second of my life that I haven't paid for that night."

"I know that now," she said softly.

"Are you sure? I couldn't take it if—"

"I knew it that night at the party," she interrupted, "though I wasn't ready to admit it."

"And now?"

"I love you, Yancy," she whispered.

"Ah, could you say that a little louder? I didn't hear you."

Her lips twitched, then she all but shouted, "I love you, Dr. Yancy Granger!"

He leaned over and kissed her. Then, pulling just a hair's breadth away from her lips, he whispered, "And I love you, Dana Bivens."

"To think we wasted so much time."

"We'll make up for it." Yancy paused, his face suddenly pale. "What about that article and your job? You promised that magazine a sensational story."

Dana had been waiting for this moment. Pulling away from his embrace, she reached for her purse on the bedside table. "I wrote two articles, two different versions. Here's a copy of the one that April FedExed to *Issues* for me." She handed it to him.

The room was quiet while Yancy read. When he finished, he lifted eyes, wide with shock. "You don't mention the automobile accident—" His voice sounded choked.

She smiled with love glowing from her eyes. "I know. Your secret is safe with me."

"I really do love you, Dana Bivens."

"I know," she whispered, then cleared her throat. "Wade Langely called this morning and was ecstatic. But then, why wouldn't he be. What with your work, Shelby's murder, and Vida Lou's trial, what more could he want?" She paused. "Of course, I can't speak for your ex-wife."

"She's no problem."

Dana looked doubtful. "Since when?"

"Since I told her that if I won the Nobel she could have all the glory and the money, that all I gave a damn about was you and the hospital."

"I bet she nearly fainted."

He gave a sheepish grin.

"Somewhere along the way, the tiger of old has turned into a big pussy cat."

He kissed her. "It's all your fault."

"Mmm, you taste good. And I'll take full credit."

Yancy's eyes were filled with love. "I owe you my sanity and my career. What can I say?"

" 'Thank you' would suffice."

"I have a better idea." He kissed her long and hard. "How's that?"

"Mmm, much better."

"Back to Langely," Yancy said. "I figure he wants you on staff."

"You're right, he does. The job's mine."

"So I guess that means you'll be living in D.C.?"

Dana's eyes pinned his. "That all depends."

"On what?" His voice had that choked sound again.

"If a certain doctor decides to make an honest woman out of me."

A hot flame leaped into Yancy's eyes, and he leaned over and kissed her again. "Oh, Dana, I want to marry you more than anything, but I was afraid that you'd never forgive me."

"I forgave you a long time ago, only I couldn't admit it. I fell in love with you that night in the restaurant, that first time you kissed me."

"And I you." Yancy's eyes darkened with sudden pain. "But can you ever forget . . . forgive me for—"

"Touching my mother? Yes. When you touch me, I never think of her."

"Thank God. I don't think I could bear it if she came between us anymore."

"So where do we go from here, my darling?" Dana asked.

He smiled."Well, since we can't go to a preacher, he'll just have to come to us."

"When?"

"Tomorrow."

Dana caught her breath."You really mean that?"

"With all my heart."

"Oh, Yancy, I do love you."

"And I love you." He placed his hand on her stomach. "And I love our baby."

Her face clouded. "Do you really think it will make it, that I can carry it to full term?"

"As a doctor, I've done all I can. And you're doing your part. Now, it's up to a fate higher than us."

"Hold me, Yancy," she whispered in a broken voice.

"Not to worry; I'll never let you go again."

Epilogue

"I wish that were me."

Dana looked down at her two-month-old son, who was sucking on her breast, then back up at her husband. They had been married almost a year now, and every day she pinched herself to make sure she wasn't dreaming. She had never known such contentment and happiness. She knew Yancy felt the same.

"Go ahead," she teased. "I have another one, you know."

With glistening eyes, Yancy lay down beside her on the bed, then propped his head on his hand. "Believe me, I'm tempted," he whispered in a guttural tone, "only I don't want milk all over me."

She laughed. "Chicken."

"I'll make you think, chicken." He leaned over and tongued the side of her free breast.

"I have goosebumps all over me."

"And I have a hard-on."

She tapped him on the nose. "You'll just have to wait for that."

"How much longer is that little bugger going to eat?" Yancy ran a finger across the tiny cheek.

"Until he's full. Isn't that right, Adam, love?"

Yancy chuckled. "Hell, he's already like his old man. He likes his titties."

"You're perverted," Dana said, rolling her eyes.

"And you're precious."

Dana's breath suspended, and they looked at each other with love radiating from their eyes.

"Have I told you that I love you, Mrs. Granger?"

"Let's see, not more than four times today and it's only noon."

"Damn, I'd better get with the program."

Dana laughed. "By the way, what are you doing at home? I figured you'd be at the construction site, giving the contractors hell, as usual."

"I'm headed that way, only I had something to tell you."

"What?"

"Vida Lou filed her first appeal today."

If there had been a dark time in their lives, it had been during the trial. Even after Tyson Peters, Vida Lou's lover, had admitted to having been paid to lie for her, she continued to claim her innocence. Only at the end had the district attorney finally broken Vida Lou.

"The first appeal in a long line of many, I suspect," Dana finally said.

"Yep. But she'll eventually have that date with the needle."

"I still find it hard to believe she's on death row."

"She deserves it, Dana. Don't feel sorry for her."

"I do and I don't, if that makes sense."

"It does."

The baby moved, claiming Dana's attention. After quieting him, she smiled at Yancy and said, "Well, I have some news myself."

"Oh?"

"Wade Langely called again today."

"And he wants you back at work?"

"Right, only I'm going to work out of the house."

"Hot damn! That means you won't have to leave Adam."

"I thought you told me you understood."

"Would you be mad at me if I said I lied?"

Dana punched him in the ribs. "You're impossible."

"You know I'm just teasing. Whatever you want to do, I'm behind you one hunderd percent."

"You know I'll never let my work or anything else come before you and Adam."

"I know, and I'm trying to live up to that same standard."

"And you're doing just fine, too." She was quiet for a moment. "I'm still disappointed that you didn't win the Nobel Prize."

"I'm not. Oh, don't get me wrong—it would've been extra gravy on the meat and potatoes, so to speak. But hell, I've got more than any man deserves." He leaned over and kissed Dana on the nose.

"I know but—"

"No 'buts,' Mrs. Granger." Yancy grinned. "Just because I didn't win the prize, my work goes on. For instance, the congressman and his wife are pregnant."

Dana smiled at his choice of words. "I'm glad. Miracles do happen."

"That's because I make 'em happpen."

She rolled her eyes.

"Hey, our son's stopped sucking."

Dana peered at Adam again. "He's asleep." She eased him away from her nipple, then leaned over and placed him in the crib beside the bed.

When she turned around, Yancy's arms were outstretched. "It's my turn now, my love."